SPREAD

Serene Franklin

Cover Artist: Jay Aheer at Simply Defined Art

Editing: Keyanna Butler at The Indie Author's Apprentice

Proofreading: Judy Zweifel at Judy's Proofreading

Formatting: Rainbow Danger Designs.

Paperback ISBN: 978-1-9994727-0-2

Ebook: 978-1-9994727-1-9

To my mom. For just being her.

And I had too many flash fires
That I just let them burn
— EDEN, "Drugs"

CHAPTER ONE

S NOW WAS BEGINNING TO fall as Theo's wandering gaze caught the open window to the left of the bed. The cool night air rolled in through the window in gentle waves, caressing Theo's exposed dampened flesh. The city was particularly still that night, the only sounds that reached Theo's ears were the rhythmic creaking of the bed, the steady breaths of a stranger, and his own hurried breaths. Theo lay on the bed on his stomach with his hands gripping the thin cotton blend sheets on either side of his head. His legs were spread wide across the middle of the queen-sized mattress in the unfamiliar room; a pillow was securely tucked under his hips, the cheap fabric roughly brushing against his sensitive skin. Despite the friction, Theo was soft.

Above him was a nameless young man around twenty years old with a moderately muscled body. His long blond hair flung back and forth over his eyes while he greedily fucked Theo, pushing his body deep into the mattress. Theo felt the weight on the bed suddenly shift. Hands moved from his hips and up over his back until finding their destination in the sheets alongside his own. In this new position he could feel the full weight of the blond against his body and felt a new depth to the hard, erratic thrusts.

The deeper thrusts caused Theo to cry out, his voice starting to become hoarse and dry. The pain was intense; this was not an endeavor for pleasure. Despite the pain, Theo arched his back, allowing the blond even more access into his body. He wanted to feel this. After a couple minutes of the unsustainable pace, the blond grunted and rolled off of Theo, lying next to him on the bed. Theo did not shift his gaze from the falling snow.

Through gasps, the blond finally spoke. "Fuck—that was great." Theo turned his head from the window and looked at him for a moment. The impetuous boy continued, "I haven't had a fuck like that in months."

"You're welcome."

"Wanna go for a third round?"

"Tempting, but I'll have to decline. I have an important meeting in the morning," Theo replied dryly.

"It's already late, you should just stay over. Besides, it's snowing now. That walk is gonna suck."

Theo turned his head back toward the window and sighed deeply. "I'll be fine. I have to face it at some point."

"What?"

"Never mind."

"So, uh, since we go to the same gym and everything, wanna hook up again sometime? I mean, I was a bit shocked when you came over, I totally thought you were a top. But I really had fun and I'd like to see you again."

Theo furrowed his brows at the proposition then sat up. He slid over to the edge of the bed, grabbed his black boxer briefs from the floor and slid them on while standing. "I don't fuck guys twice. Personal rule, sorry." Theo grabbed the rest of his clothes and dressed quickly while the blond stared at him dejectedly. "You should go clean up before *that* leaks,"

Theo said, nodding toward the blond's flaccid penis, still encased in a condom.

"Yeah, of course." The blond got up and disappeared into the bathroom without closing the door. Theo made his way around the bed and put his shoes on by the front door. He picked up his gym bag and reached for the doorknob, exiting the unit without a second glance.

It's that time of the year again.

Exiting the front door of the apartment complex, Theo gripped his bare neck as the chilled air assaulted his flushed skin. He hadn't planned on walking that night and wasn't wearing a scarf, let alone a proper jacket. He slung his black gym bag over his shoulder and started walking toward the busier part of the city, back toward the gym and his car. The snow was starting to collect on the streets and sidewalk, coating everything in a light dusting of pure white. Theo's hurried footsteps marred the otherwise unspoiled snow while he continued on alone. His thoughts began to wander, a pastime he'd been trying to avoid.

What am I doing? What would he say if he could see me like this? Would he recognize the man I've become?

"Do you think it hurts much to die? I've never had a high tolerance for pain. I'm not strong like you, Theo," he says, smiling faintly.

"We don't have to talk about this. Everything is going to be okay. I won't let anything happen to you. Just like when we were kids, I'll protect you."

"We're not kids anymore, you can't—"

"Don't, Isaac. Please. Have faith in me."

Isaac shifts on the bed, moving closer to me where I'm sitting in the chair adjacent to the bed. "You're my best friend. You've always been there for me and never let me down, but this is bigger than us. Right now, more than anything, I need your strength. I can't do this without you."

I grip the denim over my thighs as tears begin to well up in my eyes. "Okay. I'm so sorry."

I'm so sorry.

When Theo snapped out of his daze he was in the sparsely occupied parking lot of the twenty-four-hour gym standing in front of his car, a BMW M3. The black company car was coated in several inches of snow, much to Theo's dismay. In addition to not having a scarf or jacket, the snow brush was in the closet of his condo in summer storage. Cursing his lack of meteorological prowess, Theo brushed the snow off the car in wide strokes using the sleeve of his sweater. Once cleared enough, he got in the car, engaged the brake, and gently pushed the start button with his right index finger. The car quietly came to life, the parking break was disengaged, and Theo sped off fast enough for the tires to spin a bit in the slippery lot.

Driving in silence, Theo pulled up to a red light and noticed the first sign of life in the city since leaving the blond's apartment. A group of four college-aged men were exiting an apartment building, much like the one Theo himself was just a guest in. The young men were all attractive to Theo; tall and well built—they were likely athletes—just as Theo had been in his high school and university years.

Four, huh? Even that might be a bit much for me.

Once the light turned green, Theo ripped his gaze from the group and drove away—much more carefully than before. He flowed through uncharacteristically quiet streets for a few minutes before he felt his thoughts begin to drift again. Unwilling to let his memories take control, Theo turned on the radio. The distraction from mundane ads and sterilized music was enough to keep him occupied for the remainder of the fifteen-minute trip home.

By the time he reached his underground parking spot it was nearly four in the morning. He rode the elevator and was inside of his eighth-floor condo within minutes. Inside the dark entryway, Theo set his keys down on an otherwise unoccupied tall, black stand against a wall. Without turning on the lights he walked down the corridor, past the kitchen and living room areas, and entered the bathroom. He stripped off his soiled gym clothes and took a quick shower. Once finished, he wrapped a white towel around his waist and walked up the hall to his bedroom. He dropped the towel, climbed in bed, and was asleep before the beads of water on his upper body fully dried.

CHAPTER TWO

*W*HY AM I SO COLD? *Did I leave a window open last night? No, I didn't open any.*

"*Open your eyes,*" *a familiar voice calls out to me.*

"*Ahh,*" *I say as realization strikes. I am standing on the snow-covered ledge of my balcony. I didn't anticipate it ending like this, but I suppose this way is as good as any. A bitter laugh escapes me.* "*Eight stories should be high enough.*"

Enjoying the feeling of the snow crunching between my toes one last time, I close my eyes and step off the ledge.

Theo woke with a start. He was covered in sweat and his chest heaved deeply. *Another nightmare, huh? At least that one wasn't painful.* He took several long breaths to steady himself and ran his hand through his short, wavy hair, roughly tugging at the shorter hair at the back. *Wake the fuck up!*

The sun was shining brightly through the large windows in the room. The motorized white, opaque shades were rolled all the way up, inviting in the blinding natural light. The rays warmed Theo's fair skin, which was largely unmarred save for a fading shark tooth tattoo on his right lower hip, and a few small scars from his youth. Theo glanced at the clock on the bedside stand and saw that it was just after six. As much as he wanted to close the shades and sleep in, he had an important meeting scheduled for that morning. He flung back the black comforter and got out of the low, queen-sized bed. He picked up the towel he'd dropped on the floor hours before, wincing a bit from the lingering ache from last night's activity. He shook it off and walked down the hall to the bathroom to take another shower to wake himself up.

Afterward, Theo stood in front of his bathroom mirror, carefully eyeing his face. His dark blue eyes focused on his well-groomed, short beard. His beard matched his dark brown wavy hair, wet from the shower. He stroked his jaw before picking up an electric trimmer and trimmed away a few fractions of an inch for a sharper look. Pleased with the results, Theo focused his attention on his hair. He picked up a bottle of argan oil and squeezed out a dot. He rubbed it in his hands and applied it to his hair, focusing on the longer section on top. He reached for a small comb and gently brushed the curls to one side, achieving a very sleek, but natural look. Satisfied, he gathered up the dirty laundry from the floor and exited the bathroom clad in a fresh white towel.

He opened a closet door at the end of the hall and pulled out a clouded plastic bag before continuing on to his room. He put the soiled laundry, including the towel he'd just used, into the bag and zipped it closed. He set the bag down on the bed and walked past the foot of it to a black hardwood dresser, opened the top drawer, and pulled out a pair of black Calvin Klein boxer briefs. Theo slipped into them with ease and walked out to the kitchen.

His kitchen was very modern and minimalist, in keeping with the rest of the condo's décor. Polished concrete countertops sat atop black wooden cabinets; the upper cabinets were black glass. Two stools sat on the living room side of the kitchen at a dining bar area on the other side of the sink, just to the right. Spotless stainless steel appliances gleamed in the light from the open shades over the living room windows. Theo opened the fridge and took out almond milk, celery, kale, baby spinach, and apples. Starting with the almond milk, he put the ingredients into a Vitamix blender, along with ginger, ice, and flax seeds. He wasn't particularly fond of the taste, but that was inconsequential; he drank it down in large gulps directly from the blender. Once emptied, the blender was washed, dried, and put back in its place on the counter.

Theo had many expensive suits hanging in his walk-in closet. They were color coordinated for convenience. He usually wore a black or dark grey suit to work but opted for a bolder choice that day. He settled on a navy blue Tom Ford three-piece suit. He paired it with a plain pale blue Zegna dress shirt and a dark blue patterned Zegna tie. The suit, like all of his, had been tailored for a perfect fit, and accentuated his tall, toned figure; the jacket rested comfortably over Theo's broad shoulders, the lapels lay flush against his pronounced chest, and the bottom of the jacket tapered down to accommodate his thirty-three-inch waist. The ensemble was finished off with navy blue socks and a matching chestnut-brown leather Gucci belt and laced, polished shoes. It was an outfit that screamed grace and confidence, two things Theo knew he would need to embody for the day to go smoothly. He gave himself a once-over in front of a full-length mirror in his bedroom before leaving the condo and driving to work.

"D'you remember that tall girl from Austin's party last weekend? The brunette with the freckles."
"Umm, did she have green eyes or something?"

"Hazel, actually." Just like yours. No, not just like yours, yours are far more beautiful.

"I remember she was hot, what about her?"

"Apparently she's in med school with Jamie, she asked him about me."

"Yeah? You should get Jamie to set up a meet. You've been single for a long time, man."

"What the hell is that supposed to mean? You don't have a girlfriend right now either."

"That's different. I'm not like you, Theo. You're your best when you've got someone to take care of. Don't take this the wrong way, you know I love you, but we're getting older... and I don't want to hold you back from settling down with someone, just because it's not in the cards for me." Isaac, what are you saying?

"I'm not sure I follow." You were just supposed to tell me to forget about her.

"This girl is going to be a doctor and *she's gorgeous* and *she's into you. That's the jackpot, man. We're almost thirty— I've dragged you around enough on my whims, don't you think?"*

"Isaac, you're my best friend. You might as well be my brother. Truth be told, I do like you more than Jamie." I force a laugh to lighten the mood. *"You haven't dragged me anywhere. I willingly chose to accompany you and I'd do it again in a heart-beat. I'd have beaten your ass if you took off without me. Asshole."*

Isaac is smiling. *"All right, all right, I get it. Even if you say that, I'm pretty sure your parents thought I was a bad influence."*

"Oh, are you kidding? My dad definitely still hates you." We're both laughing now.

"I'm not saying you're going to marry this girl, all I'm saying is start taking chances. If you won't do it for your parents, do it for me so I can have peace of mind that I didn't fuck up my best

friend's life." He's always got a smile on his face. "Anyway, what's this girl's name again?"

Ting. The elevator doors opened to the thirtieth floor of Rey Financial corporate headquarters and Theo was greeted by his assistant, Leah. She was tall, slim, and had straight blonde hair which ran past her shoulders. "Good morning, Theo," she said while handing him a large, glass mug of black tea.

"Thank you," Theo said enthusiastically before he took a sip of the hot tea, steeped to perfection. "Have our guests arrived yet?" Theo and Leah walked out of the reception area and down a long hall toward Theo's office.

"They are en route. I received a call from Mr. Tanaka about fifteen minutes ago."

"Excellent. I have a good feeling about today's meeting." Theo smiled at Leah and took another drink.

"You're going to awe and amaze them, I can tell. You only wear that suit when you're gearing up to do the impossible. You're unstoppable when you set yourself to the task."

Theo laughed, caught off guard by the compliment. "I appreciate your faith in me, but I can assure you I am just a man. There's only so much I can do. Luckily for this company, negotiating is one of my skills." Theo pushed open the door to his office and motioned for Leah to enter first.

"Thank you," she said, as she entered the large, modern office. Theo followed behind her several paces back. She walked to the middle of the room and sat on a black leather couch. Across from it was an identical couch. A thin glass table sat between the two fixtures. Theo's desk was at the back of the office, by the floor-to-ceiling windows. There was not a chair for guests in front of it. Theo sat on the opposite couch and set his tea down on the table.

"I need a fucking vacation after this." His tone no longer carried the joyfulness it did out in the reception area.

"You're well overdue for one. It's been a tough year for you; you deserve a break more than anyone."

"You do too."

"I'm fine. I've got the world's best boss. He just neglects himself sometimes, but that's why I'm here. I need to remind him to take time for himself."

Theo broke eye contact with Leah and stared at the now half-full glass mug. *Why is she always right?*

"Promise me you'll take time off soon. I'll start fucking with your morning tea if you don't."

"My, you mean business."

"Damn right, I do. I don't want to see you this unhappy day after day. I know a short vacation isn't going to change things right away, but it's a step in the right direction."

"No, you're absolutely right." Theo leaned back into the couch and cupped his hands on either side of his neck before entwining his fingers in the back. "I'll take some time off after the meeting today. I want you to as well. Spend some time with Josh, take a vacation on the company card, and send me any additional expenses. I wouldn't have made it through this last year without you. If I deserve a break then so do you."

"Thank you, Theo, but that's way too much."

"Enough. I won't hear any more of it." Theo sat forward and took another drink. "Fuck me; you really do make the best tea."

"One of my many talents." Leah was grinning playfully. "Do you have any laundry today? You didn't have the bag with you when I greeted you."

"Ah, I forgot it in the car again."

"Ever forgetful," she teased. "I'll go get it after the meeting."

"You don't have to do that, Leah. Fetching my dirty clothes is not part of your job."

"I don't mind. Oh, shit! I forgot! Your father wanted to see you as soon as you got in this morning."

"What does that ornery old man want?"

"He didn't specify, but his tone made it sound urgent."

"He called you personally?"

"Yes."

Theo sighed. "Fine. I'll bite." He stood up and finished the rest of his tea. Leah took the empty mug from him.

"Did you have a smoothie for breakfast?"

"I did."

"I'll order you lunch later. Japanese or Thai?"

"In keeping with the theme of today, I'll take Japanese."

"Good choice. Now go, don't keep the vice chairman waiting."

"You're too good to me."

"I know."

"You wanted to see me?" Theo asked, looking at his father. He sat behind his mahogany desk, reading what looked like a report of some sort.

The man took his glasses off and threw the report on the desk. "Where have you been lately?"

Thoroughly confused by the question, Theo sat in the chair across the desk from his father. "Excuse me?"

"Your mother has been trying to call you for weeks and you don't answer or return her calls." He looked Theo square in the eyes and asked again, "Where have you been?"

"I haven't gone anywhere, Dad. I've been working on the Amagi proposal and have been busy. Tell Mom I'll try to make it home for Thanks—"

Theo was interrupted by a raised hand. "You can call her and tell her yourself. You're thirty-one years old, start acting like it and take some responsibility." He put his glasses back on and picked up the report again. "How is the Amagi proposal coming along? They are going to be an important partnership in Tokyo. It's imperative to our stats next quarter that we reach an agreement."

"I know. I have it handled."

"Now isn't the time for you to be distracted, Theodore."

"I *said* I have it under control. Mr. Amagi is on his way over now for negotiations. He will not be leaving until I've closed the deal."

Theo's father looked up from the report, pinning Theo with the same dark blue eyes he himself possessed. "Good."

Theo stood next to Leah while Mr. Amagi and his entourage of five stepped off the elevator. *"Konnichiwa, ohayo gozaimasu, Amagi-sama."* Theo bowed slightly while he greeted his guests in their native tongue, Japanese. He'd read it was a polite thing to do. *Oh God, please let me be pronouncing this properly.*

"Ohayo gazaimasu, Rey-san," Mr. Amagi greeted Theo in kind. "Your Japanese pronunciation is very good, thank you for your efforts."

"Thank you for the compliment. It is a pleasure to finally meet you, Mr. Amagi. I am Theo Rey; I have been spear-heading negotiations with a Mr. Akaashi." Theo held out a hand toward Mr. Amagi, which the older man firmly shook. Mr. Amagi appeared to be in his early fifties and was a slender man around five foot eight—four inches shorter than Theo.

"Thank you for having us, Mr. Rey. The accommodations your company arranged have been very comfortable."

"Excellent, I am glad to hear everything is to your satisfaction. Shall we continue in the boardroom?" Mr. Amagi nodded and Theo motioned toward Leah. She smiled and began walking away from the lobby. The group followed her down a short hallway and into boardroom two. "Can my assistant get refreshments for anyone? We keep a wide assortment on hand."

"No, thank you." Only Mr. Amagi spoke. He proceeded to introduce the rest of his party, including Mr. Akaashi, three men from the sales department, and an advisor, Mr. Tanaka.

Without further delay, Theo launched into discussing the financial benefits to the Amagi Group partnering with Rey Financial. He explained market trends and supplied each of Mr. Amagi's men a booklet with statistics and charts to support his claims. Things seemed to be going his way although Mr. Tanaka had been occasionally whispering into Mr. Amagi's ear. Theo paid it no mind and continued with his practiced pitch until Mr. Tanaka interrupted.

"This deal is unacceptable," he said sternly.

Theo looked at Mr. Amagi who remained silent. He shifted his attention over to Mr. Tanaka. "You're unhappy with the terms of the deal? While I cannot speak to any other offers you received, I can assure you that—"

Mr. Tanaka leaned forward and cut Theo off. "All of your competitors' offers are significantly higher. Unless your company is willing to amend your proposal, we have nothing more to discuss."

Give me a fucking break.

"I hear your concerns, Mr. Tanaka. Give me the opportunity to—"

"Fix it or negotiations are finished." *Calm, stay calm. I need to separate Amagi and this asshole.*

Theo switched his gaze back to Mr. Amagi and in a steady tone said, "Mr. Amagi, would you mind joining me in my office?" The man nodded.

"Thank you for granting me a private audience," Theo said as he closed the door to his office. "Please, have a seat."

"It is the least I can do after your company flew us here for this meeting. I have every intention of listening to your proposal." He paused for a moment before continuing. "Mr. Tanaka can be a bit abrasive at times. He has reviewed your written proposal and finds some of the terms and projections to be unsatisfactory. I apologize for one of my employees being rude to our host." Mr. Amagi took several steps and sat down on the black couch closest to the door. Theo sat on the opposite couch, where he'd sat earlier that morning.

"Please, an apology is not necessary. Mr. Tanaka seems to be a very loyal, albeit spirited, man. He cares about the Amagi Group and its longevity and does not want you to make a rash decision. I completely understand that."

Mr. Amagi nodded his head. "He certainly is spirited. I have known him since we were boys. He hasn't changed in the slightest."

Theo smiled at Mr. Amagi's admission. *I can still turn this around.* "I'm going to be completely candid with you. I didn't request privacy to go over the proposal with you." Theo carefully gauged the man's reserved reaction before he continued. "The numbers in the proposal are not going to change. Mr. Tanaka is correct in saying that partnering with another financial institution would yield higher profits, but at what cost?" Mr. Amagi narrowed his eyes at Theo. "It is my understanding that you established the Amagi Group when you were around my age, correct?"

"That's right, I was thirty-two."

"Good, I've still got a year to catch up to you." Mr. Amagi laughed.

"You've built quite the name for yourself without aid from others. You've maintained total control of the way you run your business and have generated significant gains in a very short time in the banking sector. You're competitively competing with the well-established national banks in the Tokyo area. Without a doubt, it is impressive. But, correct me if I speak out of turn, your ambition isn't sated by these accomplishments." Amagi silently listened to Theo. "You realize the only way to branch outside of Tokyo, and internationally, is to partner with a bank like Rey Financial; to partner with a company that already has extensive networks in place to carry upon the momentum that you've worked so hard to build." Theo paused for a moment to make sure Mr. Amagi was still with him. "One of the big three banks will definitely have more money to offer in a partnership, but both of us know that's not what you're solely looking for. A bigger bank will try to rebrand the Amagi Group; it would serve as a true acquisition. What Rey Financial are proposing is a strategic partnership, which leaves the Amagi Group wholly in your control but gives mutual use of markets and resources. What we're offering are the means by which you can achieve your goals without forfeiting ownership or suffering rebranding. To a man like you, Mr. Amagi, I know that integrity and pride are much more important than the numbers. Given the means that we can offer, you will more than make up for the fiscal differences in a quarter or two."

Mr. Amagi's expressionless face formed a smile and he laughed. "I see now why they sent you. You are a very capable young man, Mr. Rey."

"Theo, please. My father is Mr. Rey around here." Theo smiled.

Mr. Amagi nodded; he seemed to do that often. "Theo, I appreciate you being upfront with me and for taking the time to understand the vision for my business." He paused and looked down for a moment before extending a hand across the table. "I'd like to formally accept your offer." Theo flashed a winning smile and shook the man's hand.

"Congratulations!" All of Theo's colleagues and most of his superiors congratulated him on the success of the Amagi meeting in an upscale hotel bar. Theo played the gracious recipient and thanked everyone with a smile, tilt of his head, and a raised glass of champagne. Most of the praise had been given to him earlier individually. This was just for show more than anything. His colleagues joined him in taking a drink and then the attention passed from Theo. He leaned back into the leather booth and downed the entire flute. *How soon can I leave before they notice my absence I wonder?*

"Can I refresh your drink, sir?" Theo's thoughts were interrupted by an attractive young waiter.

Hmm, he'll do. "Absolutely, thank you."

The young man refilled the glass with a smile. "It seems like you're the man of the hour. Congratulations."

"Thank you." Theo drained the glass again. "Can I get another refill please?"

"Of course." He filled the glass once again. Theo drank the contents once more and motioned with a nod of his head to the empty glass. The waiter cocked an eyebrow and obliged.

"It must have been a *really* good day," he waiter commented. He was still smiling.

Theo emptied the glass again and looked the waiter in the eye. "It was okay, there's still time for it to get better. Fill me up." He slid the glass away from the edge of the table and the waiter had to lean in to reach it. He carefully filled the glass again. In closer proximity to him now, Theo said in a quieted tone, "I'm feeling a bit dizzy. Is there a room in the hotel you recommend?"

The waiter's eyes went wide for a moment then he smiled and nodded. "Eight oh one has superb amenities. I can have it prepared for you in fifteen minutes." Theo shrugged his eyebrows and downed the last glass of champagne. The waiter bit his lower lip and asked, "Would you care for a top up?"

"I'd love one—in about fourteen minutes."

It always ends up like this.

Theo's muffled screams filled the unfamiliar room. His silk tie was balled and stuffed deep in his mouth. The waiter from the party stood at the edge of the bed, Theo lay on his back with his knees pulled close to his chest. His shirt and vest were unbuttoned and spread wide open. His jacket had been tossed on the back of a chair. The waiter gripped the underside of Theo's muscular thighs while he rammed his cock into him repeatedly. With each thrust Theo felt like he'd be split in two. His partner was average length and girth at best, but Theo had insisted that lubricant was not necessary. He *really* wanted to feel it that night. *Go ahead and break me.* The all too eager younger man had obliged without hesitation.

The waiter leaned down and bit Theo's left nipple almost hard enough to break the skin. Theo bit down hard on the tie in response as the pain quickly spread through him; his body tensed reflexively. The sudden tightness immediately made the waiter cry out and he went still.

"Fuck, dude. You're gonna make me come if you tense up like that," he said, panting. *You tried to bite my nipple off, what the fuck did you expect?* He looked down at where his body connected to Theo's and smirked. He watched intently as he started moving again, his cock sliding in and out as he gently rolled his hips. He'd been fucking Theo for quite a while now, but Theo wasn't the least bit turned on, contrary to how flirtatious he'd been downstairs at the party.

The younger man's pace quickened rapidly, causing Theo to forcefully exhale through his nose, his jaw muscles were clenched. The waiter reached down between Theo's thighs and started pumping his cock in rhythm with his fast thrusts. Theo squirmed and shot him a sharp glare which he seemed to pay no heed to, and continued stroking. Despite his efforts, Theo did not get hard.

The waiter scoffed and moved his hands to Theo's hips and pulled him into his thrusts. He seemed frustrated, but Theo didn't care. Theo closed his eyes and continued to bite down on his tie as the friction from the condom rubbed him raw. He'd definitely be feeling this for several days.

Theo felt the hands on his hips grip tighter and knew what was coming. The waiter's hips now moved with an urgency that wasn't there before.

"Ah, ah!" He abruptly pulled out and tore off the condom in a quick motion. He took his cock in hand and jerked himself off. The frenzied stokes didn't continue for long before he threw his head back and came on Theo's stomach. He took a couple steps to the side and collapsed on the bed, frantically panting.

Theo removed his tie from his mouth and slowly sat up to inspect the damage. His shirt and vest appeared to have escaped unscathed but his Zegna tie wasn't so lucky. *Truly a shame, I loved that tie.* He looked down at his stomach and sighed. Cum was sliding down his abs and catching in the line of hair that trailed from his belly button into his pubic hair. *My God, what a mess.*

Through ragged breaths the waiter turned his head to Theo and said, "You some kind of masochist or something?"

"Something like that," he mused.

Theo took a cab home. He'd go back to the hotel tomorrow and get his car. He took off his jacket, vest, shirt, and trousers and laid them on the dresser in his bedroom. He'd thrown the tie in the trash at the hotel. He stripped off his socks and underwear and left them on the floor before going down the hall to the bathroom and turning on the shower.

Hot water cascaded down over Theo's head and aching body. It stung his nipple where he'd been bitten, but the sensation from the heat far outweighed the mild discomfort. He grabbed a bar of goat's milk soap and gently rubbed it against his arms and torso. He paid extra attention to his stomach and pubic hair. Theo looked down at himself and slowed the motion of his hands. He put the bar down and grasped the base of his soft cock. *How long has it been? A few weeks? A month? More? I guess I could today.*

He closed his eyes and gently tugged at his circumcised cock until it started to get hard. Much to his surprise, it did not take long. Once fully erect, he grabbed the bar again and rubbed it between his hands. He used the lather from the soap as a lubricant and firmly took hold of himself, stroking from tip to base. It felt better than he remembered, and he couldn't keep himself from vocalizing. He stopped with his hand near the tip and massaged his glans with his thumb. The sensation made his legs feel weak and his bottom lip quiver. Almost at the edge, he returned to full strokes, going as fast as he could until he released with a muffled moan and curse.

Theo cleaned up the contained mess of his arousal and finished showering. He dried off, brushed his teeth, and got in his bed. The soft Egyptian cotton sheets caressed his spent body and he drifted off into sleep.

CHAPTER THREE

I LOOK AROUND MY *childhood room once more, maybe for the last time. This room is a reminder of all the things I don't want. The walls are lined with shelves holding my accomplishments. I am suffocated by swimming medals and soccer trophies. My high school career is over and so is my sports career. I am scheduled to attend U of I on a soccer scholarship this September but I am not going. Isaac and I have our own plan and are leaving this bullshit behind. I think I have everything I need. A familiar voice at the door startles me.*

"Are you ready?" Isaac is leaning in my doorway with his arms folded, smiling.

"I think so. There's not a whole lot I need to take." Or want. "My dad can keep these as proof that I was once worthy of the Rey legacy." I motion around the room to the awards.

Isaac uncrosses his arms and steps into the room. He walks past me and picks up a small silver medal hanging from a blue ribbon on a nail on the wall. "I think you should take this one," he says and extends his arm to me.

I take the medal, looking at him quizzically. "Why? Of all the ones in here this one isn't even gold. I lost this race." My voice trails off as I run my thumb over the raised text on the award.

A soft smile flashes across Isaac's face as he steps closer to me. "This is the only one that matters. Don't you remember that day? It was your first official competition."

"I remember that I lost."

"To me. It was to be expected, you were new to the sport. But that's not what I remember about that day. You were so nervous; I thought you were going to pass out." He laughs and puts his hand on my shoulder, squeezing it lightly. "But after the race you were so happy. I always knew you'd be a good swimmer, Theo. You've got the build for it and it drove me crazy that you waited until high school to start. I've been a swimmer my entire life and it didn't take long at all for you to surpass me."

I look at Isaac and feel my cheeks begin to flush. He tells me I've never been good at accepting compliments. But that's not the cause of this reaction. I do remember the day I got that award. I was nervous, but it wasn't pre-race jitters. That was the day I realized I was in love with my best friend. I probably knew before, but that was the day I stopped being able to lie to myself about it.

His uncle had driven us to the school that Saturday for the race. I got in a fight with my dad over taking up swimming and he refused to give me a ride. Mom didn't drive so I texted Isaac. I was feeling pretty down over the exchange with my father and didn't say much when I got into the car. Isaac was in the front passenger seat and he turned around to greet me, smiling. His smile fell when he saw my face. Without saying a word, he got out of the front seat and slid in the back seat next to me. He took my trembling hand, gave me a sad smile and didn't let go until I stopped shaking. It was then, sitting in silence, that I realized how much I loved Isaac in so many ways. He was my best friend —a brother to me. But these new feelings weren't of the familial variety. My despondent mood gave way to feelings of fear, nervousness, and to my surprise, happiness. I was in love with my best friend. My hand shook for the rest of the drive, but not because of my father.

Prior to the race I was a scatterbrained mess. I was reeling from my newfound awareness. Everything Isaac did caught my attention in a new way I'd previously ignored. He moved with grace and confidence, likely a result of his years of training. I forced myself to keep my eyes locked onto the back of my locker when he changed into his trunks. Just hearing the sound of the rustling clothes sent a red blush across my cheeks. I'd hurriedly changed into my trunks to distract myself. When I turned around Isaac was fully changed and holding his swim cap. I swallowed hard when I saw him. It was a sight I'd seen countless times before but I remember it felt like I was seeing him for the first time. His strong legs led up to the fitted trunks which sat low, exposing his hip bones. His torso was long and toned, leading up to strong shoulders almost as wide as my own. My eyes traced his collarbone to his Adam's apple and up to his face. Full sculpted lips, high cheekbones, and the most beautiful hazel eyes were framed by his nearly shoulder-length, shaggy, brown hair. I recall thinking, "Why hadn't I noticed how hot he was before?"

How I managed to focus on the race is still a mystery to me. I was so giddy, seeing the water run down his abs and drip from his lips post-race made me—

"Theo! Hello, you still with me, man?" *Isaac is waving his hand in front of my face.*

Oh God, how long was I zoned out? My cheeks feel hot. Fuck. I'm probably blushing. "Sorry, man, what did you say?"

He smiled that all-encompassing smile of his. "Thinking of something good, yeah?"

I shrug. "Something like that."

Isaac taps on my chest with the back of his hand. "Come on, we should get out of here before someone comes home." *I nod, stuff the medal into the front pocket of my jeans, and we leave.*

We take my car and set out on our thirty-hour drive along the I-80 to California. Isaac always said he'd move there when we graduated and I'd steeled myself to go with him, without my father's permission. He'd never permit such a thing. It was common knowledge that I was expected to study finance and commerce and work at the family business, Rey Financial. Being a banker of any sort was never something I wanted to do, let alone work in that stuffy downtown building. My great-grandfather founded the company and my uncle is the current CEO. My father serves as VP. It is a guaranteed easy life of luxury and stability, but my time with Isaac made me realize that there's more to life than that—that I could live by my own rules and feel a sense of adventure, feel alive.

We'd been driving around 300 miles before my phone starts ringing. I glance down to see "Dad" flash on the call display. I hit "ignore" and keep on driving. He calls six more times over the next two hours. Isaac has been hitting ignore for me and keeping me distracted by telling me again about his plans to pick up surfing and how easy it would make meeting new girls. It makes me laugh, but also pains my heart to be reminded once again that he is straight and will never be more than my best friend. Straight. *I guess I can't think of myself that way anymore. Am I gay? I only have eyes for Isaac right now but will that change?*

My thoughts are interrupted by the phone ringing again. "Isaac, can you just turn it off? I don't want to talk to him." I roll my head back and grip the wheel tighter.

"It's Jamie. Didn't you tell him we were leaving?"

"I did. We agreed I'd contact him once we got set up in Cali." I pause for a moment and hope my father wouldn't try to use my brother's phone to get to me. I swallow hard and hit the answer key. "Jay, what's up?"

"*Where the fuck has your phone been?!*" *Jamie is borderline screaming.*

Isaac shoots me a quick worried glare and says, "What's wrong, Jamie?"

"*Mom was in an accident earlier. Theo, she was hit by a fucking car, she's in the hospital.*"

If either Jamie or Isaac are still speaking, I don't hear it. My mind begins to race with thoughts of my mom's welfare. I don't know how long has passed before I feel a hard impact on my cheekbone followed by the sting of being struck. I open my eyes and Isaac is leaned over and has his hands on the steering wheel, steadying the car. I don't hear Jamie anymore. "I-I'm sorry. I'm okay now." I put my trembling hands back on the wheel.

"*Theo. Did you hear what Jamie said? All of it?*" *His voice is full of concern as he slowly lets go of the wheel.*

"*Mom was in an accident...*" *My voice trails off.*

"*Pull over.*" *I look at Isaac and part my lips to speak, but no words come. I nod my head, signal right, and pull onto the gravel shoulder. It is dark now and traffic is light.*

Isaac takes a deep breath before speaking. "Your mom was involved in a hit-and-run downtown a few hours ago. She's still in surgery right now but Jamie said the nurses said it was pretty bad. Compound fractures, probably nerve damage."

"*Oh God.*" *I put my head against the wheel and feel tears begin to well in my eyes.*

I am quiet for a moment before he speaks softly. "We have to go back, Theo." Hot tears are streaming down my face when my eyes meet Isaac's. I close my eyes slowly and weakly nod my head.

When I open my eyes Isaac's familiar face is gone. His full lips are cracked, his long hair is now short and thin, his cheeks are sunken in, his tanned skin is pale, and his beautiful hazel eyes are now clouded over.

"*No, no, no, please, not again.*" *I turn from Isaac and shake* my head. I look back to him and he's looking in my general direction, but not directly at me.

"I'm sorry you have to see me like this. I'd have dolled myself up if I knew you were coming." He smiles weakly. His voice is hollow and cracked. "Come closer, I can't see you clearly, man."

I turn away once more and force my hands over my ears. "I can't. I can't do this again!" He doesn't reply so I open one eye and look to the passenger seat, but Isaac is gone. I drop my hands from my ears and place the palms of my hands over my eyes to stop the falling tears. The only sounds I hear are the infrequent flowing traffic and my own harsh breathing.

After what feels like an eternity, I let my hands fall to my lap. I grip the tops of my thighs in an attempt to stop the trembling. I glance in the rearview mirror and realize that my entire body is shaking. Am I losing my fucking mind? No, I must be dreaming. I have to be.

I take a few deep breaths to try and steady myself then unbuckle my seatbelt and open the car door. I drag myself out of the car and walk to the middle of the empty highway. I sit down facing away from home with my knees pulled tight against my chest and wrap my arms around my legs. The pavement is cool but warmer than the breeze biting through my t-shirt. My tears have stopped but the tremors remain. The trees in front of me are becoming illuminated and I can hear a distant car engine.

I don't look back. I can't look back. I am scared of what's to come but I know it needs to happen. I close my eyes and think back to when life was simpler, back before everything went wrong, before I lost Isaac. Before the vibration on the road coursed through me, before the sound of screeching tires took my breath away.

THEO WOKE WITH A START. After thrashing in his bed, he

shot up to a sitting position, gasping and sweating. His voice was ragged, his throat dry and constricted. He clawed and gripped at his throat while trying to catch his breath before he found his bearings and realized he was in his bed. The room was dark but the shade was down so he wasn't sure what time it was. Recognizing the familiar sights in his room helped calm his erratic breathing and Theo released his hold on his neck. He took deeper, steadying breaths, and ran his hands through his hair. He leaned to the left of the bed to look at the alarm clock: it was just before two thirty in the morning—if you could even consider that morning. After groaning, he swung his legs off the bed and retrieved a small black box from his top nightstand drawer. He flung back the blanket, stood up slowly, and started down the hall, holding the box, stark naked.

Once in the kitchen, Theo grabbed a black mug from a cupboard and filled it with water from the stainless steel tap. In the quiet of the kitchen he could hear Isaac's voice reverberating in his head. "*We have to go back, Theo.*" He shook his head, took a drink by the sink, filled the mug again, and started toward the glass sliding door off of the living room. Without stopping, he grabbed a black blanket from the back of the charcoal fabric couch. When he reached the glass door he set the mug and black box down on a tall, white table and flung the blanket over his shoulders. He opened the door, collected his things and stepped out onto the modest balcony, closing the door behind him.

The balcony was five by seven feet and completely barren, save for a black deck chair with a grey cushion and a matching glass table. Theo sat in the chair and placed the box and mug on the table while he adjusted the blanket to shield his bare skin from the cold. It hadn't snowed again since the first snow, but it was cold enough that Theo was certain it would start at any moment. Once settled, he picked up the box and removed the airtight lid, revealing two rolled joints and a silver Zippo lighter.

Shit. I'm going to have to go see him soon. Theo grabbed one of the joints and placed it between his lips while he picked up the smooth metal lighter with his other hand. The flame came to life on the first flick and Theo brought it to the tip of the joint. The sound of the paper burning met his ears before he inhaled deeply, making sure it was lit fully, and getting a lungful of smoke. He held his breath for a few moments before gently exhaling through his nose, quieting Isaac's voice in his head. The back of his throat burned but he didn't hesitate before taking another, longer drag. After the second one he coughed shallowly and took a drink. The cold water instantly soothed his dry, burning throat and he finally began to feel the tension bleed from his shoulders. The rest of his body soon followed suit as he continued to smoke and sink into the chair.

Theo sat on the balcony and smoked both joints. By the time he'd finished the second, his mind was quiet. Isaac's voice faded away and Theo was able to fully relax his mind as well as his body. He sat and gazed at the clear night sky. He watched his breath dissipate into the darkness. His mind was weightless yet his limbs felt heavy, but he lifted himself out of the chair, gathered up the mug and box, and went back inside. With the blanket still draped over his shoulders, he made his way down the hall to his bedroom. He dropped the blanket next to the bed, set the mug and box on the night-stand, and crawled into bed. He drifted off into sleep without a wandering thought.

The sound of the alarm woke Theo. He felt moderately refreshed after soundly sleeping for a few hours. He got up, followed his morning routine, and stood in his closet while he contemplated what to wear. It wasn't a special day, but dressing well was part of the façade he needed to maintain. He chose a black, two-piece Tom Ford suit with a matching belt and shoes. He paired it with a static-patterned Armani dress shirt and called a taxi to pick him up. The ride was over fairly quickly as Theo left early to avoid traffic. Upon arriving at the hotel Theo paid his fare, gave the valet his ticket, and waited a few minutes before his car came into sight. He tipped the valet a fifty, got in the car, and drove to work. The detour to the hotel landed Theo at the beginning of down-town Chicago traffic, but he made it into the office before eight.

Like so many days before, Leah greeted Theo and handed him a mug of tea when he exited the elevator. They put on their usual show of smiles, overly warm tones and business-related small talk for the receptionist and any prying eyes until they were in Theo's office with the door closed.

"So!" Leah said enthusiastically while taking a seat on the couch closest to the door. Theo sat across from her, as he usually did. "How was the party? I heard you pulled a disap-pearing act fairly early." It wasn't a question.

"Yes, I had another engagement last night which required my undivided attention." Leah looked at Theo without speaking, urging him to continue. "The party was as you'd expect. Champagne, speeches, congratulations, and fake smiles."

Leah nodded and studied Theo's expression before continuing. "Kelsey was looking for you."

Theo looked at her and narrowed his eyes. "I'm sorry, who?"

Leah rolled her eyes and sighed deeply. "Chairman Scott's daughter, Theo."

Oh. "I must have missed her." Theo smiled weakly. *And thank fuck I did.* "And how do you know? You had plans with Josh last night, did you not?"

"*Oh*, I did," she said, perhaps a bit too enthusiastically.

Theo winced and shook his head.

"Ally told me," Leah clarified. She studied the searching expression spread across Theo's face. "Oh, God, Theo. Allison. The VP's secretary."

"I know who Allison is," Theo muttered defensively. "I didn't realize there was such a gossip network here between staff."

Leah grinned and winked, causing Theo to shake his head in defeat. "You're a hot commodity around here, Mr. Rey." Theo shot his eyes at her, unamused by the address. "Nearly every woman in the building is hoping for a shot with '*one of the city's most eligible bachelors.*'"

Theo recoiled. "Ugh, do *not* mention that article ever again."

"But you were so handsome in the spread!" Theo growled and threw his head back. "All right, boss-man; down to business. I—"

Theo held up his hand and sat up. "Please add 'boss-man' to the list of things not to say to me."

Leah smiled and continued, "I cleared your schedule for today. I was thinking you might want to take it easy."

"Thank you."

"Your calendar is open on your computer and ready for you to input your vacation." Theo started to protest, but was promptly interrupted. "Nah-uh! This is non-negotiable. You already agreed to it anyway. One of us should be here, so I'll take my time once you've returned. Lastly, your clean laundry is in your desk chair."

Theo smiled genuinely. "Thanks, Leah. Expect a huge bonus this year." She smiled from ear to ear.

Theo sat at his glass desk and opened his laptop. Just as Leah had said, his calendar was open with several weeks highlighted over the next few months. Feeling rather over-whelmed by it all, he sighed and started to close the lid.

"We have to go back, Theo."

Theo froze with his hand on the partially closed lid and tightly shut his eyes. He shook his head and opened his eyes. "Perhaps some time off is what I need," he whispered. It was the beginning of November and the next several weeks in the month were available, including the week surrounding Thanksgiving. Theo took a deep breath, highlighted the entire month, and sent it off to Leah for processing.

At the gym Theo decided on a lighter cardio workout than his usual weight training or high intensity circuits. He got there just after nine in the evening, after having to work late in preparation of his upcoming vacation. After spending more than twelve hours at work and not sleeping all too soundly, he was exhausted. He changed and did some light stretches as a warm-up. After doing several standing stretches, he lay down on his yoga mat with his back flat against the ground. With his arms outstretched straight and palms resting on the floor, he inhaled deeply and twisted at the hips, his right knee touching the floor over his left knee. He held the position for thirty seconds before rotating his hips and doing the same thing with his left knee. While holding the position, his gaze wandered to the other patrons.

There were several new faces sprinkled in amongst the regulars Theo had come to recognize. The new members were mostly female so Theo paid them no mind. What caught his attention were a few familiar faces. Not just the faces of regulars, but the faces of men he'd picked up. Two of them smirked at him when they made eye contact and Theo immediately looked away and pretended to focus on his stretches. *I guess I have to start picking up guys somewhere else. Probably for the best, I'd rather not have to stop coming here due to my poor decisions.*

Theo finished his stretches and ran intervals on a treadmill for an hour and a half. Seeing *familiar* faces killed any plans he'd had on picking someone up that night so he quickly showered and went home after his workout. After depositing his gym clothes in his laundry bag, Theo made a protein and fruit smoothie, plunked down on the couch and watched *Jaws*.

CHAPTER FOUR

T HEO WOKE UP JUST after three thirty. Another nightmare had stirred him from sleep and without any more weed, he was unable to calm down and fall back asleep. He quickly climbed out of bed, stripped off the sweat-soaked sheets and pillowcases, and threw them on the floor. Clad only in black boxer briefs, he raced out of the room to the hall closet. A black jump rope hung on a hook just inside the door, which Theo grabbed before returning to his room. He firmly gripped the two ends of the rope and started to skip. The first five minutes were slow, merely a warm-up for his muscles. His labored breathing began to even out and he took deep controlled breaths. Once Theo's muscles were warmed up, he increased his speed from seventy skips per minute to one hundred sixty. The pace was maintained until he stopped at the hour mark, panting and dripping sweat. His calves ached and burned, relishing the brief reprieve.

Theo took a few deep breaths then tossed the rope onto the pile of soiled sheets and dropped to the floor. He landed hard on the palms of his hands on outstretched arms and proceeded to do deep push-ups with his chest nearly touching the floor; he did them in sets of fifty reps. Upon completion of the second set, sweat was dripping from Theo's nose and forehead onto the dark hardwood floor beneath him. During the fourth set his arms trembled and his pace slowed, but he did not stop. By the middle of the fifth set, Theo's trembling arms gave out under his weight and he collapsed.

He rolled onto his back and started doing sit-ups before he had time to catch his breath. He did sit-ups with the same reps and sets as the push-ups, but was unable to continue during the fifth set. Splayed out on the floor on his back, Theo's whole body was ablaze. He tried to do side planks but was too exhausted to hold himself up for more than a couple minutes. He fell to the floor again and lay there until he caught his breath. The events of the nightmare were now pushed from his thoughts and all focus was on his tired, aching body.

With every ounce of energy he could muster, Theo pulled himself to his feet, using the edge of the bed for leverage. Once standing upright, he gathered up the soiled sheets and tossed them into a black, metal, wire chair against the wall by the door. He stripped off his boxer briefs and did the same to them before staggering down the hall to the bathroom and getting in the shower.

Standing was a painful endeavor, but Theo's throbbing muscles were rewarded by the soothing heat from the spray. Moving the bar of soap over his body was tiring, but he managed to finish and get dried off without too much trouble. Putting clean sheets on the bed was a much more difficult task but the reward of feeling his body fall into fresh sheets was worth the work.

WORK WAS BUSIER THAN USUAL, which was good, as it helped to distract Theo from how much pain his body was in from his late-night workout. Leah had gotten Theo's schedule sorted out before he'd arrived that morning. Taking nearly the whole month off meant several meetings had been pushed forward and others had been changed to telephone and Skype conferences. Theo was greeted the usual way when elevator doors opened, but his unrestrained banter with Leah, once inside his office, was replaced with a thorough game plan for every second of his extremely busy day.

Leah had Theo booked into back-to-back meetings until early afternoon. By the time he returned to his office he was exhausted and starved. He walked in to see Leah laying out takeout containers on the table between the couches.

"What's all this?" Theo asked after closing the door behind him and walking over to the table.

"After the morning I planned for you, I figured you'd be hungry." Leah smiled and motioned for Theo to take a seat, which he did. "I knew better than anyone that you didn't have time for a lunch break so I ordered some Chinese. There's steamed chicken and mixed vegetables, with that brown sauce you like on the side, chop suey, beef and broccoli, and steamed rice. I also got you a half order of chicken balls in case you were feeling like having a super cheat day." Theo's eyes lit up at the mention of chicken balls—his favorite guilty pleasure. "It looks like I made the right choice. Come on, sit down."

Theo sat down in front of a bottle of Fiji water and a pair of chopsticks set out on the table. "Thank you," he said with a smile. Leah returned the gesture and nodded in response then started toward the door. "Leah, where are you going?"

She stopped in her tracks at the sound of her name and glanced back to Theo. She smiled again and said, "You've been occupied all morning, I figured you might like some privacy before your afternoon appointments."

"Get back here and sit down. If you make me eat all of this by myself, I'll be in a comatose state, unfit for any business later." They both laughed and Leah took her usual seat. Theo looked about the table expectantly then at Leah. "Is there by chance…"

Leah held up her index finger and reached into the brown paper bag on the table and pulled out a jug of Sriracha. Theo's eyes lit up and Leah laughed. "What kind of amateur do you take me for? I wouldn't forget your hot sauce."

"I'm sorry I ever doubted you."

"You should be."

Leah left after they'd finished eating, giving Theo about fifteen minutes alone until his next engagement. He pulled his iPhone out of his pocket and opened up a folder titled "Backup." Inside the folder was a single app: Grindr. It had been about a month since Theo had last opened up Grindr, but after his realization at the gym he knew it was time to do something different.

Ignoring all of the unread messages, Theo began to browse active profiles. Bombarded by a sea of headless bare torsos and screen names like MagikMike and Todd69, Theo quickly lost interest and closed the app. His own profile was not much better; his username was "God's Gift"—the meaning of his very name. It wasn't very clever, but it was the best he could muster. His headline was simply "Discretion is key" and conveyed nothing fun or flirty. The rest of the profile was minimalist, much like most things in Theo's life outside of work. His picture was a full body shot from the neck down in his fitted gym clothes. The picture itself said more than enough and he had no shortage of interested users, but he didn't have time for that when an afternoon of appointments loomed over his head. Slipping his phone back into his pocket, Theo tidied up the mess on the table he'd insisted Leah leave for him to do, and made his way to boardroom three to meet with the young man who would be assuming most of his responsibilities during his absence.

Despite how sore his muscles were, Theo went to the gym after work for light cardio and his usual circuits. He ran for half an hour on the treadmill after stretching and once again noticed too many familiar faces in the gym. The circuits consisted of a mixture of body weight exercises and weight machines: pull-ups, burpees, pendulum lunges, sumo squats, high box jumps, tricep curls, lateral raises, tricep dips, and oblique dips were among the roster of exercises Theo cycled through. The whole circuit lasted an hour on average, depending on how good Theo was that day. Today's session would be a longer one.

After finishing up his workout, Theo hit the gym shower then changed back into his work clothes, minus the tie and jacket. In an attempt at looking casual, he'd rolled his sleeves up just below his elbows and undid the top two buttons on his grey button-up. Pleased with his comparatively relaxed look, Theo went out to his car and opened up Grindr.

After browsing for a few minutes and receiving a few uninteresting messages, one came through which caught his eye from a user going by Conquistador. *Conquistador, huh? Let's see.* Theo opened the profile and raised an eyebrow when he saw the picture expanded; light brown skin, big brown eyes, toned abs, and a sizable bulge in grey sweats. Theo opened the message.

Conquistador: Hey there.
God's Gift: Hey. What're you up to?

Conquistador: I just got out of class. I'm a university student. Wbu?

Wbu…? What the… oooooh.

God's Gift: I just finished up at the gym. Feeling pretty lonely.
Conquistador: I have trouble believing someone with a body like yours is ever lonely.

Oh, you cheeky fuck.

God's Gift: How about you come keep me company, then? See if you've got what it takes to conquer me.

Theo audibly groaned over his part in this exchange, but he needed this to hurry along and was getting tired of messaging.

Conquistador: I'll gladly lay claim.

Perfect.

God's Gift: Meet me in the lot behind the Whole Foods by the pier in half an hour. I'll be waiting by a black BMW M3 in a grey dress shirt and black dress pants.
Conquistador: Okay.
Conquistador: Sounds hot.
God's Gift: Just hurry up.

The sun had nearly set by the time Theo parked behind the Whole Foods. Theo arrived early; it hadn't taken more than ten minutes for him to drive over. He'd said half an hour to give Conquistador a chance to bus over from the university. At the twenty-minute mark Theo got out of the car and leaned against it. He still hadn't retrieved his winter coat from storage so wind chilled him to the bone. His fuck showed up early, dressed properly for the weather. His smile was wide as he approached Theo, stealing glances between the man and the car. Theo curled one side of his mouth into a smirk to reassure the boy that he'd found the right person.

"Hi," the boy said quietly.

"So," Theo started, slowly eyeing the boy from head to toe. He was taller than Theo by about an inch. "You're Conquistador. I can't say I'm disappointed."

The boy's gaze quickly shot to the ground and he smiled.

Good God, is he shy?

"It's nice to meet you. I'm actually Santiago. But everyone just calls me Santi. I mean... you can call me Santi if you want to. What's your name?"

Theo cocked an eyebrow at him. "You don't have to be so nervous."

"I-I know. I just haven't met up with anyone quite as attractive as you. You are really good looking." Theo smiled at the awkward compliments. "Is your name Theodore by chance?"

Theo's eyes widened and shot to Santi's in a panic. He took a small, reflexive step back. "How do you know my name?" His tone was sharp.

"Ah, it was just a guess. See, I have a cousin named Teodoro and my aunt made a big deal about when he was born, saying he was 'a gift from God.' She'd been trying to have a baby for a long time with no luck and she finally got pregnant so they named him Teodoro—God's gift. He's a couple years younger than me and oh my God, I'm sorry, I'm ranting. I'm so sorry. I didn't mean to catch you off guard or anything. I-I'm just going to stop talking now."

"Santi, how old are you?" Theo ran his hand through his hair.

"Twenty-two," he answered immediately.

Theo took a step closer and Santi gasped. "How old are you?"

"I told you, I'm twenty-two."

"Cut the shit, kid. How old are you?"

Santi looked down at his shoes and whispered, "Eighteen."

Theo nodded and took a deep breath. "Are you a university student? Do not lie again."

Santi hesitated before answering. "No. I'm a high school senior. I swear I am eighteen, though."

Oh my God, no.

"What are you doing here?"

"Well, it's my birthday and I figured I'd like to meet up with someone. I haven't really... no one knows that I like guys, so I figured I'd try Grindr and your pictures looked really good. And discretion! No one knows about me so I thought I'd like to be discreet too."

"Look, you seem like a really nice kid, but believe me when I say that I'm not the type of guy you want to associate with. It sounds like a brush-off, but trust me."

Santi's face fell but he still managed a smile and nodded his head. "I'm sorry I lied."

"It's okay. Go home before you stress your parents out." Santi turned to leave and still wore that sad look on his face.

Fucking hell.

Theo grabbed Santi's wrist, pulled him close, and in one fluid motion he kissed him; Santi returned the kiss once his shock subsided. He put his left hand on Theo's neck and ran his right up the side of Theo's chilled body. Theo broke the kiss with a laugh. "Easy there, Conquistador."

Santi's cheeks flushed and he spoke softly. "Thank you."

"Get going before it gets dark."

Theo waited until Santi was out of sight before going in the Whole Foods. He bought his usual fare of vegetables, fruits, lean steak, skinless chicken breast, and eggs. He drove home, unloaded the groceries, and sat down on the couch. The wall clock indicated it was just after nine. Theo considered going out to try and meet someone the old-fashioned way, but he was tired. He pulled his phone out and sent his brother, Jamie, a text.

T: Hey, Jay. I need to pick up, when can I see you?

Before Theo could put the phone down a message came through.

J: Oh, things are going great, thanks for asking.

Theo rolled his eyes.

T: How're you doing, Jay? How's school?
J: How's school? Really?
T: Shut up.
J: hahaha
J: I can hook you up tomorrow, bro.
T: Perfect. What time?
J: Noon. You can buy me lunch.

Theo snorted.

T: Fine. Text me in the morning once you've picked a place.
J: K. See ya tomorrow. I gotta go smash.
T: Gross. Have fun.

Theo threw his phone on the table in front of the couch and made a protein smoothie. He left the mess and returned to his spot on the couch, putting on Ridley Scott's *Alien* while he drank his smoothie. *It's just like old times, right, Isaac?* He smiled sadly to himself and focused his attention on the movie.

CHAPTER FIVE

THEO WAS AT THE GYM by six in the morning. His sleep was once again interrupted and his mind a mess. On top of his usual thoughts of Isaac, he was hit with a wave of anxiety over not having work to distract him and occupy his time. His body was still very sore from being pushed a few nights prior, so he was thankful that it was a cardio day. He stretched, ran for an hour and a half, showered, returned home, and went to sleep.

He woke up a few hours later and sat in bed, pondering what to do until Jamie called. Jamie didn't wake up early unless he had to, so Theo figured he probably had around three to four hours to kill before he had to go out again. He reached for the remote on his nightstand and rolled up the shade. Bright light slowly filled the room and Theo winced when it reached his eyes. Once he'd adjusted to the new lighting, he eyed the pile of sheets in the chair by the door. He groaned, got out of bed, collected the sheets and took them to the laundry room across from his bedroom. Laundry wasn't a particularly enjoyable task and he often had his clothes professionally laundered while at work, but he was bored and wouldn't be back at the office any time soon.

With the sheets and a few clothing items in the washer, Theo set about making his bed. Finished with the bed, Theo glanced around his room to see what else could be done. The walls were painted white and were unadorned with the exception of an abstract black-and-white print with geometric patterns above the bed. There was only one night-stand which matched the black stain that was on the frame of the bed and the dresser. The top of the dresser was completely bare, as was the rest of the room. The silence in the room slowly evolved into familiar voices which caught Theo's attention.

"What're you doing this weekend?" I ask.

"Probably something with your stupid ass." Deadpan. What an asshole.

I lean forward, grab the pillow behind me, and throw it at Isaac's head. "Asshole."

He's laughing now. He turns to look at me before flicking his eyes back to the TV. "This is the best part."

I rip my gaze from him and look back at the movie. We're watching Jaws *for about the hundredth time. I'm not particularly fond of old movies, but it's Isaac's favorite so I never say no when he wants to throw it on. Right now Brody, Hooper, and Quint are sharing stories over scars.*

"'Tiger. Thirteen-footer. You know how you know that when you're in the water, Chief? You tell by lookin' from the dorsal to the tail.' This is one of the greatest scenes in cinematic history."

"Oh, I know. You've only made me watch it about a million times, dude." We sit in silence until Quint is finished telling Hooper and Brody his story then I remember why I started talking in the first place. "So, do you have plans this weekend or not?"

"I thought I already answered you," he says, smiling smugly. "No, I don't have anything planned. Why, what's up?"

I hesitate for a moment. I know what he's going to say. "Blaine and Jake Krazinski are having a party this weekend." I pause but Isaac remains silent. "I guess their parents are flying to New York for the weekend. So, do you think you wanna go?"

He's quiet for what seems like an eternity. "They invited you?"

"Yes."

"Do they know you're asking me?"

"Look, I know you guys didn't get along in the past, but I won't let anything happen. They're not bad guys. They've grown up a bit." He's totally going to say no, I shouldn't have mentioned it at all.

"Okay."

"What?"

"I said okay. I'll go with you."

I try to hide it, but I don't think my smile can be contained.

"No!" Theo violently pulled at his hair and shook off the unwanted memory. Needing to keep busy, he retrieved some cleaner and a roll of paper towel and proceeded to clean every hard surface in his room that he could reach. He moved on to the laundry room, and then scrubbed down the shower and rest of the bathroom, paying extra attention to the grout between the tiles on the shower wall.

Theo moved on to the kitchen and living room then sat on the couch. He pulled his phone out of his pocket and saw that it was just after noon. *He should be up soon.* Theo stood and paced around the room until his phone pinged a few minutes later. He ran over to the table, picked up his phone, and saw a new message from Jamie.

J: Yo, you up?

T: Of course I am.

J: Yeah, dumb question.

J: I think I want fajitas, cool with you?

T: That's fine. When and where?

J: Pick me up and we'll find a place.

T: Okay. I'll be there in 20.

J: Uh, I'm not at home.

T: Where are you?

Theo impatiently waited for a reply, which was delayed.

T: Jamie, I swear.

J: Chill, bro. Downers Grove.

T: What the fuck are you doing out there?

J: I told you, I had plans last night.

T: Whatever. Text me the address. I'll be there in about 40 minutes.

J: See ya then!

I'm going to fucking kill him.

JAMIE JUMPED IN THE CAR, a blur of shaggy, wavy hair and big blue eyes. He resembled Theo in the way that siblings often do, but Theo took after their father where Jamie had more of their mother's softer features. His cheeks were a bit fuller and his eyes a bit lighter. He thanked Theo for picking him up and gave directions to a close by restaurant. Things were quiet before Jamie broke the silence.

"So, how was traffic?" he asked in an almost singsong tone.

"It's Saturday, Jay. You know how it was."

"Come on, bro. Don't be cross with me."

Theo sighed. Jamie always got his way. "Is this place on the right or left?"

"It's just past the second set of lights on the right. There should be parking out front."

The restaurant was much smaller than Theo expected it to be. It seemed to be a low-key, "ma and pa" type of establishment with a clean, yet warm interior. The walls were a creamy off-white with one burnt orange accented wall and there were about twelve honey-colored wood tables; each table had a napkin dispenser and a bottle of Valentina hot sauce. Theo and Jamie sat at the table closest to the accented wall. Not a moment after they were seated, a middle-aged woman with long black hair came over with ice waters, menus under her arm, and a warm greeting. She introduced herself as Salma and placed the menus in front of Theo and Jamie.

"Can I get you boys anything else to drink?"

"I'll have a Sol, please. No glass."

Theo shook his head gently. "No, thank you, the water is perfect."

Salma smiled and walked behind the bar. She returned a few quick moments later with the beer and placed it in front of Jamie. He thanked her and she smiled appreciatively. "I'll give you boys a moment with the menus." She walked away from their table and into the kitchen.

"You're not going to have a drink with me?"

"I'm trying to watch my carbohydrate intake." *I think? When did I stop drinking beer?*

"Order a shot of tequila then."

A laugh escaped from Theo's lips. "I do have to drive your sorry ass home. I'd rather not get a DUI doing so."

Jamie rolled his eyes and took a swig of his beer. "Ugh, fine. You have to promise me a few drinks next time, though. Perhaps during a time you're *not* watching your carbs." Theo ignored the condescending tone in Jamie's voice. "In all seriousness though, you're looking pretty fit, dude. I think you're in the best shape I've ever seen you in."

"Shut up." Theo smirked.

"Learn to take a compliment."

Before Theo could reply, Salma reappeared. "You boys decided on what you'd like?"

"Absolutely. Medium rare beef fajitas for me and he'll have chicken fajitas." Jamie handed both menus back to Salma and took another drink.

"So now you're ordering for me?"

"Let's not pretend you weren't going to get them anyway."

Theo nodded. "Fair enough." A silence fell between them for about a minute before Theo broke it. "Cute place. It doesn't seem like your style."

Jamie took a swig of beer and smiled. "You're totally right. D brought me here about three months ago." Theo saw the moment Jamie realized what he'd said. His brother stilled and winced while Theo's own jaw tensed. "I'm sorry, bro. I said that without thinking."

"That's okay, Jay. H-how is Dani doing?" Theo was looking off at the window, the clock on the wall, the label on the hot sauce; anything to avoid making eye contact with his brother.

Jamie was quiet a moment, like he was choosing his words. "Do you really want to know?"

"I do."

"She's doing great, Theo. She's seeing someone now, so don't feel bad, okay? She doesn't hate you. Not anymore at least."

A deep sigh left Theo. "She doesn't hate me, huh? Perhaps she should."

"Look, bro. I don't know exactly what happened between you two, but she's okay. You though... you don't seem all that happy these days."

"I'm fine. Work is busy. In fact, I'm actually taking a bit of a vacation right now."

"Really?! That's awesome. You deserve a break more than anyone I know. Are you going to go anywhere?"

"Leah said the same thing. I don't think I'll go anywhere; I'm not really in the mood for travel. I think I'll just stay close to home and try to relax."

"Have someone special you'll be spending the time with?"

Theo nervously looked at Jamie, unable to speak. He opened his mouth, but the words did not come. He took a drink of water and felt like he was suffocating under Jamie's waiting stare. He managed to shake his head, indicating that no, there wasn't anyone.

"Sorry for the wait," said Salma as she set down two large platters on the table. The food smelled amazing and looked just as good. "Is there anything else I can bring? How about another Sol?"

"Yes, please."

"Thank you for the food, it looks great," Theo managed to say.

Salma winked at Theo. "Just wait until you taste it, love." She turned her head back to Jamie. "I'll be right back with your drink."

Salma was right; the food was even better than it looked. Jamie jam-packed his tortillas with beef, peppers, onions, guacamole, and sour cream. He scoffed them down as if he hadn't eaten in days. Theo on the other hand didn't touch his tortillas. He instead ate the chicken and vegetables doused in hot sauce with a fork and knife.

"Jesus, hungry much?"

Jamie wiped his messy fingers on a napkin then finished the first bottle of beer. "You have no idea. School is getting crazy and food like this is a luxury."

"Mom and Dad won't front you lunch money? Really?" Theo teased.

"Shut up." Jamie snorted and began adding toppings to another fajita. Salma brought his second drink over with a smile and a top up for Theo's water. "I'm in my third year— the shit's getting real. I'm on rotations now. I just started my surgical last week, actually. So it's not a question of money for food, but one of time." Jamie took a huge bite of food and audibly groaned his approval.

Theo shook his head and smirked. "It sounds like it's going well for you. I'm glad to hear it, Jay. But answer me this—am I going to have to call you doctor next year?"

"You bet your fucking ass you are."

The annoyed sigh that Theo reflexively made caused both brothers to erupt into laughter. For the duration of the meal, Jamie spoke of his duties in the hospital, about how he and Dani were lucky to be on the same surgical, and Theo listened intently. He paid the bill and they set out for some "light shopping at Nordstrom" as Jamie had put it. *I'm sure I'll have to pay for that too.*

Jamie told more stories about his patients for the car ride back to downtown Chicago and the time passed much faster than it had for Theo when he drove up solo. Although he gave him a hard time, Theo truly did enjoy spending time with his brother. Hearing of his happiness and success made Theo feel a sliver of the happiness he had once felt.

"Are you still listening to me?" asked Jamie.

"What?" Theo looked around and saw that they were parked and the engine was already off.

"I asked you where you bought that sweater." Theo looked down at the black hoodie he was wearing. "Theo, are you sure you're okay?"

"It's Michael Kors. I got it at Neiman Marcus last month. We should probably go inside, I'm sure you have other things you'd like to do today considering how busy you are with school." Theo turned and started to get out of the car. He stopped when he felt Jamie's hand on his shoulder.

"Theo, wait. Are you really okay? You haven't really been yourself since... Isaac." Theo's body stiffened at the mention of the name he'd been trying so hard to not think about. "I don't mean to upset you, I really don't. I just want you to know that if you want to talk about it, I'm always here."

Theo looked at Jamie and relaxed the tension in his shoulders a bit. "Thanks, Jay."

Jamie gave a half smile and clapped his hand on his brother's shoulder. "Come on. There are some clothes you need to buy me." *I fucking knew it.*

Jamie dragged Theo around Nordstrom for over an hour. He ended up buying a new Zegna tie for himself and a down duvet as well as three dress shirts and a pair of Gucci high top sneakers for Jamie. By five in the evening they were making their way up to Jamie's loft.

Theo followed Jamie in and took in the massive open-concept kitchen and living room area. The perimeter walls were all restored brick, while there were white walls to the right which had been put up for a bedroom and washroom. The walls were adorned with various framed pop culture posters and a few framed record sleeves. A considerable mess was atop the quartz countertops, but the living room was free of clutter. Theo took a seat on a crimson leather couch and waited as Jamie disappeared in his bedroom. Theo was looking at a beat-up copy of Hemingway's *The Sun Also Rises* on the table when Jamie returned with a tray of marijuana paraphernalia unfamiliar to Theo. He sat on the matching chair adjacent to the couch and turned on the TV. He slid the remote over to Theo.

"Feel free to watch whatever. I've got everything."

"I'd actually like to hear more about what you're doing, if you don't mind telling me." Jamie flashed Theo a wide grin and told him about his classmates, the doctors he worked with, and more about how Dani was on his same rotation. Theo listened keenly and loved hearing these small details.

It took Jamie half an hour to roll twenty joints. When he finished, he put them in a Ziploc bag, handed it to Theo, and they said their goodbyes. Theo was home by six and feeling drained. He collapsed into the couch in a seated position and rested his head back on the cushions. He'd tossed the bag of joints and his new tie on the coffee table when he came in.

WE'RE LATE SHOWING up to the party and I can see that everyone is already out back as Blaine leads us through the house. We reach the back door and my soccer buddies are sitting around the fire pit. I feel an arm around my shoulders and the weight of someone against my body before I see who it is.

"Rey! You made it!" I can tell by his voice that it's Jake.

"I told you I was coming."

"Yeah, but you've been known to bail on us, which is kind of a dick move, but you're here now." He gulps the cup of what's presumably beer he's holding with his free hand.

"Whatever, man. Hey, I brought Isaac with me." I turn to

see Isaac standing behind me, looking off to the side of the yard. He flicks his eyes to mine and gives me a quick half smirk.

"What? Jones is here?"

"I'm right here, Jake," Isaac says. "Nice to see you again. It's been a while." Isaac extends a hand to Jake, which he swats away.

"What the hell, ma—" Jake cuts me off. The arm that was once over my shoulders is now pointed at Isaac's chest. His right hand is jabbing into my own chest, spilling beer on my shirt.

"Shut up, Rey." He shifts his stare over to Isaac. "What the fuck do you think you're doing here?" Before Isaac says anything, Jake yells out, "Hey! Blaine! Why did you let him in the house?"

Blaine walks over from the now onlooking crowd by the fire pit and stands between Jake and me. "He's Teddy's guest, of course I let him in. Don't be an asshole."

"This motherfucker needs to go back to the gutter he crawled out of before we need to clean the tiles."

I step forward and grab Jake's favored arm. "That's enough. You told me you were cool with him now."

"'Cool with him'? This piece of shit thinks he can go out with my girl and I'm just going to be okay with that?"

"Jake, don't be petty. You guys weren't even dating at the time," I say in an attempt to make him see reason.

"Fuck you, Rey." Jake pushes me and I stumble over Blaine. When I look back at Jake I see he's dropped his drink and is making a fist. Isaac sees it too, but he doesn't run. Please, please move!

"Try not to get your mongrel blood on the grout." Jake pulls his arm back and I see red. I don't know exactly what happened, but when I regain my bearings I'm kneeling over Jake's chest with my right fist feeling heavy against his bloodied face. The guys are pulling me off him and everyone is shouting. I'm thrown back and land hard on the tiles. I look at my fist and I see that the skin over my knuckles is broken and it is shaking uncontrollably.

I can't move my own body and start to panic. Why am I so angry?

That's when I feel it; a familiar hand gently wrapping itself around mine. My eyes shoot up and Isaac is standing above me. His bottom lip is split but he otherwise looks unharmed. Physically at least. He pulls me to my feet and quickly leads me out of the house the way we came.

Out front, he sits me down on the curb and examines my knuckles. "You shouldn't have done that, Theo."

Before I can think to hold it in, tears are running down my face. "I'm sorry. I'm so fucking sorry, Isaac."

"Don't apologize. You saved me from a hell of a beating and for that I am grateful. But dammit, Theo. These are your friends and teammates. I shouldn't have come here tonight."

"I'm not going to associate with anyone who talks to you like that. You're more important than all of those assholes." I look at the blood flowing from his lip. "I'm sorry I didn't react sooner."

Isaac smiles then winces from the pain. "Come on, let's go for a walk then get a cab. You can get cleaned up at my place while we think of a cover story for why your hand is so torn up."

"I'm so sorry."

"Let's go, Mike Tyson. Remind me to never piss you off." Despite how shitty I'm feeling he makes me laugh, just like he always does.

THEO WOKE with an all too familiar unpleasantness lingering. It was dark outside now and when he checked his phone he saw it was just after ten thirty. He wasn't remotely tired and didn't want to be in the house any longer so he opened up Grindr. Before the app could fully load he thought back to his meeting with Santi and closed it. *Fuck this, I'll just find someone the old-fashioned way.*

He bolted off the couch, went to the bathroom, and stripped down. He retrieved a black silicone bulb from under the sink and gave himself a warm water enema before showering. With his hygiene no longer a concern, Theo dressed in a fitted light grey Tom Ford henley and dark wash, straight leg Diesel jeans. It wasn't snowing, so he slipped on a pair of black Armani suede boots, grabbed his phone, called a cab, and left.

The club wasn't the overcrowded sweaty mess it would become in a couple hours. There were a lot of people, mostly men, inside but there was still a respect for personal space, which Theo valued. It was insanely dark, with the only light coming from dimmed blue overhead lights and colored strobes. Theo approached the neon red lit bar and ordered a gin and tonic, paid in cash, and made his way around the open dance floor.

He noticed plenty of eyes on him, but didn't see anyone who fit the bill of what he was looking for. He wanted to hurt. It's what he felt he deserved, so he ignored their stares and continued walking the perimeter. After about twenty minutes of no luck, he finished his drink and returned to the bar for a second. He downed that one at the bar and ordered a third. Taking the glass in hand, he went out searching again, figuring it might be easier if he were drunk. After a few minutes of roaming around, Theo stopped and leaned against a support beam. He bitterly finished his drink and looked out to the dance floor when he noticed someone looking back at him. Not just looking, but boring holes into him with his unwavering stare. The stranger was tall, about twenty-five, and had free-flowing long black hair that stopped a couple inches past his shoulders. He looked Japanese and was dressed in what appeared to be a white t-shirt under a black leather jacket, black jeans, and black leather boots. He was definitely hot. His shoulders looked broad and Theo guessed he was pretty strong from what he could see of his build. *Oh yes, he'll do.* Theo set his glass down next to a collection of dirty glasses on a ledge by the wall and made his way over to the handsome stranger.

CHAPTER SIX

As Theo got closer to his prey, his features became clearer into view; full lips, determined eyes, high cheekbones, he was *definitely* Japanese. Theo smiled confidently as he reached the stranger. *"Konbanwa."* He stood just a few inches from him now. *I'll get him out of here quickly and get this over with. "Saikin dō?"*

The stranger stared back at Theo, seemingly amused, and lifted an eyebrow. "I don't speak Japanese."

His words hit Theo like a Mack truck and deflated his bravado. *Oh shit, oh shit, oh shit. Was I seriously that wrong?* "I-I'm sorry. I thought you were... Japanese." Theo broke eye contact, feeling heat spread across his face and up to the tips of his ears. "Excuse me." Theo turned to leave but stopped at the sound of snickering over the loud music. He dared to glance back and saw the stranger's body lightly convulsing with his fist up in front of his mouth. Behind the fist he wore a wicked smile. *Did I say something funny?* Theo was curious about what the man found so amusing about the situation, but he was too mortified to stick around and chat about it.

He looked ahead and started toward the bar. He didn't even make it four steps before he felt a firm grip on his forearm.

"Wait, please." Theo stopped and turned to see the source of his deflated ego. The man released his grip. "I'm sorry, I shouldn't have laughed. Please, stick around for a sec."

Theo wanted to say no. He wanted to retreat and go home. But something about the man before him held him in place, something he couldn't quite define. "Okay."

The man smiled, seemingly relieved. "Good." A silence fell between them for a few beats, their eyes remained locked and the man snorted out a faint laugh before he spoke. "How about we start over? Name's Masamune." His voice was low, smooth.

Wait, what? I thought he wasn't... Theo studied Masamune's face and mulled his name over in his head. His face must have relayed his confusion because Masamune spoke again before Theo could focus enough to form words.

"I know what you're thinking. You weren't completely off the mark before. I *am* Japanese." Theo just stood there, listening to the words roll off of his tongue. He didn't hear a hint of a Japanese accent, but he definitely heard something. Over the thumping music, it was difficult to tell. "Although I can't speak or understand much of the language."

Theo nodded. "Ah, okay. I shouldn't have assumed. I am sorry."

Masamune raised his hand and waved it casually. "Don't worry about it." He put his hands into his jeans pockets. "So, are you going to tell me your name? Or should I start guessing?" He smirked.

Masamune's smile was disarming. Under normal circumstances Theo would never give his name to a trick, but nothing about this encounter had gone as planned. "I'm Theo."

Masamune's smile got even wider. "Pleasure to meet you. What do you say we go get a drink?"

Just say no. "Sure."

"It's a bit loud down here, do you mind if we head up to the lounge upstairs?"

Just say no. "Lead the way."

Theo sat alone on a bar stool at a high table. The lounge was a large dark room with soft lighting. The music from downstairs resonated in the room, but Theo could at least now hear himself think. *I need to get control of this situation.*

His thoughts were interrupted when Masamune returned to the table holding a gin and tonic and bottle of Budweiser. "Double gin and tonic, as requested." Masamune slid onto the empty stool across from Theo and took a swig of his beer. "Let me start by saying that you were very charming downstairs. If your plan was to seduce me using my native tongue, it would have worked marvelously. You know, had you chosen the right language." He laughed again and took another drink.

Theo felt the flush return, crawling up his neck and face. "Okay, you've got me. As if I wasn't embarrassed enough already, I don't need to relive the experience." He drank half of his drink in one go. "I'm going to need another one of these if you keep bringing that up."

"I'm sorry, I'll stop teasing you."

"You apologize a lot considering you're *not* the one who just made a complete ass of himself a few minutes ago."

"Yeah, I guess I do. I'm Canadian; it's kind of our thing." He winked at Theo.

Canadian, huh. Ah, the accent. "Are you a native French speaker by chance?"

"Indeed I am. Not many people notice, though."

"My great-grandparents were from France. My grandfather taught me the language when I was a kid. I can usually spot a French accent right away, but it was pretty loud down there." Theo's voice trailed off at the end and he took a drink to silence himself. "So, what's a French Canadian doing in Chicago?"

"Just passing through actually. I've been to a few cities already, just taking in the sights and the people, but Chicago is my first stop stateside."

Perfect.

"How do you like it so far?"

"It's big. It didn't seem too different from Toronto but then I met this really hot guy who agreed to have a drink with me, so I'm liking it a bit more than Toronto right now."

Theo choked on the last gulp of his drink and locked eyes with Masamune for the first time since leaving the dark downstairs; they burned with just as much intensity as they did downstairs, but his eyes appeared different now. Theo noticed that they looked lighter. Light brown, maybe. The contrast from what he perceived downstairs caught him off guard. "You don't have much of a filter, do you?"

"I'm afraid not. Restraint has never been one of my strengths. Especially not when there's something I want."

Theo's lip twitched. "What do you want?"

"Well, Theo," the name rolled off of Masamune's tongue so easily, "first I'd like to buy you another drink. Then I was hoping we could talk some more."

Theo's heart was pounding. His mouth was dry and all he could do was nod. Masamune took his leave and headed over to the bar. *Pull your shit together already.*

Masamune returned with two drinks and a smile. Theo took his glass from Masamune before he could set it down on the table. He tossed it back in one go and steadied himself. "How about we skip the talking and get out of here?"

With an eyebrow cocked, Masamune lifted his beer to his

lips and drank it faster than Theo had ever seen anyone complete the act. He watched the way Masamune's lips formed around the opening, the rise and fall of his Adam's apple, and bit his bottom lip. "I need to stop off at the coat check then I'm yours."

Theo watched as Masamune flashed the coat check guy a smile and a twenty. The guy slid him a note with what looked like a phone number on it and Masamune took a large black backpack and the paper off the counter. He slung the bag over one shoulder and pocketed the paper with a half-hearted grin. He walked over to Theo and they headed outside. At some point it had started snowing and Theo regretted his choice in footwear.

"Is your place far?" Masamune asked.

"What?"

"I just got into the city tonight. I don't have a room yet. It was too late to check in at a hotel and I'm not sure of the area yet so a motel seemed a bit sketchy. But it's totally cool if you'd be more comfortable with that. You can maybe point me in the right direction."

Bringing a guy home wasn't something Theo had ever done. He'd always kept this particular proclivity out of his personal life. But Theo also didn't have the patience to check into a skeezy motel in the middle of the night. *He's just passing through. I need this tonight.* "Let's head inside over there and I'll call us a cab." Theo motioned to a Dunkin' Donuts across the street.

The cab ride was silent. Theo caught Masamune unabashedly staring at his lips the entire time. He felt naked, exposed. As if the mask he wore had suddenly been ripped off. The feeling normally would have had him retreating in solitude, but the gin worked its magic in mellowing him out.

When they were in the privacy of the elevator Masamune backed Theo against a wall and kissed him hard. Before Theo could protest, he found he'd opened his mouth and was kissing back. Masamune's hands slowly explored Theo's body as he let his bag fall to the floor. His caresses were frenzied, just as much as his kiss. He slid a hand up Theo's shirt and gently rubbed his nipple while he deepened the kiss. Theo groaned into Masamune's mouth and put his hands on Masamune's to still them.

Masamune pulled back and asked, "Am I going too fast?"

"No. We're just at my floor." Theo couldn't look at Masamune; he didn't trust what his face might say about what just happened. *Holy shit, holy shit, holy shit!*

"Ah, I suppose we should get off then." Masamune reached down and picked up his bag. He slung it back on this shoulder and lifted Theo's head with his free hand. He stared into Theo's eyes for a few moments before gently kissing him again. Although this time Theo's mind ran wild. Until then, Theo had been too distracted to notice Masamune's eyes. Prior to being kissed again he saw them clear as day; striking hazel eyes which saw nothing but him.

His eyes... they're just like—

His thoughts were interrupted by the kiss followed by a lip-biting grin. "It's your turn to lead the way, Theo."

"You have really beautiful eyes." He just blurted it out mindlessly.

The compliment caught Masamune off guard. The lust in his eyes faded for a moment and he looked genuinely happy to Theo. "Thank you. Come on; show me where we're going."

Theo felt Masamune's body heat radiating behind him while he unlocked the door to his condo. His hands shook and he fumbled with the key. *Come on, get your shit together.*

He steeled himself and opened the door, motioning for his guest to enter first. Masamune complied and entered the dark corridor without hesitation. Theo closed the door behind him and Masamune turned back around as Theo launched himself onto him. Masamune was pinned against the wall while Theo kissed and bit at his neck, Theo's hands palming Masamune's already erect cock over his jeans. Masamune vocalized his pleasure over the touch and grabbed the back of Theo's head then drew him in for another all-encompassing kiss. *Fuck, he feels big.*

Feeling Masamune's arousal made Theo deeply conscious of his own semi-hard dick. He didn't ever get hard during a hookup, let alone offer up kisses. He knew this was different from his usual encounters from the start, he knew he should stop. But he liked the way it felt with Masamune—and that scared him.

Theo abruptly stopped the kiss as well as his wandering hands, leaving Masamune panting and stricken with unsatisfied lust. He toed out of his shoes and slinked around the corner and down the hallway, leaving Masamune frozen in place against the wall.

When Theo reached his room he paused long enough to hear the sound of clothing and heavy boots hitting the floor. Theo smiled to himself and continued toward his bed. With an unprecedented feeling of urgency coursing through him, he undid his pants, shoved them down under his ass before quickly climbing on his bed on his hands and knees. Masamune's heavy footsteps started down the hall in a steady rhythm that faltered for a step about halfway to the room by the sound of the echoes. The footsteps continued to fill the narrow space followed by Masamune's deep voice.

"Hey, we haven't really discussed what's going to happen, but I just want to let you know I'm vers and down for whatever you—"

Masamune's voice cut off and Theo set his head down and turned back to see Masamune frozen in the doorway with his eyes wide and his mouth agape. The sight of Theo on all fours with his pants around his thighs and his face against the bed, looking at the doorway seemed to stop him in his tracks. He had a pleading look on his face, one of lascivious intent.

"Crisse, mon dieu…"

"Masamune."

He groaned low in his throat and palmed his cock through the black jeans he still wore. Theo locked eyes with him and shivered from the intensity of the gaze.

"Fuck me up."

In a few long strides Masamune was at the edge of the bed. He pulled his shirt over his head, grabbed a condom from his back pocket and tossed it on the bed, undid his pants, and let them drop to the floor. He kneeled on the bed behind Theo and ran his hands up the sides of his thighs and ass, to his hips. He gently kissed Theo's dimples of Venus and trailed soft kisses all the way up his spine until he reached his neck. He buried his face in Theo's nape and inhaled deeply, the anticipation sent a chill down Theo's spine and he flinched. Theo's movement was slight, but his body was flush against Masamune's, so the other man was sure to have felt it. Masamune inhaled Theo's scent again before running his tongue from Theo's neck up to his ear. He bit down on his earlobe gently and whispered, "I like the way my name sounds on your tongue."

Masamune gripped Theo's hips again and rolled his own slowly against Theo's ass. His boxer briefs were stretched tight over his rock-hard cock but he kept them on as he moved on top of Theo. He took in Theo's scent once more while he moved and let out a deep, throaty groan. The contact drove Theo crazy. He writhed about beneath

Masamune, seeking more, but Masamune continued his agonizingly slow pace.

"Hurry up and fuck me." His voice was strained, desperate.

"In due time." He stilled his hips and reached between Theo's legs and gently cupped his balls. Theo cried out once before stifling the reaction. He bit down on the comforter as Masamune massaged his balls, rolling them slowly in his palm and rubbing with his thumb. Theo was fully erect now and his body was aching to be touched. His desire for pain was replaced with an intense sexual need he didn't know he was capable of feeling. Every time he closed his eyes he saw those familiar eyes burned into his memory. *They're just like his.*

"Please." *I am not above begging for it right now.*

Masamune pulled his hand back and tapped the side of Theo's hip. "Turn over for me and I'll give you what you want."

Theo quickly complied. He lay on his back with his eyes closed and his head turned toward the window. The snowfall had picked up and the sky was a flurry of white. *It really is that time of the year, huh?*

"Hey." Theo snapped out of his momentary daze when Masamune's lips touched his neck and trailed up to his jaw. "You still with me, or has all the gin gone to your head?"

"I'm fine." Theo shifted under Masamune and noticed his pants had been removed. He tilted his head to meet his lips with Masamune's. Their tongues met in a soft embrace but Masamune took control after a few moments. He pulled Theo's head back and licked and nipped at his bottom lip before sliding his tongue back into Theo's welcoming mouth. With his other hand, Masamune ran his hand down Theo's chest and gently fingered the sparse patch of hair between Theo's pecs before circling his right nipple with his middle finger. Theo moaned into the kiss, which Masamune seemed to take as encouragement; he slowly rolled Theo's nipple between his finger and thumb.

Masamune released his hold on Theo's hair and slid himself down Theo's body. He looked up and met eyes with Theo and smiled before he took Theo's nipple into his mouth. Theo squirmed at the unexpected sensation and bit down on his bottom lip when Masamune tweaked his other nipple while he rolled his tongue around the right. It was as if his nipples were hardwired directly to his cock; he felt like he could come just from this sensation. But that wasn't the type of gratification he craved.

The sound of Theo's hitched breathing signaled that he was close. Masamune released his nipple and licked all the way down Theo's tight abdomen. He brushed his thumb over the shark tooth tattoo on Theo's left hip then slid it lower. With his hands rubbing Theo's thigh and stomach, Masamune took him into his mouth and swirled his tongue around the tip of Theo's cock, lapping up the beads of pre-cum present. Theo sighed loudly at the unexpected warmth and pleasure he felt on the tip of his cockhead. A shock went through his body when Masamune's mouth hummed and vibrated around his cock and Theo tried to thrust his hips up, deeper into Masamune's mouth, but he kept pulling away. Theo whimpered, partly in frustration, and partly in the pleasure from Masamune's circling tongue.

After one more swirl of his tongue, Masamune took Theo into his mouth and down his throat. He pulled back and plunged all the way down to the root repeatedly and Theo rewarded his efforts with exquisitely unrestrained moans, grunts, and thrusts. His hand held Masamune's head in place, his other clung to his own hair. Masamune worked off his boxer briefs while he maintained his rhythm and stopped when Theo's voice became a higher, softer pitch. He pulled his mouth from Theo's cock with a slurp and a pop and brushed his hair back from his face. He took Theo's slicked cock into his hand and firmly stroked the full length of his shaft. With his free hand he grabbed the condom he'd previously tossed on the bed.

"Where do you keep the lube?" His voice was gravelly and low.

"There isn't any, you don't need it. Just fuck me," Theo said with more urgency than he liked.

Masamune's eyes flicked down toward his cock and he cocked his head. "I don't mean to brag, but that's just not going to happen." Masamune looked around the dark room, but didn't make a move to get up. He finally sighed and turned his gaze back to Theo. "Pass me a pillow."

Theo grumbled and threw a pillow at Masamune's head.

"Behave."

"Just fuck me," Theo repeated.

"Se comporter." Masamune folded the pillow and pulled Theo's hips up onto it. He spread Theo's legs wide and pushed them back toward his chest. He wet his lips, leaned in, and flicked his tongue over Theo's hole. Shock and an unfamiliar sensation caused Theo's body to freeze while Masamune continued to stimulate his tight opening. He wrapped his hands around Theo's thighs and probed him with his tongue, slowly pushing in and out. Theo had started moving his hips and moaning again, unable to muster up the control he usually had over his body. Masamune let go of one of Theo's thighs and sucked on his index finger. Wet with spit, he worked it inside of Theo and mimicked the probing he'd done with his tongue. He occupied his mouth with Theo's balls, after running his face along Theo's pubes. He groaned and pushed in deeper, making Theo wonder for a moment which of them was enjoying this more—which of them needed it more.

He added another finger to help loosen Theo up, then a third after some time. Once Theo comfortably accepted three fingers, Masamune withdrew his digits and ripped a condom packet open with his teeth. He rolled the condom down his length and returned his mouth to Theo's hole, adding some much-needed lubrication. He gathered up some spit with his fingers and slicked up his sheathed cock before pressing the tip against Theo's hole.

"Are you ready?"

"Masamune, please."

"I *really* do like the way my name sounds on your tongue." He pushed into Theo's hole slowly but steadily and held the backs of his thighs. Theo cried out, unable to stifle his reaction this time. Once buried to the hilt, Masamune stilled his hips, taking measured breaths. "Is it too tight?"

"It's fine, you don't have to worry about me. Fuck me as hard as you like."

Masamune started to speak but stopped himself. Instead, he pulled almost entirely out of Theo, spit on his cock again, and shoved it back in to the root. His next thrusts weren't as deep but the relaxed pace was maintained.

With each push Theo closed his eyes tighter in protest. He enjoyed the physical aspect of what was happening and that enjoyment held no place in these types of hookups. He tried to form the words or move his body to resist, but the carnal pleasure he experienced overwhelmed his other wishes. *Why, why is he being so kind to me?* As if Masamune could read Theo's mind, he leaned down and kissed him tenderly, his hips never breaking their tempo.

Masamune pulled back from the kiss and Theo caressed his face now that it was a few inches away and then gripped his hair. His angular features were obscured in the darkness, but Theo remembered them well. He slid his thumb between Masamune's lips and the other man sucked on it eagerly. Theo ran his other hand through Masamune's thick black hair then slid it up under his arm and felt the muscles working on his back. He removed his thumb from Masamune's warm mouth and kissed him again.

As their tongues collided and massaged each other, Masamune quickened his pace and pushed deeper. He took Theo's cock in his hand and jerked him in time with his pelvic movements. The feeling was sensational and unlike anything Theo had felt before. In a matter of minutes he felt the pressure in the tip of his cock release and he shot hot cum between their bodies.

Masamune leaned back upright and pounded into Theo harder and faster than before. Theo's lustful cries filled the room, effectively spurring Masamune on. He reached down and smeared the cum on Theo's chest over his nipple before pulling his fingers back and licking them clean.

"T'es crissement sexy."

Theo experienced an aftershock from his orgasm and his body contracted, causing Masamune to cry out and still over him. Theo felt Masamune's cock pulse inside him before he thrust back in a few more times. He shivered then carefully pulled out and rolled onto his back. Both men lay sated and panting without a word until Masamune propped himself up on his elbows and turned his head to Theo. "Where is the bathroom?"

"Second door on the left."

Masamune got up, grabbed his boxer briefs and exited the room. Once he was gone Theo sat up and swung his legs over the edge of the bed. He was sore, but not like with his usual encounters. More than pain, he'd experienced intense pleasure quite unlike anything he'd had before. And more than that, he felt a strange familiarity with Masamune—a familiarity that left him unprotected. He cast his gaze to his feet on the floor and heard footsteps coming from down the hall.

Masamune returned and animatedly spoke of how nice the tiles in the shower were. He sounded like he was smiling, but Theo didn't dare lift his head. "I think you should go."

I am such a coward.

CHAPTER SEVEN

"EXCUSE ME?" The tightness in Masamune's voice conveyed the confusion that had to be written on his face.

"I said, I think you should go." Theo kept his eyes cast down.

"I heard what you said." Masamune started to speak and stopped himself several times. Theo hadn't known the man long, but this seemed odd to him considering how forthcoming and direct he'd been earlier. When Masamune finally spoke his voice was quiet, resigned. "Okay."

Theo heard him pull his pants on and shifted his eyes up enough to see Masamune's silhouette. It looked like he was pulling his t-shirt down over his chest. An instant later the shadow disappeared and Theo heard heavy footsteps down the hall followed by more rustling clothes at the front door. The door opened and closed a few moments later.

Theo lifted his head and looked to the dresser mirror. Half of his face was obscured by shadows but he could see enough to be disgusted by the sullen expression on his face. Unable to stomach the sight of himself, he turned in the bed toward the window and watched the heavy falling snow. *I'm such an asshole. I threw him out in a borderline storm and now I'm the one sulking? Pathetic. I shouldn't have been so cold. No, I never should have brought him here.* Theo sighed to himself before he crawled under the sheet and blanket and tried to fall asleep.

For what felt like an eternity Theo tossed and turned in bed. Despite how sated and tired his body was, he couldn't fall asleep. Restless nights were nothing new for him, but his usual sleeplessness could be attributed to his nightmares. As he lay in bed his mind raced with thoughts of the handsome stranger he'd broken his rules for. Theo wondered where Masamune ended up going. It was too late to check into any respectable hotel, after all.

He sat up and saw that the snowfall had gotten even heavier. Theo sighed and looked at the clock to see it was just half past one in the morning. Resigned to the fact that he wasn't going to fall asleep of his own volition, he got out of bed and pulled on a pair of charcoal sweatpants and a matching zip-up sweater. It was a bit cooler inside than it had previously been and Theo imagined the usual couch throw wouldn't take the edge off of the cold that night. He'd left the bag with the joints and his new tie on the living room table, so he grabbed his Zippo out of the dresser door and headed out to the living room.

Through the glass sliding door Theo could see that several inches of snow had collected on the balcony so he slipped on some leather boots before going out with one joint. And cold it was. There wasn't a hint of wind to scatter the snowfall so it fell straight down and collected quickly. The streak of unusually quiet nights had come to an end with the sound of sirens from many blocks away reaching Theo's ears. Sirens, car engines, distant voices, coughing.

Wait, coughing?

Theo leaned over the ledge and scanned the street. He saw a hooded figure standing inside the glass confines of the bus stop across the street. *Saturday night* and *shit weather? They'll be waiting a while.* Theo dusted the snow off of the chair and sat down. He sparked up the joint and took a deep inhale. The joint was gone in a few long drags; it was too cold to linger outside, so Theo made quick work of it. He went to the door to go back inside when he heard another cough. His hand froze on the handle and something inside him told him to take another look. He walked back over to the ledge and tried to take a closer look. He couldn't see the man's face, but the set of his shoulders under his leather jacket and bag slung over them were all too familiar.

Shit. Why is he still down there? It's freezing out.

Theo shook his head and groaned when he remembered that Masamune was new to town. He didn't have a place to go, especially not at that hour. Theo glanced up and down the street and didn't see any other people. He put his hands in his sweater pockets and called out loudly. "What are you doing down there?"

Masamune's body stilled for a moment then stepped out of the bus stop. He looked up until he noticed Theo through the snow. "Just waiting for the bus."

"It's late. The bus only comes down this street every hour and with this weather it'll probably be delayed. You might want to call an Uber or a cab."

"Thanks." His tone was flat. He stepped back inside out of the snow.

Theo watched with curiosity as Masamune continued to stand still. He didn't go for his phone which struck Theo as strange. He figured Masamune had to be cold, so why the hell was he waiting for a damn bus? *What if he's broke? Or you know, he was telling the truth about not having a place to go…*

Theo wanted to go back inside and go to bed, but he hadn't been obeying his head that night, so he didn't see why he should start now.

"Masamune." He stepped out of the shelter at the mention of his name. He looked directly at Theo but didn't say anything. "Come back up here."

"Why?"

"Why? It's snowing and it's freezing out."

"It was both of those things when you told me I should go."

Okay, that's fair. "Look, don't be stubborn. Just get back inside. It's suite eight oh five, I'll buzz you up." Theo went inside and waited.

And waited.

And waited.

At least ten minutes had gone by before he grew impatient, grabbed his keys, and stormed out of the condo. He took the elevator down to the lobby and exited the building. The snow on the street was pristine, save for a trail of footprints, which were mostly filled in, leading across the street. Theo followed them until he reached the bus stop and stood before Masamune. Theo took a good look at him and the worst of his anger dissolved. Masamune looked like he was half frozen. His body infrequently trembled and Theo was sure he'd heard his teeth clatter before Masamune clenched his jaw.

"What the fuck are you doing?"

"I told you, waiting for the bus."

"Cut the shit and come with me."

"You made it very clear that you don't want me in there."

"Look, I'm sorry, okay. I was being an asshole before but right now you're being stubborn. The cold must have gone to your head."

Masamune scoffed and smirked but he nodded his head slowly. "You really don't mind?"

"It would weigh better on my conscience if I didn't let you freeze to death in front of my home." Theo shivered. He was standing just outside of the bus stop's cover and his clothes and hair were covered in snow. "Come on." He walked back inside with Masamune trailing behind him.

The elevator ride was silent and lacking the intensity of the previous one. Masamune stepped inside Theo's dark entryway again and closed the door behind him. Theo toed out of his boots, brushed the snow off of his clothes and started down the hall toward his room. He stopped after a few steps when he didn't hear footsteps behind him. He turned back and called out, "Masamune, are you coming?"

Masamune kicked off his boots and pulled his hood back but left his jacket on. "I figured I'd sleep on the couch tonight." He sounded uncertain.

Theo walked back around the corner and crossed his arms. "I don't have spare blankets. It's too cold to go without one tonight. Besides," Theo eyed him up and down, "you're too tall for the couch." The last remark garnered a snort of laughter from Masamune. Theo felt a smile pull at his lips, but quickly clenched his jaw. He nodded his head down the hall and Masamune followed.

Inside the room, Theo stood by the bed and started to undress. He grabbed a fresh pair of trunks from his dresser and slipped them on before crawling in bed. Masamune stood on the other side of the bed with his gaze cast down until Theo was under the covers.

"For someone who had his face between my legs not too long ago, you're acting awfully shy over there." *Is it mean to tease him? Why do I even want to? Just shut up and go to bed.*

"I'm invading your privacy. The last thing I want to do is overstep your boundaries."

"Enough. You can hang your jacket on the chair by the door. Don't worry about your wet clothes. I've got an in-suite washer and dryer you're welcome to use in the morning."

Masamune nodded and shrugged off his jacket. He hung it on the chair and piled his wet clothes next to his bag. He unzipped the bag and pulled out some boxer briefs and slid them on before getting in the bed. He tried to stay close to the edge but a queen-sized bed really wasn't all that spacious with two grown men in it. Masamune chanced a glance over at Theo and caught his eyes for a moment until Theo looked away and rolled over away from him. They lay there in a heavy, awkward silence until Masamune broke it.

"Theo, are you sure you don't want me to sleep on the couch? I don't want you to feel uncomfortable."

Theo sighed and sat up. He ran his hand over his face and up through his hair and looked over at Masamune. "You being here isn't an issue."

Masamune propped himself up on his elbows with his eyebrows drawn together. The sheet slid down his chest revealing a large tattoo on his bicep and chest Theo hadn't noticed before. He figured he'd been too caught up to have paid attention.

"Then what is the issue?"

"The fact that I don't mind you being here *is* the issue." He looked down at his hands in his lap and entwined his fingers. "I kicked you out earlier because I was scared. I always leave immediately after… encounters, but this is my place and I didn't feel like I had to get away from you. But I knew I *should*. Then I saw you out there looking like a lost puppy and realized what an asshole move that was. I'm sorry."

Masamune wore a serious expression while he listened to

Theo. He relaxed his features when Theo stopped. "Apology accepted."

"Just like that?"

"Just like that. Well," Masamune flashed a smirk, "you *could* make it up to me with breakfast in the morning."

Theo huffed a short laugh. "Fine." His answer made Masamune smile like a fool. *What did I say to make him so happy?* "Hey, why didn't you call a cab or something earlier?"

"Ah, my phone battery died just before you approached me at the bar."

Theo furrowed his brow. "You didn't think to charge it before you went out?"

If Masamune noticed the bite in Theo's words and tone, he didn't show it. "I charged it this morning at the hotel in Toronto. Then I spent the day wandering around the city before getting on a plane to come here. I went straight to the bar from the airport."

"Betting on your charm to get you a place to stay, huh?"

"It worked, didn't it? And don't forget my dashing good looks," Masamune said as he waggled his eyebrows.

"Do *not* get cheeky."

"Okay, okay. I told you, restraint isn't one of my strengths."

They both laughed easily and Theo forgot for a moment that he just met Masamune. He didn't know his last name or where he was even from. Despite this, he felt almost comfortable with Masamune in a way that unsettled him. He was too tired to think about it further and pushed the thoughts to the back of his mind for another day.

"It's late." Theo let the words linger while his eyes greedily took in the expanse of Masamune's bare chest. He bit his lip involuntarily. "We should go to sleep."

"Okay." His voice was low and seeping with the lust Theo was trying to hide.

Theo swallowed hard and forced himself to look away as he wished Masamune a good night before ducking under the covers. Masamune echoed Theo's words, lay flat on his back, and closed his eyes. They lay in silence for several long minutes until Theo heard soft, open-mouthed breaths from Masamune. He chanced a peek over at his bedfellow to make sure he was truly asleep before he rolled onto his side to watch the rise and fall of Masamune's chest. He watched and listened to Masamune breathe until sleep finally took him.

THE SOUND of the waves coming in fills my ears. We went swimming in the ocean earlier and air-dried in the hot sand. Isaac went and got us a bottle of spiced rum from the bar so we've been draining that for the last hour while shooting the shit. To put it bluntly, I am fucking hammered.

The sun is setting now, offering a slight reprieve from the relentless heat of the day. I'm already sunburnt to a crisp but Isaac is a fucking golden god. He's always tanned so well. He looks gorgeous in his sandy-colored shorts and wind-tousled hair. I grin to myself and take a quick drink from the bottle. The rum burns my throat and warms my stomach as if it is the sun itself contained inside the bottle. I pass the bottle back to Isaac and watch him gracefully wrap his lips around the opening. The rum slides down his throat effortlessly and he doesn't even flinch. If not for the movement of his Adam's apple, I'd think he was a statue—a perfect marble sculpture made to appease my eyes and shatter my heart. He pulls the bottle from his soft lips and sets it down in the sand between us then turns to me and squints when the sun hits his eyes.

"This place is so fucking gorgeous."

Without taking my eyes off of him I say, "The view is

perfect." His hazel eyes glow in this lighting. The sun is intensi-
fying the large golden specks in his irises.

Isaac doesn't seem to notice my drunken leering and gestures
around us with his hands. "I could get used to this. Chicago is
fucking miserable."

And it had been for Isaac. I wasn't particularly fond of the
city and what living there meant for my future, but Isaac had
nothing but bad memories of the place. We tried to get away but
fate had other plans for me. I told Isaac to leave, to go to California without me, but he said he wouldn't leave me to deal with
my father after my mother had her accident. "What kind of best
friend would I be?" he'd said to me. I appreciated it deeply but
now I sometimes feel like I'm holding him back from living his
own life. He abandoned his dream to stay with me and he hasn't
mentioned it since. I know he still wants to go, but he'd never
admit it.

He suggested Mexico last year as a grad gift to us. He'd said
we deserved a break away from reality. To my father's dismay, I
worked a part-time job with Isaac and paid for the trip myself
instead of asking him for the money. He'd have shot me down as
soon as I said I'd be going with Isaac anyway. We worked at a
bar not too far from the university. Isaac turned out to be a
fantastic bartender. I was shit at pouring fancy drinks and
flirting with girls so I was moved to the door.

I see a smile spread across Isaac's face suddenly. He's looking
in my direction, but through me. His eyebrows rise and he nods
his head over my shoulder. I tilt my head to the side in an
attempt to understand, like the lost puppy I am when he's
around. Then I hear it. Voices. High-pitched voices with thick
accents; some local girls are coming our way. From the look on
Isaac's face I can tell the girls are very attractive and it makes me
want to take him by the wrist and retreat back to our room. I
steal a glance over my shoulder and see them about twenty yards
away; long black hair flowing past their shoulders, wide smiles,

and smooth brown skin concealed only by bikini tops and tied shawls around theirs round hips. They were the type of girls Isaac liked—petite and curvy. Features which were the complete and utter opposite of mine in every sense. I look back at Isaac and force a smile to hide my sudden panic. Unconvinced that my face can keep up the charade, I grab the bottle of rum and take several long gulps and grimace. Isaac laughs at my foolishness and licks his lips. I don't even think he realizes that he does that, let alone what it does to me.

"Trying to work up some liquid courage, man?"

"Something like that." I force another smile but only end up curling one side of my mouth.

"¡Hola, chicos!"

My shoulders tense when I hear her voice and my fingers grip the neck of the bottle to the point where I wouldn't be surprised if it shattered. Isaac stands up and steps closer to the girls, flashing his best smile. He would hate me if I acted outwardly rude and ruined his shot with one of them, so I take another drink and pull my sorry ass to my feet to stand beside him.

"Buenas tardes, damas." It isn't often that I got to hear Isaac speak Spanish, but my God, is it ever sexy—even if it isn't directed at me. "What are you lovely girls up to tonight?"

They both fucking giggle. Fuck me.

The taller one says, "We were just going for a walk and we saw some tourists who looked lonely."

"So you've come over to keep us poor boys company?"

"Sí," the shorter girl says.

Isaac claps his left arm over my back. "I guess that makes us extremely lucky. I'm Isaac." He pats my back again. "This is Theo, he's a bit shy so be nice to him."

I feel my face flush so much that I bet it's even visible through my sunburn. I shoot daggers at Isaac and he laughs it off and turns back to the girls. They're all laughing at me now.

"I'm Mariela."

"Ana," says the taller one.

"Such beautiful names. But I really shouldn't have expected any less from chicas bellas such as you."

Ana and Mariela got all giddy on cue and fall right into Isaac's cheesy pick up. I take another long drink to stifle an exasperated groan.

"Whoa there, buddy," Isaac says as he pries the bottle from my hand. "Let's get that under control."

But it's too late. I've always been a lightweight with alcohol. The amount of rum I've had will for sure put me on my ass. But it's not enough. I don't want to remember what's going to happen tonight.

"I'm fine, give it back, Isaac." I reach for the bottle but he pulls it away.

"Come on, Isaac, let him have a little fun," Mariela says.

"Yeah, maybe we can have some fun too." Ana. Fuck.

Isaac raises an eyebrow and hands the bottle back to me. He leans in close to my ear so the girls can't hear and says, "Don't lose control, Theo."

He turns back to the girls and smiles. I take another gulp.

My head is pounding. Not just figuratively, it literally sounds like my head is pounding. I think I'm back in the room on the resort. It's dark now so I must have passed out from drinking like an idiot. I try to sit up but my body feels heavy and I'm still way too drunk. My mouth is dry so I reach for the bottle of water I left on the nightstand this morning. My hand-eye coordination isn't as good as I think it is right now, so I knock the bottle onto the floor. Suddenly, some of the pounding in my head stops. I shuffle in bed and turn far enough to see Isaac naked in bed with Mariela and Ana. My eyes go wide and I turn my head back toward the wall. It was only for a moment, but I saw everything. Isaac's bare flesh and his hips buried between Ana's thighs while kissing Mariela.

If I thought my mouth was dry before, it is a desert now. I hear Isaac's voice whispering something then springs from the mattress. In a few moments the weight on my bed shifts and I turn to see Mariela kneeling on the bed by my legs. She's smiling and eyeing me with lust that I want nothing to do with. I try to wet my mouth to speak, but when I open my mouth I'm silenced by the pounding sound again. I glance over and see it's the headboard of the bed slamming into the wall while Isaac fucks into Ana. My eyes snap shut and I want to die. Between how drunk I am and how much my heart hurts, I feel like I am dying. I'm reminded of my mortality by Mariela undoing my pants. I want to stop her, but I'm too fucked up and pissed off to function and think clearly so I just grit my teeth. She takes me into her wet mouth eagerly and I keep my eyes closed. Ana is moaning like a porn star but I can hear Isaac's grunts in rhythm with the banging of the headboard. I focus on his voice and imagine it is his mouth around me, his hands raking up and down my thighs and I get hard as steel. After only a few minutes of the illusion, I shoot into Mariela's mouth and shiver in the aftershock of my orgasm. It isn't long after when I hear Isaac groan out his release, almost in unison with Ana.

Mariela slides up my body and rests her head against my chest. I can smell the sweet scent of her hair product and the illusion that she is Isaac shatters. I know I'm going to feel terrible about what I've done in the morning, but right now I'm just too drunk to fucking care.

"Ça va bien aller."

"Shhh. Ça va bien aller."

As Theo regained consciousness, he felt an arm wrapped around his chest and a warm body against his back. He went rigid for a moment until he felt long fingers running through his hair and he relaxed into Masamune's gentle touch.

Masamune's breath tickled the back of Theo's neck and he could have sworn he felt him purposefully smell him, like he had the night before. Theo's suspicions were confirmed when Masamune let out a sigh of contentment from deep in his throat. Theo stirred.

"Are you awake?"

"Yes." His voice was dry.

Masamune released his hold on Theo, but Theo didn't pull away. He shifted onto his back, most of his body still touching Masamune's.

"You give off a lot of body heat."

"There are more direct ways for you to tell me I'm hot."

Theo rolled his eyes and flinched when he felt Masamune's morning wood twitch against his hip. "Were you seriously snuggling me with a hard-on?"

"Well," Masamune started, "it was only a semi when I started but you were pretty squirmy in your sleep."

"Have you no self-control?" Theo's attempt at an indignant reply failed and came off more playful than intended.

"I told you last night. Twice. Restraint isn't one of my strengths." His lips curled up into a smirk. Theo couldn't help but grin at Masamune's direct and unabashed nature.

"I guess not."

Masamune's smile faded and his eyebrows drew together before he spoke again. "Are you okay? You were dreaming about something that seemed pretty intense. I didn't want to startle you awake."

Theo's body went stiff again for a moment before he made himself relax. He didn't want Masamune to know what he was dreaming about. "Just a bad dream. I get them sometimes."

Masamune didn't do anything but a look of concern spread across his face.

"It's not a big deal. I'm fine."

Masamune didn't look convinced and Theo wondered if he'd said something in his sleep. He hadn't spent the night with anyone over the last year and he wasn't sure if he still occasionally talked in his sleep, especially with the caliber of the nightmares he'd been having over the past year. He debated whether or not he should say anything more. The desire to know won. "Did I say anything?"

"No." Masamune answered immediately—too fast. Theo had grown accustomed to reading people from his job and noticed the subtle changes in Masamune's body language as he uttered the short lie. Masamune was an open book up to that point and his lie came out rushed and without the usual ease in his deep voice. Deciding it best to change the subject, Theo rolled onto his side to face Masamune.

"Forget about that. How about you just focus on making me feel better now that I'm awake?"

Masamune cocked an eyebrow. "And what do you propose I do to accomplish that?"

"You can start by putting that morning wood to good use and fucking me senseless."

The worry etched on Masamune's face instantly faded and his eyes glazed over with a look Theo was very familiar with: lust.

Masamune leaned forward and grabbed Theo's chin before kissing him. His tongue slid into Theo's mouth and twined with his own. Neither seemed perturbed by morning breath or the fact that Theo was sweating out the alcohol from last night. Masamune rolled on top of him without breaking the kiss. He pulled Theo's head by his hair flat against the bed and slowly licked the roof of Theo's mouth. Theo moaned and jerked his hips off the bed, which seemed to be all the encouragement Masamune needed to escalate things. He shifted down Theo's body and latched onto his neck, treating the salty flesh to pecks, licks, and playful nibbles while his free hand slid down Theo's body to the band of his trunks.

"T'as un beau corps. Et ta peau..." He ran his fingers along the band once then slid his fingers into the trail of hair leading down from Theo's belly button. Theo arched his hips upward to meet Masamune's hand and whimpered when he finally cupped Theo's stiffening length. *"Magnifique."*

Theo shivered as Masamune ran his thumb over the thin fabric covering the head of his cock. Theo reached to push his underwear down, but Masamune let go of his hair and grabbed his wrist before he reached the waistband. He pushed Theo's wrist into the pillow above his head and smiled.

"Nah uh, no touching."

"Then hurry up."

"Man, if I had a dollar for every time you said that, I'd—"

"You'd have too much goddamn money." Theo reached down and squeezed Masamune's right ass cheek and bit his bottom lip hard enough to make Masamune wince. The pain seemed to spur him on as he ground his hips into Theo's while staring into his eyes. Masamune leaned back and rested his weight on his haunches. Without breaking eye contact with Theo, he pulled Theo's trunks off and bit his sore bottom lip when Theo's cock slapped against his abs. He looked down to see Theo's hard cock resting just to the right of his belly button. He stared at Theo for several beats without saying a word. The anticipation of getting his cock sucked caused Theo's dick to twitch against his stomach, but when Masamune leaned down he kissed the faded shark tooth tattoo on Theo's hip before taking Theo's length into his mouth.

The sudden sensation had Theo breathless, grunting, and thrusting up into Masamune's mouth and down his throat.

Just as he was coming undone, Masamune dragged his tongue from Theo's base to his tip and leaned up. He shimmied out of his underwear and lifted Theo's legs off the bed, pushing his knees nearly flat against his chest. Theo panted restlessly and longed for that familiar stretch and burn.

"Where are the condoms?" Masamune gritted out.

A sudden realization hit Theo like a punch to the face. "I don't have any."

"What?"

"I told you, I don't bring people up here. Condoms are in the car."

"Where is the car? No, you know what, fuck it." Masamune released Theo's legs and inched up his body until their cocks were aligned. He took both in his right hand and pumped them slowly while keeping his grip firm.

It shouldn't have felt any different than when Theo jerked off alone, but something about his cock rubbing against Masamune's set his desire ablaze. It was new and felt salacious in nature to what he was used to. He was brought out of his daze by Masamune's mouth crashing onto his. He was moaning into Theo's mouth between erratic breaths. Theo bucked his hips up into Masamune's hand in time with the other man's movements.

Masamune leaned down and licked Theo's collarbone, neck, and earlobe before basking in his scent again. He groaned in response to the smell and gritted his teeth. His breathing quickened and a low grunt escaped his lips as he shot his load all over Theo's chest. His groans resonated in Theo's ear, sending a shiver directly to his dick. He closed his eyes and tensed his body as his orgasm rocked through him, sending his own release to mix with Masamune's.

When he opened his eyes he saw Masamune kneeling between his legs. He had some cum sliding down his taut abs and he was smiling. Theo blinked the post-orgasm haze out of his eyes and took a good look at Masamune in the light of day. He was even more attractive than he'd appeared last night at the bar. His uncircumcised cock lay against his thigh, still semi-hard. He was definitely a lot thicker than Theo in that department, but Theo figured he had him on length. His body was fit and had enough definition and mass to show that he was pretty consistently active. His abs and pecs weren't as defined as Theo's, but he was definitely sexy. He had shoulders almost as broad as Theo's and a tattoo of some sort of tree over his well-toned left bicep. The branches extended onto his chest, far enough to be visible if he wore a low-cut shirt.

Theo was right in his first impressions that Masamune had nice full lips. He'd seen those very lips wrapped around his cock and tasted them. His plush lips contrasted his strong jaw, which was decorated with a sparse, trimmed goatee along the bottom of his chin. It looked less like a style choice and more like a natural growth pattern that suited his face. Masamune's long black hair was brushed back from his face save for a few stray strands clinging to the sweat on his brow.

Theo had been trying to avoid it, but the only place left to look was at Masamune's eyes. He swallowed hard when he locked his blue eyes with Masamune's hazel. They weren't just hazel. They were the same as the ones he'd grown accustomed to seeing nearly every day of his life; the outside of the iris was light brown with dark green swirled around the pupil with gold flecks scattered about. Theo sat up and leaned in close to Masamune's face. He carefully studied his eyes and sighed in relief when he noticed the positioning of the gold flecks was different from Isaac's.

"What are you doing? Do I have something on my face?" Masamune had regained his breath and his voice was steady. He grinned nervously.

"You really do have beautiful eyes."

CHAPTER EIGHT

MASAMUNE'S EYES LIT UP at Theo's words. A wide smile crossed his face and Theo flicked his eyes down, suddenly feeling embarrassed.

"Thank you." Masamune lifted his hand to Theo's chin and guided it up to meet his mouth. The kiss was short and sweet and eased Theo's discomfort. Masamune drew back and sighed contentedly.

"What was that for?"

"You smell like sex and the most appetizing meal."

"You really don't have a filter."

"I told you—"

"Right. Restraint."

A long, satisfied sigh passed Theo's lips as Masamune rolled off of him and onto his side. Theo arched his back off the bed in a stretch before letting his limbs go limp and crashing back onto the mattress. He started to inch away and get out of bed but was stopped by Masamune's gentle grasp on his wrist. Theo looked back and was greeted by Masamune's kind eyes. His features were relaxed and he licked his lips before he spoke.

"Stay for a bit."

"I'm a mess." *In so many ways.* Theo waved his other arm over his torso.

Masamune chuckled. "I am too, but a couple more minutes won't change that."

"I haven't been this messy since high school. I need a shower. You do too."

"Is that an invitation?" The side of Masamune's mouth curled up and he started to pull Theo toward him.

"No." Masamune released Theo's arm and he pulled it back.

"So cold." He feigned sadness.

"Colder than outside?"

"Ouch. Touché."

Theo bit back a smirk. "I won't be long." *Why did I say that? This is my house.*

Masamune smiled and rolled onto his back as Theo left the room.

The hot water felt good on Theo's aching body. He gently guided the bar of soap over every inch of his skin and shuddered. His skin seemed to be more sensitive than usual, likely a result of him coming not too long ago. He quickly washed his hair and stepped out of the shower. He toweled off before wrapping a towel around his waist and stood in front of the steamed-up mirror. Theo wiped the mirror clean with his hand and gave his beard another quick trim.

He left the bathroom and started toward his bedroom, but stopped when he heard a yawn come from the living room. He followed the sound and found Masamune sitting on his couch with his arms and legs sprawled out, his head back, and his eyes closed. Theo noted that he'd put on comfortable-looking pants and that his bare chest looked clean of any evidence of what they'd done earlier in bed. He stood stock still watching the other man's chest rise and fall, admiring how the muscles in it formed and connected. He wasn't sure how he'd dropped his guard enough to let Masamune into his home, but he was certainly enjoying the eyeful of his smooth, slightly swarthy skin.

"Are you just going to stare at me all day?" Masamune's head swayed to the side and he opened his eyes.

Theo flushed at the suddenness of Masamune's voice and instantly cast his eyes to the ground. "I didn't realize you were awake."

"So, you were watching me *because* you thought I was asleep?" There was a playful edge to his voice.

"That sounds really creepy—I'm sorry, Masamune."

He tried and failed to stifle a giggle. He rose to his feet and closed the gap between them in a couple long strides. "No worries. This is your home," Masamune gently held Theo's chin in his fingers and tilted his head up, "you can look wherever you want."

Masamune's gaze burned through Theo. He felt his dick twitch beneath his towel and tried to think of a way to flee the situation before he embarrassed himself further. Masamune bit his bottom lip and Theo's own lips parted. Masamune's lips twitched into a faint grin and he ghosted his lips over Theo's before giving him a soft, slow peck.

"Masamune," Theo started. He bit his tongue and withdrew himself from the hazel eyes staring into him. Masamune dropped his hand when Theo turned his head to the side.

"Call me Masa."

Theo cleared his throat and continued. "Masa," he drew out, testing the new nickname on his tongue, "you're welcome to use the shower if you'd like to get cleaned up before we go out." *What the fuck is wrong with me?*

Masa's face fell and his brows knitted together before a

look of confusion overtook his clear disappointment. "Wait, what? Where are we going?"

"I promised you breakfast last night. I don't have too much here for feeding someone else, so I figured we could go eat somewhere or pick something up." Theo realized the implication of the latter part of his statement after the words were out of his mouth. It was too late to take them back and he wasn't sure he even wanted to.

Masa seemed to pick up on what was implied and his expression brightened again. He nodded and departed to the bathroom. Theo breathed a deep sigh of relief when he heard the bathroom door click shut. He rubbed his chin then squeezed the semi under his towel, cursing his newfound lack of self-control. He still felt a bit off-balance being around Masa but the anticipation and excitement he felt was much stronger than his apprehension. He'd given up on trying to identify why he was so at ease with Masa and decided to just enjoy it for the day. Masa would be gone tomorrow and he could get back to his routine. *But I'm supposed to be taking this time to not be such a miserable fuck. Do I even deserve to feel happiness?*

Not wanting to think about it further, Theo turned on his heels and went to his room to get dressed. He pulled on a pair of jeans and slid a ribbed pale grey sweater on. He was looping his tan leather belt through his jeans when Masa walked into the bedroom with a white towel hanging danger-ously low on his hips. Theo stole a glance and swallowed hard before focusing his attention on fastening his belt.

"I'll give you a minute to get dressed."

Masa giggled under his breath, but didn't say anything as he walked past Theo. Theo took a few steps toward the door and stopped to steal another glance at Masa over his shoulder while he was in the doorway. Masa had his back to Theo and was reaching into his bag on the floor. He stood and Theo caught a clear look at his broad, strong back. What caught his attention most were a series of circles and semicircles tattooed down his spine, starting from his shoulder blades and going down to the dip in his lower back. Theo wanted to ask about them, but he swallowed his words and headed to the couch to give Masa some privacy.

He sat on the edge of the couch, leaning forward, with his knee bouncing impatiently. Before Theo could get lost in his head, Masa came down the hallway wearing slightly distressed dark wash jeans and a black long-sleeved henley with a deep V-neck and his bag dangling from one hand. His chest was bare underneath the shirt and some of his tattoo was showing. The tease of ink, muscle, and smooth skin shifted Theo's thoughts to last night and earlier that morning. A smile tugged at his lips but he took a deep breath and suppressed it.

"You ready to head out?"

"In a minute," Masa said. He walked over to the couch and kneeled by the wall to unplug his phone and collect his charger. He stuffed the cord in his bag and the phone in his pocket after standing. "Okay, I'm ready."

"Fully charged?" Theo teased.

Masa scoffed out a laugh. "One hundred percent. I'm good for the next two days."

"I sure as hell hope you get a hotel room before then."

"Aww, you worried about me?"

"I dragged my ass out in the cold last night to keep you from freezing to death—"

"Much appreciated," Masa cut in.

"—I don't need you being reckless now and having that weigh on my conscience."

"You feeling responsible for me?" Masa smiled.

Theo flushed. *Why am I making such a fuss over this? He can do whatever the fuck he wants and it's none of my business or concern. I'll never see him again, anyway.* "Just don't be stupid."

Masa had his hands clasped behind his back with a knowing smile on his face. "Noted." He nodded his head.

Frustrated, Theo pushed to his feet and walked past Masa, ignoring him entirely. Or at least he tried. He flinched when he thought he heard a familiar whisper fall from Masa's lips.

"What did you just say?"

"Ah, nothing. Just mumbling to myself."

"Let's go. I imagine you're hungry."

And hungry he was. Theo took Masa to IHOP after they'd driven past it and he'd nearly died of excitement. There wasn't too much traffic on the road for a Sunday, likely due to the unplowed roads and how early it was. The restaurant was about half full.

They were seated at a booth against a wall of tall windows with the blinds half drawn. A hot cup of coffee sat in front of Masa while Theo had a cup of tea. He took a sip of the tea while Masa spoke animatedly.

"I can't believe it! There isn't an IHOP at home and I've *always* wanted to go. This is my first time in the US and this was definitely on my list. And the Olive Garden!"

"Olive Garden? Good God. I can give you a list of a hundred better places to get Italian food in the city."

"Hey, I'm a simple guy—I see ads for unlimited bread-sticks and I'm interested."

"You're such a child."

"You weren't complaining last night. Or this morning." Masa winked.

"I stand by my earlier declaration. How old are you anyway?"

"Twenty-four. What about you?"

Jesus, he's younger than Jamie. Well, I suppose others have been too. I just didn't ask. "Thirty-one. Last night I think you said you were from Toronto?"

"I just came from Toronto," he corrected. "I was visiting there for a couple days before coming here. I'm from Montreal."

Ah. "That explains it."

Masa cocked his head to the side. "Explains what?"

"I can understand more French than I can speak. But I didn't follow some of what you said last night." As soon as the words left his mouth he wished he could take them back.

Masa narrowed his eyes and licked his lips. "I can give you a repeat performance if you want to hear those words again."

Theo shifted in his seat. He knew this type of reply would come, but the reality of having heard the words still took him back to the context in which they were spoken. Back to the way Masa had looked at him, touched him, melted against him, and breathed him in. It was intoxicating. Remembering it was almost enough to take Theo over the edge. Almost. He was able to resist getting roped into his fantasies by clinging to the part of him that didn't like to lose. Masa sat across from him with a smug smile pulling at his lips—as if he was well aware of his ability to turn Theo into a bumbling wreck. Theo sat up straight in the booth and looked Masa in the eye.

Masa seemed to notice his shift in body language and adopted a more serious expression. Theo observed that he opened his eyes wider than the heavy-lidded looks he'd been giving and he sat up straighter, as if he were very eager to hear what Theo was going to come at him with.

Theo opened his mouth to speak but abruptly stopped at the sight of Masa's eyes. The sunlight hit them just right and the gold flecks shone bright. They truly were beautiful, even if they painfully reminded him of Isaac. He looked away and took a sip of tea as his bravado faded.

"You're awfully bashful for your age." Theo forced a half smile and soft grunt. Masa sat quietly then sighed. "My eyes freak you out, don't they?" His tone was tinged with a sadness that felt out of place coming from someone as bright as him.

Theo shot his gaze back to Masa and saw that not only his voice carried sadness. "No, no, no. That's not it at all. I was serious when I said I liked them. It's just…" Theo ran his palms over his thighs. "I used to know someone with eyes like yours. When I look at them, it reminds me of them sometimes." He'd sounded a lot less confident than he'd hoped and dropped his gaze to his lap. If Masa's silence was any indication, he'd gone and made things awkward. Theo tapped his fingers on the tops of his thighs while he tried to think of a way to get the easy conversation back on track. He stole a tentative glance at Masa and saw that he didn't look awkward or uncomfortable at all, but he did look like he was really thinking about something. His brows were drawn together and his jaw was tight. Was he holding something back again? Instead of potentially dredging up talk of his nightmare and what he *could* have said, Theo focused his attention back on Masa's now serious eyes.

"You act a little funny when I mention your eyes." Theo left his question implied.

"Let's just say not everyone thinks they're as nice as you do." A tight smile pulled at his lips.

The heaviness at the table lifted when the server returned carrying two large plates. She placed an omelet with spinach, tomato, and bacon and a side of whole wheat toast in front of Theo and he thanked her. Masa's eyes lit up when she set four blueberry pancakes with blueberry compote and whipped cream on top in front of him. He thanked the server with over-excited graciousness that made Theo smile. The server left and came back a few moments later with a tray of butter and different syrups.

"This is going to be the best breakfast ever!"

"I take it you like pancakes?" Theo picked up the small bottle of hot sauce on the table and doused his omelet before cutting off a piece and savoring the flavor.

"About as much as you like hot sauce. Welcome but unexpected."

Theo's eyes shot up to meet Masa's. He was smiling so earnestly that Theo couldn't help but grin back at him. "You must really like pancakes then."

"Dude, pancakes are my favorite. Well, for breakfast. Oh my God, this looks amazing."

Theo laughed quietly to himself and returned his attention to his plate.

"What? You don't like pancakes?"

"It's not that I don't like pancakes. I haven't had them in a long time, but they are good. It's just that your enthusiasm is reminding me of someone right now."

"Who?" Masa asked quickly, his jaw tensing immediately after.

Theo answered without a hint of discomfort as he sliced off another piece of egg. "My brother, Jamie."

"Is he older or younger?"

"He's a year older than you." He took a bite. "Enough with the inquisition. Eat your food before it gets cold."

"Yes, sir," Masa teased.

Theo scoffed and Masa shot him a quick smile before he took a bite of his pancakes. He groaned and his eyes rolled back when the explosion of flavor mixed with the fluffy texture hit his tongue. Theo snorted a short laugh then resumed eating his own food.

The rest of the meal carried an ease and lightness the

prior conversation lacked. They made small talk between bites, mostly about music, and Theo found that he enjoyed Masa's company. When the bill came, Masa tried to pay, as a way to thank Theo for his kindness, but Theo insisted against it.

"I owe you breakfast, remember? I try to make good on my promises," Theo said as he slid his Visa into the handheld machine for payment. After the server walked away Masa spoke.

"I wasn't entirely serious about what I said last night. You really didn't have to buy me breakfast. But thank you, Theo."

"It was really the least I could do after what I did." Masa's mouth twisted up into a small smile. "You do that a lot."

"Do what?"

"Smile. You must be a pretty carefree guy."

"I just had the best pancakes of my life in the company of a really sexy guy. I don't have a lot to complain about right now."

Theo rolled his eyes and shook his head, but the compliment made him feel good. He found Masa to be extremely attractive as well, but he couldn't bring himself to vocalize it.

"So," Masa started, "when am I going to get to see you again?"

When, huh. The confidence in this one.

"You're assuming I want to see you again."

"Nah, that's not going to work. I *know* you want to see me again." Masa sat back in the booth and wore an expression as confident as his tone.

"I don't fuck a guy more than once."

"Well, it's too late for that. In fact, you *asked* me for it this morning." His confidence didn't waver.

Theo felt backed into a corner. Masa was absolutely right. Theo *had* solicited sex again. He told himself it was only to distract Masa from asking questions about his dream, but he wasn't entirely sure that was accurate. Despite how much he tried to resist it, he was attracted to Masa and even now, wanted to have him again.

"How about this: Let's exchange numbers and work something out. I won't put you on the spot to decide right this second." Masa leaned forward and rested his crossed arms on the table. "It's no secret that I had a good time with you, and I hope you did too. I think we could have more fun together if you're willing to give it a chance."

As much as he didn't want to admit it, Theo knew Masa was right. Masa had proved to be a great distraction from Theo's typical morose thoughts and state, but he wasn't sure that was a reprieve he deserved. In the short time Theo silently deliberated, Masa's expression softened and he looked less certain of himself. His eyes conveyed a vulnerability that made the words flow easily from Theo's mouth.

"Give me your phone."

Masa eyed Theo for a moment before he retrieved his phone from his bag, unlocked it, and pushed it across the table. Theo set his own phone on the table then picked up Masa's and sent himself a text message. Theo's phone vibrated on the table and he handed Masa's phone back to him. Masa accepted it with one of his big smiles.

"Now you've got my number. I can't make you any promises, but you can message me sometime." *He gets it, just stop talking.*

"Awesome. I will. You better not dodge my texts either."

"I promise I won't." They both laughed and Theo checked his watch. It was just after eleven. "You ready to head out?"

"Yeah. Again, thank you for breakfast."

"You're welcome. Do you know which hotel you want to stay in? I can give you a lift if you'd like. It's still pretty gross out there and transit will likely be running behind."

"I'm really not sure... Maybe somewhere around here so I can come back for pancakes."

The seriousness in Masa's tone made a laugh erupt from deep within Theo. He hadn't laughed that hard in months.

"What?" Masa asked confused.

While his shoulders still shook with amusement, Theo said, "It's nothing. I know a decent place not too far."

Theo drove Masa to a hotel just a few minutes away from the IHOP. It was close enough to walk, but Theo had insisted. Masa called ahead to book a room for three nights. On the drive over Theo asked about Masa's luggage, or lack thereof, and Masa explained that the airline had lost it on a connecting flight and that they would be contacting him today to send it to him. Theo really felt like an ass for throwing him out last night, but Masa truly didn't seem bothered by it anymore, so he tried to ignore it.

He pulled up to the front lobby entrance of the hotel and put the car in park. They sat in silence for a few moments before Theo looked at Masa and started to speak. "Listen, I'm not really good a—"

His words were cut off by Masa's lips on his. Theo answered the advance by slipping his tongue into Masa's mouth and taking control of the kiss. Masa broke off first and gently bit Theo's bottom lip before opening the passenger side door. "You communicate your feelings just fine when you let your body do the talking. I'll talk to you later, Theo." Masa exited the car and closed the door behind him.

Theo watched him disappear into the turnstile leading to the lobby and in that moment he desperately wanted to follow Masa inside. He abandoned the thought almost just as fast as it had crossed his mind and he drove home.

The condo seemed quieter than usual. It possessed a

disturbed stillness that Theo wasn't used to. He instantly noticed some things on the kitchen counter slightly out of place but ignored them and made his way to the bedroom with the duvet in hand. More signs of a guest were found in the bedroom. The sheets were disheveled and stained and the pillows were spread about on the bed. Theo walked over to the bed to strip it but stopped when he stepped on something. He picked it up and came face to face with the principal reminder of the prior night's guest: a large, gold condom wrapper. He sighed, suddenly more aware of the ache in his ass, and started cleaning up.

Before he could fully strip the bed of the soiled sheets, his phone buzzed in his pocket. He withdrew it from his pocket to see a text from Masa's number. A smile pulled at the edges of his mouth as he read the words.

M: Miss me yet?
T: This is your idea of "later"?
M: Don't act like you're not happy to hear from me.
T: Whatever.

Theo paused to wait for a reply but one didn't come after a minute, where the other replies had been instant. He worried that he'd been too standoffish and scrambled to send another message.

T: Do you like the hotel? Have you heard from the airline?

Jeez, you don't sound desperate or anything.

M: The hotel is REALLY nice. I'd say it's too fancy for me, but there's nothing wrong with spoiling myself once in a while.

M: The airline actually called me while I was checking in, it was perfect timing! I should have my bag by tomorrow night.

T: That's good.

M: When can I see you again?

Theo inhaled and exhaled deeply and sat on the bed.

T: Can I think about it? I don't mean to come off as a flake, I just need some time.

T: To think.

God, I'm horrible.

M: Sure thing. Anything that happens will be on your terms. Is it okay if I still text you while you're thinking? I promise I won't be pushy.

Theo's smile returned.

T: I wouldn't mind that. I have to go right now. I've got some things to do today.

M: Take care. I'll msg you tomorrow.

Theo couldn't think of a send-off that sounded adequate and not awkward so he pocketed his phone without replying and went back to the task at hand.

CHAPTER NINE

T HE NEXT COUPLE of days were agonizingly boring for
Theo. He found himself pacing around his condo,
watching movies, working out, and meticulously cleaning
any surface he could find several times over. His nightmares
persisted and without work as a distraction for most of his
day, his mind slipped back into the past more often than it
normally would have. He knew he was supposed to use this
time off to try and clear his head and sort out what happened
with Isaac, but he just couldn't bring himself to confront his
pain. When the memories wouldn't let up, he conceded to
his weakness and smoked to avoid thinking about it. The two
week supply of joints Jamie had given him was almost
exhausted by the third day.

His stress was compounded by phone calls from his
mother. She'd called him several times a day and left just as
many voicemails, but he didn't dare pick up or listen to
them. He already knew it was about Thanksgiving and didn't
have it in him to tell her he wasn't going to come to dinner
that year. The idea of spending an afternoon with his parents
shook Theo to the core and only worsened his already melan-

cholic mood. Although his relationship with his father had always been strained, he didn't have that issue with his mother until after her accident, just after he'd graduated. Her spinal cord was torn in the accident which resulted in paralysis below the waist. Theo had been on his way to California with Isaac when Jamie called and told him what had happened. The accident derailed the move to California and Theo and Isaac went home. Logically, Theo knew that it wasn't his fault and that being home wouldn't have changed anything, but he still felt an immense sense of guilt over what happened to his mother. That guilt festered over twelve years to the point that now even just hearing his mother's voice made Theo want to dissolve into oblivion. He didn't know how it got so bad or how to fix it, so he just avoided her as much as he could. He knew it was cowardly, but he couldn't bring himself to face it—like so many other things in his life. Jamie used to bring it up, but he stopped several years ago when he saw how much it upset Theo.

On Tuesday morning Theo received another call. He'd avoided looking at his phone all day Monday, save for when he heard a text message alert. Masa had been checking in to say good morning, goodnight, and ask how Theo's day was going. The messages weren't anything pushy or invasive, which Theo liked. In fact, Theo found that he looked forward to Masa's messages, perhaps more than he felt he should. He'd constantly resisted the urge to invite Masa over again for three agonizing days. During that time Theo noticed a significant change in his body and his thoughts. While he still drifted back to the past and Isaac, he now caught himself remembering the way Masa had touched him and how his body craved more of him. Being with Masa was unlike anything he'd ever experienced and he wanted another taste.

It was because of this insatiable feeling that Theo actively made an effort to not invite Masa back over or let on that he wanted to see him again. Theo did *not* want to think about Masa as he was. The desire he felt for Masa, a man he barely knew, alarmed him. He relaxed too much around a relative stranger and did not want his lust to deepen or twist into something more. He didn't even know Masa's last name, although the urge to ask him gnawed at Theo every time he read a text from him. So Theo stayed away—or at least he tried to. He was too eager to reply to Masa's texts and forced himself not to initiate contact, despite how much he wanted to. He wanted to tell Masa how much he wanted him, how much his body longed to be filled again. The thought of it made his dick swell and ache with need. He'd been jerking off more in the last three days than he had in the last three months.

The sound of the phone ringing again broke Theo from his trance. He leaned forward from his spot on the couch to see the phone display on the table. A part of him dreaded that it was his mother again while a small part of him hoped it was Masa. Neither name appeared on the screen, but a familiar one did: Leah. Theo cocked his head to the side, cleared his throat, ragged from smoking, and answered.

"Theo speaking."

"Oh, good morning, Theo! I've been trying to get ahold of you since yesterday."

"I'm sorry; I've been... away from my phone." Theo paused for a moment. "Is everything okay?"

"Yes, everything is fine. Lucas is proving to be very capable and there are no disasters to report. I just wanted to remind you about your quarterly checkup with Dr. Kinley tomorrow at ten."

Theo groaned into the phone which elicited a laugh from Leah. "You're going! You bailed on the last one and I am *not* letting you skip out again. I need you healthy. I'll drive you myself if I have to."

"Fine." Theo raked his hand down his face. "Has the office moved?"

"Nope, same place. Should I arrange a cab for you?"

"No, thank you. I'll drive. Wait, who is Lucas?"

"Oh for heaven's sake, Theo. Lucas is the junior associate handling your files. The one you personally briefed."

"Ah, right."

"How have you been?" Leah's tone shifted and became softer.

Theo sighed. "I'm okay. This time off is driving me batshit, but I'm okay."

"Are you sure? You sound a bit off, dear."

Damn her and her active listening. "My throat is just a bit dry, but I'm really okay. Besides, I'm going to see Dr. Kinley tomorrow, anyway."

"That's my boy. All right, I won't keep you. I just wanted to check in and remind you of your appointment. If you need anything call me, okay? You're on vacation, but I am still the world's best assistant."

Theo smiled. "That you are. Thank you, Leah."

"Bye, Theo."

Disconnect.

Leah's warm tone usually put Theo at ease, but at that moment he just felt alone, more so than he had before the call. He'd had trouble sleeping the night before so he went to the gym early and had already been home and showered for several hours. There wasn't anything left in the condo to clean and with only having slept for a few hours, Theo was very tired. He lay down on the couch, pulled the throw over his body, and closed his eyes.

I never thought my life would end up like this. Here I am at an upscale restaurant with Isaac and my fucking girlfriend, Daniella. Dani is a great girl, she really is, but she isn't the one I want. We met at a party a few months ago and we got along pretty well. She goes to school with Jay and he said she had a bit of a crush on me. I told Isaac about her to gauge his reaction. Part of me was hoping he'd be at least a little jealous or sad, but he was enthusiastic and supportive that I'd finally shown interest in someone. He encouraged me to give things a shot with Dani and told me he essentially felt guilty about fucking up my life and monopolizing my time. And that broke my heart. Even more than pretending to fall in love with Dani was doing right now.

So, here the three of us are at some French restaurant I don't want to be at and that I know Isaac will hate. Isaac detests fancy food—says it's all pretentious pomp and circumstance. But tonight he's wearing his best smile as well as his best suit with a black and burgundy paisley silk shirt and no tie. And fuck, he looks so handsome. The hints of green in the shirt really bring out the green in his hazel eyes. We're here to tell him we're moving in together. It's the last thing I want, but I couldn't think of a reason to say no when Dani and I talked about it. In that moment all I could do was think about Isaac and how much harder it was going to be to pretend to have feelings for Dani. I froze in front of her and couldn't speak. She took my speechlessness as a good sign and started to smile so I did the most I could muster and nodded my head.

She looks stunning tonight. She's wearing a dark brown satin dress with a halter top which is extremely low cut in the back. The earthy tone is perfect with her smooth, tanned skin, long brown hair, and hazel eyes. She's got freckles over her nose which come out more after she's been in the sun. In another life I know she would be perfect for me. In a life where I didn't want Isaac. In a life where I wasn't attracted to men.

"Baby, are you in there?" Dani's soft but assertive voice knocks me out of my thoughts.

"Sorry. What were you saying?"

Isaac giggles under his breath and gently shakes his head. "Some things never change, man." He directs his gaze to Dani. "He's been like this for as long as I've known him, you can't take it too personally."

Dani smiles at Isaac then looks back at me. "I was asking you how work was going with your new promotion."

Work is the last thing I want to discuss, but I answer anyway any explain that it's a bit stressful because of the workload but that I prefer negotiations a lot more than the purely desk job I had before. It isn't that I hate my job. I hate that I work for my family's company. It's something I swore I'd never do when I was younger yet here I am. I'm working at Rey Financial under my father's management and dating a woman; I'm a fucking walking contradiction.

We eat our food, drink wine, and conversation flows easily. Isaac really likes Dani and they get along great. As the desserts come I feel sick to my stomach. Not from the food, but from what I'm about to say. Dani and I arranged this dinner to tell Isaac about us moving in together. I couldn't bring myself to tell him before and I'm not sure I can do it right now either.

"Isaac, there's something Theo and I would like to tell you."

No, not yet. Please, no.

Isaac cocks an eyebrow and looks between Dani and me before settling on me. "Spill it, Theo."

I'm sweating, oh God. I reach for my wine but Isaac must have seen me look at it because he grabs the glass off the table and holds it out of my reach. Goddammit, why does he know me so well?

"Nah-uh. I'm not letting you nervous-drink your way out of telling me whatever it is you came to say."

My throat is so tight. I close my eyes and go to loosen my tie *but, like Isaac, I'm not wearing one. I feel like I'm suffocating when I feel a hand squeezing mine. I open my eyes and see that Isaac is holding my hand, like he used to when we were younger. I instantly feel better and start to relax until the sound of glasses clinking snaps me back to reality. We aren't in my room or the back seat of a car right now. We're in a full restaurant and we're grown men now. I glance around the room expecting to see disgusted eyes staring at me. But no one is watching. Everyone is in their own little bubbles and not one person is looking at me. Another squeeze to my hand jerks me back to the situation at hand and I look up to see that I was wrong before. Someone is watching me. Isaac has his eyes set on me. He brushes his thumb over the scars on my knuckles and my eyes flutter closed. I swallow deeply and nod at him. When I open my eyes Isaac smiles back and removes his hand from mine. Suddenly I remember why we're here and that we're not alone.*

I turn my head and Dani's eyeing me intently. Her lip is trembling like she wants to say something, but she doesn't. I force a smile at her and she rubs my lower back in small circles. The contact is comforting, but pales in comparison to when Isaac touched me. I turn back to him and take a deep breath.

"Dani and I have been discussing moving in together. I mean, we are." The words are a whisper and come out cracked.

Isaac's eyes go wide with genuine surprise and happiness and he looks at Dani and smiles. "Guys, that's fucking amazing! I'm so happy for you two. Damn, Theo, no wonder you were so nervous. But, Jesus, I thought you were going to tell me something horrible."

I force a laugh, but my throat is still too tight so a shallow sound comes out. He doesn't know just how horrible the news is. Then again, he can't know.

Theo woke coated in sweat and out of breath. He sat up on the couch and dragged both hands down the sides of his face. His beard hadn't been trimmed in a few days and was starting to get too long, but he didn't care. Theo dropped his hands from his beard and held them out in front of him. He examined the scars on his knuckles and bit back the taste of bile in his mouth.

It was still early in the day, just after noon, but Theo couldn't stay inside anymore. He needed to get out. He needed to get fucked and not think about anything else. His mind instantly wandered to Masa but he shook the thought off and opened Grindr. *It doesn't have to be him; it doesn't have to be him.*

It turned out that a cold Tuesday afternoon wasn't the liveliest time to find a hookup. Theo was in no mood for games so he closed the app, prepared himself and showered, dressed in a black sweater with the sleeves neatly rolled up his forearms, dark blue cuffed jeans, and was out the door.

Theo walked into a dimly lit bar in Lakeview, the area known as Boystown. He usually didn't venture there in broad daylight for fear of being noticed by a business associate, but he was desperate. The establishment was just as nondescript as he'd hoped it would be. The kind of bar that the hipster crowd didn't frequent. The clientele in a place like this weren't there for social media bragging and a trendy setting.

There was nothing remarkable about the interior and Theo paid it no mind. What he focused on were the patrons. There were about twenty men inside. Some stood and talked, some played pool in the corner, but most sat at tables and were nursing drinks. Theo made his way to an empty stool at the bar and ordered two fingers of Canadian Club Whisky. He'd never had it before but he couldn't help but notice the name. He knew it was silly. Canada was a big country, not some quaint little idyllic village where everyone was nice and drank Canadian Club. Hell, maybe Masa had never even had it before. Even though he knew these things, the amber liquid still brought warmth and comfort to Theo, in more ways than whisky typically did. Theo grinned like an idiot over the sensation and the memories it evoked before he was interrupted by a deep laugh.

"You must really like the whisky to be smiling like that." The man appeared around forty and was tall with a thick, muscled build. He had jet-black hair and wore a dark maroon plaid button-up and blue jeans with Doc Martens.

"It's actually shit. It's my first time having it."

"You sure ordered enough of it."

"Trust me when I say it takes more than two fingers to knock me out."

The man shifted on his stool and raised his eyebrows. "You're here on a mission, huh?"

Theo shrugged his shoulders and cocked his head. "I guess you could say I am. And what about you?"

"I'm not here for the conversation."

Theo threw his drink back and nodded back toward the bathrooms.

THEO LOCKED the door behind him, kicked off his shoes, and walked straight to the bathroom. He winced with every step and cursed himself. He'd wanted rough sex and the man at the bar hadn't disappointed on that front. He'd taken Theo rough and hard in the bathroom without any preparation or kindness. It was the kind of cold, emotionless fuck he'd begged for on Saturday night and hadn't received. Now that he'd received it he was filled with shame and regret. Casual sex usually made him feel numb, but at that moment he was disgusted with himself.

Theo stripped in the bathroom mirror and saw a vicious

bite mark on his collarbone which was sure to bruise. He was also certain there would be bruises on his hips and ass, but that was an issue for tomorrow. Theo got in the shower and tried to wash away his shame.

After having the remaining joints out on the balcony, he made his way to his bed and curled up under the comforter. The sun hadn't set yet, but he needed the day to be over one way or another.

About half an hour later Theo's phone dinged on the dresser. He reached for the phone and saw a text from Masa.

M: Hey, how was your day? I saw some pretty cool shit today. There's a ton to do in this city.

Theo locked his phone and slid it back on the nightstand. He couldn't face Masa right now and felt he needed some solitary time with his agony. He wanted to talk to Masa, but what would he say? What could he say? Another text came through around ten. Theo knew what it said without having to look, but he looked anyway.

M: Goodnight.

CHAPTER TEN

"It's been a long time, Teddy." Dr. Kinley closed the door behind him and sat down at a wheeled stool by his desk in front of Theo. The office was large, but there was only about five feet of distance between them. The walls were plastered with medical dioramas and charts as well as some PSAs about the dangers of smoking and the benefits of a balanced diet and activity. Dr. Kinley's degrees were framed above his birch desk. He smiled at Theo, his once black hair now greying at the sides. His stubble was also greying, but he still had the same warm smile Theo remembered from his youth.

"Good morning, Dr. Kinley. It's Theo now, actually. No one calls me Teddy anymore."

Dr. Kinley nodded his head and smiled. "Sorry about that. You're still that shy kid with a sprained wrist when I see you." Dr. Kinley opened a file on his desk, Theo assumed it was his. "Perhaps if you were consistent in your checkups I'd remember your new nickname."

Theo held up his hands in defeat. "You've got me there. I've been really busy with work."

"Nothing is more important than your health, son. How

are your parents doing? It's been a while since I've seen them."

"They're doing fine, thank you for asking. Jamie is doing great as well."

"Oh, yes. I'm very familiar with Jamie. That little shit is in here too much."

Theo laughed before he realized what he was doing. He was curious why Jamie was seeing Dr. Kinley so much, but he knew better than to ask about privileged information. Besides, it was none of his business.

"All right, it's been a while and you look healthy as ever, but I'd like to run a full spread of tests to just make sure. Sound good?"

Theo nodded.

Dr. Kinley proceeded to run the typical tests and exams on Theo. His blood pressure, temperature, respiration and heart rate were measured and yielded great results. The heart, lung, head and neck, abdominal, extremities, and neurological exams also went on without a hitch. Dr. Kinley commented several times on Theo's peak physical condition and praised him for his hard work and dedication to his health, but warned him not to take it too far. When Theo's physical appearance including skin, eyes, hair, his posture and his walk were examined, he faltered for the first time. Theo was still particularly sore from the previous day's activity, and his discomfort did not go unnoticed.

"Have you sustained a lower back injury?"

"No, I'm just a bit sore. It's nothing to be concerned about." Theo tried to brush it off and walk without conceding to the pain. He winced quietly and looked to the floor, away from Dr. Kinley's concerned eyes.

"Have a seat, son." Dr. Kinley pulled Theo's chair closer to his stool. Theo sat down and winced again. "What's going on with you?"

Theo shifted in the chair and absently jiggled his leg up and down, a nervous habit he thought he'd broken in university. He looked at Dr. Kinley but remained silent.

"Theo," Dr. Kinley started, "you've been my patient since you were ten years old. Anything you tell me is covered under doctor-patient confidentiality. More than that, as your primary care physician, I need to know what's going on with you so I can provide you the best care that I can."

Theo inhaled deeply through his nose and nodded. "I engaged in rather rough anal sex last night." He paused to gauge Dr. Kinley's reaction, but the man's expression didn't give anything away. "I... I'm..."

Dr. Kinley put his hand on Theo's shoulder and gave it a gentle squeeze. "It's okay, son. I understand." Theo nodded silently and looked down at his feet. "I need to ask you some questions about this and I don't want you to feel alarmed or embarrassed." Theo nodded again, as if it was all he remembered how to do. "Are you seeing anyone right now?"

"N-no."

"You are sexually active. How many partners do you have?"

"Um, it's pretty casual. Someone new a couple times a week, sometimes once a week if I'm busy."

"Male and female?"

"Male."

"How long has this been going on?" Dr. Kinley's voice was even.

"Almost a year."

"Are you using protection?"

"Yes, consistently."

Dr. Kinley marked something down in the file on the desk before he continued. "Have you been tested for STDs in the past year? Your last test according to my records was three years ago."

"I—no, I haven't."

Dr. Kinley scribbled more in the file. "Okay, I'd like to collect blood and swab samples from you today as well, Theo. I want to issue you a full clean bill of health, all right?"

"Okay. Thank you." Theo's tone conveyed everything that he couldn't voice, but Dr. Kinley seemed to understand and he smiled.

"Don't thank me yet, we haven't done the more intrusive exams yet." Theo laughed and marveled at Dr. Kinley's uncanny ability to make him feel like a kid again. He'd been nervous about being honest with the man, but he felt better now that he had. He couldn't bring himself to say the actual word, but it was a start.

Theo felt extremely awkward leaned over the exam table with his pants dropped. Dr. Kinley had done this exam with him several times before, but he felt self-conscious about it now. He knew it was silly, but he couldn't help it. Dr. Kinley seemed to sense his discomfort and illustrated just how good his bedside manner was by talking to Theo and distracting him. Before he knew it, the invasive physical exams were over and his blood was being carefully drawn. The cotton swab in his mouth was dry, but Dr. Kinley gave him some orange juice after, just like he did when Theo was a kid.

Theo left the office with a smile on his face and felt like the utter hopelessness he experienced the day before was vanquished. His test results were expected back in about a week so another appointment was scheduled to pick them up. The past few days had been mild, making the walk back to the car an easy one.

Theo parked in a garage several blocks away. There was no conceivable way he'd have been able to find a meter on a Wednesday morning, but he had no issue walking. Once he was in the driver's seat he pulled his phone out of his pocket and turned the ringer back on. He had a good morning text from Masa which made him grin and a text from Jamie. Theo opened Jamie's text before replying to Masa.

J: Hey, bro. Mom is trying to call you. She called me to tell you.

Theo's mood deflated.

T: Did she say what she wanted?
J: She's wondering if you're coming to Thanksgiving dinner.
T: I see.
J: So?
T: So?
J: Are you coming to dinner?

Theo hesitated for a moment before he replied. He wanted to talk to Jamie in person. He wanted to tell him what Dr. Kinley now knew but didn't have it in him to do it via text and he didn't trust himself to not hang up a call.

T: When is your next day off? I need to pick up.
J: I'm free this Sunday.
T: Okay, I'll come to your place with food around 1.
J: Sounds good, bro.

Theo started to put his phone down when the notification went off again.

J: You should really call Mom, Theo.
T: I'll see you on Sunday, Jay.

The good mood Theo just had was shattered. He now felt guilty over having dismissed Jamie's concern for him in addition to ignoring his mother's calls. He'd hoped Jamie would understand and forgive him after they spoke on Sunday, but Theo still didn't feel right at the time. He leaned back in the seat with his head back and closed his eyes. He tried to calm himself by controlling his breathing and clearing his head, but it didn't work. Before he could stop it, his mind slipped.

Isaac and I are waiting in the doctor's office. They wouldn't give the results over the phone so we came in as soon as we got the call. My leg is jiggling uncontrollably, but Isaac is a stone. I stand up and pace the room while running my hands through my hair and pulling at the roots.

"What's taking them so fucking long?"

"Theo, sit down." Isaac pats the chair next to him and I do as he asks. "They'll be in here as soon as they can. Try to calm down." Isaac starts to rub my lower back and it definitely helps, but I still feel like an unstable bag of nerves.

The door to the office suddenly opens and in walks Dr. Thiessen. Her mouth is set in a hard line and she looks tired.

"Mr. Jones, Mr. Rey, good evening." She walks over to her desk and sits on the edge in front of us. "I'm afraid I have some terrible news. There's no easy way to say it, so I'm going to give it to you straight." The pounding in my ears is so loud; I can barely hear Dr. Thiessen. Isaac's hand has stilled on my back. I look over at him and he looks serious, but collected. He smiles tightly at me then flicks his attention back to Dr. Thiessen.

"Fuck!" A blaring car alarm ripped Theo from his memory. He felt the sting of impending tears in his eyes, but gritted his teeth and held them back. He refused to show that kind of weakness in a fucking parking garage of all places.

He reached for his phone to find that it had fallen on the floor. When he picked it up the screen was unlocked and his texts were still open. He saw the message from Masa again and didn't hesitate to open it and reply.

T: Are you busy?

Theo had a white-knuckled grip on his phone and impatiently waited with his eyes glued to the screen. Masa's reply came through about a minute later.

M: Nope, I just got out of the shower. What's up?
T: Come over.

Theo realized how weird and desperate that sounded. He might *be* desperate but he didn't want Masa to know that.

T: I mean if you're free and have nothing else to do.

Ugh, now I sound insecure and *desperate. Great.*

M: Okay. I can do that.
T: Come in about half an hour.
M: All right.
M: Just to be clear, why are you inviting me over?
T: I want you to fuck me until I can't think or stand.
M: I'll be right over.

Theo anxiously paced around the living room. He'd only been home for a few minutes but it felt like a lifetime. About twenty minutes later, a knock at the door froze Theo in place. *You invited him, don't be ridiculous.* He walked over to the door and took a deep breath before he unlocked it.

He was greeted by Masa's friendly smile and hungry eyes raking him up and down. Masa looked even better than Theo remembered. His hair was still damp and hung around his face, some strands over his eyes. He had on his leather jacket with a black waffle cloth shirt underneath and charcoal drop crotch pants. In place of his boots were black high-top sneakers with thick black soles. He was holding two grocery bags and looked so much more youthful than Theo remembered, but this look was just as good on him.

"Hey, sexy." Masa bit his lip in that way that made Theo's breathing hitch. Theo stood there in silence and took the sight of Masa in. He eyed him up and down several times without uttering a word or gave no indication that words were on his mind. Masa smirked and licked his lips. "So... Am I invited in? Or are you just going to eye-fuck me in the hallway."

Theo shot his eyes up to Masa's. He grabbed the collar of his jacket and hauled him inside. He pushed Masa up against the closed door and kissed him hard. Masa's bags thudded to the floor and his arms were wrapped around Theo's waist in a heartbeat. Theo kissed him with a desperation he couldn't put into words and Masa returned the intensity with fervor of his own. Their teeth clashed together until they found a rhythm, but the passion of the kiss did not diminish.

Masa tried to pull away first, but Theo held him firmly against the door and kept his mouth on his. Theo was strong. He figured he could easily best Masa if they both tried.

Theo's head was swimming with equal parts lust and confusion. He couldn't identify what exactly he wanted from Masa, only that the longer he kissed him that want felt more like a need. He pushed those thoughts away and focused on the slide of Masa's tongue against his. Masa slid his hand through the back of Theo's hair and forcefully jerked his head back, exposing his neck. Theo stopped kissing Masa to wince and suck in a sharp breath. He pulled against Masa's grip, ignoring the sting of pain. He sought out Masa's eyes and the man seemed to be contemplating something beneath his obvious lust. Theo unconsciously relaxed as he watched Masa's eyes and Masa used the distraction to reverse their positions, pinning Theo to the door with more strength than he'd been using earlier. He breathed against his neck, moistening the skin, then licked from Theo's Adam's apple to his ear. Masa bit down on Theo's earlobe then growled out, "Tell me what you want."

Theo struggled against Masa, but his grip did not falter. To secure his hold on Theo, Masa drove his legs between Theo's and spread out his stance. Theo panted through gritted teeth and tried half-heartedly to flip Masa back against the door. Masa let go of his hair, grabbed Theo's hands, and held them above his head. With only one hand on both of Theo's wrists, he could have broken free without much of a struggle, but Theo remained trapped under Masa's hold. With his free hand, Masa lifted the hem of Theo's shirt to expose the taut muscles on Theo's stomach. Masa cast his eyes down to take in the sight then licked his lips and smiled. It wasn't his usual playful smile, but one which told Theo Masa liked what he saw.

Masa ran his free hand up under Theo's shirt and gently brushed his fingers over the smooth skin until they reached his chest. He leaned down to kiss Theo but stopped just fractions of an inch from his lips. Theo groaned and jerked his head forward to kiss Masa, but Masa pulled back. He brushed his thumb over Theo's left nipple in tight circles and spoke again when it became erect.

"Tell me what you want."

A shiver ran down Theo's spine and his skin broke out in goose bumps. Masa's thumb stilled then continued after a brief pause. Theo remained silent, but his body's reaction said more than enough.

Masa ground his body against Theo's and shuddered at the sensation. He kissed and nipped at Theo's neck and jaw until finally claiming his mouth with soft pecks. Theo answered Masa's actions with advances of his own, despite his limited mobility. He rocked his hips against Masa's and groaned in frustration over the lack of pressure.

"Touch me," Theo choked out.

"I *am* touching you." Masa gave Theo's nipple a hard pinch.

Theo cried out and shook his head. "Touch me more."

Masa leaned in and whispered against Theo's ear, "I'm going to need you to be a bit more specific." He kissed Theo's neck again. Theo didn't say anything more, but he struggled against Masa's grip. He started to feel the anxiety from earlier creep back and his breathing became shallow. Masa cocked his head and kissed Theo's neck one more time then looked him in the eyes. Theo hoped his anxiety wasn't clearly written on his face, but he knew better than to cling to wishful thinking. Masa released Theo's hands and cupped his face while he brushed his thumbs along Theo's cheeks.

"Hey, it's all right. We don't have to do anything you don't want to do." Masa smiled then took a step back from Theo. Theo grabbed Masa's forearm and pulled him back against him.

"I want this. I just… can't say it right now. But I do want this."

Masa nodded but didn't look convinced. "Okay. Come on, let's go somewhere more comfortable."

Theo didn't move or release Masa. He could see in his eyes that Masa felt guilty about having thought he made Theo feel uncomfortable. Theo wasn't doing so well expressing himself verbally, so he resorted to a more base method of communication and undid his belt buckle and the button on his jeans. He pulled Masa's hand into the front of his pants, wrapped his free hand around Masa's neck, and kissed him slowly. Masa gently squeezed Theo's balls while he kissed him back, making him moan from deep in his throat.

"Do... what you... want with me," Theo said between kisses.

"Wrap your arms around my neck." Theo eyed Masa quizzically through heavy-lidded eyes but obeyed.

"Hang on tight," Masa said before he slid his hands down Theo's ass and hoisted him up around his waist. Theo was shocked at first and worried about 1) getting dropped, 2) getting dropped, and 3) how he felt being carried around by another man. Another kiss from Masa quelled the latter concern. Then Masa started down the hall. Theo wrapped his legs around Masa's lower back and ass and clung on for dear life, but Masa seemed fully capable of supporting his weight. Once Theo realized this he relaxed some of the tension in his body just in time to be thrown down on his bed.

"Don't move a muscle," Masa said as he backed out of the room and went back down the hall. Theo heard him kick off his shoes in a rush and the rustling of one of the grocery bags. Masa was back in sight in less than a minute, holding a box of condoms and a tube of what appeared to be lubricant. Masa flashed a self-satisfied smile and said, "I came prepared this time."

His genuine enthusiasm made Theo laugh. Just like at breakfast the other day, Masa's eyebrows drew together and he looked a bit confused. His tone was uncertain, just as it had been the last time he was in Theo's bed. "What?"

"It's nothing. Get your clothes off and come here." Theo scooted back further on the bed and looked at Masa with appreciation. Masa tossed the box and lube on the bed and started to strip. As Masa stripped off his clothes, the last shreds of Theo's anxiety melted away until the only things that mattered were Masa and his eyes on Theo.

Once Masa was completely naked, he kneeled on the foot

of the bed and crawled over Theo, kissing him again once their mouths lined up. He palmed Theo's erection through his boxers while their mouths were connected and ran his other hand down the back of Theo's pants. He gave Theo's ass a good, hard squeeze then broke the kiss.

"You're wearing too many clothes."

"You told me not to move."

Masa smirked then leaned back so he sat upright. He pulled Theo's pants off one leg and at time and kissed his ankles and calves on each leg as they became bare. He left Theo's boxers on and opted to remove his shirt next. Masa started to lift up the hem but Theo sat up enough to pull the shirt off and lie back down on one elbow. He balled the shirt up and tossed it over by the window, which was wide open and letting in the sun. Theo looked back at Masa and expected to see hunger in his eyes. Instead he was met with concern.

Masa's brows were drawn together and his mouth was set in a hard line. His gaze was directed at Theo's neck, but Theo couldn't think of why.

"What's wrong?" Theo asked.

"Your neck…"

"My neck…" Theo's voice trailed off when he remembered the bite mark from last night. "I-I—"

"Who did this to you?"

Theo remained silent for a few moments while he decided how to best explain what happened. *I got lonely and wanted to have sex with you, but was disgusted with myself for wanting to rely on you so I went out and got roughed up by some bear instead and immediately regretted it.* "It was consensual."

Some of the tension in Masa's face relaxed, but returned as if he thought about something else. "When did this happen?"

"Last night."

"Are you sure you're okay?"

"Yes." Theo put his arms around Masa's tense neck. "Come on, don't worry about that. I gave you carte blanche to do whatever you wanted with me, remember?" Theo brushed the hair back from Masa's forehead and kissed the tip of his nose. He didn't know why, but it felt like the right thing to do, even if it did feel a bit more intimate than just kissing him on the mouth. The next kiss was directed at Masa's lips. Masa kissed him back and Theo took that as a sign to advance things. He slid a hand down and grasped Masa's thick cock and marveled over the fact that it was his first time touching it without clothing as a barrier. It was short-lived though, as Masa grabbed Theo's wrist and pushed him down on the bed. He lay over Theo in silence for a few drawn-out moments and stared into his eyes, searching for something.

When Masa touched Theo again, it was with a tenderness Theo had only ever come close to receiving from Dani when they were together. Masa explored every inch of Theo's exposed skin with his hands while he brushed his tongue against Theo's in a rhythmic back and forth. He leaned back once more and dragged his hands down Theo's body, catching the waistband of his boxers along the way. Theo's fully erect cock sprang free from its confines and rested against his stomach. That pained look crossed Masa's face again and he carefully ran his fingers along Theo's hips. Theo leaned up on his elbows and glanced at his hips and saw a plethora of fingertip-sized bruises. He hadn't noticed those, but wasn't surprised to see them.

Masa's shock subsided a few moments later and he slowly took Theo into his mouth from tip to root. Theo threw his head back, thrust his pelvis upward, and inhaled a quick sharp breath at the sudden overwhelming pleasure. Masa slid Theo almost all the way out of his mouth then plunged back down and burrowed his nose in Theo's pubic hair repeatedly. When Theo took hold of Masa's head and fucked his mouth, Masa reached for the lube and squeezed an ample amount on his fingers. He swallowed around Theo's cock as he eased a finger inside of him. The sensation mixed with the pain from the pounding he'd taken the day before caused Theo to cry out sharper than he normally would. Masa seemed to know how much it hurt so he very slowly moved his finger inside Theo, almost as if searching.

He stopped his exploration when Theo nearly yelled.

"Oh, fuck!"

Masa pulled off of Theo's cock and licked it from base to tip. "Does that feel good? Right here?" He brushed his finger over the spot again and Theo hissed in a breath. "Has anyone massaged your prostate before?"

"Ah! No."

"I wanted to do this to you last time, but I couldn't hold myself back." Masa licked the slit of Theo's cock, collecting the pre-cum oozing forth. "I needed to get you stretched so I could fuck you."

Theo's uninhibited cries filled the room while Masa continued to massage his prostate and slid another lubed finger inside. Theo dragged his teeth over his bottom lip and held his head up to see that Masa had started stroking his own cock with his free hand. His foreskin slid over his sensitive head and he moaned around Theo's cock in his throat. The vibration and the sight of pre-cum leaking from Masa's cockhead drew more moans from Theo, the kind of desperate ones that signaled he'd come soon.

Masa eased off of Theo's cock and withdrew his fingers from his hole. The loss of sensation left Theo writhing in frustration.

"Be patient," said Masa as he tore open a condom. He rolled it down his hard length and rubbed more lube on himself and Theo's opening. He gripped Theo's hips with care and rotated them so they were turned to the side. He guided Theo's top leg up onto his shoulder and positioned himself on either side of Theo's other leg, which lay on the bed. Masa lined up his cock with Theo's hole and slowly pushed inside.

Masa held on to Theo's legs as he eased inside. He went slow, giving Theo's body time to adjust. Given how sore Theo was, a part of him was grateful for the gentle treatment. Another part of him wanted to be used. But Theo didn't ask for it harder or faster, taking only what Masa gave. Once the initial sting and burn wore off, he was completely immersed in the slow, cadenced thrusts Masa gave him. Every single one was aimed for his prostate and sent electrifying jolts throughout his entire body.

Masa changed positions and leaned down over Theo with his leg still up on his shoulder. He kissed him while rocking his hips into Theo with one destination in mind. Theo moaned into Masa's mouth as his body trembled with pleasure.

"I've missed this—the sounds you make. The way your body shakes for me." Masa buried his face in Theo's hair, just behind his ear. "Your intoxicating scent." He kissed Theo again, softer this time and ran a hand over the bruises on Theo's hip. "Come to me next time. I promise I'll give you what you need."

Theo tried to process Masa's words, but all he could do was focus on the building pressure at the base of his spine and in his balls. His breathing changed and his moans got louder, but Masa's pace maintained. He kept up the same tempo of slow, deep, thrusts and brought Theo over the edge when his cock brushed against Theo's prostate once more.

Theo's body tensed and shook while he shot all over himself and Masa. The contractions around Masa's cock ripped his orgasm out of him shortly after with muffled cries into Theo's neck. After a couple more rolls of his hips, Masa slowly pulled out, released Theo's leg from his shoulder, and rolled over onto his back, panting.

"I'll be right back." He got up and left the room, presumably to go to the bathroom. Theo lay in bed completely sated and unable to stand due to light tremors in his legs. He'd never experienced an orgasm that intense before nor had he imagined it possible to actually come without touching his dick.

Masa returned a minute later without the condom and with the second grocery bag. He climbed in bed next to Theo and pulled one of Theo's washcloths out of the bag. "Do you mind? I thought you might want to get cleaned up a bit?"

Theo told himself he should say no, that he'd do it in a minute, but that would mean explaining that he couldn't stand or walk at that moment. He nodded his head and closed his eyes. When the damp cloth touched his skin the heat felt amazing on his hyper-sensitive skin. Masa wiped up the cum and lube from Theo's body and he was a lot more comfortable after. He ignored the discomfort he felt from being touched so intimately and just reveled in how *good* he felt.

When Masa finished he tossed the cloth on the floor over by Theo's shirt. "Are you hungry? I picked up a couple gyros and a sixer on the way over. It sounded a hell of a lot like donair—which is amazing by the way—so I figured I'd grab a couple."

"I'm actually starving. And gyros are fantastic."

Masa smiled and handed Theo his food and a beer. They had the first few bites in appreciative silence until Masa spoke. "This is fucking delicious and tzatziki is great, but this *needs* donair sauce."

"Wait, what is a donair?"

"It's basically this exact same thing, just with a few

different spices and donair sauce, which is kind of sweet, but garlicy, and perfect."

"Sweet? Hmm, I'm not sure how I feel about that. I don't typically mix sweet with meat." Theo took another bite.

"You have to trust me. It sounds weird, but it complements the meat impeccably."

"So, they're pretty popular in Canada?"

"Well, they're an Atlantic Canadian thing. There are now a couple places in different provinces that make them, but the Maritimes is the best place to get one." Masa told Theo about when he visited Nova Scotia one summer and that he didn't care for the lobster, but fell in love with donair and that he tries to visit a couple times a year just to buy them. Theo enjoyed Masa's story, but more so he enjoyed how he told it. Masa's enthusiasm for something as simple as some kind of sauce or pancakes was exceedingly endearing to Theo.

When the food was gone and the story of his first summer in Nova Scotia ended, Theo and Masa were lying down on their sides in front of each other, heads propped up in their hands. Masa looked over his shoulder out the window at the setting sun for a minute before he lowered his voice and looked back at Theo. "It's getting late. Do you want me to leave?"

Theo's reply came out as barely a whisper. "Stay."

CHAPTER ELEVEN

MASA SMILED FROM ear to ear, lines crinkled at the corners of his eyes. Theo kept his gaze cast down, avoiding direct eye contact with Masa. His breathing was labored, and his ears burned hot. Masa chuckled softly and lifted Theo's head by the chin. He leisurely pressed his lips to Theo's for a peck on the lips. Theo flicked his eyes up to meet Masa's when he broke the kiss. He still felt off-balance looking into Masa's eyes, but somehow he also felt comfortable. When Theo looked past his own hang-ups and self-doubt, being with Masa felt easy. Theo barely knew him and he knew how ridiculous the notion sounded, but that didn't lessen the truth of it. He looked at Masa and saw someone who could have made him happy in another life—in a life where that happiness wouldn't be tainted by Theo's thoughts and transgressions. He accepted that he didn't deserve what Masa could possibly offer him, but he wanted a taste of it anyway.

"What are you thinking about?" Masa's brows were furrowed, but his voice was soft.

"Nothing."

"Come on, you expect me to believe that?" Masa pressed.

"I was kind of thinking about you."

Masa cocked an eyebrow. "Oh? What about me?"

Theo sat up on his elbows and looked at Masa. "Well, I don't really know anything about you."

"What would you like to know?"

"For starters, what's your last name?"

"Kuroki."

"Kuroki." Theo rolled the name over his tongue a few times. "Masamune Kuroki. I like it."

"Thank you. What about you? What's your last name?"

"It's Rey."

"Mmm, sexy. You said your family comes from France?"

Theo nodded.

"Does Rey come from *roi* by chance?"

Theo nodded again and hummed "mhm."

"That's sexy," Masa purred.

Theo scoffed out a laugh. "What's so sexy about it?"

"It's strong. A king is absolute."

"I think you're thinking of a god," Theo muttered.

"Fancy yourself a god?"

Another scoff. "Hardly."

"Just a gift from one then?"

"What?" Theo drew back from Masa slightly and narrowed his eyes.

"I saw you on Grindr the other day. At least, I was pretty sure it was you. I guess I was right."

Theo was quiet for a moment with his jaw clenched tight. "How did you know it was me?"

"Um, I recognized your body... and I might have Googled your name and saw that Theodore, I'm assuming that's your full name, means God's gift. I was certain it was you at that point."

"You didn't send me a message."

"You've got my cell number. If you wanted to reach me you could have. I wanted to give you some time and space. Besides, you did eventually contact me, so it worked out okay."

"Why were you so sure I would?"

Masa shrugged his shoulders. "Why did you?"

Theo shook his head. "Nah-uh, don't answer a question with a question."

Masa smirked and lay down flat on his back with his hands behind his head. "I thought we had a connection. Clicked, if you will. And we're definitely sexually compatible, which is important." Masa glanced over at Theo just as he was rolling his eyes. "In all seriousness, I'm really intrigued by you and I feel like you're into me too."

Heat spread across Theo's cheeks, coloring them in a faint blush. He looked down at the space between himself and Masa and clenched his jaw.

"Relax, Theo. I don't mean to put words in your mouth and you don't have to say anything in response to what I just said. Those are my thoughts and feelings and I know they're not necessarily yours."

Silence hung between them while Theo pondered what to say. Masa looked on patiently while Theo waged an inner war on whether he should be honest or not. One look into Masa's eyes told him to speak honestly.

"I messaged you because I wanted to see you. I…" Theo trailed off and considered his words. "I needed to see a familiar face. I don't really have anyone except Jay and I can't bother him while he's so busy. I don't know you very well, but I turned to you because," Theo swallowed but his throat was dry, "talking to you is easy. It's an ease I'm not used to and that kind of makes me uncomfortable, but the talking part is easy."

"Thank you for being honest with me." Masa leaned over

and kissed Theo while he stroked his thumb over the scruff on Theo's cheek. "I like your beard. It screams masculinity, but not in a, um, lumberjacky kind of way. It's refined and elegant, but still really manly. I'm not really explaining this well, but it looks really hot. I like it." Masa smiled and bit his bottom lip.

"You don't have to compliment me."

"No, I don't have to. But I want to. I want you to know how," Masa scanned his eyes up and down Theo's body, "appreciative I am of your hard work."

Theo smiled and gently shook his head. "I think I know how appreciative you are."

"I'm being serious. You're in insane shape. How often do you work out?"

"Every weekday. Most weekends. Sometimes twice a day."

"Jesus. You're making me feel like a slob. I haven't done a workout since I left Montreal two weeks ago."

"I think you're in great shape. You're really, uh, strong." The blush crept across Theo's cheeks again as he recalled being carried.

Masa had to have noticed the flush on Theo's pale skin, but he didn't draw attention to it or tease. "I used to go hard at it, kind of like you do. I did gymnastics for eight years when I was a kid and really started training hard when I was fourteen."

"You did gymnastics?" Theo asked skeptically. "I can't picture that."

"What's that tone for?"

"Well, you're kind of, uh, big. For a gymnast, I mean."

"… Big…"

"I mean not in a bad way or anything, it's just—"

Masa started laughing at Theo's panicked tone. Theo

abruptly stopped talking once Masa started laughing and he shot daggers at him.

"I'm glad my social missteps are so amusing for you."

"I'm sorry for laughing, I really am." Theo pointed his eyes at Masa and he giggled again. "Okay, I'm not really sorry at all."

Theo mumbled the word asshole under his breath, not caring if Masa heard or not.

"You're not entirely wrong though. I was a gymnast for years then I hit puberty and had to stop."

"Why?"

"Growth spurts. I grew way too fast and the strain on my joints was too much so my doctor banned me from training vigorously and competing. I was pretty bummed about it because I wanted to aim for the Olympics, but it is what it is. After I was done growing I got back into fitness and kept up with my training, to a degree. I'm not nearly as disciplined as I used to be, but that's okay. I'm never going to be a professional athlete so I'd rather just be happy and healthy. Did you play any sports?"

"Swimming and soccer. What do you do?" Theo quickly changed the subject.

"Huh?"

"Like, for work. What do you do?"

"I'm actually a student. Well, not right this second. I finished my master's degree in philosophy back in June and I'm enrolling into a doctorate program for July."

"Dr. Kuroki, huh? Shit, I'm going to be calling everyone fucking doctor." Masa cocked his head and Theo elaborated. "Jamie is in med school. He's made it very known he's going to expect me to call him doctor."

Masa chuckled from deep in his chest. "I think I like your brother. He sounds like a riot."

"Oh, he is. You would probably like him. He's a lot more interesting than me."

"Hey, I think you're plenty interesting. You intrigue me to no end."

Theo laughed in disbelief and threw his head back into the pillow. He shook his head and looked over at Masa. "Please tell me what you find so interesting or intriguing about me. One thing."

"I could go on at length, but you want just one? Take your pick. You don't like talking about yourself and deflect the conversation more often than not whenever the topic focuses on you. You're insecure about yourself for some reason, but I can't understand why. You're pleasant company, you're hot, and I can infer that you're successful at whatever it is you do for a living, but you're also guarded. And I can't figure why." Theo went still and Masa seemed to notice. He reached for Theo's hand and brought it up to his lips to kiss Theo's fingers. "But I want to—figure you out, that is."

"I can promise you I'm not hiding anything fascinating."

"We'll see, won't we?" Masa's voice was tinged with something Theo couldn't quite place. Hope, maybe. A feeling he'd let go of a long time ago. "Your tattoo also intrigues me." Masa snuck his hand under the comforter and traced his finger over the inked flesh on Theo's hip. "Why a shark tooth? It is a shark tooth, right?"

Theo pushed the blanket down enough to expose his tattoo while still maintaining some modesty. He had no issues with his body, but was feeling particularly naked at the thought of talking about his tattoo with Masa.

"Yeah, it is a shark tooth. A great white, to be exact. As for the significance? Well," Theo brushed his hands up and down on his face and up through his hair, "my best friend growing up was obsessed with the movie *Jaws*. He loved aquatic wildlife in general, but great whites held a special place in his heart because of the movie. He was a swimmer too and one day he convinced me we needed to go get matching tattoos, and I went along with it, like I always did. He got his on his bicep," Theo rubbed his hand over his upper arm, "but I had to be a bit more discreet. My parents would never have let me get a tattoo. I managed to hide it from them for a couple months but my mom came to one of my races and saw it when my trunks slid down after the race."

"I take it she wasn't too pleased?"

Theo groaned. "It was a disaster. I practically had to stay with Isaac for a month until my parents calmed down."

Masa cocked his head at the mention of Isaac. It was subtle, but Theo saw it. He was almost certain now that Masa had heard him talking in his sleep.

"Isaac. Is that your friend's name? The swimmer?"

Shit. "Ah, yeah."

"What's he up to these days?"

"He's, uh, actually not in my life anymore. He hasn't been for some time." Theo's voice trailed off, hoping Masa would drop the subject. Theo chanced a look at Masa and saw that serious expression again. The one he now associated with Masa deep in thought or lying. Before Masa could think of something else to say, Theo spoke again.

"What about your tattoos? Do they have any significance?"

Masa sat up and crossed his legs, the blanket loosely draped in his lap, leaving one leg exposed. "They're actually representations of my parents." He looked so full of pride, but also a bit sad. "This one here is an out-of-blossom sakura tree." He rubbed his hand over his bicep and shoulder. "It's for my father. His name was Takahiro Kuroki. In Japan, you're addressed by your family name far more frequently than by your given name. My father would have gone by

Kuroki most of his life, so I decided to honor that as well as his family's name with the tattoo. Ah, I should probably explain the meaning behind the name." Masa smiled in a way Theo hadn't seen him do before. He looked how Theo felt most of the time. Vulnerable.

"A lot of last names in Japanese culture are derived from nature. *Kuro* is black and *ki* is tree. So Kuroki can be read as black tree. The tattoo is pretty self-explanatory beyond that." Masa smiled to himself as if he'd remembered something sweet. "The branches extend onto my chest," Masa slid the back of his fingers from his arm and onto his chest, "and stop here, just above my heart. Saying it out loud is a bit cheesy, but the idea is that I carry my family in my heart and they protect me. It's a reminder for me to be the kind of man my father would be proud of."

Theo slowly shook his head and brought his knees up to his chest. He wrapped his arms around his legs and rested his head on his knees. "I don't think it's cheesy at all."

Masa rubbed the back of Theo's neck and brushed his fingers through the back of Theo's hair. "The tattoo on my back is for my mother, Tsukiko. Tsukiko can be read as moon child. The tattoo is the lunar phases. It's a literal representation of my mom, but it also describes what a complex woman she was. I was really close with my mom, she always supported me and the stupid things I wanted to do or create. She was beautiful."

"Can I see it?"

"Of course." Masa uncrossed his legs and spun around, swinging his legs off the bed. He sat on the edge with his hands on either side of him, holding the edge of the mattress. Theo crawled over and kneeled down behind him. He grazed Masa's soft skin along the width of his shoulders with his fingertips and settled on the first of seven tattoos trailing down Masa's spine. He ran his hand down the length of

Masa's spine, touching each tattoo, and rested his head on the back of Masa's shoulder.

"What happened to your parents?" Theo didn't miss how Masa spoke of them in the past tense.

"They died in a car wreck when I was five."

"Oh, God. I'm so sorry."

"It's okay. It was a long time ago. My aunt raised me after that—my mom's half sister. See, Mom was half Japanese, but her dad was French Canadian. It's why I have hazel eyes; they're just like my mom's and my granddad's." Masa laughed to himself for a moment. "Other than family, you're the only person to say my eyes were beautiful. It caught me off guard a bit when you said it and I saw on your face how much you meant it. Thank you."

"You don't have to thank me. Your eyes *are* beautiful."

A comfortable silence drifted between them. Theo continued to stroke Masa's back and allowed himself to relax against it, listening to Masa's steady breathing.

"Theo, I meant what I said earlier."

Theo's hands stilled. "Which part?"

"All of it. But I'm talking about you reaching out to me for anything you need. I know it's not my place, but I'm saying it anyway. Anything you need, please just ask me. I… I won't hurt you."

"What if I want to be hurt?" Theo's voice was hollow.

"I wouldn't be here right now if that was what you wanted, Theo."

Theo remained quiet as his pulse quickened. His body tensed as a spike of panic ran through him, rendering him unable to move or speak. Masa turned around, rested his forehead against Theo's, and cupped his hands in his.

"It's okay, just relax. I won't push." He brushed his lips to Theo's knuckles and planted a quick kiss. "So, what do you want to do?"

"I-I usually watch a movie or two at night. Or work out." *Or pace frantically and stew in my neuroses.*

"I'll be honest, I'm a bit too drained to work out right now," Masa flashed Theo a playful smile, "but I can definitely watch a movie with you."

"Do you want to come with me tomorrow?"

"Where?"

"Ah, to the gym. I missed it today and really need to get back to my routine."

"Of course, I'd love that. What time do you usually go?"

Theo shrugged. "Around five or six in the morning on a good day. Earlier or later if it's not."

"What the fuck? I want you to have a good day, but can you *please* let me sleep in? Until at least nine?"

Laughter erupted from Theo and he looked Masa in the eye. "If you give me a reason to be tired, I'll consider letting you sleep in."

The look in Masa's eyes shifted from playful to smoldering as quickly as the words were out of Theo's mouth. Masa pressed his mouth to Theo's with frenzied urgency and bit at his bottom lip. He slid his tongue into Theo's mouth and ran his fingers through Theo's hair at his nape. He gave a quick tug, drawing a sharp sigh from Theo's lips. Masa groaned into the kiss and raked his teeth down Theo's taut neck. He settled on Theo's collarbone, just above the bruise. He brushed the bruise with his thumb and planted a series of kisses over it, before looking back up at Theo's face.

The kiss-drunk look that was surely on Theo's face spurred Masa on and he pinned Theo to the bed, holding his hands above his head with one of his own. He ground his bare hips into Theo's and Theo felt Masa's arousal against his thigh, signaling that a movie would have to wait.

Ah, the virility of youth.

Theo and Masa arrived at the gym late the next morning looking refreshed and relaxed. They stopped off at Masa's hotel room to pick up his sneakers and gym clothes. Thursday mornings weren't a particularly lively time in a gym, so Theo was hoping he wouldn't see any *familiar* faces. He scanned the thinned-out crowd and felt a wave of relief wash over him when he didn't recognize anyone who could make things awkward.

"What's your routine like? I'll follow your lead today."

"Yesterday was supposed to be weights and circuits. Today is cardio. I usually run on the treadmill after some stretches."

"I don't know, I'd think you'd be stretched enough already, what with what I did to you last night and this morning."

Theo glared at Masa, but the younger man was undeterred and had no shame in laughing at his own crude joke.

"Anyway," Theo started, "come on. There's a spot I like over by the windows."

"By the windows, huh? I'll remember that you like an audience."

"If you behave, I'll buy you lunch when we're done here."

Masa's face lit up and he smiled as he nodded his head in such an over-exaggerated display that Theo laughed and shook his head. They made their way over to the open space and laid down their yoga mats. Theo had an extra in his closet for Masa to use for the days he was too lazy to have his main mat cleaned.

With the mats side by side, they sat down facing forward and began doing a series of stretches. Masa shamelessly gawked at Theo's body and Theo pretended to not notice. He resisted the urge to steal glimpses at Masa, despite how much his eyes were screaming for the sight of him.

While Theo was seated doing tricep stretches over his

head, Masa was lying on his back doing hamstring stretches. With one leg flat against the mat and the other being pulled back toward his stomach, Masa grunted at the stretch of his muscles. The sound piqued Theo's interest and he couldn't help but take a glance over. Masa's eyes were closed tightly and his head was flat against the mat, tilted up slightly. From Theo's position, he had a clear view of Masa's muscles in action; and he took advantage of his vantage point.

He skimmed his eyes over Masa's strained face and marveled at how he managed to be so effortlessly handsome. His gaze drifted down Masa's long, toned body, across his torso and rested on his shorts. They were sliding up his raised leg, revealing a muscular inner thigh that made Theo's pulse race. He leered at the exposed flesh without any qualms, like a starving man to a feast.

The sounds in the room seemed to fade away until the only sound that reached Theo's ears was the sound of his own quickening heartbeat. He began to salivate and felt a stir in his shorts. With heavy-lidded eyes and parted lips, Theo was—

"If you keep ogling me like a deranged pervert I'm going to take you on these mats and we're going to get thrown out of here."

Oh, fuck. Masa's gravelly words broke Theo from his daydreaming. He was no longer stretching and was lying on his side, facing Theo.

"Um," Theo started and shook his head. "I don't know what to say. I'm sorry for staring."

Masa tilted his head to the side and eyed Theo curiously. "Are you sorry for staring at me like I'm a piece of meat, or are you sorry you got caught?"

"Both," Theo blurted out.

A deep laugh rumbled out of Masa. He glided his hand down the front of his shirt and slid it underneath the fabric.

He brought his hand back up to his chest, with the shirt along with it, revealing his toned abs. Theo's eyes went wide and he ran his hand through his hair, giving a hard tug at the back before letting go.

"Fuuuuuck."

"You don't have to feel guilty about looking at me. You can watch me any time you'd like." His voice conveyed a hunger that Theo felt all too well in that moment.

Theo swallowed hard and balled his fists into the fabric of his shorts. His eyes darted back and forth between Masa's exposed stomach and his eyes. He was about to speak when the PA system cut over the music Theo forgot was playing and announced that a blue Civic was parked in a fire lane. The momentary break from his concentration on Masa brought Theo back to his senses. He cleared his throat and shrugged off his urge to pin Masa to the mats.

"I think that's enough warming up." Theo stood and held his hand out to Masa. Masa took his hand and was hauled up to his feet. They rolled up their respective mats and set up at two side-by-side treadmills. They ran in silence for ninety minutes with Masa following Theo's fast pace. Masa's legs were longer and his strides larger than Theo's so he had no problem keeping up.

Both of their chests heaved when they stepped off the treadmills, sweat beading on their skin. Theo led Masa over to a water fountain where they took turns.

"I didn't think to bring bottles. I never do."

Masa leaned up from the fountain and brushed the back of his forearm over his mouth. "It's fine, I wasn't thinking about water anyway."

"You're such a horndog."

"What else is new?"

Theo crossed his arms and rolled his eyes. "Whatever. You kept up with me pretty well back there."

"Pretty well? Please. We could have gone faster," Masa teased. "I run a lot for cardio, just not usually on a treadmill. I'm more of a sneakers-on-the-pavement kind of guy. Oh, and body weight exercises. I go to the gym in the winter, but never in the summer, so I like exercises I can do without gym equipment."

"You sound like you're pretty dedicated to it."

"I am. Not as much as you, clearly, but I do love it."

"What's your favorite workout? I figure you must do some interesting body weight ones."

"I do, but ironic enough, my favorite is done with gym equipment. It's the salmon ladder."

Theo looked at Masa incredulously and cocked an eyebrow. Masa snorted a laugh and shook his head. "Hey, don't look at me like that."

"You actually use that *thing*? I only ever see crossfitters and college dudebros on that," Theo replied.

Masa laughed out loud and held his hand over his mouth when a young woman on an elliptical cut her eyes in their direction. "Shut up, it's fun. Have you ever tried it?"

"Hell no, I'd rather not fall on my face or ass." Theo waved his hands in front of him.

Masa scanned the room and smiled when his eyes found their target. "Come on, I'll show you how to do it."

The salmon ladder was empty so they made their way over to the industrial-looking equipment. Masa picked up the long metal bar and hooked it into the second rung from the bottom, about six feet off the ground.

"Before you get started, let me just say that I am not trying that today. I *will* watch you do it, though."

"All right, next time. For now, feast your eyes." Masa gripped the bar and tucked his knees back, dangling above the ground. He swung back and forth, building momentum, and blew Theo a kiss before he lunged upward and hooked the bar into the next ascending set of pegs. He climbed two more pegs in quick succession then looked down at Theo. "Sure you don't want to try it?"

Theo cleared his throat and crossed his arms. "I'll admit, you look pretty hot right now, but no, I'm okay on the ground today."

"If you insist." Masa climbed the remaining five pegs then descended at such a fast pace that Theo felt uneasy watching. Masa dropped to the ground with a smug smile on his face and waggled his eyebrows.

"Show off," Theo scoffed.

After showering and changing at the gym, Theo took Masa out for lunch, as promised. Masa had insisted on the Olive Garden but Theo ignored his desperate pleading and took them to an authentic Italian bistro a couple blocks from downtown to avoid most of the business lunch crowd.

The restaurant was at half capacity and had beige brick walls and wooden tables draped in red and white checked tablecloths. There were a few high-backed leather booths against the side wall and a bar with eight stools sporting an impressive wine selection for a place so small. Soft mandolin music flowed from unseen speakers and added the perfect backing for conversation. The lighting was dimmed and lit tea candles decorated every table. Not in a romantic, candlelit dinner kind of way, but it was a nice touch to the ambiance of the place. It was warm and intimate, but still casual. Theo had been there with Jamie a dozen times. And Dani a few times. He had never thought twice about the candles or the intimate setting until he sat in a booth across from Masa and saw how his eyes caught the flickering flame from the small candles.

God, he is gorgeous.

Masa took the room in and looked back at Theo with a

smirk on his face. "This is a nice place. If you were trying to impress me, it's working."

They both laughed and Theo shook his head. "I'll be honest here, I've never noticed how, uh, datey this place is. The food is really good and they have a great wine list."

"You know, you're not making it sound any less datey," Masa teased.

"I know. I usually come here with Jamie. Actually, I don't go to restaurants with anyone else but Jay."

"So you're telling me you've never brought a guy to this place? It's a sure way to get laid."

Theo hesitated for a moment and chose his words carefully. "I've never brought a guy here." He felt a little guilty about omitting his involvement with Dani, but he didn't have to explain himself to Masa. He knew he didn't, but he still felt a pang of guilt. "But this place really is great. I couldn't let you eat that fake Italian shit when the real deal is so close."

Masa opened his menu and mumbled something about unlimited breadsticks under his breath. Theo shook his head and lightly chuckled at Masa's childlike grumbling.

Masa closed the menu and set it down on the table deliberately. "What is it now? And *don't* say it's nothing again. You laugh at me when I say certain things."

"Okay, okay." Theo held his hands up in surrender. "It's nothing bad, I swear. Sometimes you just act a bit like a kid."

Masa furrowed his brows and strained his voice. "What?"

"No, no, no. That's not right. I mean… sometimes your reactions to things that excite or upset you are just so honest and that makes me smile. You don't care about trying to hide how you're feeling in any situation and I admire that about you. Like, how excited you got over the pancakes the other morning… that was something I wouldn't be able to let myself experience. Your reactions are unfiltered, that's what I meant when I said you acted like a kid. It came out wrong at first, please don't take offense. I didn't mean anything bad by it. It's actually something I really like about you. It's kind of adorable and sweet." *Oh God, stop talking.* Theo looked down and rubbed his sweaty palms on his pants. After enduring the silence for too long, he looked up to see Masa sitting with his arms crossed and looking like he was seriously pondering something.

Finally, Masa unfolded his arms and let one rest on the table while he brushed his hair back with the other. Theo braced for his words, but the tension left his body when Masa giggled.

"So, you think I'm adorable and sweet, huh?" The shit-eating grin Masa wore was the biggest Theo had ever seen, surpassing even Jamie's.

"That was your takeaway from what I just said?"

"Yes."

"Unbelievable."

"I'll add that to the list of things you love about me." Masa winked and Theo rolled his eyes. "Now tell me, what's good here?"

Theo relaxed into the booth and pointed out his favorite dishes and wine pairings. When the server came, Theo ordered mushroom risotto and a bottle of a Valpolicella blend and Masa got lasagna, stating it was one of his favorite foods. The wine came a few minutes later and they took a slow, appreciative sip.

"Shit, this is really good. I'm not usually a big red wine drinker, but this is pretty smooth."

"I'm glad you like it."

Masa set his glass down and looked Theo in the eye. "So, what do you do? I meant to ask you last night."

"I work for my family's company."

"Doing what exactly? Actually, no. I don't mean to pry.

You don't have to answer if you don't want to."

"It's fine. I gave you a vague, asshole answer. It's a bank. Rey Financial."

"Are you an investment banker or something?"

"Oh God, no. I work in mergers and acquisitions. I do a lot of negotiating and drafting proposals day to day. And market research. There are interns for that, but I like to do it myself. I can have more confidence in what I'm presenting if I didn't rely on someone else's research. If that makes sense."

"No, I totally get it. I admire that you're so hardworking. I knew you had to do something important, I just couldn't figure out what it was. Wait, shouldn't you be at work right now? It's Thursday."

"I took a few weeks off—just before we met actually. I'd just closed a lucrative deal with an important client from Japan and I was... Well, you know what I was like."

Masa laughed at the mention of Theo making an utter ass of himself. "Yeah, I do recall you being pretty puffed up compared to how you've been since then. It was charming, but I like this you better."

"What me is that?" Theo asked in amusement.

"Who you are without the mask. You're not actively trying to impress me, but you're unknowingly doing just that. You did it the morning after we first met too. Like I said before, you seem unsure of yourself, but you shouldn't be."

"I'm not like that at work," Theo said quietly. A short silence fell between them and Theo noticed Masa was deep in thought again. Just as suddenly as the seriousness appeared, his eyes went wide and his head perked up.

"Wait, Rey. Like the huge building a couple blocks away?"

Theo took another sip of his wine and nodded his head. "That's the one. How do you know about it?"

"I've spent a lot of time walking around downtown since

I checked in and I've seen the building a bunch as well as ads all over. Holy shit, that's, like a big deal. No wonder you didn't want to talk about it."

"I never wanted to work there, but it is what it is. Anyway, what brings you to Chicago? I asked you before and you said you were just passing through. That was nearly a week ago."

"Well, the plan was to travel to a bunch of cities and enjoy my winter break, but also find a school to attend for my doctorate. Chicago is high on the list of potential cities for that."

"Why here?"

"There's a professor whose work I really admire at UIC on a five-year term. I've been following his work since my second year of studying philosophy. I've been over to the university a couple times to check out the department, but I haven't had the chance to catch Dr. Kirstein yet."

Theo nodded. "What do you plan to do once you're finished with your degree?"

"I'd like to be a professor. I love teaching and everything, but the research aspect is really the big draw for me. If I could be paid to do research and write papers... that would be the dream."

The server returned to the table before Theo could reply and set down a basket of sliced bread and two saucers with olive oil and balsamic vinegar, respectively. The server informed them their food would arrive in a few minutes before topping up their water and excusing himself.

Masa looked at the bread with anticipation and a toothy grin then back up at Theo.

"It's not unlimited breadsticks, but homemade focaccia with rosemary is pretty fucking great." Now it was Theo who wore the shit-eating grin.

"This smells *amaaaaaaazing.*"

Theo smiled and enjoyed Masa's reaction. He couldn't wait to see how crazy he went over his entrée. "Shut up and try it."

Theo pulled into the hotel parking lot to drop Masa off. Lunch had been thoroughly enjoyed and Masa ended up forgiving Theo for not taking him to the Olive Garden after he tried the dark chocolate almond gelato for dessert. Masa had made some embarrassingly obscene noises that garnered a few looks, but Theo was glad he enjoyed himself.

He'd been fairly quiet for the duration of the drive, but stopping in front of the hotel lobby drained the joy out of Theo entirely. He put the car in park and turned to Masa, but couldn't find any words.

"Time for another awkward goodbye," Masa said.

"I guess so." Theo gripped the wheel tighter.

"It doesn't have to be if you don't want it to be." Theo's eyes found Masa's and found hope in them. "You're more than welcome to come up to my room if you'd like to. In fact," Masa leaned over and whispered in Theo's ear, "I'd like it very much if you would." He kissed Theo's neck and bit his earlobe before sliding back into the passenger seat.

Theo didn't say a word. His skin was hot where Masa had touched him and he needed more. He needed it more than oxygen in that moment. He didn't want to go home and be subjected to his usual foray from his past. A few more hours of peace wasn't asking too much, was it? *No, it is. Why should I get to have a reprieve? When did I get so fucking greedy? How much longer until I crash and burn?* He put the car in gear and put his foot down on the gas.

"Where are we going now?" Masa asked.

"I can't leave my car parked in front of the lobby if I'm going with you." He turned to Masa and hoped his smile hid how scared he was.

CHAPTER TWELVE

"WHY WON'T YOU ANSWER Mom's calls?" Jamie asked as Theo cleared a spot and set a bag of Thai takeout on the cluttered counter. Theo stood behind the middle of the island, close to the sink, while Jamie was at the end, near the door. Theo looked away from Jamie and out the large windows in the living room area at the light falling snow. It had been clear the past three days, and was only a touch more than flurries now. "Hello? Earth to Theo."

Theo locked eyes with Jamie and shrugged his tense shoulders. "I brought Thai, I hope that's okay."

"No, you're not doing that avoidance thing this time. Answer me." Jamie's tone was stern, unlike his usual playful tone.

"Sorry. I've just been really busy lately and not up to talking with Mom."

"Busy? You're still on your vacation aren't you?"

Theo nodded but didn't reply.

"Look, I get that you find it difficult to talk to Mom sometimes, but you really can't keep avoiding her like this. It's been years since her accident."

"I know. And I know it's not fair to her. I *know* that, believe me, I do. But…" Theo trailed off with a pained expression.

Jamie leaned down on the counter and gripped the edge with his hands. "But what? Talk to me."

"Jay, I," Theo stammered. "It's not something that's easy for me to talk about."

Jamie's expression softened. "I know. But I'm your brother. You can talk to me about anything. You know that, right?"

Anything? I hope so.

"I promise we'll talk. Can we just sit down and have a bite first, please?" Theo motioned to the containers he'd laid out.

Leaning back and crossing his arms, Jamie sighed and the fight fled his body. "Fine. I am pretty hungry." Theo gave him a half smile and sighed in relief. Jamie walked around the island, past Theo, and opened the fridge. "You want a beer?"

"Yeah, sure." Theo turned around and retrieved two plates from the cupboard. He began dishing out pad Thai and cashew chicken in equal portions with a small serving of jasmine rice. Jamie set Theo's beer down next to him and cleared his throat while eyeing one of the plates. Theo snorted a laugh and shook his head, but he still scooped more rice onto Jamie's plate. Jamie smiled in victory.

They sat over on the couches and ate in what Theo hoped would be relative silence, but Jamie insisted on making porny groans to show his satisfaction with how good his food tasted. He was just like Masa in that regard, showing unbridled appreciation for the simplest of things. It made Theo smile and shake his head.

Jeez, they're exactly alike.

Theo turned his attention to the TV where Jamie had put on *Game of Thrones*. Theo watched as a platinum blonde young woman tiptoed around what appeared to be her new, hulking husband. He didn't quite understand what was going on, but Jamie was enthralled.

"I love this show. I'm rewatching it again for the new season."

"I've never actually seen it," Theo said between bites.

"Excuse me?" Jamie forcefully set his fork down and it clanked against the plate. "How is that even possible?"

Theo shrugged. "I don't watch much TV. TV shows I mean. I watch quite a few movies, but usually just some oldies."

Jamie picked up his fork and shoveled a heaping forkful of noodles into his mouth. "You're unbelievable."

The scene in the show changed and now the blonde girl and hulking guy were starting to become intimate. Theo stopped paying attention and drained his beer. He stood and went to the fridge to get a second. He called out to Jamie and asked if he wanted another to which Jamie yelled an enthusiastic "yes."

Theo sat back down on the couch adjacent from Jamie and picked at the label on the bottle. Moans and grunts from the TV began to fill the room and Theo glanced over to see that Jamie's undivided attention was still on the show. He decided now was as good a time as any to talk to him. If things got awkward, at least the show would be there as a distraction and an excuse for them to not speak to each other after.

"Hey, Jay. There's something I need to tell you."

Without looking from the TV Jamie continued eating and said something around a mouthful of food that sounded like "yeah."

"I like guys," Theo choked out.

"You disguise? Huh?"

Theo cleared his throat and tried to speak louder. "I like guys."

Jamie's eyebrows twitched and he leaned closer to Theo, but he didn't break his gaze from the TV. "What are you talking about?"

Theo chewed his bottom lip and slung back a gulp of beer. "I like guys, Jay," he said, louder than necessary.

Jamie's body went rigid. He cocked his head over at Theo then muted the TV and spun in his chair to face him. He pursed his lips and spoke slowly. "What exactly are you telling me?"

Theo ground his teeth and focused his attention to his hands in his lap. "I'm gay, Jamie." He closed his eyes as a wave of relief washed over him. It was the first time he'd ever said that word out loud in relation to himself. It was both terrifying and liberating to finally voice it. His internal celebration was cut short when he opened his eyes and saw Jamie; his eyes were wide and the disbelief on his face was evident.

"Hooooly shit."

"Yep." Theo nodded and smiled tightly.

"Since when?"

Theo tried to stifle an awkward laugh. "Always, I guess."

Jamie groaned in frustration and rolled his eyes. "No, you idiot. I mean when did you realize it?"

"Oh. I guess when I was fifteen."

"I see." Jamie went quiet and Theo could practically see the gears turning in his mind. Suddenly, Jamie gasped and his eyebrow quirked up. "Were you and Isaac—"

"No," Theo interrupted. He softened his tone and couldn't hide the sadness in his voice. "It wasn't like that with Isaac. He wasn't like that."

"Did he know?"

"No one did."

Jamie nodded. "I'm sorry. Wait, what about Dani, then?"

Theo knew this question was coming. Dani was Jamie's best friend and Theo had essentially lied to her, wasted her time, and broke her heart. "That was a mistake. It's complicated but I know it's no excuse for what I did to her. She's a great girl and she deserved better than me."

Instead of arguing, Jamie just nodded his head again. His lack of fight surprised Theo but he visibly relaxed when he saw Jamie wasn't going to jump down his throat.

"I get it. Yes, lying to Dani was a dick move, but I can see how difficult it was for you to tell me this and I'm sure you had your reasons for lying. It's not my place to judge you or pretend I understand what it must have been like for you. But, Theo, fuck, I'm sorry you had to be alone in this for so long. You're my brother and I love you more than anything. I wish you'd have told me sooner so I could have been there for you." Jamie slumped back in his chair, looking more serious than Theo had ever seen him.

"I know what you're thinking, but please don't blame yourself. You didn't ever do anything to make me think you wouldn't support me. To be honest, Jay… I couldn't even admit it to myself properly, let alone say it out loud. Today was the first time I've ever said it."

Jamie leaned forward and rested his forearms on his thighs. He folded his hands between his knees. "I'm glad you told me. I'm really fucking glad, Theo. I wish it happened years ago, but I get that you weren't ready. Thank you for trusting me."

"You're going to make a great doctor. You've got the bedside manner down already."

"Don't give me that shit, man. I mean it, Theo. You're my brother. I fucking love you no matter what. There's no bullshit or acting in that."

"Fuck, I'm sorry. I didn't mean anything by that. I love you too, Jay. Thank you. Really, thank you. You don't know how important your approval is to me."

Jamie glanced back at the TV to see bare breasts on display and he scrambled for the remote to shut the TV off. He looked from the black screen to Theo and shrugged his shoulders. "Sorry, bro."

His sincerity and the absurdity of what just transpired made Theo double over in laughter. When his voice was even enough to speak he said, "Jesus, Jay, I've seen a naked woman before. I've *slept* with women. You don't have to get worried about a show offending me."

"Okay, that makes sense. Aaaaand now I feel dumb." Jamie stood up and clapped his hands together. "All right, it's time for another drink. Finish that beer and I'll break out the hard stuff. I'm getting you drunk."

"Drunk? Why?"

"You said you would last time I saw you. I'm not letting you renege."

"Fine. Do you have scotch?"

"Just who the hell do you think I am? Of course I do."

They took their plates and empty bottles to the kitchen where the drinking continued. Jamie poured liberal drinks, filling the tumblers to the rim. Theo recoiled when Jamie slid the full glass across the island to land in his hand.

"I said I'd drink with you, not die with you."

"Aw, come on. Calm your tits; no one is going to die. I'm a doctor, you'll be fine."

Theo lifted the glass to his lips and swallowed a mouthful. The scotch warmed his belly instantly. "You're not a doctor yet, you cocky asshole." Theo took another drink.

Jamie smirked and waggled his eyebrows. "Choice words coming from you." Theo choked on his drink and started coughing. He set down the glass while the fit continued and shot a death glare at Jamie, who was leaning over the counter and laughing obnoxiously.

"I'm sorry, bro. You just made that too easy."

"Whatever. Asshole." Theo fought off a smile and took another drink.

"So tell me something. D'you have a boyfriend?"

"What? No."

"Really? Why not?"

Theo set his glass down and crossed his arms. "I'm not really into dating. I've never dated anyone seriously aside from Dani. And, well, I don't know if that really counts."

"What the hell, don't you get lonely? A man has needs." Jamie held his hands in front of him and squeezed them into fists as if that were the universal nonverbal indication of a man having needs.

"Ah, hell. Are we really having this conversation?"

Jamie squared off against Theo from the other side of the island. "Yes, we are. I've always told you about my girlfriends, this is no different. I just want to know that you're okay and not lonely. I mean, I know you live alone, but I don't want you to be lonely."

Goddamn him. "I see people casually."

Jamie perked up. "Ouu, tell me about them."

"Ah," Theo hesitated, "I mean *very* casually. As in I don't catch names." He took a longer drink and winced, from the words being spoken or the liquor, he wasn't sure.

"Oh. *Ooooh.* I gotcha. You little minx." Theo began to protest, but Jamie held up a finger and shook it. "Nah-uh, I'm not done. So you're doing the whole casual thing. What about friends? I haven't heard about you hanging out with any of your old crew since things with Isaac."

The name pained Theo, but he shook it off. "I stopped

seeing everyone last year. I don't really have any friends anymore. Well," Theo hesitated, "no, never mind."

"Whoa, whoa, whoa, 'well' what?"

"It's nothing," Theo mumbled.

"Bull-fucking-shit! Tell me." Jamie stared Theo in the eye.

Theo emptied the glass and slid it back over to Jamie, who filled it back up to the brim. "You're going to fucking kill me," Theo whispered. He took another drink and set the glass down, trying to be as casual as possible. "I met someone—"

"I knew it! You lying—"

"No, no, no. We're not dating. It's just sex."

"Yeah, okay, whatever. What's his name?"

Theo sighed in defeat. "His name is Masa."

"Masa?"

"Yes, he's Japanese—kind of. He's Canadian. Japanese Canadian, I guess."

"Really?! That's awesome!" Jamie buzzed with excitement, which amused Theo.

The next hour consisted of Jamie asking a thousand questions about Masa and Theo's newly revealed sexual identity. Day faded into dusk and the bottle of scotch was emptied into their glasses. As the alcohol relaxed Theo's tension, it also relaxed his tongue. He answered *every* question Jamie asked him, especially things he'd never admit sober. He'd described Masa as both cute and adorable and Jamie beamed like the fucking sun.

The drinking moved back into the living room and Jamie put on a Spotify rap playlist filled with songs Theo mostly didn't know, but he was too far gone to care. Conversation continued to flow as easily as the honey-colored liquor, and soon enough Theo and Jamie were recounting stories from their childhood, working up to adolescent transgressions. Theo's speech started to slur first and his movements became sluggish. He sloppily removed his pullover sweater and swayed on his feet. His head was spinning, Jamie's distant laughter echoed in his head.

The last thing Theo remembered was the satisfying pop of another bottle being uncorked.

I'M PACING around the apartment in the dark, just waiting for Dani to get home. I can't keep pretending anymore and I'm going to end things. It's just too much to keep up with and I need to be with Isaac right now. I feel like shit and I know it's not fair to her, but Dani is the only expendable thing in my life right now.

Fuck me, I'm despicable.

Dani walks in just after ten. She texted me that she was going to be studying late with Jamie. Of course, I didn't reply. I couldn't. She looks exhausted, but she's still happy to see me. Her smile morphs into a concerned look when she lays eyes on me. I must look like a wreck; I've been stressing for hours. And drinking. I'm a drunk fucking asshole about to break an innocent girl's heart.

Dani approaches me and gently embraces my arm, winding her arms around my bicep. "Baby, what's wrong?"

I pull my arm back and shake my head, fists clenched. I can't look her in the eye so I'm looking at my feet. "Dani, I," I choke on my words.

Dani touches me again. She cups my face in her hands and forces me to meet her gaze. "Theo, what the hell is wrong? Oh God, is it Isaac?"

I shake my head and feel warm tears run down my face. Great. "I can't do this anymore."

Her eyebrows crinkle together as she tries to understand what I'm saying. "What are you talking about, baby?"

"I can't be with you anymore. I can't do this." I don't have to

pull away from her again. Her hands drop from my face and slide down my chest before she takes a step back. Then another. Tears are filling her eyes, but she doesn't speak to me. She can see in my eyes and hear the finality in my voice that talking about it would be pointless.

She disappears in the bedroom for a couple minutes then comes out holding her overnight bag. She walks up to me and holds my cheek in her palm for a fleeting moment before snuffling back tears and walking out of the apartment with her head held high. If not for the tremble in her shoulders, anyone who saw her wouldn't know she'd just had her heart smashed to pieces.

But it wasn't just her. My heart was breaking too. Only mine had been breaking for fifteen years.

THEO'S CELL rang and woke him from his dream. The volume was set low, but to his sensitive hearing, it sounded like a police car siren in his head. A hangover was something Theo had been very familiar with in university. It wasn't an earth-shattering issue. Life went on. What he was feeling when he woke was worse than an average hangover. He was positive he had some degree of alcohol poisoning and felt like a sack of run-over shit.

He sat up abruptly to find his phone, but the pain in his head sent him back onto the couch. Theo took a few moments to groan and suffer before memories from last night came flooding back. He opened his eyes and saw that he'd spent the night at Jamie's and was still wearing his clothes from yesterday. Most of them. His sweater and one sock were missing, though all else was in place. As comfortable as Jamie's couch was, Theo longed for his bed and used that as motivation to will himself to sit upright. He grabbed his phone off the table and saw several unread texts from Masa and a missed called from Leah. She left him a message, but his head couldn't handle hearing it so he opened the texts instead.

He read that last night Masa had watched a *Jaws* marathon, including the awful *Jaws 3*. He'd fallen asleep during the fourth installment, but Theo took that as a good sign. As awful as the third film was, the fourth was unspeakably terrible. Masa sent some commentary on the first film but stopped after the shark attack at the beach, likely too enthralled to continue looking at his phone. There was a goodnight text around two in the morning, probably when Masa had woken up and went to bed properly. Theo smiled at the screen and closed the SMS app. He figured he'd reply when he got home. It was almost ten and Theo wanted to get home. He decided that the gym was entirely off the table for the day. He'd make up for it tomorrow.

Theo stood up slowly and made his way to the washroom before heading to Jamie's bedroom door. He knocked and called out to him and was met with silence. Not having the patience to wait any longer, Theo opened the door and walked in the bedroom to find Jamie faceup and passed out with his clothes half off. It seemed he made a valiant effort at getting undressed but ultimately failed. Theo snapped a few pictures and laughed to himself then strode over to the edge of the bed and gently shook Jamie's shoulder.

"Wake up, Jay." A reply came in the form of a deep intake of breath and a pained groan. "Come on, get up."

"What time is it?" Jamie's eyes were still closed and his voice was seeped with sleepiness.

"It's almost ten."

Another groan. "What the ever-loving fuck, man? Let me die."

Theo rolled his eyes. "You're not dying. You're probably dehydrated, but you'll be fine."

"Tell Mom and Dad that I went out with pride and dignity." Jamie rolled onto his side, tangling his legs in his pants before kicking them off.

"If you don't get up in the next thirty seconds I'm going to distribute the pictures I took of you a moment ago. All sprawled out and tangled in your clothes."

"You'll delete those pictures if you know what's good for you," Jamie warned.

"Like hell I will. These are good enough for the family album."

"Then I suppose the video I took of you singing 'Bohemian Rhapsody' last night would be a good addition to the next family get-together. Oh, wait! That's this Thursday, what a treat."

Theo blanched. "Okay, okay, I'm deleting them." He unlocked his phone and deleted the photos. "Done. Now delete that video."

"Please, as if there was one. I was too busy singing it with you, you idiot. Sorry, but you've been duped again."

"Whatever. Look, I need more joints. The last batch didn't last as long as I'd hoped."

"Am I turning you into a pothead? I'm not sure how I feel about that."

"No, it just helps me sleep sometimes. It's nothing to be concerned about."

Jamie mulled it over for a few seconds then sighed. "Fine. I'll roll you twenty more but you can't have them unless you pick them up—"

"That's fine."

"—from Thanksgiving dinner." Jamie folded one arm behind his head and pointed the other at Theo. "Don't even think about not showing up. I'll go to your place first and drag you if I have to."

Theo sighed in defeat. "All right, I'll come. Anyway, I need to get home."

"Why? Got a hot date?" Jamie teased.

"Nothing like that."

"I don't know, by the way you talked about him last night I'd wager money that you're going to see him today."

"Shut up." Theo rolled his eyes.

"Whatever. I'll have the joints ready for Thursday. Go on and have fun with your little *adorable cutie* while I lie here and die."

Theo got home half an hour later and immediately took a hot shower. He was hungry, but the smell of alcohol seeping through his pores won the battle over his hunger. After showering and brushing his teeth he felt somewhat alive and got in bed with his phone. He'd received a good morning text from Masa while on his drive home from Jamie's.

T: Ugh, it's not so good.

M: What's wrong?

T: Everything. Jamie got me drunk last night.

M: Ah, are you hungover?

T: More than a little.

M: We can postpone going to the gym today until you're feeling better.

T: That's probably a good idea. You can still come over later if you want. Maybe tonight after I've slept the worst of this off.

M: Sure thing. See you around 7? I can bring dinner.

T: Sounds good. Now, excuse me while I go suffer.

M: Feel better.

Another bad dream woke Theo up just before six. Or perhaps it was the need to vomit, which had him running down the hall to the bathroom. As terrible as throwing up felt, he felt ten times better after he'd done it. He brushed his teeth and swished mouthwash twice to rid his mouth of the awful taste.

Theo went back to his room and sat on the edge of the bed. The notification light on his phone was flashing: another text from Masa. This one was just double checking to make sure Theo was awake. Theo thumbed out a quick reply saying he was and he checked his messages, remembering there was one from Leah. Theo still had a bit of a headache so he didn't open the message.

He fell back into the sheets once more, but instead of feeling relaxed he crinkled up his nose. The sheets smelled awful, as did he. He figured he'd had the sweats while he was asleep. He stripped all of the bedding and threw it in the washer. He put on a spare set of white damask striped sheets and brought out a white down duvet for the colder weather. He didn't have a cover for it yet, but it would have to be fine for the night. Once the bed was made Theo checked the time and decided he should take another shower. Masa would be arriving in less than twenty minutes so he had to hurry. He douched prior to the shower to ensure a thorough cleanse and was just drying off when he heard a heavy knock at the door. Theo wrapped his towel around his waist and rushed out to answer the door.

"Hey."

Masa's eyes scanned Theo up and down and he bit his lower lip, discretion be damned. "Hey."

Theo stepped aside and motioned for Masa to step inside. Masa obliged and Theo saw he was holding a medium-sized pizza box. He also noticed the way Masa's jeans hugged his ass and strong thighs. *Not yet.*

Masa set the box down on the counter and took off his jacket and scarf, placing them on one of the stools at the bar. "I know it's not particularly healthy, but I figured you might want some hangover food. I skipped the beer this time."

"You're a godsend."

"I believe that title already belongs to you."

"Shut up."

Masa laughed and closed the distance between him and Theo. He placed one hand on Theo's hip, brushing his thumb over his tattoo, and cupped his chin with the other. "You look really sexy right now." He ghosted his lips over Theo's then kissed him slowly. "But at the same time you kind of look like shit. You've got bags under your eyes and your coloring is all off. I think I can even still smell alcohol on you. Jeez, how much did you drink?"

Theo whacked Masa's shoulder and stepped away. "You're an asshole." His tone held no malice.

"Aww, *soit pas comme ça, nounours.* I brought you pizza. That's *got* to give me some points, yeah?"

Speaking French gives you more points than pizza ever will. "Thank you," Theo muttered.

Masa smiled, knowing he'd won. "I wasn't sure what you liked aside from mushrooms, spinach, tomatoes, and bacon. So I got pepperoni with bacon and mushrooms to be safe. Well, mushrooms on half. I don't like mushrooms, but this isn't about me."

"Thank you, Masa." Theo's voice was sincere this time. "Come on, let's eat on the couch. We can watch a movie or a game if you're into sports."

"Are you?"

"Not really."

"Good. Because I'd rather watch static. Unless it's Olympic swimming, I can manage that." Masa winked.

Theo rolled his eyes, but he couldn't disagree.

They had pizza on the couch and watched an episode of Archer. Laughing felt good, but the pizza in Theo's stomach felt glorious. Theo was so hungry that he'd forgotten to change and still had the towel wrapped low around his hips. He'd caught Masa eyeing him several times while the episode was on, but Masa hadn't made any advances. As the credits played, Theo was tired of waiting for Masa to make a move. He spread his legs and bumped his knee to Masa's. The towel remained tied at his hips but parted to display his thighs. Before Theo could even look at Masa he heard him swallow hard.

Ah, this is too easy.

"Are you going to just sit there all night? I'm over here in a towel if you hadn't noticed."

"Trust me, I've noticed. Several times. I didn't want to do anything in case you were still feeling off."

"I'm hungover, I'm not dead."

"*Fine.* But I'm not going to fuck you. Just a hand job."

Theo scoffed. "Jesus, are you twelve?"

"You're in trouble if I am."

"For the love of God—do I have to beg?"

Masa brushed the backs of his fingers down Theo's cheek. "I'm just worried."

"I'm a big boy, I can handle it." Theo stood in front of Masa and squeezed his filling cock through the towel. "Besides, I spent all that time getting *ready* before you got here. It would be a shame if it was all for nothing."

"Fuck," Masa growled. He grabbed Theo's wrist and pulled him down onto his lap. Theo straddled Masa and kissed him with the hunger he felt earlier. Masa ran his hand down Theo's back and cupped his ass over the towel. He slid his other hand up Theo's thigh, under the towel, and rubbed his perineum. Theo gave an encouraging sigh then a frustrated one when Masa removed his fingers. A moment later,

Masa's fingers were in Theo's mouth and he sucked them as Masa groped his ass.

"Good boy." Masa pulled his fingers from Theo's mouth and slid them back under the towel. He bypassed his perineum and inserted two fingers inside of Theo. "Sorry, gotta do this quickly." Masa kissed Theo as he worked his fingers in and out of his hole in a steady rhythm.

Theo ground his hips down onto Masa's and winced from the pleasure of the pressure and from the pain of the friction on his sensitive skin. "Lose the pants, now." Masa withdrew his fingers and rolled Theo onto the couch. He stood to remove his pants, but stopped once they were unzipped.

"*Ah, tabarnak!*" Masa growled and walked over to grab his bag off the stool by the kitchen. On his way back he inched out of his jeans, but they snagged on his foot. "*J'ai aucune patience pour cette merde!*"

What the fuck did he just say? Thoroughly amused, Theo sat up and watched Masa with a smile on his face.

"Oh, you think this is funny?" He finally kicked off the jeans and whipped his shirt off over his head, revealing his smooth, broad chest.

"More than a little. Get over here."

Masa dropped the bag by the foot of the couch then dropped to his knees. He grabbed Theo's ankles and pulled him to the edge of the couch. Masa pushed Theo's legs back, spreading him wide. The towel was still tied, but was now bunched underneath Theo, leaving him exposed. He dropped greedy, sloppy kisses on Theo's inner thighs and balls, but didn't touch his aching cock. He slipped his tongue down from Theo's balls until he reached his hole. Masa's tongue danced over Theo's crease while his hands held Theo's legs back. Theo writhed and moaned on the couch and had both hands fisted in Masa's hair.

"Hold your legs back for me."

Theo did as he was told and the feel of Masa's hands disappeared from his longing skin. Masa's tongue never stopped working Theo over so he didn't think too much about the missing hands. He didn't have to wonder too long. The sound of a foil packet being ripped and the cap snapping on a bottle of lube were welcome sounds to Theo's ears. Masa replaced his tongue with slicked fingers and quickly pressed them deep inside Theo.

"You ready?"

Before Theo could form words, Masa pulled his hips over the edge of the couch and guided Theo down onto his thick cock. Theo cried out sharply and his body tensed.

"Lean back and relax. I'll go slowly until you're ready for me."

Theo leaned back against the edge of the couch cushion, which was in the middle of his back. His legs were bent at the knees and hooked around Masa's forearms, effectively pinned. Masa leaned in and kissed him tenderly, keeping his hips still. He drew back a few inches and looked searchingly into Theo's eyes. Theo nodded and Masa began to drive his hips up into Theo. The position allowed for deep penetration, deeper than Theo was used to.

"Oh fuck," Theo hissed.

"That's it, just breathe, baby." Masa continued his slow thrusts, working the tension out of Theo's body. "That's it. You ready for more?"

"Give it to me."

Masa smiled and slammed his hips into Theo. On each thrust Theo had the urge to cry out, but he clenched his teeth and grunted instead. The angle of Masa's movements targeted Theo's prostate perfectly and he was quickly overwhelmed by waves of sensation. He wasn't going to last long. Masa wasn't either, going by his more frequent sighs and quickening pace.

His hips moved in a frenzy of uncoordinated spasms, nailing Theo's sensitive gland until Theo's own orgasm tore through him, splattering cum on Masa's chest. Masa's eyes rolled back and he grunted, his cock pulsing deep inside Theo.

They panted in a heap on the floor until Masa lifted Theo up onto the couch and went down the hall, holding his boxers. He returned wearing them and with a clean chest. In his hand he held a damp cloth. Masa kneeled on the floor and proceeded to clean Theo up as he'd done the other night. Theo didn't have a working bone in his body or the voice or will to stop him. When he was finished he tossed the cloth into the sink then dried Theo's damp skin with his towel. He pressed his lips to Theo's and they shared a slow, lazy kiss.

"Do you want to stay out here or do you want to lie in bed?" Masa asked. Theo still couldn't speak so he just moaned. Masa nodded, seeming to understand. "Bed it is, then. Can you walk or do you want me to carry you?"

That gave Theo some energy. He sat up slowly and groaned. "I can walk."

Masa shrugged. "Pity. I was hoping to princess-carry you down the hall." He had that shit-eating grin on his face again.

Theo found the strength to kick him in the shoulder, which made Masa cry out. "Shut the hell up."

Once in bed, Masa curled up into Theo's side under his arm. He was radiating heat and felt really good so Theo put his arm around him and gently fingered his hair. The soft strands ran through his fingers like silk and Theo reveled in the sensation. After a few peaceful moments, Theo's phone dinged on the dresser, which reminded him about Leah's message.

"Sorry, I have to listen to a message." He leaned over for

the phone and opened up the message. Not having the energy to hold the phone up to his ear, he put the phone on speaker and set it on his chest.

"Good morning, boss-man. Wait, no. I'm not saying that. Anyway, I'm just calling you to remind you that Thanksgiving is on Thursday. And your mom called the office looking for you. She sounded a bit sad and she doesn't usually call your business line, so I figured it might be important. Anyway, I need to get back and check on Luke. I'll see you in a few days."

Theo groaned.

"She sounds nice."

"She is."

"Who is Luke?"

Theo sighed. "*Lucas* is the young associate who is in charge of my files while I'm on vacation. I guess he's *Luke* now."

Masa snorted a laugh. "It sounds like someone is jealous. Don't worry; I'm sure she likes you best."

"Shut up." Theo exhaled deeply. "I wasn't planning on going to Thanksgiving dinner, but Jamie kind of changed my mind last night."

"Why wouldn't you want to go?"

"I've been kind of avoiding my parents for a long time. I see my father at work, but it's been a long time since I've been able to face my mother."

"I see."

"The tension is all my fault, but I don't know how to fix it any more. Shit, I don't know why I'm telling you this."

"Don't worry about it. I'm sure you'll figure it out if you go see her." Masa snuggled in deeper. "What was the occasion for last night anyway?"

Theo stilled his hand in Masa's hair for a moment before

continuing to thread the inky black strands between his fingers. "I, uh, told Jamie I was gay."

"Shit, really?"

"Yeah. He took it extremely well—too well if my hang-over has anything to say about it. After I told him he cut off the beer we were drinking and broke out a bottle of scotch. And then a second bottle, which is why I hate him right now."

Masa laughed and held Theo tighter. "How do you feel now that you've told him?"

"Surprisingly better. Lighter maybe? I'm not sure how to best describe it. He wants to meet you," Theo blurted out before he could stop himself.

"You told him about me?"

"Well, kind of." Theo ground his teeth while debating how much more to say. "Jamie asked me some things and he could tell I was withholding something. So I mentioned you. Apparently, he asked me all sorts of questions when I was drunk and I don't remember what I said."

Masa buried his face into Theo's side and giggled. "Now I want to meet Jamie so I can hear what you said about me."

Theo fought back a laugh. "Shut up."

"You tell me that a lot lately. How do you plan on making me?"

Theo grabbed Masa's hand on his chest and dragged it down under the blanket to cup his semi.

"Oh," Masa hummed. Taking the hint, he shimmied down Theo's body and dragged his nose through Theo's pubic hair before whispering, *"Oui, monsieur."*

CHAPTER THIRTEEN

PARKED IN THE DRIVEWAY of his parents' Lincoln Park home, Theo sat with a vise-like grip on the wheel. Last time he'd been parked in this driveway had been last Christmas. It was a disaster so he didn't stay long before leaving to be with Isaac. Theo didn't even remember why it turned south so quickly, but it had and he wasn't looking forward to experiencing a repeat. But he was here and he didn't want to abandon Jamie with his parents. Jamie might not have had the strained relationship that Theo had with them, but he was not impervious to their father's manipulations. Jamie's decision to go to medical school had created enough friction that he moved out of the house, but their father eventually decided that a medical practitioner was an *acceptable* career path outside of the family business.

Remembering how much worse he had it in this house took Theo's mind to dark places. He thought back to when he returned home with Isaac from trying to move away. The day of his mother's accident. They went straight to the hospital and were greeted by a bleary-eyed Jamie and Theo's father, white with grief. The color quickly returned to his face when he'd laid eyes on Theo and Isaac. The man chided his son with more vehemence than he usually did, even raised a hand and struck him across the face. It was the only time his father had ever hit him and Theo's guilt began to fester. Isaac stepped in between Theo and his father and received a cruel tongue lashing before dragging Theo away to sit next to Jamie. It was one of the worst days of Theo's life, one that he hadn't thought about in years. Yet it all came rushing back clear as day while he peered through the windshield at the front door to the house.

He took several deep, calming breaths and tried to regain control of his thoughts before they rendered him unable to move. Breathing techniques weren't going to be enough to calm him, so Theo pulled his phone out of his pocket and thumbed out a text to Masa.

T: I don't know if I can do this.

A reply came almost instantly and Theo released a breath he hadn't realized he'd been holding.

M: What's wrong, baby?

Baby. Masa had called Theo that a few times since Monday. He wasn't sure how he felt about it just yet, but that was the least of his concerns at the moment. He didn't want to get into the whole fucked-up mess via text, though he knew he had to say something considering he'd initiated the conversation.

T: My parents. I don't know if I can see them today. I promised Jay I'd come for dinner, though. I can't disappoint him.

M: I see. If you're really not feeling up to it, I'm sure

Jamie would understand. If you think you can handle it, maybe just try going in and seeing how it feels.

M: If it's not going well you can leave. But you won't know if you don't try.

He's right. I know he's right. But I still have this sinking feeling...

T: You're right. I should at least try for Jay.
M: Try for you, Theo. Jamie will be fine.

Theo knew Masa was right, but he couldn't bring himself to say anything in reply. He pocketed his phone and headed for the door.

He walked inside the house and into the vast entryway. The foyer had thirty-foot ceilings painted a creamy off-white and polished white marble flooring. Fresh flower arrangements in harvest colors housed in transparent glass vases adorned the foyer as well as the hollowed areas in the wall up the curved staircase. Soft orchestral music flowed quietly from what sounded like the dining room several rooms to the right. Off to the left was an unused sitting room with pristine Victorian-style furniture and a large floral print rug. Theo took off his shoes and made his way past the sitting room and into the even bigger living room. The Victorian-style décor continued into this room, which also had a sixty-inch flat screen TV held in a grandiose dark stained wooden entertainment center. Arranged in front of the entertainment center were a couch, loveseat, and chair set with matching dark stained tables. Theo's father, James, sat on the couch with a tumbler of scotch in front of him on the table. Jamie was slumped in the chair with an open Pilsner in hand. The Vikings-Lions game played on, holding Theo's father's attention. Jamie was never a big football fan so he tapped away on his phone wildly. His fingers stilled when he noticed Theo standing in the archway.

"Hey, you made it!"

Theo nodded and walked in to stand between the couch and the chair. He nodded toward his brother and turned to address his father. Before he could speak, his father's authoritative voice reached his ears.

"You actually came. How shocking." Theo's father didn't look away from the game.

"Hi, Dad." Theo looked at the man and tried to keep his voice steady. "Where is Mom?"

"She's up in her room. Dinner will be ready shortly."

"Which service was hired to prepare dinner this year?" Theo's father cut his eyes at him but did not reply. Jamie spoke up.

"Cara's I think, man. The one with those creamy garlic mashed potatoes."

Theo grunted. They were indeed good. "Is Uncle Charles coming?" Theo didn't feel awkward around his uncle or his wife.

"Nah, Uncle Chuck took the fam down south," replied Jamie.

"Oh." Theo had been hoping his uncle would be present to serve as a buffer between him and his father. The news that he wouldn't be there sparked Theo's anxiety again. He reached to loosen a tie he wasn't wearing and ended up scratching at his neck instead. The high ceilings closed in on him and he felt crushed. Unable to be in the room any longer, Theo excused himself and went up the rounded staircase and down the hall to his old room. He locked the door behind him and took in the familiar yet foreign room.

The spacious walls felt just as oppressing as they had when Theo was growing up, although now the space was used as a guest bedroom and his old belongings were long gone. He dragged himself over to the queen-sized bed and sat down on the edge. Being out of the house for so many years didn't lessen the surge of memories this room brought forth, but Theo determined that was better than being down in the living room with his father. He lay down on top of the neatly made bed, curled onto his side, and closed his eyes.

NERVOUS DOESN'T COME close to describing how I'm feeling. Isaac's uncle is out of town for work so I invited Isaac over for Thanksgiving dinner. He reluctantly said yes and I can understand why he'd be feeling apprehensive. After my dad found out about my tattoo he was furious and he hadn't nice things to say about Isaac's influence on me. I told Isaac about it and he's been avoiding coming over to my house for the last couple months to let my father cool down.

We're up in my room playing XBOX right now, Dad and Jamie are watching the game in the living room, and Mom is putting the finishing touches on dinner. After about half an hour, Jamie knocks on the door to tell us dinner is ready.

Everyone is at the table when we walk into the dining room. Dad is at the head of the table with Mom and Jamie to his left. I take the seat on the right closest to my father to put some distance between him and Isaac, just in case. Dinner passes with a relative ease for the first half hour. Jamie loves Isaac and Mom always engages with him. Dad hasn't said much, other than one-syllable replies to questions directed at him. Once the plates are cleared, I see my father set his shoulders and look directly at Isaac.

"Isaac, I haven't seen you around in a while."

"Yes, it's exam time so I've been spending a lot of time at home, Mr. Rey."

"I heard you boys looked good at your competition a few

weeks ago," my father probed.

"Thank you, sir. We've been practicing hard." I was on edge listening to Isaac engage with my father, but Isaac answered with ease.

"Those tattoos sounded especially intriguing. I hear you've got one on your arm."

Isaac brushed his hair back behind his ears. "Yes, it's fairly new."

"Where did you go? I'm curious to know which respectable shop put their gun on a minor."

"My uncle signed a consent form for me." A lie. Isaac's uncle almost had a heart attack when he saw us with our bandages on.

My father leaned back in his chair and scoffed out a self-satisfied laugh. "I shouldn't be surprised. Your sort is always making poor decisions. Although next time you decide to lower your social standing even further, leave my son out of it." He picked up his tumbler of scotch and went into the living room to finish watching the game, leaving everyone at the table at a loss for words. I look over at Isaac and his jaw is clenched. He meets my gaze for a moment and flashes me a smile that doesn't meet his eyes. I start to stand to head into the living room and rip into my father but my mom calls my name and I freeze.

"Stay here, dear. I'll go talk to your father." She stands and walks into the living room, leaving Jamie across from us.

Jamie looks between Isaac and the living room a few times before asking, "Why does Dad hate you so much?"

Fuck, leave it to kids. Isaac laughs and smiles genuinely at Jamie. "He just thinks I'm a bad influence."

Jamie ponders this for a moment before he smiles and says, "Well, I think he's wrong. You're awesome, Isaac. I even like you more than Theo."

That little fucker. That makes Isaac and me both laugh, dissolving the prior tension.

"I love you too, Jamie," Isaac says. My face must contort with

the hurt and petty jealousy I'm trying to hide because Isaac looks
at me with concern and says, "I love you too, Theo."
  I can't stop my heart from skipping a fucking beat.

A knock at the door brought Theo back to the present.
He cleared his throat and called out cautiously, "Yes?"

"It's me." Jamie's voice eased some of the tension in
Theo's gut. "Food is ready and everyone is at the table. I tried
to text you but you didn't reply."

Theo stood and was opening the door after a few long
strides. "Sorry, I must have dozed off."

"It's all good, man." Jamie clapped Theo on the shoulder
and gave it a squeeze. "Come on, let's get this over with."

Theo flashed a tight half smile.

The long rectangular table was largely cleared and Theo's
family sat at the far end, with his father at the head of the table.
Theo sat side by side with Jamie, across from their mother. He
hadn't spoken to her yet other than a tight hello when he hugged
her briefly upon entering the room. The caterers brought out
trays of overly complicated plated food and set one in front of
each member of Theo's family. Theo avoided making eye contact
with his mother but he could feel her pleading eyes burning
through him, piercing his walls. When the caterer left the room,
Theo reached for the glass of cabernet sauvignon in front of him
and drained it in one go. He filled the glass past the point of
being socially acceptable and drank half of it before Jamie placed
his hand on Theo's knee and gave it a squeeze. Theo looked over
at Jamie whose brows were drawn together with concern and
flashed him a tight smile that didn't reach his eyes.

"Mom, when did you get your hair cut?" Jamie said,
breaking the awkward silence in the only way that Jamie
could.

She smiled bashfully and tucked her bobbed sandy-blonde hair behind her ear. "Last Thursday. Jane suggested it."

"Shit, Mom, it looks really good!"

"Watch your mouth, James."

"Ew, Dad. For the millionth time, can you please not call me *James*?" Jamie rolled his eyes and stabbed his fork into the ornate mashed potatoes.

"Thank you, dear," Theo's mom said as she stared down into her plate.

"Suzie, your food is getting cold."

"Yes, Jim." She picked up her knife and fork and cut up a piece of turkey.

Theo scoffed and gripped the stem of his wine glass. "I see nothing here has changed."

Jim set his knife and fork down, put his elbows on the table and knitted his fingers together. "What is that supposed to mean?"

"You've always ordered Mom around. She's a grown woman and can take care of herself, Dad."

Jim sneered. "You're right. Nothing has changed. You're still the same ungrateful, self-righteous child you've always been. You, who ignores your family then has the gall to come into my house and tell me how to treat my wife? The woman you've so actively avoided for years? Boy, don't you dare tell me how I should act."

Theo flinched at the words. They held so much truth that hearing them felt like receiving lashings. He had been a terrible son. He had been shutting his mother out and didn't know how to stop. She'd done nothing wrong to him and he'd treated her with disregard and not the love and respect a son owes his mother. He knew this—he *knew* it. And that made him feel even worse. The fact that his father, and probably Jamie, knew it too wounded Theo's already dismal view of himself.

He couldn't say anything. Even if he thought his voice would work, he didn't have anything to defend himself with. Theo lifted the wine glass to his lips once more and threw it back, emptying its contents down his throat.

"Such weakness. I thought you'd be rid of it once that *boy* was gone. But I see that your shortcomings run deeper than poor associations."

That caught Theo's attention. He jerked his head toward his father and narrowed his eyes. "What the hell is that supposed to mean?" Theo did not try to mask the bite in his words.

Jamie turned in his chair to face Theo and grasped his shoulder. Theo shrugged it off without taking his eyes off of his father.

"You insisted on wasting your time associating with that dreg and defied me at every turn. I'd hoped you would have matured a bit over the past year, but it seems that was wishful thinking."

"Don't talk about Isaac that way. I'm warning you and I'm only going to do it once."

"Theo, look at me." Jamie snapped his fingers in front of Theo's face, drawing his gaze from their father. "Calm down, just calm down."

"You're warning me? You don't get to waltz back into this house and police what I can and cannot say." Theo fumed, but his father maintained the same cool and collected demeanor he always adopted. "Unless that wasn't an empty threat? Do you intend to bash my face in like an uncontrolled animal? Just know that I won't be there to keep your sorry ass out of jail and free of a criminal record again. No, Theodore, if you want to act like an animal, I have no qualms over letting you rot in a cage."

"Jim, ple—" Suzie started.

"No. Theodore thinks he has some sway in this house and he needs to be educated otherwise. He needs to understand that coming in here full of piss and vinegar isn't going to accomplish anything. His attachment to that *parasite* wasn't healthy." Theo's dad directed his attention back to Theo with a pointed finger. "The fact that he's still got his filthy talons in you is pathetic. Now, you can either act like a fucking man or get the hell out of my house."

Theo was a stone. His father calmly resumed eating his dinner while Theo felt like he'd been gutted. Talking about Isaac was nearly impossible for him and there his father was, throwing it in his face with the same unaffected countenance he might have if he were reading sales reports. Theo's mom sat with her head cast down while Jamie had his hand on Theo's shaking right hand. He looked concerned and remorseful and was rendered uncharacteristically quiet. His eyes darted back and forth, as if he was trying to think of the right thing to say.

Avoiding eye contact with his father, Theo looked across the table to his mother. Her head was still down and her cheeks were damp with silent tears. He knew dinner would be a disaster. He *knew* it. But he hadn't expected his father to be quite so ruthless. Theo didn't have it in him to rise to his father's ultimatum. He stood on shaky legs, excused himself, and started toward the front door. Before he reached his car, Jamie was running down the driveway in just his socks.

"Theo, fuck, please don't go."

"I have to. I ca—" Theo took a deep breath. "I can't go back in that house. I won't. I can handle him pointing out my shortcomings. It's nothing I haven't already told myself a thousand times. But I... I can't listen to him talk about Isaac like that. I just can't, Jay." Theo's eyes stung, but he wouldn't cry.

"I'm sorry I didn't say anything. I've never heard him go off that bad; I just didn't know what to say." Guilt clouded Jamie's ordinarily carefree eyes.

Theo shook his head and grabbed Jamie's sweatshirt, pulling him in for a hug. "It's all right. It's better if you don't get in the middle of it."

Jamie pushed off of Theo and dropped his arms. "You're my big brother. I'm already in the middle of it."

"Please, Jay. Just leave it be for today. I'm going home, but I really think you should stay. Mom is really happy to see you."

"She was happy to see you too."

A tight smile pulled at Theo's mouth. "Please tell her I'm sorry." Theo opened the car door and started to get in when Jamie snatched the keys out of his hand.

"You're not driving."

"I appreciate your concern, but I'm not drunk."

"Maybe not. But you're not in any shape to be driving. Theo, look at your hands."

Theo held his hands out and looked down at them to see they were still shaking, like they used to when he was younger. He balled his hands into fists and winced at how much more pronounced the scars on his knuckles looked when the skin was strained. "I won't drive. I promise. Can you please grab me the joints? I'm pretty fucking sure I'll smoke half of them tonight." Theo tried for humor, but failed.

Jamie pocketed the keys and motioned over his shoulder toward the house. "They're in my bag in the house, just give me a minute. And I'm taking the keys with me."

"Fine." Theo got in the car but kept the door open. When Jamie was out of sight, Theo pulled out his phone and called Masa before he could think twice about it.

"Hello?" Masa's deep voice filled Theo's ears.

"Hey." *Ugh, I'm such a fucking idiot.*

"What's going on? Aren't you at dinner?"

"It was cut short."

"Theo, what's wrong?"

How can he tell already? "I really need to get out of here. I don't really want to be alone right now." Theo regretted the words as quickly as he'd spoken them. What if Masa was busy? What if he didn't want to see him? "I-I mean, if you're not busy and if you want to."

"Where do your parents live?"

"Lincoln Park."

"Did you drive there?"

"Yes."

"Have you been drinking?"

Theo shifted in his seat. "Yes, some."

"Okay. Please just stay there and wait for me. I can take an Uber or Lyft or whatever. Just send me the address and please wait."

"All right." Theo looked up and saw Jamie coming down the driveway holding a small black plastic resealable bag, the kind used in university examinations for cell phones. "I have to go. I'll text you the address. And, Masa... Thank you."

"Don't worry about it. I'll be there shortly."

Theo disconnected the call and thumbed out a text with the address for Masa as Jamie handed him the bag. He took it and tossed it in the glove compartment.

"Thank you."

"Don't sweat it." Jamie flung Theo's key ring around his index finger as he spoke. "Did you figure out how you're getting home?"

"A friend is coming to pick me up."

"A friend, huh?"

Theo bowed his head. "Yeah."

Jamie nodded knowingly and didn't push further. Seemingly satisfied that Theo wasn't going to drive, he reluctantly surrendered the keys. "Okie. Text me when you get home." He went back inside after Theo assured him he would.

About twenty minutes later a silver Honda Accord parked on the street in front of Theo's childhood home. The door flew open and Masa rushed out in a flurry of baggy black and dark grey clothes. His hair was a mess, visibly tangled and haphazardly pushed back from his face. His eyes settled on Theo's car and he closed the distance in a few long strides until he reached Theo's still open door. He kneeled in front of Theo in the dusting of snow coating the driveway and cupped his face in one of his hands. His other hand held Theo's left hand. Masa brushed his thumb over Theo's knuckles.

"What happened, baby?"

There it is again. "I don't really want to talk about it right now if that's all right."

"I understand. Come on, I'll take you home." Masa withdrew his hand from Theo's cold cheek and stood, taking a step back. Theo got out of the car and shivered when a gust of wind blew through his thin button-up sweater. He'd been too distracted to even consider closing the car door while he waited for Masa and was only now realizing just how cold it was.

Theo's discomfort didn't go unnoticed by Masa. He pulled Theo close and kissed his forehead while he rubbed his upper arms gently. "You're freezing, Theo. Hurry up and get in."

Theo walked around to the passenger seat and got in. Masa did the same once Theo's door closed. Once inside, he held Theo's key and looked between it and the ignition quizzically. His confusion was clearly displayed on his face by the set of his eyebrows—drawn together yet also raised—and him biting the left side of his bottom lip. The sight pulled a giggle from Theo he didn't know he was capable of given the circumstances and he showed Masa how to start the car.

Traffic was heavy on the drive back to Theo's place. The majority of the drive was spent in silence until Masa asked if Theo had eaten anything. He shook his head to indicate no and Masa made the executive decision to stop at Wendy's, the first place they could find on the way back. Theo shrugged when asked what he wanted so Masa took a chance and ordered him a spicy chicken sandwich and a bacon double cheeseburger for himself.

Inside the condo, Masa led Theo over to the couch and sat him down. He pushed the sandwich in front of him and instructed him to eat. Theo wasn't particularly hungry, but he ate it anyway without a fight. Masa finished his burger first and went to the kitchen to get them a couple glasses of water. Theo drank his in one go and handed the glass back to Masa's outstretched hand. He crouched down in front of Theo again and entwined his fingers in the space between his knees. He took a deep breath to steady himself.

"We don't have to talk about it right now. And if you want me to go, I will. Just tell me what you need."

Theo remembered hearing Masa speak similar words before and felt comforted by his willingness to do whatever Theo selfishly needed. "Please don't go."

"Okay. Are you tired at all?"

"Exhausted."

Masa bowed his head and stood. "Come to bed." Theo rose from the couch and they made their way down the hall and stripped down to their trunks before sliding into the clean sheets. Masa pulled Theo into his arms and set Theo's head on his chest. He curled the arm Theo used as a partial pillow and ran his long fingers through Theo's hair at the back of his head.

"*C'est bon, nounours. Je t'ai eu.*"

CHAPTER FOURTEEN

THEO WOKE WITH Masa's arms wrapped around him and his face snuggled firmly into Theo's nape. His body was snug against Theo's, his inevitable morning wood pressed against the crack of Theo's ass. Tempting as it may be, Theo still felt a bit shaken from the prior day's turn of events. Part of him wanted to sit in bed all day and do nothing, while another part of him wanted to wake Masa and get pounded into oblivion. He knew it wasn't healthy, and that Masa would never go for hurting him like that, but he couldn't reconcile his emotions to find a middle ground. Masa always touched him like he was something to be cherished, but Theo couldn't figure out why. He wondered if perhaps Masa was just an affectionate person. He couldn't imagine the man being cruel to anyone, in any capacity. Masa had said he'd give Theo what he wanted, but was that something he would be able to follow through on? Theo wasn't sure he wanted to taint Masa with his pain like that. He wasn't sure of anything in that moment other than how good Masa's warmth felt on his back and the way his breath tickled the sensitive skin on the back of Theo's neck.

"You're awake, aren't you?" Masa whispered, his voice thick with sleep.

Theo startled at the slight rumble against his neck and goose bumps spread across his skin. "Yes."

Masa groaned and buried his face deeper into the hair just above Theo's neck. He inhaled deeply and Theo felt Masa's dick twitch against his ass. "*Mmm, tu sent crissement bon.*"

"You're snuggling me with an erection again."

"Ah, *nounours,* come on. *Je ne peux rien y faire.* It's the morning."

That I understood. "You might not be able to help it, but you don't have to grind it into my ass."

"Really? I thought you liked it when I did that." Masa rolled his hips into Theo.

Theo felt him smile against his neck and smiled himself, glad he was facing away from Masa so he wouldn't provide fuel for his smug smile. "Whatever." Theo had no comeback so he resorted to a childish dismissal. Masa noticed and laughed in earnest, vibrating against Theo's body. "Shut up." Theo bucked his hips back hard, making Masa wince.

"Hey now, behave." Theo thrashed in Masa's arms, but Masa maintained his hold on him. "*Nounours,* come on, it's early."

Theo could have easily broken free, but he stopped resisting at Masa's words. "Why do you call me that? *Nounours.*"

"Why do you ask?"

"My grandmother used to call my grandfather that. I'd always thought it was some kind of nickname for him, but I never asked. Then again, eight-year-old me was more interested in the cookies my grandmother baked for me when I did well with my French lessons."

"Your grandfather, was his name Theodore?"

"Yes, how did you know?"

Masa giggled. "*Nounours.* It means teddy bear. I assumed it was a safe bet you were named after him if his wife called him that too, of all pet names."

Theo jerked forward and rolled over to face Masa. "*Teddy bear?* You've been calling me teddy bear?! Are you fucking kidding me?"

"Shh, don't yell. Does it really bother you?" Masa had concern all over his face and traced over Theo's shoulder with his fingertips.

"It's not that it bothers me per se." Theo paused and sucked in a deep breath while he thought of the right words. "It's just not very... manly."

Masa bit his lips and studied Theo for a moment. "So you're worried about not being perceived as manly?"

"Isn't every guy?"

"Tell me, what was your impression of your grandfather? What kind of man was he?"

"Well, I remember him always being kind. And strong. He used to always have Jamie and me grab on to his arms and he'd lift us up while we laughed, which of course made my grandmother worry. He was a good man."

Masa smiled knowingly. "And his wife called him *nounours.* It didn't make him any less of a man, did it? Theo, trust me when I say that a lack of masculinity isn't an issue for you. You're probably one of the most masculine men I've ever met, without being a dreaded dudebro or toxic about it. No one who looks at you would see anything else. Even if they did, there's nothing wrong with that. You're sexy as hell and drive me crazy. But if you don't want me to call you that, I'll try to stop."

Theo could tell Masa meant no disrespect by the look on his face and his tone. He shuddered to think his identity as a man was fragile enough to shatter over being called a nickname. "It's okay. On two conditions. Don't say it in public, and don't you dare say it in a smug or condescending tone."

Masa laughed and looked into Theo's eyes. "Damn, those are two of my favorite tones to employ."

"I know. Asshole." Theo reached behind him to grab a pillow and whacked Masa with it. Masa protested in a flurry of French that Theo couldn't make out, but hearing it brought a smile to his face. He ceased his attack and threw the pillow back behind him.

"You're gorgeous, but you're cruel," Masa pouted.

"Tell me something I don't know."

"You really do drive me crazy."

"What?"

"You said to tell you something you didn't know." Masa looked at Theo without a hint of playfulness in his eyes.

Theo stared at Masa blankly and burst out laughing. "You're so literal sometimes."

"Yeah, I've heard that. I'm a pretty simple guy."

"It's refreshing in a way. I don't have to guess with you. I don't have to worry about what you're thinking and if I've upset you. It shows very clearly on your face and in what you say."

"Wearing a mask takes up too much energy," Masa eyed Theo up and down, "and I can think of several ways I'd rather use my energy."

"You're a walking hard-on."

"Ugh, don't say that. I'm trying to be good."

"What do you mean?"

"I've got plans for us today. Sort of. I need to shower first, though." Masa rolled out of bed and stretched with his arms over his head. Theo shamelessly stared at his tented boxers and bit his bottom lip.

Masa glanced down and caught Theo staring at his crotch

and he scoffed while he adjusted himself. "*Se comporter.* I'll be back." He walked out of the room.

Once Theo was alone he adjusted the erection in his boxers he'd been hiding from Masa moments before. He leaned over toward the nightstand and glanced at the clock to see it was just after nine in the morning. Theo grabbed his phone and hit the first number on speed dial and put it on speaker.

"Theo! Where the hell have you been?!" Leah's voice filled the room from the tiny speaker.

"Hey, I'm sorry. I've been having a busy couple of days. But I did want to wish you a Happy Thanksgiving."

"Thanks, same to you. But don't for a second think that that excuses you from dodging my calls."

"I know, I know. We'll talk about it when I get back in tomorrow."

"Is everything okay? You sound like you're just waking up?"

Theo sighed and sat up further in bed. "Yeah, I'm good. Some shit happened yesterday, but I'll tell you about it on Monday." Leah was silent for an uncomfortably long time, which unnerved Theo. "Leah?"

"You have someone there with you, don't you?"

"*What?*" *Holy shit, how can she tell?*

"I know you, Theo. You sound *different*. If you haven't met someone, it's something."

Theo heard the shower shut off and shuffling in the bathroom. "I have to go. We can talk about this on Monday."

Leah laughed. "Oh, there is totally someone there! You scoundrel—"

"Goodbye, Leah." Theo hung up the phone and tossed it back on the nightstand. He rubbed the heels of his hands into his eyes and groaned as heavy footsteps made their way into the room.

"What's up? You look kind of annoyed."

"Can *everyone* tell how I'm feeling? Fuck." Masa looked at Theo with his head cocked to one side, clearly trying to understand why he was being defensive. "I just got off the phone with my assistant. She pushes my buttons sometimes. Not in a bad way. She's just always right and it's frustrating sometimes."

"Ah, I see." Relief flooded Masa's face and he carried on with his usual carefree ease. He walked over to the edge of the bed by the window and pulled out a fresh pair of boxers from his bag, sliding them on under the towel tied at his waist. He dropped the towel to the floor and hopped back in bed, shimming up against Theo.

"Come on, your hair is still wet."

"But you're comfy." Masa squeezed Theo tighter and nuzzled in deeper under his arm.

"Whatever. I probably stink, you shouldn't do that."

"*Décâlisse.* You smell amazing. I can't get enough."

"What's so good about it?"

Masa moaned and rubbed his face on Theo's chest. "I don't know exactly. It's probably your pheromones. I can't describe the scent but it's intoxicating. I can't wait to get my hands on you after a workout."

"Ew. You're weird."

"Maybe. But you're still sexy." Masa kissed Theo's chest and smiled against his skin. "What do you want to do today? My plans for you aren't until this evening."

"You," Theo deadpanned.

Masa huffed and smiled. "That sounds great, but I meant, like, outside things."

"Outside things?" Theo asked skeptically.

"Yeah. Like some shopping or sightseeing. I figured you might be able to show me around the city a bit. I'll probably go to school here, so it would be nice to get to know downtown."

"I'd love to, but it's black Friday and we might get trampled to death."

"Oh shit, that's right. I forgot about that. I've seen some videos of people fist fighting over vacuum cleaners. It's crazy."

"Mhm. So I'd prefer not to go shopping or sightseeing today, but if you wanted to catch a movie or something, that would be nice I suppose."

Masa lifted his head and smiled so wide Theo thought his cheeks must hurt. He leaned up and kissed Theo on the lips.

Jesus, he's adorable.

THE MOVIE WAS some action flick with Tom Cruise and a bomb. It wasn't bad, however neither Theo nor Masa paid much attention to the screen. They spent the duration of the film with their eyes locked on each other, escalating from stolen glances to full-fledged eye-fucking complete with heavy breathing. As strong as the urge was, neither man touched the other, aside from Masa's knee bumping Theo's a few times.

Once the movie ended they looked away from each other. When the theater was empty Masa turned to Theo and choked out a single word, almost a command.

"Car."

Theo nodded, and they headed out to the parking garage.

"How fast can you get us back to your place?"

"Not fast enough," Theo said as he pulled the keys to his BMW from his pocket. Before he could open the driver side door, Masa grabbed his arm, spun him around, and leaned him back against the closed door.

"I can't wait," Masa growled.

Theo frantically looked around the garage, seeing no one else in sight. He could hear tires squealing in the distance, but they were relatively alone. He met Masa's lust-filled gaze and melted. Speech was nearly impossible, but he swallowed and managed to choke out two words. "Back seat."

Masa pulled Theo against him and opened the rear door. He shoved Theo inside and he landed on his back. Theo scooted back and rested his head and shoulders against the passenger side door. Masa climbed in on top of him, immediately grinding his body against Theo's and seeking out his mouth. Theo opened up to Masa as soon as their lips touched, and he threaded his legs around Masa's. It wasn't comfortable and was very cramped, but that wasn't important. The only thing that mattered to either man was the other.

Masa leaned back and undid Theo's pants, pulling them off one leg at a time. Theo's shoes got in the way and Masa tossed them, rather aggressively, into the front seat. He hooked his thumbs into the band of Theo's boxers and started to pull.

"Masa, wait." Masa froze and looked up at Theo's blissed-out eyes. "The door." Masa cocked his head and furrowed his brow. "Close the door." Theo flicked his eyes past Masa to the open car door.

Masa followed Theo's eyes and looked behind him. "Oh, shit, sorry." Masa turned back to pull the door closed and whacked his head on the roof of the car.

"Ostie d'câlisse de tabarnak!"

"Masamune," Theo pleaded, his eyes heavy-lidded.

"Right." Masa closed the door and picked up the keys off the floor to lock the doors before settling back against Theo. "Better?"

Theo bit his lip and nodded. He ran his hand down

Masa's back, worked it into Masa's pants, and squeezed his ass. "Come on, don't make me wait." He slid his other hand down his own chest and gripped his stiff dick, giving it a firm squeeze.

"Shit," Masa said before he crashed his lips back down on Theo's in a consuming kiss. Theo only felt one of Masa's hands on him and longed for more contact. The sound of a zipper and rustling fabric caught Theo's attention and he broke the kiss to glance down. He sucked in a sharp breath and was stunned to see the tip of Masa's dick disappearing and reappearing in his foreskin as he quickly stroked himself.

After a few tantalizing strokes Masa swatted Theo's hand away from his own cock and held both of theirs, stroking them hurriedly and returning his lips to Theo's. When pre-cum slicked Masa's hand he stopped stroking and pulled back from kissing Theo.

"You said you keep condoms in here?"

"Glove compartment," Theo said while panting.

Masa leaned into the front seat and opened the glove compartment. He reached for the box of condoms and jerked, fumbling the box when Theo suddenly started stroking him from root to tip. "Jesus Christ," Masa ground out as he shifted back into the back seat between Theo's bare legs. Theo smiled up at him roguishly while Masa tore open a condom and rolled it down his length. "Baby, this is gonna be rough." Masa sucked on two fingers and penetrated Theo with them one at a time. He stroked Theo's prostate and tried to quickly stretch him. He slicked up the condom with more spit and slowly pushed past Theo's tight ring of muscle until he was buried balls deep.

Theo's lips parted with a sharp sigh and his eyes flitted and rolled back as Masa filled him. It did hurt, but his arousal outweighed the pain tenfold. He needed this, to feel claimed by Masa in such a visceral manner. He leaned up and nipped at Masa's earlobe before whispering, "Fuck me up, Masa."

The words spurred Masa on and he fucked Theo harder and faster than he ever had before. Both men clawed at one another and panted and moaned at every erratic thrust. Masa jackhammered his hips into Theo like his life depended on it and Theo took everything Masa gave him. It wasn't pretty, and it didn't last long. Masa came first and stilled over Theo, pulsing his seed into the condom. He gave a couple more deep thrusts before pulling out and taking Theo's still hard cock down his throat.

Theo threaded his fingers in Masa's hair and bucked his hips up off the car seat, forcing his dick further down Masa's throat. Masa grasped Theo's thighs and moaned his approval around his cock. Theo took the sweet vibration as encouragement and fucked Masa's throat in earnest until the pressure in his balls released and his cum spilled down Masa's throat. Masa swallowed everything Theo gave him and pulled off of his cock with a lick of his lips.

When Theo caught his breath enough to speak he brushed his fingers through Masa's hair, twirling some over his index finger. "Are you all right?"

Masa looked up with a curious smile. "Better than all right. Why wouldn't I be?"

"I don't know, I just throat-fucked you with no warning. Oh, and with no courtesy heads-up about coming."

Masa laughed at that and ran his fingers through Theo's pubic hair. "You don't have to be worried about me. That was fucking hot and you can have my mouth any time you want it. Are you feeling okay? I didn't really prep you too well."

"I'm great. A bit sore, but it was worth it."

"Good." Masa took a gratuitous sniff of Theo's pubes and moaned his satisfaction. Before Theo could comment Masa spoke again. "I know. I'm weird. Don't worry about it. As much as I'd like to stay tangled up back here with you for the rest of the weekend, we should get going before someone sees us and calls security."

"Oh, God. Yeah, let's go. I need to get home and get out of these sweaty clothes."

"Do you mind if we stop somewhere first? There are a few things I wanted to pick up."

Theo waited in the car at Masa's request during the stop he'd asked for. Masa had asked Theo where he usually bought his groceries, to which he replied Whole Foods. This was how Theo ended up waiting in the car in the Whole Foods parking lot. Masa emerged from the store about ten minutes later with two half-full reusable bags. Masa put the bags in the back seat and then hopped in the front.

Theo craned his neck to look in the back, but Masa caught his chin and he leaned in to quickly kiss him. "Nah-uh, no peeking."

Theo rolled his eyes. "It's a grocery store. There's only so much you could have bought."

"Yeah, well, you'll just have to wait and see."

Theo changed into dark grey Lululemon sweatpants when they got back to his place. Masa had banned him from the kitchen while he unpacked the groceries. Masa was poking around in the lower cabinets looking for the right pans when Theo came back down the hall.

"Are you going to tell me what you're making?"

Masa looked up as Theo was sitting on one of the high stools are the bar. "I wasn't planning on it, no."

"I can help you cook if you tell me."

"You cook?" Masa asked skeptically.

"I can prep food."

Masa smirked and set a skillet and deep sauté pan on the

counter. "I appreciate the offer, but I'd really like it to be a surprise."

"Okay."

"I'm going to go change. Can I trust that you won't sneak a look?"

"At you or at the food?" Theo teased.

Masa smiled and shook his head. "Don't start. I really want to cook for you today."

Theo held up his hands in defeat and spun around on the stool as Masa walked around the counter and headed for the hallway. "I promise I'll *comporter*."

Masa groaned and went down the hall to get changed. Theo thumbed out a reply to a text from Jamie while he patiently waited. Jamie had texted him the previous night, asking if he was okay. Theo assured him he was fine and didn't offer anything more. He set his phone down on the counter when Masa came back with black sweats, a black tank, and his hair tied back. His bangs still hung over his eyes, but the newfound view of his jaw and neck sent Theo's thoughts racing straight to the gutter. Masa brushed his bangs back behind his ears, but several stubborn strands refused to stay in place and fell back in his face. Theo watched Masa like he was putting on a performance. He studied how his body moved, how each action seemed to be performed with so much deliberate intent, and he admired the beauty and grace before him.

Masa pulled out a package of what looked like two chicken breasts as well as several small bags of unmarked spices. He set the meat on a cutting board and drizzled olive oil over them before sprinkling on several spices and herbs. "I can see you peeking."

"Guilty."

"Funny, I wouldn't have pegged you for a voyeur, but I guess you couldn't resist watching me rub my meat."

They both laughed, and Theo shook his head as Masa worked the seasoning into the meat. "You're ridiculous."

Masa winked at Theo and flipped the meat over. "Do you mind putting some music on?"

"Sure thing. What are you in the mood for?"

"Surprise me."

"I thought that was your job today?" Masa flashed Theo a playful look and Theo could already hear Masa's deep voice rumble in his ear. *Se comporter.* The thought sent a shiver down his spine. Theo shook it off and walked over to the table in front of the TV to grab the remote. He turned the surround sound on and synced it up with the Bluetooth on his phone to stream Sixteen Stone by Bush.

"Everything Zen" filled the room while Masa peeled and chopped some kind of vegetable after rinsing another. Theo tried really hard not to ruin Masa's surprise, so he sat across at the bar and worked on a word search on his phone. He and Masa made comfortable conversation while Masa cooked, and he occasionally helped Theo with recent pop culture questions. Theo hadn't felt this comfortable with someone since Isaac. He tried not to think about it too much, but one look into Masa's hazel eyes sent him spiraling back to thinking about Isaac and how much it hurt to have someone close to you leave.

Masa will leave too.

Theo was enjoying this time with Masa, but he knew it was transient. It had already gone on longer than it should, but Masa made Theo feel good and he selfishly didn't want to give that up just yet. As if Masa could read Theo's mind, he smiled at him.

"What's on your mind?"

"A lot. Dinner smells really good." *Obvious much?*

"It's almost ready. Would you like some wine?"

"You bought wine? Are you even old enough to do that in the States?"

"Whatever. I got a red and white. I wasn't sure what you'd be in the mood for. Either will complement dinner."

Theo folded his arms and raised an eyebrow at Masa. "When did you become such a wine connoisseur?"

"Ha, cute. I might have done some research on Google. Let's start with white."

Masa bowed his head and fished two stemless wine glasses out of the cupboard and uncorked the bottle with a satisfying pop. He poured more than a socially acceptable amount of wine in each glass and set one down in front of Theo. Theo picked up the glass and grinned.

"Do I look thirsty?"

Masa's eyebrows drew together. "Is it too much?"

"No, no. It's absolutely fine for me. It's just about double what you'd get in a restaurant. But I like how you pour." Theo brought the wine to his lips and took a sip of the cool liquid. "You picked a good wine, even if it wasn't wholly intentional."

Masa smiled and tried the wine himself. "You're right, that's not half bad." Masa took another sip and set the glass down when the timer on the oven went off. "Ah, great timing. Where do you want to eat?"

"Umm, right here?"

"Okay." Masa jerked his head to the end of the bar. "Do you mind if I sit there next to you?"

"Not at all." Theo got up and moved the stool he was sitting on around the edge of the counter and pulled the one to his right beside him. With this arrangement they'd be seated perpendicular to each other instead of side by side.

Masa grabbed a tea towel and asked Theo to close his eyes for the plating. Theo took another sip of wine and sat patiently with his eyes closed. Theo focused on the sounds and scents that filled the kitchen as he fought the urge to open his eyes. Whatever Masa made smelled *amazing*.

"You can open your eyes now."

Theo opened his eyes and gasped when he saw the meal in front of him. Set on a square plate was a feast of what looked like roasted chicken breast, a roasted squash and carrot mixture, and sautéed asparagus. He tried to stifle the gasp by taking a quick drink of wine, but he was sure it had been audible to Masa. "Holy shit."

"Is that a good holy shit, or is it too much?" Masa was now sitting at the end of the bar with an identical plate of food in front of him.

"Masa, I," Theo started, "I don't know what to say."

"Please say you're hungry for starters. Shit, and that you like squash."

"I love squash. Masa, thank you. You really didn't have to do this." Theo's voice was tight.

Masa smiled and rubbed his hand over Theo's thigh. "I know. But I wanted you to have a good Thanksgiving. I know it was yesterday, but I hope this is still okay."

Theo laughed to himself and held Masa's hand on his thigh. "It's perfect. Thank you. Wait, is that turkey?"

Masa sighed in relief and withdrew his hand from Theo's thigh. He picked up his knife and fork and started to cut into the turkey breast. "It sure is. Eat up before it gets cold. You can stare longingly at me when we're full and drunk off this awesome wine."

"Shut up," Theo said with a huge grin.

The easy conversation continued over dinner and Theo praised Masa's cooking skills. Masa, of course, took the compliment with as much modesty as Dorian Gray would have while admiring his reflection. Once they were finished eating they lay out on the couch, with Masa leaning on Theo, and watched *Jaws: The Revenge*. Masa held Theo's hand in his and occasionally brushed his thumb over Theo's knuckles. After nearly an hour of both men internally cringing at the movie, it was Masa who finally spoke up.

"Good God, you weren't kidding when you said this was bad."

"I tried to tell you."

"I'm sorry I ever doubted you," replied Masa in a mock-horrified tone. He quieted for a few minutes and continued to rub Theo's knuckles. "Can I ask you something?"

"Yeah, of course."

"How did you get these scars?"

Theo took a deep breath and exhaled loudly. "I used to get in some fights when I was younger—in high school mostly."

Masa craned his neck to look up at Theo's face. "Really? I don't picture you as the fighting type. Someone must have really pissed you off."

"It wasn't for me. I was protecting a friend."

"Isaac?"

Theo huffed out a breath, as if remembering something about the man Masa was so curious about and said, "Yes." His voice sounded pained.

Masa kissed Theo's knuckles individually while Theo watched him closely. That look was there again. Masa was holding something back.

"Do you want to talk about what had you so upset yesterday?"

To both their surprise, Theo answered immediately. "My father, mostly." Theo explained the guilt he felt over what happened to his mother the day he and Isaac decided to leave. Masa listened intently and did not interrupt or try to fill any silences Theo left. When Theo was ready to continue, he did. "I was already on edge over seeing her after so long. I barely even said five words to her yesterday. Jesus Christ. I've never had an easy relationship with my father. He's always been a very straightforward person, but in a very cold, calculated way. He doesn't sugarcoat his words and they're his ultimate weapon. They're sharpened daggers aimed right at your weakest spots. He tore me up over how I've treated my mother and believe me, it's nothing I didn't already tell myself. But just hearing it out loud somehow made it more real. I was forced to acknowledge how much of a coward I am, not just in the recesses of my mind, but in broad daylight and at my family's fucking dining room table." Theo ran his free hand through his hair and pulled at the roots in the back. He laughed to himself dryly. "That wasn't even the worst part, though. No, after being stripped bare he started in on Isaac and I felt like I was in high school again, like I had to protect him. He said some pretty hateful things and I felt myself start to slip. You see," Theo's voice cracked, "I got most of these scars at a house party of some rich kid who I used to call a friend. There had been tension with him and Isaac for several months, but I was foolish and wanted everyone to get along and insisted that Isaac come with me to the party. It was a disaster. They argued and the guy decked Isaac. I-I can't remember what happened after that. My next memory of that night is when I was pulled off of the guy who hit Isaac. I'd bashed his face in and probably would have killed him if I wasn't stopped. How fucked up is that?

"My father took care of the incident and we never spoke of it again. Then he brought it up again last night. After he'd insulted Isaac I started to see red, just like that night. My father must have seen it in my eyes too. He called me out on it and essentially told me that if I wanted to act like an animal he'd let me rot in jail like one. He told me to man up or leave. And, well, you picked me up yesterday, so you know how the story ends."

Masa sat up and searched out Theo's eyes. "*Mon dieu,*

Theo." Theo braced himself for platitudes appropriate for what he'd just shared. The type of remarks he had no interest in hearing. Instead of hearing them, he felt Masa stroke his knuckles again and Theo instantly relaxed his shoulders.

"What's your dad's problem with Isaac? You said he was your best friend."

"My father thought he was a bad influence on me. We were pretty inseparable growing up and Dad thought Isaac would bring me down and hinder my future prospects. Isaac's parents died in a car wreck when he was eleven. He moved in with his uncle after that and we met a couple years later. His uncle didn't have much money and was a blue-collar worker. All the insurance money from his parents went toward Isaac's schooling. He attended the same private schools I did. Isaac also had this carefree attitude my father despised. But he mainly disliked him for his social standing. And how our friendship reflected on the family."

"That's fucking ridiculous."

"Oh, I know. He was like a brother to me. Nothing my father said kept us away from each other."

"Where is he now?" Masa asked eagerly.

Theo tensed his jaw and looked back at the TV. "He, uh… we're not friends anymore."

Masa rubbed Theo's knuckles again, but Theo couldn't relax. He didn't want to talk anymore for fear of how his voice might sound. He leaned into the end of the couch, away from Masa's warmth. Theo heard Masa shift on the couch and he thought he heard Masa suck in a sharp breath. He was tempted to look over, but he doubted he'd be able to conceal the depth of his anguish from Masa if he did.

They watched the rest of the movie smothered by a heavy silence. Theo sat with his arms crossed and his legs tucked up under him. His eyes didn't leave the TV once for the rest of the movie. He knew he was being an asshole, but he didn't trust himself to not break down in front of Masa if he kept talking. So he did what he always did when he didn't want to show his weakness, he shut himself down.

Masa looked over at Theo when the movie ended and Theo met his gaze. He'd felt Masa's eyes on him during the movie, but he ignored the urge to look his way. He flashed Masa a tight smile that didn't quite reach his eyes. Masa smiled back and stood.

"I should get the dishes done."

"Masa, wait." Theo jumped to his feet and grabbed Masa's wrist.

"You cooked. It's only fair that I at least do the dishes."

Masa sighed in defeat. "If you insist," he said as he sat down at the bar. Theo smiled at him more genuinely then headed into the kitchen. He stood before the sink and rolled up his sleeves before turning on the hot water and going to work on the dirty dishes. He threw himself into the simple task, hoping to divert his attention from the serious turn his conversation with Masa had taken. He hoped the brave face he was putting on would convince Masa. All he wanted to do was sink into the man's arms and be held. Theo stole a glance at Masa and he looked just as pained as Theo felt. Theo flashed him a smile but he was sure it appeared weak.

Masa suddenly got off the stool and sauntered around the bar and stood right behind Theo. He wrapped his arms around Theo's waist and rested his bowed head on the back of Theo's neck. They both remained quiet, but Theo spoke volumes when he leaned his head slightly to the side and relaxed his body against Masa's. Masa softly kissed his neck while he held him coaxing Theo further into relaxation, exposing more of his neck to Masa's exploratory kisses.

Theo turned in Masa's arms and leaned his head into his neck. "I'm sorry," he whispered.

"I am too. I don't know when to shut up sometimes."

Theo shook his head softly. "You didn't do anything you have to apologize for." Theo balled his fists in the sides of Masa's shirt. "Thank you for today, Masa. This was the best Thanksgiving I've had in years."

Masa pulled Theo closer and ghosted his lips over Theo's before kissing him tenderly. "You're welcome. Come on, fisticuffs. Let's go to bed."

"Wait. Did you just call me fisticuffs?"

"Mhm."

"That's not how that word works."

"Shh, sure it does."

Theo smiled into Masa's neck as he slid his hands up his back and hugged him in earnest. "Thank you, Masa."

CHAPTER FIFTEEN

"**G**OD. I'VE MISSED THIS," Theo said after he slouched into the leather couch across from Leah and took a sip of hot tea.

"Don't get too comfy, you'll wrinkle your suit."

"Do I have any appointments today?"

"No, I figured I'd ease you back into things."

"Then I have no one to impress." Theo smiled and took another sip of tea. He groaned from deep in his throat to express his contentment.

"Jesus, Theo. Do I need to give you a moment?"

Theo cocked his head to the side. "What do you mean?"

"You've only been gone for a couple weeks, but I see a serious change in you. Looks like I was right after all."

"It's not like that, we're not serious," Theo said quickly.

"Who are you not serious with? And you're assuming I was talking about your mystery date, which basically confirms that it is in fact serious." Leah sat back with a self-satisfied smile on her face.

Jesus. Her, Jamie, and Masa with that goddamn smile.

Theo set the glass mug on the table before him and

spread his arms across the back of the couch. "If I ever went up against you in negotiations I wouldn't stand a fucking chance."

"Exactly. So why do you even bother to try and hide things from me?"

"A man needs to have some mystery and—"

"Puh-leeeease. Don't get me that BS."

"Fine."

"So, are you going to tell me about them?" Leah probed.

Theo shrugged, trying to look casual while sweat started to form on his forehead and back. "What's there to tell?"

Leah scoffed. "Quite a lot. I'm very intrigued to know who was special enough to grab your attention."

Theo tapped his fingers against the couch and stared down at the mug on the table. "You're not going to let me off, are you?"

"Nope," Leah snapped back as she smiled and shook her head.

"Can we talk about Thanksgiving instead?" Theo sounded desperate now. Leah just shook her head again.

"We met at a bar," Theo muttered. Leah inhaled sharply but didn't say anything, so Theo went on. "I was kind of an asshole, but we ended up getting along and going home together. The past couple weeks have been fun. It's pretty casual. Not much more to tell." Theo regretted the words after they'd left his mouth. Masa was so much more than a fun time, but he couldn't say that out loud. Saying it would make it too real. Saying it would open him up to getting hurt.

"Ooookay. What is she like?"

Theo shifted on the couch and drained the rest of his tea. His hand was unsteady returning the glass to the table and Leah noticed. Her eyebrows drew together, and she leaned forward, as if she wanted to touch Theo. He held up his hand to let her know he was all right and she settled.

Shit. It's now or never I guess.

"He's a man." Theo paused to look into Leah's eyes, but her expression never changed so he continued. "His name is Masamune." Sweat was now dripping down Theo's back and forehead. He took his jacket off and looked back at Leah nervously.

"So, tell me about him."

Theo wearily sat forward and leaned his forearms on his thighs. He rubbed hands together between his knees. "You don't look surprised. Did you know about this too?"

Leah flung her long blonde hair off her shoulders. She usually wore it tied back, but today it was down and covering the top of her lavender chiffon blouse. "I'd suspected it for a while, but I wasn't certain."

Theo sighed. "Did you purposefully use female pronouns in hopes I'd one day correct you?"

"Guilty," Leah replied as she raised her right hand.

"Why didn't you just ask me?"

"Oh, Theo. It wasn't my place." Theo sucked in a breath, about to speak, but Leah cut him off. "I know, I know. That's rich coming from me. Me prying into your personal life as I've been doing is one thing, but this is another matter. This is something about yourself you kept from me intentionally and it wasn't my place to outright ask you. I shouldn't have poked and tested either, but I couldn't help myself." Leah shrugged and flashed a half smile.

Theo smiled in return. Telling Leah felt good and that feeling of heaviness being shed returned. She wasn't looking at him any differently; she didn't even flinch when he told her. Relieved, Theo leaned back into the couch again.

"I still want you to tell me about him."

"Damn, I thought I'd sufficiently distracted you."

"No dice."

"Well, he's really nice. He makes me laugh and is frustrating as hell sometimes. He, uh, is also really considerate. And he's smart. He's going to school for his doctorate."

Leah beamed. "He sounds great. What does he look like?"

"He's Japanese and French Canadian. He's got black hair down to his shoulders and these really nice hazel eyes. They," Theo paused, "they actually remind me a lot of Isaac. Ah, he's tall. I'm not sure exactly how tall, maybe around six foot three. He's got some tattoos as well."

"Jesus, Theo."

"What?"

"He sounds hot as hell!"

Theo turned a shade of red reserved only for roses. "Yeah, I guess he is. But I meant what I said before. It's just casual."

"Okay," Leah said skeptically. "What about Thanksgiving then? Did you bring him with you?"

"Oh, God no. That was a big enough mess on its own without me dropping that on my father."

"Does Jamie know?"

"Yeah, I told him last week. He took it really well and insisted we get hammered on scotch. It was a mess." Theo shuddered at the memory.

"I can imagine. Jamie is a handful."

"He's something. Anyway, Thanksgiving was a disaster." Theo explained the exchange with his father and how Masa ended up coming to pick him up. Leah nodded solemnly and came over to sit next to Theo. She wrapped her arms around one of his and leaned her head on his shoulder.

"I'm sorry, Theo. You didn't deserve that."

"I kind of did, though."

"No. No one deserves to be treated like that, especially

not by their own family. Jeez. No wonder you didn't want to talk about it when you called."

"It ended up okay, though. Masa made me dinner the next night and it was really sweet. Turkey breasts too."

"Theo. This doesn't sound all that casual. That's like, a really grand gesture."

Theo shook his head and waved a hand. "No, it's not like that. I told you, he's just a really nice guy."

Leah sighed in a way that let Theo know she was not at all placated by his denial. "If you insist, dear."

An awkward silence filled the room before Theo cleared his throat. "Anyway, catch me up on everything I've missed."

"Very smooth."

"Shut up," Theo said without an ounce of malice.

"For starters, Lucas is amazing. He's extremely capable and a quick learner. If I ever get tired of you, I know who your replacement is going to be."

"You're pure evil sometimes," Theo said with mock horror. Leah just grinned back from ear to ear.

After the briefing with Leah, Theo started on the files stacked up on his desk. Shortly before noon his phone vibrated in his pocket. He pulled it out and unlocked it with the fingerprint censor to see a text from Masa.

M: Good morning, sexy.

T: You're pushing the boundaries of what can be considered morning.

M: Yeah, well, I'm a rebel.

T: What're you up to today?

M: I have a bunch of appointments at UIC.

M: I'm meeting the department head at 5 and am pretty nervous.

M: He's kind of a rock star in the field.

T: Haha, you should get up soon so you're not late.

M: I know, but the hotel sheets smell like you and I can't get enough.

T: You're ridiculous.

M: You're hot and you make me so hard.

"Jesus Christ." Theo smiled and bit his lip.

T: Come on. You can't say stuff like that to me when I'm at work.

M: I put the "do not disturb" sign on the door so house-keeping doesn't change the sheets.

OhmyGod.

M: I'm thinking about what I'm going to do to you next time you're in this bed.

M: How I'm going to make you scream out my name.

Theo shifted in his chair and tried to think about anything other than what Masa was suggesting. He still had more than half a day to get through and doing so with a hard-on was not an appealing idea.

T: Please, Masa. Don't do this when I'm at work.

T: I'll do anything you want later if you stop.

M: Anything?

Shit.

T: Yes…

M: Are you going to the gym after work?

T: Yes.

M: What time do you think you'll be finished?

T: I should be home around 7.

M: Does that include shower time?

T: Yes…

M: Skip the shower and go straight home. I'll meet you there.

Theo wanted to protest. He hated leaving the gym without a shower, but it wasn't a long drive and he'd live. Enduring ten extra minutes in gym clothes was better than being tortured by Masa all day in the office. Theo sighed in defeat and thumbed out his reply.

T: Okay.

T: Look, I've got to get back to work. I'm sitting in front of a stack of files I need to review before tomorrow afternoon. I'll see you around 6:45?

M: I'll be looking forward to it.

The rest of Theo's work day consisted of him buried in files. Leah brought lunch about half an hour later—chicken pitas and baby spinach salad with a light vinaigrette dressing on the side. The meal was typical of Theo's usual diet, but he'd had more cheat days than not on his vacation and he needed to get back into his old habits. That included killing his body at the gym tonight with cardio and circuits.

Typical for after a major holiday, the gym was packed, and Theo wasn't awarded the privacy he was used to from going very early or late at night. At this hour the gym was filled with business types and a few university students. Why they didn't just use the campus gym, Theo didn't understand, but he didn't spare it more than a moment's thought.

He started with his normal stretching then hit the treadmill and ran hard for close to an hour. He nearly lost his grip near the end of his workout while doing the last set of pull-ups. He finished the set then headed to the locker room to get his bag, change into sweats, and leave. The drive home had him a jittery wreck. Theo wondered what could be so important that required him to go straight home and began to *really* regret telling Masa he'd do whatever he asked. The last time Theo had given Masa explicit control and freedom like that was when Theo invited him over after getting roughed up. Masa had been really tender with him and Theo could tell that he wasn't happy about the whole situation. This time wasn't going to be like that. Masa was in a devious mood based on the texts he sent Theo. Theo didn't want to imagine what Masa might make him do—or what he might do *to* him. The thought gave Theo a semi that he tried his best to ignore for the duration of the drive.

When Theo stepped off the elevator and rounded the corner to his door he spotted Masa. He was sitting on the floor with his knees drawn into his chest and he had earbuds in. He was dressed rather dapper in fitted dark blue cotton trousers, a white button-up shirt with the top three buttons undone, and his leather jacket. He wore new-looking brown loafers and a matching brown belt. His hair was neatly tied back and reminded Theo of how carefree and sexy Masa had looked a few nights before when he'd made him dinner.

Masa noticed Theo approaching and smiled in that all-encompassing way only he could. He stood up as Theo put his key in the lock and leaned against the doorframe.

"Hi," Theo said. Masa waggled his eyebrows and cocked his head toward the door. "What? You're not going to talk to me?" Masa motioned toward the door again. "*Fine.* I was going to tell you that you looked really nice," Theo opened the door and stepped inside, "and ask you about how your meeting went, but you can forg—"

Masa grabbed Theo's upper arm and flung him hard against the wall. He pressed his body tight against Theo's and held him by the throat with one hand and by the arm with the other. Theo's pulse was racing, and his breaths were hurried and short. Masa breathed calmly through his nose and continued to hold Theo in place.

"You're still wearing your gym clothes. Good." Masa's voice was rough.

Theo swallowed around the tight hold on his throat. "You told me to go straight home."

"And you listened. Good boy." Masa leaned into Theo's neck and tilted his head to the side. He ran his face along Theo's throat and collarbone and inhaled deep enough for Theo to feel coolness on his sensitive skin. Masa groaned, the vibration against Theo's neck made him break out in goose bumps. *"Saint ostie,* you smell so fucking good." Masa licked Theo's neck and pulled his head forward to smell Theo's nape. "God, you taste great too." Masa pulled back from Theo with a love-drunk look on his face and mischief in his heavy-lidded eyes. "Follow me." Masa turned and went down the hallway to Theo's room. Theo followed once he remembered to tell his feet to move.

He walked into the dark room to see Masa sitting on the edge of the bed. He was leaning back on the palms of his hands and looked like he may pounce at any moment. The thrill of uncertainty grew Theo's semi to a full erection, which tented his sweatpants. Masa leaned forward and bit the corner of his bottom lip.

"Close the shade and turn on the lights." Theo did as he was told and returned to stand in front of Masa, who eyed him up and down. "Lose the clothes." Theo hesitated, but the look in Masa's eyes conveyed just how serious he was. He stripped off all his clothes except his trunks. When he was able to stand up straight again Masa said, "All of your clothes. Toss me your underwear."

Theo took a deep breath, closed his eyes, and slid his

trunks off. He tossed them to Masa and he caught them in one hand. Theo stood and watched as Masa balled the boxers in his hand and drew them up to his nose. His eyes flitted open and closed and he let out a desperate, guttural moan that almost brought Theo to his knees. Theo was mildly disgusted by what he'd just seen but also egregiously turned on; the pre-cum pooling at his slit being all the proof needed to ascertain which reaction had won out.

Masa laughed quietly as he watched Theo's reaction and he ordered him to stand in front of the wall-mounted full-length mirror by the door. Theo looked at his naked reflection and felt bashful suddenly. As if he could read his thoughts, Masa got up from the bed and walked over to Theo to whisper in his ear.

"Don't be shy. Give me everything." Masa rubbed his hands all over Theo's chest and stomach and kissed his shoulders, adding in the occasional nip. "Turn around for me and close your eyes." Theo complied.

With his vision gone, Masa's caresses felt like so much *more*. The anticipation of being touched, but not knowing where or when drove Theo crazy. He panted and whimpered at the slightest of grazes. When the contact stopped he tried to focus on what he was hearing—the floorboards creaking under shifting weight and the sound of Masa sucking on his lower lip between his teeth, like he might do after just licking them.

"Oh, fuck, fuck, fuck!" Masa's hot mouth was on Theo's cock before he could process what exactly he was feeling. He stumbled back but Masa grabbed his hips before Theo hit the mirror. Masa held Theo firmly in place while he took him deep. He went slow, every teasing flick of his tongue deliberate and aimed to dissolve Theo's faculties. Theo occasionally jerked his hips in search of more of Masa's mouth, but Masa kept his rhythm. He pulled off Theo and licked the underside of his cock from his balls up to the tip to collect the leaking pre-cum. Masa kissed his way down the top of Theo's length and nestled his face in Theo's pubic hair, taking deep breath after deep breath. He pulled back from Theo entirely, leaving him whimpering and twitching in anticipation.

A smothered laugh reached Theo's ears before Masa took all of him into his mouth in one motion and swallowed around him. Theo's moan was so needy that Masa had to know he was close to losing it. Masa gave one last slow swallow before releasing Theo's cock and hips and standing.

"Open your eyes, baby." Theo opened his eyes not even halfway and stared into Masa's with a desperate need he hadn't experienced before. "Turn around and place your hands on the wall on either side of the mirror."

Theo did it. Of course, he did it—he'd do anything Masa asked of him in that moment. In the reflection he could see Masa undo his pants and give himself a few slow strokes before he sheathed his cock in a condom. Theo bit his tongue and bowed his head, unable to watch any longer for fear of losing his fleeting composure. He heard the cap of the lube bottle and knew this torture would be over quickly. Masa stepped close behind Theo and slid two slicked fingers inside him without warning. Theo gasped, but because he was still biting his tongue it wasn't nearly as loud as it could have been, for which he was thankful.

"What's the matter? I didn't stretch you out enough this morning in my room? Well, you'll just have to bear it for tonight." Masa withdrew his fingers and replaced them with his cock. He slid into Theo quickly and all control Theo had over the volume of his cries was shattered. Theo watched himself come undone in the mirror while Masa relentlessly slammed his hips into his. It hurt. It felt amazing. It was everything that Theo wanted and everything that he feared.

Masa grabbed Theo's throat again and squeezed it harder than he had in the entryway.

"Take a good look at yourself, don't shy away from it. You're gorgeous. And you are *mine.*" Theo couldn't even think about Masa's words. The feel of being stretched open and the firm grip on his throat were all he could process. His legs began to tremble, and Masa pushed even harder. "Jerk yourself off. Now," Masa ordered.

Theo stroked himself so hard and fast his forearm burned. He didn't stop until he felt himself tip over the edge. He gritted his teeth and tried not to scream as he shot jet after jet all over the mirror. His now sensitive prostate continued to take a beating until Masa came with a shaky, strangled cry. He collapsed against Theo's back as his cock continued to pulse inside him. Once he had his bearings, he wrapped an arm around Theo's waist and drew him backward toward the bed. He pushed Theo back first onto the bed and disappeared from the room.

Masa returned after what could have been twenty seconds or twenty hours to Theo. Time seemed a concept he couldn't fathom as he lay naked and completely boneless on his bed. Masa got in bed and pulled Theo up into the pillows, settling him against his chest. Theo felt bare skin and inched closer to Masa, discovering he was now nude. When their breathing evened out Masa sighed.

"How are you feeling?"

"I think you fucked the life-force out of me."

Masa laughed, and the sweet sound rolled through Theo. "Last I checked I wasn't a succubus, but thank you."

"I'm not convinced you aren't."

"Come on, be nice to me."

"Fine. How did your meeting go?"

"Really good, actually. Dr. Kirstein is remarkable. I went

in for a consult, but we got caught up discussing theory and he invited me out for coffee next week."

"Did you just seriously dumb that down for me?"

A laugh burst out of Masa and he squeezed Theo tighter. "Maybe a little. Okay, a lot."

"Thank you. I'd love to hear about what you study a bit more in-depth, but I'm pretty useless right now. It's great that he likes you, though. But I guess you're kind of likeable."

"Only kind of? You compared me to a puppy before and I think they're pretty damn adorable."

Theo sighed. "A *lost* puppy. Jeez, you don't forget anything, do you?"

"Not really and don't change the subject."

"Masa…"

"Just tell me how likable I am, and I'll drop it."

Theo groaned and buried his face in Masa's chest. "You're just as adorable as a puppy—when you're not smelling my underwear like some deranged pervert. What the hell was that?"

Masa scoffed. "To be honest, I don't even know. I promise I've never done that before. It just felt like the right thing to do. Besides, I saw how much you got off on it so don't you dare lie here and play the innocent prude."

"'It just felt like the right thing to do'?" Theo asked dubiously.

"Leave me alone. It's your fault anyway. I told you that you drive me crazy." Theo grumbled against Masa's chest but made no attempts to move away. "Forget about that. Tell me about your day."

"It was boring as hell. I spent it at my desk the entire time. The highlight was easily when I told Leah I was spending my personal time with a man."

"You mean—"

"Mhm. She asked about you, so I gave her a very brief lowdown. She said you sounded hot as hell." Theo laughed.

Masa perked up and his voice raised several octaves in excitement. "Did you tell her I was?!"

Theo smiled again and shook his head. He leaned up and kissed Masa. "Shut up."

CHAPTER SIXTEEN

THE NEXT WEEK went by in a blur. Masa came over and cooked dinner for Theo nearly every day. Theo got back into his regular gym routine and Masa accompanied him more often than not. They slept together, woke together, laughed together, and sweated together. It was unlike anything Theo had ever experienced before and it made him feel good. He still wasn't entirely used to having someone else around so often, but Masa was great company and he made Theo feel like someone other than himself—someone better. With every passing day he toyed with the idea that he might be able to let himself be happy.

He found himself looking forward to seeing Masa while he was at work and he longed to hear about how he spent his days. Masa had been going to the university a lot to meet with faculty in the philosophy department and always returned with stories and recollections of debates that left Theo scratching his head, but he loved to listen to them. Masa started explaining basic ethics theory to Theo, exploring a different ideology each night, building up enough of an understanding to explain his PhD thesis. Theo didn't understand all of the high-level stuff, but he loved how passionate and animated Masa was when he explained the theories. He spoke with such vigor and poise and it drove Theo crazy. He'd try to focus on Masa's words, but the man was just so sexy when he, as Theo put it, got all academic.

Theo's newfound happiness in his personal life extended to his professional one as well. He was energetic and brimming with enthusiasm he hadn't had in nearly a year. He worked quickly and competently and enjoyed a lot of downtime in his office with Leah. Jamie had called several times wanting to know about Masa, he'd even asked to speak with him a few times. Theo, of course, declined and told Jamie to mind his own business.

On Friday night Masa suggested going out so they went back to the Italian bistro they'd gone to before. Masa once again, made inappropriate sounds while he ate but Theo wasn't put off by it. In fact, he found it to be a bit charming. They spent the rest of the weekend rotating between visits to the gym and having sex in every room of Theo's condo. The amount of laundry Theo was left with on Sunday night was staggering so he made a mental note to buy a few more sets of sheets.

His nightmares remained, but waking up with Masa proved to be beneficial. Masa helped soothe him, so he didn't spend the entire day loathing himself and dwelling on the past. During waking hours, less and less did Theo's mind wander back to painful memories. Isaac was always in his head, but not in a way that plagued him. Theo was truly starting to believe that maybe being with Masa was okay. That maybe it was something he could allow himself to have. The thought both terrified and exhilarated him.

Monday morning was a bit frantic. Theo spent the night in Masa's room and headed straight to work from the hotel. The night before, Masa picked out a grey Armani three-piece suit, a black Versace tie, and a white John Varvatos shirt for Theo to wear. Theo had nearly been late for work because Masa wouldn't let him leave his hotel room. While Theo was getting dressed Masa pulled on his clothes and said some filthy things to try and entice him. And it had almost worked. Theo distracted Masa by promising a good time after work if he left him alone to get ready. Masa pouted, but lay back down on the bed, propped up against the headboard with his hands behind his head. He watched Theo get dressed with fire in his eyes. A fire that was sure to engulf Theo with one misstep. To distract himself, Theo looked anywhere else in the room and tried to ignore Masa's piercing stare. As Theo scanned the room, a thought occurred to him.

"Hey, how much is this room per night?" Theo asked.

"I'm not entirely sure. It's billed directly to my Visa."

"You were only supposed to spend a couple nights here and it's been weeks. Do you have a work Visa and a secret job I don't know about?" Theo flashed Masa a quick smirk.

Masa chuckled and shook his head. "No, I'm not sneaky enough to pull that off. I worked during my undergrad and masters, so I've got some money saved up."

"You didn't use that to pay for tuition?"

"I had scholarships. I'm kinda smart, you know," Masa teased. "I also got some money from my parents' life insurance. They had my aunt as the beneficiary and instructions to put the money in a trust for me until I graduated from university. Or turned thirty."

"So, you've had access to it for a few years now but still chose to work and save? That's admirable." Theo smiled at Masa and popped the collar on his shirt to feed the tie through. "You're a good man, Masamune. I'm sure your parents would be extremely proud of what you're making of yourself." Theo folded his collar down and started to work on his tie.

Masa looked down at the bed and chewed on his bottom lip while his forehead crinkled, like he was deep in thought. He turned to Theo again and smiled, though tension was still in his brow. "Thank you. I really appreciate you saying that. I really miss them sometimes. I know they would be proud of what I'm doing, I know it. But it feels really nice to hear someone else say it. It makes it real, maybe. I don't know what I'm trying to say."

Theo walked over to the bed and sat on the edge next to Masa. He took hold of his hand and rubbed his knuckles the way Masa always did for him. He hoped it would soothe him as much as it did when Masa did it to him. "It's okay. I get what you're saying. Look, I really have to head out. We can talk about it later if you want, though?"

"So, you're not sick of me yet?"

"What do you mean?"

"You've seen me every day for the last week. You're not sick of seeing me?" Masa sounded just as uncertain as he looked.

"Of course not. I've had a lot of fun with you, even if you are an insatiable succubus with an occasional, mild sadistic streak." Masa barked out a laugh and gave Theo what he loved to see: him smiling and happy. Theo didn't consider himself to be an overly affectionate person, but in that moment he wanted to reach out, grab Masa, and kiss him with everything he had. Instead, he buried the notion and stood up. "I really do have to go. Text me later if you'd like to come to the gym." Theo got up and flung his jacket on and toed into his shoes. He opened the door to leave but Masa's hand reached out from behind him and pushed it closed. Theo spun around and was face to face with lust-filled hazel eyes. Masa gently held Theo's chin and tipped his head up, stroking Theo's cheek with his thumb. He leaned in and kissed him, slowly at first, then he deepened it, swiping his tongue over the roof of Theo's mouth. It was something they'd both discovered made Theo's knees weak and this time was no exception. Theo leaned back against the door for support and kissed Masa back, matching every swipe of his tongue. Masa broke the kiss first and took a step back so Theo could open the door.

"Have a good day, *nounours*."

Speechless, Theo nodded his head and left.

WORK STARTED out just like any other day. Leah briefed Theo on the day's agenda and they caught up on weekend gossip over tea in his office. Theo spent the rest of the morning doing research at his desk for a new potential client Rey Financial had its sights on. Leah knocked on the door around noon with dolmades and Greek salad for lunch. They took a long lunch while Leah told him about the Christmas trip to Jamaica Josh had surprised her with.

The rest of the afternoon was peaceful until another knock came at the door hours later. Leah re-entered the office and closed the door behind her. Instead of coming over to the desk like she normally would, she stopped a few steps inside.

"What's going on, Leah?"

"The vice president sent for you personally."

Theo nodded. "When?"

"He's on hold right now. He asked me to let him know when you left your office. He sounds a bit, um..." Leah trailed off.

"Impatient?" Theo offered.

"Fucking pissed."

"Shit. Okay." Theo stood and closed his laptop. "You can tell him I'm on my way down."

Theo knocked on his father's office door and heard the man's voice beckon for him to enter. He was nervous as hell, but refused to let his weakness show in front of his father at work. Theo never let their personal relationship affect their working one and his father seemed to respect that unspoken rule as well. Why he would be upset right now was beyond Theo. Everything at work had been going beyond great this quarter and Lucas had done a fantastic job handling Theo's files while he was on vacation. Theo shook the thoughts off, took a deep breath, and stepped into his father's office.

"Leah said you wanted to see me," he said while approaching the chairs in front of the desk and taking a seat.

Jim Rey's face was twisted. He looked scornful and tired. "I'm going to keep this brief and be direct with you."

Theo's chest tightened but didn't flinch. "What is it?"

"Upon much consideration, I've made the executive decision to remove you from some files." The words were so unexpected that Theo was speechless. He stared blankly at his father as the words sunk in. "I've noticed that your... priorities seem to have wandered off from what is best for this company as of late. Until that is remedied, someone more capable will handle your affairs."

"Someone more capable? That's absolutely absurd. There isn't anyone more capable than me in this department and you know it."

Jim sighed, as if he was exhausted that this conversation was happening. "That may have once been true, Theodore. Things have changed."

Theo waved his hand in front of him and shook his head. "Nothing has changed. Nothing negative, anyway. If anything, securing the Amagi Group contract proved I've gotten *better*. Dad—"

"Do not call me that here."

"I don't understand where this is coming from. If it's because I took a vacation, who hasn't? Everything was taken care of in my absence and I've already started research on the Madero file. I'm failing to see what the problem is with my work." Theo was defensive. He tried to remain calm, but couldn't when his work ethic and reputation were effectively being slandered. He had the utmost confidence and pride in his work and not even his father's disapproving words would take that from him.

"Why did you take time off? Of all times, why now?"

"*What?* This is about me taking a couple weeks off?"

"Answer the question, Theodore."

Theo tapped his fingers on the armrest. "I had some things I needed to think about. I just needed to clear my head for a bit."

"Some things, you say. That man who picked you up from the house. Is he one of those *things*?"

"What are you ta—" *Fuck.* Theo shifted in the chair and looked away from his father. He'd had the fight completely knocked out of him and didn't know what to say. *How much did he see? Think, think, think!* "He is a friend of mine. I'd been drinking, and Jamie suggested that I didn't drive."

"Do you allow all of your *friends* to embrace and kiss you? That does explain your unnatural obsession with that useless Jones boy. I should have seen it from the start."

"No. Isaac wasn't like that."

"You expect me to believe anything you say? You're not the man I thought you were, Theodore. You're not the man I raised." Jim shook his head, but his expression remained unchanged. "I'd always wondered what it was you saw in that Jones boy, although this filthy perversion had never crossed my mind. I'm glad that southside swine is gone. I'd hoped you'd have pulled yourself together by now, but it seems I was mistaken in placing that much faith in you. You're just as misguided as ever."

"No! He wasn't like that. I told you."

"But you are." Jim stared Theo down, daring him to deny what they both knew to be true.

"Yes. I am." Theo choked out the words and stared at his shoes. How ridiculous he felt now, all dressed up in clothes another man had chosen for him. This was happening because he'd been too weak to stick to his own rules and foolish enough to entertain the notion that maybe—just maybe— he could be happy. He cowered in the chair and wanted to disappear. Putting on a brave face was no longer an option. Not when his father *knew*. Theo felt completely exposed and spread open for the entire world to see.

His father scoffed as he eyed Theo. "You can have your assistant drop off the Madero, Johannes, and Baker files to my assistant by the end of the week. See yourself out." Just like that, Jim Rey turned his attention to his monitor and the conversation was over. Theo forced himself to his feet and left his father's office.

As soon as Theo rounded the corner, he saw Leah. Her face fell immediately; the pain he felt was all over his face. His face was contorted and he was trying with every ounce of his fleeting composure to hold back tears. She pressed a button on her desk phone then jumped to her feet to meet him in his office, away from prying eyes. She sat him down on a couch and rubbed her hand up and down his back.

"Theo, what happened?"

Theo sat stock-still, staring down at nothing in particular. "He knows." His voice was barely a whisper. "Dad knows about me. Oh, God."

"What did he say?"

"He took me off some cases. Said he'd reassign them."

Theo cleared his throat and stood up. "I-I can't stay here. Please hold all calls for me." He started for the door, but Leah held his hand and stopped him.

"Wait. Do you want me to come with you? I don't think you should be alone right now."

Theo tried to force a reassuring smile, but it fell flat. "I'll be fine. I'm seeing Masa later tonight. You don't have to worry about me. I just need the rest of today."

"Okay." Leah released Theo's hand. "Oh, wait!" She walked over to his desk and grabbed his phone off the desk. "Take this and keep it on. I'll call you later."

Leah forbade Theo from driving and called him a taxi. He was impatient while he waited for it and cursed internally. Once the car came he was relieved to not have to worry about focusing on staying on the road. He hadn't noticed his shaking hands, but he was sure Leah had when she suggested —no, insisted—on calling a cab for him.

His place was dark and quiet. It was only midafternoon, and the sun had yet to set but the curtains were closed in the living room. Theo plunked down on the couch and set his phone on the table. The notification light was flashing and he tried to ignore it. That lasted for all of two minutes.

M: I hope your day is going well. We still on for the gym?

Theo set the phone back on the table facedown and went to his room to get changed. He put on grey sweats and a white tee and came out of the room holding the black box of joints. He hadn't smoked many, as Masa had been around often, so only about one quarter were missing. Theo wanted to calm down but he couldn't bring himself to smoke in broad daylight, so he sat back down on the couch to wait.

His head was a mess. He didn't know if he hurt because of Isaac or because of how powerless he'd been before his father. It didn't matter. Either way he just hurt.

EVERYTHING HURTS. But this is what I wanted, isn't it? I don't want to feel numb anymore. I want to feel something. *Pain just seems like the most acceptable thing. I roll onto my back and sit up but my throbbing ass and hips protest. I fall back into the bed and hear snickering beside me. The tank of a man next to me looks sated and completely unaware of how much he hurt me. Or he doesn't care. But that doesn't matter. We both got what we wanted and it's time for me to leave.*

I take a deep breath and lift my heavy body off the bed. My clothes are still on for the most part. I pull my pants and trunks back up and leave the house without saying anything to the first man I've ever slept with. Under normal circumstances I'd have at least said something instead of slinking out like a whore in the night, but there is nothing normal about these circumstances. Under normal circumstances, I'd be with Isaac right now, watching some old movie or getting drunk and planning our next adventure. But things aren't normal. No, they're about as fucking far from it as can get. So here I am, wandering around in a strange neighborhood feeling like I've been ripped apart mentally and now physically. It's only fitting that my body should feel the same as my head and heart.

It wasn't like I'd imagined it to be. There was nothing pleasurable about it, but for that it was perfect. The distraction and pain are what I deserve so I should be thanking him.

I walk for over an hour and without even thinking I wind up at my old apartment. The one I shared with Dani. I suddenly taste bile and think I'm going to be sick. Why did I come here? I have no good memories of this place. Living a lie every second of the day was exhausting and lying to Dani had nearly broken me. She deserves so much better than what I was able to give her.

I'm cold and I can't walk any longer, so I call a cab to take me back to my place. I bought the condo about a month ago and everything is all moved in, but it doesn't feel like home. Everything seems foreign, almost like it belongs to someone else. In a way it does. This place holds nothing of the old me. Everything is new, in hopes that it would help me start over. Move on. Grow the fuck up. All that shit. In reality, all it does is remind me that I'm now alone.

As much as I want to just go to bed, I shower quickly first in an attempt to remove some of my shame. I'm not ashamed that I slept with a man. I am ashamed over how it happened. I didn't even ask for his name. I towel off and crawl into my bed and hide under the covers, acting out the avoidant behavior I now associate with myself. As the shock from the pain dulls, the numbness returns, and I cry myself to sleep.

That's how I remember it, anyway. But right now I hear knocking. Is someone at the door? No. No one knows I moved here except Jay and he'd have texted first. Maybe I'm imagining things. Wait, there it is again. I'm sure it's the door, but it can't be. Unless this isn't part of a dream or a memory and there actually is someone knocking...

Masa.

Theo opened his eyes and sat up. He was sweating and panting and surely looked a mess, but he didn't want to miss Masa. He got up and opened the door to see Masa standing there with those drop-crotch pants Theo liked on him. His jacket was zipped up and his bag slung over his shoulder. He smiled as soon as the door opened, though his face fell when he took in Theo's appearance.

"What's wrong, baby?"

"Come inside." Theo stepped back from the door and walked back over to the couch. He sat down as Masa entered the room and kicked his boots off. He rushed over to the couch and dropped his bag before sitting down. Masa took Theo's hands in his and brushed his knuckles with his thumbs.

"What happened?" Masa asked softly.

Theo tried to smile, but much like when he'd tried with Leah, he couldn't quite manage it. "I, uh, I had a pretty awful day you could say."

"Tell me about it."

"I don't really feel like talking right now."

"Theo, the last time I saw you upset like this was Thanksgiving. You at least reached out to me then. Today you're dodging me and I'm really worried. So, please. Please talk to me," Masa pleaded.

Masa's tone caught Theo's attention. He sounded a bit desperate, scared almost. Theo was talking before he could rethink it. "My father knows about us. About me. He saw us on Thanksgiving."

"*Oh, merde.* Theo, I'm sorry."

"He said that my priorities weren't in the right place and that until they were, he was reassigning my biggest cases."

"What? That's ridiculous."

"I know. I was fine defending my work, but when he came at me with personal stuff I just froze. To make it even worse, he said some pretty hateful things about Isaac that he just knew would hurt me. He said I could have my files back after my priorities were straight. No fucking pun intended," Theo said bitterly.

Masa pulled Theo into his arms and kissed his forehead. When he released him and looked to be carefully considering his next words, his jaw muscles clenching and unclenching.

"Babe, there's a part of the story you're not telling me. What happened to Isaac?"

Theo froze in Masa's arms. He tried to think of a way to get out of answering when Masa started rubbing small circles on his lower back, the way Isaac had done so many times before. "He died last year," Theo said in a shaky voice. Masa held him tighter but didn't say anything. "He got a late stage four diagnosis of pancreatic cancer and he died ten months later." Theo's eyes started to sting. He closed them as if he could shut out the world and buried his face into Masa's shoulder. "He was my best friend. I've felt so alone this past year." Theo leaned up and cleared his throat, and searched Masa's face. He hoped that would satiate Masa's curiosity and he'd leave the topic alone. Masa's brows were drawn together, and his jaw was tense. He was looking off into nothing and Theo knew there was more he wanted to say.

"Were you in love with him?" His deep voice startled Theo.

"We were just friends," Theo said defensively.

"But you loved him." It wasn't a question. "For how long?"

Theo sighed. "Fifteen years."

"Jesus, Theo. Did he know?"

"No."

Masa ran a hand through his hair, pushing it back from his face. "Have you talked to anyone about this?"

Theo pulled back from Masa and looked at him incredulously. This was *not* where he wanted the conversation to go and he was done talking about it. "Why do you care?"

Masa cocked his head and furrowed his brows. "Why wouldn't I care?"

Theo shrugged and crossed his arms, putting a small barrier between them. Masa's eyes followed Theo's arms and narrowed slightly at the action. "We're just fucking. You don't have to pretend to care about my fucking problems."

"Just fucking? Huh? Are you kidding me? You can't say you honestly think that?"

Theo shrugged his shoulders again and rolled his eyes. "You come over or I go to your hotel room and we have sex. A lot. I told you from the get-go that I don't fuck guys more than once. I broke that rule with you and we had fun. But don't think it was anything more than that." Theo could barely believe the venom spewing from his mouth. It hurt him to say it, so he could only imagine how Masa felt hearing it. If Masa's face was any indication, he was pretty shocked and upset. Theo felt terrible for letting himself get frustrated and defensive and lashing out as a result, but he figured this was for the best. He'd always known things with Masa had to end; that it was a pursuit of happiness he did not deserve. He regretted that it came out like it did, but it was going to come to this sooner or later.

Masa put his hands on his thighs and took a few deep breaths before he spoke. "I know you don't mean what you're saying. And it breaks my heart that you think you have to say it."

"You don't know—"

"Stop." Masa put his hands on Theo's arms and leaned in so his forehead touched Theo's. "Please, Theo. I care about you and I want to help. Won't you let me?"

Theo pushed him away and stood up. He paced around the living room and shook his head. "I can't."

"Why won't you let yourself be happy? Why are you fighting this so much?"

"I'm not a good person, Masa. Happiness isn't something I'm meant to have."

Masa stood up and approached Theo, but didn't try to

touch him. "Why are you saying that? What have you done that's so terrible?"

"Aside from that fiasco with my mom, I lied to Isaac for years. I tried to tell him after he got sick, but I didn't want him to hate me. He was dying in my arms and I stayed silent, so he wouldn't die despising me. I didn't want him to regret being my friend. I selfishly misled him to spare myself. I don't need help from anyone. I have to be strong. I can't afford that kind of weakness."

"See, that's where you're wrong. Admitting you need help isn't weak. What you're doing *is*. You're coasting through your life on autopilot." Theo turned away from Masa, but Masa stepped back into his line of sight. He was going to be heard. "You don't do anything for yourself and you keep people at a distance. Why? Because you think you deserve to be miserable because you kept a goddamn secret?! There is nothing noble or strong about being a martyr in this situation. *This* is what weakness looks like. And cowardice. True strength would be being honest with yourself and accepting that things can't stay the way they are."

Theo stepped back from Masa and with a shaky voice said, "I am trying my best to hold it together."

"No." Masa stepped back into Theo's personal space. "You're not holding shit together except for an illusion. You present this perfect idea of Theo Rey but it's bullshit. You're a mess, and there's nothing wrong with that. You're hurting and need help."

Theo snaked his head back and started to get angry. He gritted his teeth and raised his voice. "And what? You think I don't know that? I don't need some kid to tell me about my faults. I know what I am better than anyone."

"No, you don't. You're lost. You don't know how to get out of this hole you've dug for yourself and you're too goddamn stubborn to accept help, let alone ask for it."

Theo nodded his head as he felt the flush on his chest crawl up his neck. "I've listened to enough. Get the fuck out."

"No."

"Excuse me?"

"I said, no."

Theo grabbed Masa's arm and led him to the door. His grip was a vise. "Who the fuck do you think you are? Get out!" He flung Masa hard against the door. Masa remained still and quiet and just watched Theo, who had begun to pace. "Masamune, I swear to God... you need to get the fuck out of my sight."

"Or what? I'm not leaving, Theo. Not again."

Theo stopped and turned to face Masa. Rage welled inside him and he grabbed Masa's shirt collar and pushed him back against the door, harder this time. "If you don't get the fuck out of here things aren't going to end well."

Masa relaxed against the door and looked Theo in the eye without a trace of anger or frustration clouding his features. "I'm not going to leave. And I'm not going to fight you. We both know you're stronger than I am, so what's the point? Besides, hurting you isn't my goal. If you feel like you need to hit me then I'm not going to try to stop you. Just know that it's not going to make me walk out."

Masa's words—how calm and collected he was—aggravated Theo. He saw red and his hand began to shake. He clenched his fist and drew it back while Masa just stared into his eyes with a sympathetic smile on his face. Theo closed his eyes and smashed his fist into the wall next to Masa's head, shrieking from the pain emanating from his bloodied hand and the contempt he felt for himself. He let go of Masa's collar and fell onto his knees with hot tears stinging his eyes. Masa kneeled down and hugged him, brushing his hand through Theo's short hair. Theo clung to him, pulling at his clothes and sobbed. It wasn't Theo's view of manliness and it wasn't dignified, but he didn't care.

"*Shhh. Ça va bien aller, nounours.*" Masa held Theo until he stopped shaking and crying, then pulled back and wiped the tears from Theo's eyes with his thumbs. He kissed Theo's forehead and picked up his bloodied right hand, inspecting Theo's torn knuckles and sighed. "Wait here." Masa stood up and headed down the hall, out of Theo's sight. He came back a few moments later with a wet washcloth and the small first aid kit from under Theo's sink. "I'm a bit surprised you have one of these," Masa said, holding up the kit. He kneeled back down in front of Theo and dabbed the warm, damp cloth around the wounds on Theo's hand.

"I'm so—" Theo's voice cut out and he tried again. "I'm sorry, Masamune. I'm so sorry." Fresh tears formed in Theo's eyes. "I've said that so fucking much in my life that it's probably worthless by now."

Masa looked up from Theo's hand and flashed him a small smile. "It's never worthless if you mean it." Theo nodded and hung his head while Masa went back to work on his hand. "I meant what I said, Theo. I think you do need help and I'd love it if you'd let me in."

"Why do you care?" It was the same question Theo asked earlier although the intent was not aimed to cause harm this time. "I'm a horrible person. Why do you care about me?"

"You're not horrible. You're just lost." Masa opened the first aid kit and pulled out a roll of gauze. He began wrapping it around Theo's hand, keeping his eyes on the task. "I've gotten to know you a bit over the last few weeks and I really like the person I've seen. To be quite frank, I'm falling for you, Theo. Hard and fast. I don't want to force my feelings on you, and I don't want you to think I only want to help you so we can date or whatever. If you don't feel the same way about me, that's fine. I still want to help you as a friend. I'm not saying it'll be easy, but nothing worthwhile is, right?" Masa finished wrapping Theo's hand and tied off the gauze. He kissed Theo's bandaged knuckles and moved each of his fingers gently, starting with the pinkie. "Let me know if anything hurts. I want to make sure your hand isn't broken."

"My hand is fine."

"Maybe. But the wall sure isn't so I want to make sure."

Theo looked up and saw a fist-sized hole in the wall. He looked behind Masa and saw some debris lying on the floor. The realization of what he'd almost done made him want to vomit. Before he could retreat into himself, Masa's big hands were on either side of Theo's face, his thumbs grazing his cheekbones.

"I know you're sorry about what just happened, so don't beat yourself up about it, okay? But, Theo," Masa looked down and licked his lips then looked back at Theo, "if it happens again I'm gone for good. I mean that."

"It won't. I promise you it won't."

Masa dipped his head slowly. "Good. A lot has happened and been said. I want you to have some time to think about everything... About whether or not you want to be with me." Masa sighed and stood up. He walked over to the couch and slung his bag over his shoulder then returned to the front door. He started slipping his boots on but stopped when Theo grabbed his ankle.

"Please don't leave." Theo's voice was small.

"Baby, I want you to think about this. Really think about it. I need to know what you want from me and what I can expect from you. It's a lot so I don't want you to make any hasty decisions, okay?"

"I don't need to think about it. I don't want you to leave."

"And beyond tonight?

"I-I don't know."

Masa dropped to his knees and sighed. He locked eyes with Theo and didn't offer him a reassuring smile this time. "Just tell me how you really feel."

"I don't know," Theo repeated, feeling crushed under Masa's gaze. Up close his eyes were even more beautiful, but they burned through Theo's fleeting defenses and left him feeling bare.

"Theo, for God's sake—be honest with yourself for once in your life. Tell me you hate me, just tell me *something.*"

Masa sounded like he was at the end of his patience. With his defenses shattered, Theo took a deep breath and tried to voice what he was feeling. "I like you, Masa. It's not what I wanted to happen. I'm really confused, but I know that I like being around you."

"That's a good thing, Theo," Masa said, seemingly relieved.

"No! For the first time in my life my defenses are crumbling, and I feel unprotected, like I'm unsure about everything. Everything except you. I like you and I don't know what to do about it and that's fucking terrifying. I tried to convince myself that you could never want to be with someone like me so that it wouldn't hurt as much when this —whatever this is—ended. Loving Isaac wasn't even this hard. And believe me, it was pretty fucking hard. But it was different. I knew we would never be together and I accepted that. But you," Theo shook his head, "you burst into my life and no matter how hard I tried, I couldn't shut you out. When I threw you out the night we met I knew it was wrong. I felt right away that things were different with you. But I was scared, and I defaulted to what I thought would keep me protected and safe. I can't own up to anything and it makes me feel so guilty."

Masa leaned forward, closing the gap between them and kissed Theo. It was a slow, sweet grazing of the lips without urgency or pretext. He pulled back and grinned at Theo's dumbfounded expression. "Thank you, Theo. Thank you for being honest with me. Open communication from here on, yeah?"

Theo nodded his head. "I'll try. It's hard for me to speak like that. But I'll try."

"Okay. If there's something you don't think you can say, can you tell me that? Just so I'll know to give you more time with it."

"I can do that," Theo replied.

"Good." Masa kissed Theo again and rubbed the back of his neck. "Have you eaten yet, baby?"

"I had lunch. What time is it, anyway?"

"It was around nine when I got here. I've been texting you all evening, but you didn't answer. I figured you'd be home by now and wanted to make sure you were okay."

"You're too good for me."

"Enough. Come on, stand up. I'm going to get you some food then we can watch a movie or go to bed. Whatever you want." Masa stood up and pulled Theo up with him.

"I'm not really hungry."

"Theo..." Masa warned.

Theo held his hand up to silence Masa. "I know, I know. I'll eat breakfast, okay? We can go out if you don't have plans."

"I don't, but what about work?"

Theo laughed dryly. "I'm not going in tomorrow. What do I have to work on now that my father seized control of my files? I'll call Leah in the morning and let her know so she doesn't worry."

"All right."

Theo unzipped Masa's jacket and put his hands on Masa's chest. He slid them over his shoulders, pushing Masa's leather jacket down his arms, then off entirely. He undid Masa's pants and pushed the jeans down past his thighs and off each foot. In just a t-shirt, boxers, and socks, Masa stood before Theo looking as beautiful as he'd ever seen him. Theo grabbed Masa's hand and led him to the bed where he stripped off his shirt and pants before climbing in. Masa stood at the edge of the bed and watched him settle.

"Please come to bed," Theo said.

Masa reached over his shoulder, grabbed the back of his shirt, and pulled it off over his head. He toed out of his socks then climbed into bed. He lay next to Theo unmoving with his jaw set and his brows gently furrowed. Theo saw the inner debate Masa was having written all over his face. He smirked and snuggled under Masa's arm, resting his head on Masa's chest.

"You were thinking about how to hold me, weren't you?"

"Busted. I didn't know if you'd want to be the big spoon or the little spoon tonight."

"You could have asked. What happened to open communication?" Theo teased.

"*Se comporter.* Don't you start." They both laughed quietly and the tension from before finally lifted. Theo snuggled closer into Masa's side and Masa drew small circles on Theo's arm and back with his fingers. They fell asleep in each other's arms without another word.

CHAPTER SEVENTEEN

THE NEXT MORNING Theo woke in Masa's arms. His face was plastered against Masa's chest and—oh God —he'd drooled on him in the night. Theo glanced up to make sure Masa was still asleep before he gently wiped the mess away. He lay his head back down over the tattoo on Masa's chest and tried to fall back asleep. When sleep didn't come, he began tracing the dips and grooves of Masa's chest and stomach muscles with his fingertips. Masa squirmed slightly at one of the light caresses by his hip.

Theo's hand stopped, and he craned his neck to look up at Masa's face. "Did I wake you?"

"Were you trying to?"

"No. I just couldn't help it. You looked so peaceful."

"So, you thought you'd violate me while I was defenseless? How lewd," Masa teased.

Theo buried his head into Masa's side to hide his face. "God, I'm sorry. I should have waited and asked."

Masa rolled onto his side giggling and kissed Theo's shoulder. "I'm only teasing. You can feel me up any time you want."

"You're insufferable sometimes."

A smile spread across Masa's lips and he took Theo's hand in his. He kissed each of Theo's fingertips then placed Theo's hand on his chest, just over his heart. "Go ahead and finish."

"It's awkward now."

"Nonsense. I like it when you touch me. So please, carry on." Theo hesitated then withdrew his hand. Masa rolled his eyes and groaned. *"Tête de cochon."* He wrapped his arms around Theo's waist and rolled them both over so Theo ended up straddling him. Masa held Theo's thighs and snaked the tips of his fingers under the hem of Theo's trunks.

Theo shifted in Masa's lap and tried to get up, but Masa held him in place. "What are you doing?"

"Forcing you to touch me, basically."

A jolt of panic shot through Theo. Did Masa want him like *this*? Theo had never been in a position like this with another man and it unnerved him. He wanted Masa, but he couldn't—not in their current positions. Theo squirmed again in Masa's lap, but the grip on his thighs didn't let up. Theo's eyes connected with Masa's and he spotted the moment recognition of what was happening bled into Masa's expression.

Damn him. Why can he always see through me?

Masa loosened his hold on Theo and lightly rubbed the tops of his thighs. "What I mean to say is that I'm not going to touch you, but I would really like it if you'd continue touching me. I didn't mean to imply anything else."

"You'll have to forgive me for assuming, given our positions and your dick poking my ass." Theo jibbed.

"Ignore that. Pretend it's not even there."

"That's going to take *a lot* of pretending," Theo mumbled.

Masa snickered. "You flatter me. But seriously, if you

want it to go away, you need to stop moving and stop saying cute things."

Theo scoffed. "I don't say cute things."

"Okay, Rambo."

Theo rolled his eyes and grunted. "There actually is something I wanted to talk to you about."

Masa put Theo's hand on his chest and said, "Go on."

"When I told you about Isaac, I left something important out. Well, someone." Theo traced the lines of Masa's tattoo as he spoke. "I dated someone for over a year before Isaac got sick. It wasn't what I wanted, but I did it for him. He felt like he was holding me back from a happy life and felt guilty over monopolizing my time. I told him he was crazy, but he insisted I branch out and start dating. See, I hadn't dated much, not seriously, and he thought it was his fault for us always hanging out. I couldn't really explain that I chose to stay single because I wanted him, so I kind of went along with his suggestion and dated someone. We even ended up moving in together." Theo traced the tight skin around Masa's navel.

"So Isaac knew you were ga..." Masa's voice trailed off on the last word. "Sorry. I never actually asked if you were exclusively gay."

"No, I am." Theo smiled to himself and continued his exploration of Masa's chest. "Isaac didn't know."

The confusion Masa felt was written clear on his face. "So...?"

"So, I dated a girl named Daniella. She goes to school with Jamie. They're best friends, actually. She hit on me at a party one night and I told Isaac about it, hoping he'd be a little jealous. It was foolish, I know. And it backfired completely. That was when he gave me the speech about how I should branch out and date. He liked her for me, so I started seeing her. Things moved really fast and she really loved me. Before I knew it, she wanted to move in and I felt so trapped. We did it, then Isaac was diagnosed a few months later. When the cancer spread to his surrounding organs and his condition started deteriorating I broke things off with her without explaining a thing. She was devastated. She did a good job of trying not to show it, but I'd spent so much time with her that I could just tell."

"I can't imagine what that must have been like for you. Having to put on a front for your friend as well as at home? That must have been exhausting."

"What I experienced was just punishment for how I acted. I think about how I treated Dani and I feel awful."

"I think you think too much," Masa said while rubbing the tops of Theo's thighs.

"I think you think too much of me."

"You're wrong about that. I see the good and bad parts of you, Theo. I know you're not perfect, but you don't have to be. You focus solely on the bad things, babe. As a result, you're left with all this compounded guilt and a skewed vision of your self-worth. I see you for the man you are, and sure, maybe I'm not completely objective," Masa smiled, "but I'm in a much better position than you to see that you're worth a damn. And I'm going to make you see that one day."

"I appreciate the sentiment, but you just turned into an eighty-year-old man by saying 'worth a damn.'"

"At least you're not a cradle robber anymore." Theo whacked Masa's chest, generating a crisp smacking sound. "Ow, that hurts, you know."

"I don't need to be reminded of how young you are. Your youthful exuberance confounds me," Theo said sarcastically.

"You're so feisty sometimes, fisticuffs."

"You're one to talk. You're a walking hard-on." Masa winced at that and his face fell. Theo saw the change in Masa's demeanor, but he didn't understand why. He wanted to cheer Masa up and there was one tested and proven method of accomplishing that.

"Hey, how about you flip me over and we have some make-up sex? I've never had it before, but Jamie says it's all the rage." Theo smiled and brushed his thumb over Masa's nipple. Masa inhaled sharply, and Theo felt him twitch against his ass. Theo's smile grew, and he leaned down and kissed Masa's neck, making Masa fidget under him.

"Theo, wait."

Theo leaned back and a crease formed between his brows. "What's wrong?"

Masa rubbed his hands up and down his face then through his hair. "You're not doing anything wrong. In fact, it feels fucking great. But I don't think we should be having sex right now, not for a while."

Theo sighed, his voice was quiet. "This is about what I said to you yesterday. Masa, I was angry and didn't really mean that. I know what's going on here is more than cheap sex, I do. I'm sorry I said that."

"I know, baby. You didn't mean it the way it came out, but I do think there was some truth to what you said. The words came from somewhere and I think that's mostly my fault."

"What are you talking about?"

"I didn't want to scare you away with words and labels, so I didn't say anything. I'd hoped my feelings would come through, but I shouldn't have assumed. I should have said something to you, so you knew where I stood."

Theo snorted out a laugh and shook his head. "You know, you sound a lot like me right now. You're right, though. Had you tried to talk to me about feelings I would have shut you out. I knew you cared, Masa. Believe me, I could tell. But I spent so much time convincing myself I was wrong, so I didn't want to let myself believe it."

"I still should have said something. I took the coward's way out for selfish gains." Masa clapped a hand on Theo's ass and smiled. "But I want to make it right and eliminate all doubt that I'm only after your sexy body." He winked at Theo and let his hand drop to Theo's leg. "I have a plan."

Theo crossed his arms and eyed Masa skeptically. "A plan?"

"Mhm. I think it would be best if we don't have sex until you want to. We can just take things slow and go on dates and not have to worry about sex being a motivator."

Theo looked at Masa with his head cocked, trying to make sense of what he was hearing. "So, you want to date me but not sleep with me until I want it?" Masa nodded. "Easy enough, I want it right now."

"*Nounours*, I'm being serious."

"So am I." Theo reached down and squeezed his stiffening cock.

"*Saint ostie*, you don't play fair." Masa held one of Theo's legs and the small of his back and flipped them both over so Theo was on his back. He pinned Theo's hands next to his head and kissed him hard. Masa pulled back when Theo ground his hips up into Masa's.

"Theo, I mean it. As much as it *pains* me to say it, I don't think we should do this until there isn't any doubt." Masa kissed Theo's nose and sat upright. "On your terms or not at all."

Theo huffed out a breath and groaned. "All right, fine. For the record, I don't think this is a good idea."

"Oh, hush. You're just complaining because you're horny. You'll feel better about this later."

"And until then?" Theo flicked his eyes down to his crotch then back up at Masa.

"Ah, yes. I'd really love to give you a hand with that, but no touching." Masa shrugged apologetically.

"No touching at all?" Theo whined.

"Not that kind. I'm still going to hold you and kiss the hell out of you."

Theo groaned. "I can't believe you said that with a straight face. You're so corny sometimes."

"Please, don't act like you don't like it."

"Whatever." Theo groaned again in frustration and pulled his legs out from between Masa's. He rolled over to the other side of the bed and stood up to stretch. Theo threw his arms up over his head and arched his back forward as a sigh of relief fell from his lips. His erection strained against his trunks and he palmed it before craning his neck to look over at Masa, who stared back at him with his mouth slightly ajar. Theo winked at Masa then walked out of the room to go shower. He heard Masa whimper as he closed the bathroom door and quietly laughed.

After getting showered and dressed, Theo and Masa went back to IHOP for breakfast. They each ordered the same thing as the first time they went, and Masa was easily just as excited about it during their second visit. After breakfast Masa asked if they could stop to do some shopping, as the limited options in his suitcase were starting to get boring. Theo decided to take him to Nordstrom. Jamie really liked shopping there, so he figured they'd have a decent casual men's selection. Theo didn't normally pay too much attention to trendy clothes and focused more on classic pieces and suits, so Jamie's judgment was the best he had to work with.

Based on Masa's reaction to the array of designer clothes, Theo had made a good decision. Or a bad one. Immediately upon entering the men's section of the store, Masa gravitated over to what Theo thought was the most god-awful, tacky sweater in the whole store. It was black and featured a huge tiger head embroidered in white and gold. Masa essentially vibrated with joy when he held it up over his chest and turned to face Theo with the biggest smile spread across his face.

"This sweater is fucking dope!"

Dope? Jesus, it's just like talking to Jamie. "It's, uh, interesting," Theo offered.

Masa lowered the sweater and snickered. "You don't like it, do you?"

"It's not my style."

"Remember what we said about full disclosure?"

Theo stroked his thumb through his beard and chewed his bottom lip. "God, Masa, that's the ugliest sweater I think I've ever seen. A tiger? Really?"

Masa stared blankly at Theo then burst out laughing at a volume far too loud to go unnoticed by other shoppers. Masa regained his composure—to a degree—and flipped the sweater around. He felt down the arm until he found the price tag.

"*Crisse, mon dieu!* What the actual fuck?"

"What?"

"This sweater is over three hundred dollars. Jesus." Masa hung the sweater back up and picked up another, this one black with teal, yellow, and red feather designs. "Oh my God, this one is three-fifty! What kind of store did you bring me to?"

Theo eyed Masa like he had three heads and looked at the new sweater he was holding. It was decidedly better than the first. "Well, it's a department store. Prices vary but they're all designer, so I guess that's pretty standard."

"Jesus. You call this standard? This is *expensive.* It's nice as hell, but expensive nonetheless." Masa hung the new sweater up and stepped closer to Theo. "Can we go to, like, a mall or something? There's got to be an H&M or Forever21 around here somewhere." Masa brushed his hair out of his face, but it fell back immediately.

"You like the clothes here, yes?" Masa nodded. "Just pick out what you like. I'll buy it. It's really not a big deal. You can't be any worse than Jamie when we go shopping." Theo noticed how uncomfortable Masa looked suddenly. His body seemed rigid, and his jaw was clenched tight.

Did I say something wrong?

"You don't have to buy me things."

"It's not a big deal."

"I mean, I don't expect you to do it. Just like with the," Masa stepped in closer to Theo and lowered his voice, "the *sex* thing. I'm not with you just so you'll buy me things."

Theo stared at Masa blankly before realization hit. "Oh God, like a sugar daddy? Ew, no. Masa, you're being ridiculous now."

"I just want to make sure."

"Enough." Theo held up a hand to signal that he should stop talking. "You're being hypersensitive to me now and you need to relax. That didn't cross my mind at all. It's as simple as you liking some stuff and me wanting you to have it. You can't work in the States, so I realize that you've got to make your savings last and I admire your restraint—financially speaking, anyway. I didn't think of it before coming here and that's my oversight. But I knew there would be stuff here you'd like. I never imagined it would be a hideous tiger head sweater, but I guess we're still getting to know each other so I don't know everything you like yet and God, I'm going to stop talking now."

Masa stared at Theo, blinking in disbelief. He grabbed his collar, pulled him in and pressed his lips to Theo's. He kissed Theo's nose then pulled back and smiled so wide the sides of his eyes crinkled. "And you said you don't say cute things."

Theo scanned the area to make sure no one was around to see them kiss and tried to keep the flush of embarrassment from creeping up his neck. "Shut up. Do you want the clothes or not?"

"I do, but you don't have to buy them."

"Grab whatever you want. It's my treat because I like you. End of discussion."

"Mm. Yes, sir."

After collecting an alarming number of items, they made their way to the change rooms. Theo waited outside while Masa went in with both arms full of clothes. After a minute or two and a lot of shuffling and clinking sounds, the door to the room opened and Masa beckoned Theo inside. He was reluctant at first, but Masa assured him he just wanted his opinion. He sat in the chair in the corner of the small room while Masa changed again and again a couple feet away in front of a full-length mirror. Another mirror sat on the wall behind the chair. Masa had all of the clothes hung up on one side of the room, presumably to hang up the wanted items on the other side.

Theo sat quietly and tried not to stare but it was hard with Masa right in front of him and a huge mirror behind him, giving Theo a great view anywhere he looked. Masa took his time undressing and redressing, flashing smiles and winks at Theo all the while. After he'd had enough, Theo reached out and grabbed Masa's wrist just after he'd taken his shirt off and pulled him close. He looked up at Masa and licked his lips; his eyes were glazed over with need. Masa sat in Theo's lap and hooked his legs behind the chair. He slung his arms around Theo's neck while Theo wrapped his arms around Masa's lower back. Theo raked his hands up and down Masa's smooth skin while their tongues explored and entwined. Theo squeezed Masa's ass causing Masa to moan into the kiss, a softer moan than Theo was used to hearing from him. He loved it and he wanted to hear more of it, but Masa pulled back and shoved off of Theo's lap.

"What're you doing?" Theo ground out.

Masa whipped on a new shirt and brushed his hair back, catching his breath. "I'm getting hard."

"So? So am I."

"Yeah, well, we're out *and* I'm not touching you, remember?"

Shit. Theo leaned back in the chair and slumped down. "Ugh, this is a terrible idea."

"Yeah, I know." Masa turned to face the mirror but looked at Theo in the reflection. "Hey," he said. Theo perked his head up. "What do you think of this shirt?"

Over two hours passed before they made their way to the checkout. Masa tried to be choosy and limit how much Theo spent, but any time he expressed interest in something, Theo threw it in the cart. As they stood at the checkout and watched the young male cashier ring items through, Theo stole a glance at Masa and noticed he was worrying about something again. Probably the money. Theo bit back a grin and focused his attention on the clerk.

"Your total is four thousand eight hundred one dollars and twelve cents," the cashier said cheerfully.

Theo smiled and pulled out his credit card without a hint of hesitation while Masa shifted uneasily next to him. When they got out to the car Masa thanked him dearly and promised to pay him back one day. Theo kissed him and assured him it was a gift and left it at that.

They hit the gym next and Theo still refused to try the salmon ladder, but that didn't stop him from watching Masa do it several times and reveling at the sight. They showered in stalls far from each other and went out for a late lunch at a Japanese restaurant.

Various rolls, appetizers, bowls of noodles, and two bowls of spicy miso soup were brought out to the table on two large trays. Masa sat across from Theo at a small table with wide eyes when the food was laid out.

"This looks great, but I should warn you that I kind of suck at using chopsticks."

Theo's head shot up and he eyed Masa as if he'd told a complicated joke. "What? How is that even…"

"I know, the irony. I used them when I was a kid, but after my parents died and I lived with my aunt and uncle I got pretty damn acclimated to a knife and fork. I've only gone out for sushi a handful of times with my friends."

"It's pretty easy. I can show you if you need help. Or if it's hopeless you can ask the server for a fork, but I really hope it doesn't come to that."

Masa grinned and shrugged his shoulders. "I'll try, baby."

At Theo's suggestion, they had the soup first, which Masa loved, then picked at everything else. Masa's technique was atrocious, but he handled the chopsticks adequately enough to not make too much of a mess.

"Last piece of karaage, do you want it?" Theo asked.

Masa shook his head and sipped on some warm sake. "No, thanks, it's all you."

Theo effortlessly picked up the piece of chicken with his chopsticks and held it out across the table to Masa. "Come on, we both know you want it."

Masa shrugged his brows and grinned. "Busted." He leaned forward and took the parcel from the outstretched chopsticks with his teeth and moaned while he chewed, savoring the flavor. "Delicious."

Theo stared at Masa's neck and jaw as he chewed and swallowed and was enraptured. He couldn't look away and felt like a leering pervert for corrupting such a simple action. Everything Masa did had an unintended effect on Theo one way or another. Now that Theo knew Masa was more or less on the same page as him, he tried not to feel awkward about it. But that was easier said than done when all Masa had to do to drive him crazy was complete mundane tasks. Before he lost all control, Theo brought his sake cup to his lips and relished in the distraction of the warm alcohol flowing down his throat.

"This city has so much good food, it's kinda crazy."

"You haven't seen anything yet. There are a ton of great places I can take you to."

"I look forward to it. Speaking of the future—terrible segue, I know—I officially applied at UIC to complete my doctorate. The philosophy department head assured me applying was merely a formality and that they'd be thrilled to have me complete my degree there. UIC is pretty big into research and well, that's my first love."

"Masa, that's great to hear. How long will the degree take?"

"Two or three years. If my Canadian master's degree is accepted, then it'll be two years for my dissertation and oral exam. Three years if I have to take a few supplementary classes with my degree. I don't think they're going to make me take extra classes, but we'll see in a few weeks."

"So you'll be Dr. Kuroki well before you're thirty. You're amazing."

Masa smiled and bit his lip. "It's really not that special. A lot of people do it."

"I don't just mean the degree. Just in general, you're amazing. Except when it comes to using chopsticks. You're absolutely shit at that. But no one is perfect."

"You couldn't just leave it at the compliment."

"Never."

"So cold, *nounours*. Ah, shit, sorry. It just slipped out."

Theo huffed a laugh and glanced around the restaurant.

"It's okay. I doubt anyone else in here speaks French. Certainly not that made-up-sounding filth you've been using."

Masa gasped in mock shock. "Did you just insult my language? I'll have you know that *Québécois* French is a colorful and inventive piece of our culture."

Theo rolled his eyes but couldn't stop the smile pulling at his lips. "Whatever."

"Jeez, you distracted me *and* insulted the way I speak. The nerve. Oh, right, about school. Since I'll be here for a fair amount of time I can't really stay in a hotel forever. At this point it's a waste of my savings. So, I was hoping you might want to help me find a place to rent? My budget is pretty small, but I figure you might be able to help me find a place where I won't have to fight with roaches or mice. Or meth heads."

"I can definitely help with that. You're not interested in living on campus, though?"

"Nah, I like to have a degree of privacy when I'm working. I'm over the party scene and just want some quiet."

"You're twenty-four and you're talking like you're an old man."

Masa shrugged. "I'm an old soul. Eh, sometimes. Anyway, how am I going to explain your screams of pleasure to fellow students if I lived on campus?" Masa winked and puckered his lips at Theo in a mock kiss.

"Shut up."

MASA SPENT the night at Theo's but left early in the morning to meet Dr. Kirstein for coffee. After he left, Theo called Leah to get a status update on how things were going with his father. She relayed that she had not seen or heard from him and Theo figured that was good news all things considered. The idea of going to work and hiding in his office doing shit-all sounded worse than spending the day alone, so Theo told Leah to take messages for the day and stayed home. When he disconnected the call, he sank back down into the mattress and huffed out a breath. This was his first time being alone since fighting, and subsequently reconciling, with Masa. He hadn't taken any time to process everything that was said, but thinking about it now, he felt antsy, exhilarated even. Unable to sit still, and not wanting to mope around all day, Theo got up and headed to the gym.

Masa texted Theo just after noon and asked if he wanted to do lunch and work out. Theo had already worked himself to the bone earlier, but he wasn't about to turn down a chance to see Masa hot and sweaty. They met at the gym and Theo let Masa set the pace. They started out with stretches then moved on to the treadmills to run. Theo pushed himself to keep up, but Masa kept looking over when Theo was panting harder than he normally would.

"Are you feeling okay?"

"Yeah, I'm just a bit tired," Theo said through gasping breaths.

"Come on, your cardio is way better than this." Masa reached over and turned Theo's machine off then did the same for his own. As the belts slowed they dialed back to walking. "What's up?"

"I already worked out this morning. Really hard. I had a lot of energy for some reason and I might have taken it a bit far."

"Why didn't you say something? You didn't have to come with me."

"Yeah, I know."

Masa leaned in closer to Theo. "But..."

"But?"

"This is the part where you say, 'but I wanted to see you, so I came anyway.' Then I'd tell you that you're sweet and that you can call or text me any time you want to see me."

Theo was thankful he was so out of breath and flushed from running, otherwise he'd be blushing from embarrassment and Masa would know he was right. *But isn't it okay if I tell him he's right?* Theo stepped off the treadmill and picked up his towel from his bag. "I wanted to see you," he said before covering his face with the towel, pretending to mop up the sweat. When he let the towel fall Masa was beaming.

"First thing we're doing when we're alone is discussing boundaries because I really want to grab you and kiss you right now."

Theo laughed, which made him cough a bit. "I guess a kiss won't kill me. I'm sure everyone in this gym knows about me anyway by now."

Masa cocked his head as if trying to make sense of what he'd just heard, but it passed quickly. He hopped off of the treadmill, wrapped an arm around Theo's waist and kissed him like he hadn't seen him in a month—all passion without regard for anyone else in the room. Theo was caught off guard, but he didn't try to stop Masa or push him away. When Masa had kissed him at the store he was surprised but not angry. Out in public, anyone could see them. But standing in the gym, Theo wanted to be connected to Masa more than he wanted to hide. He tried not to think about where they were and gave himself over to the kiss, once again following Masa's lead. Masa bit Theo's bottom lip then pulled back and smiled.

"Jesus, I said you could kiss me, not make love to my mouth." Theo glanced around the room and saw a few sets of eyes on them. "People are staring."

"People stare at you everywhere we go. You're gorgeous."

Theo scoffed disbelievingly. "I'm pretty sure they're looking at you."

"Agree to disagree." Masa shrugged his shoulders and checked the time on his phone. "You wanna get out of here? Since you're tired we can skip eating out and I can make something?"

"I'm never going to turn down your cooking, but what about the rest of your workout?"

"It's fine. I'll make up for it tomorrow. Right now, I want to make you chicken stir fry and give you a back rub."

Masa looked at Theo like he was something to be cherished. The gold in his eyes was catching the sun coming in through the window just right and Theo was stunned by how beautiful Masa's eyes were. Not just his eyes, but all of him. Masa was a vision from head to toe and Theo wondered how he ever stood a chance at not liking the guy. "They're definitely looking at you," Theo said under his breath.

"What?"

"Nothing. Let's go."

After dinner Theo sat on the floor in front of the couch between Masa's legs while Masa massaged his bare shoulders. *Christine* was playing but Theo was too distracted by Masa's hands on his shoulders. It was still daylight out, so the curtains were drawn making the room dark aside from a floor lamp and the glow from the TV.

"How was coffee this morning?" Theo had been meaning to ask all day, but he felt awkward doing so, like he was prying and didn't have a right to know.

Masa held none of Theo's reservations and answered immediately. "It was early. Too early. Matt was way too energetic, but that woke me up too, I guess."

"Matt?" Theo asked, looking up at Masa.

"Ah, Matthias. Dr. Kirstein. He insisted I stop being so formal and claimed it made him feel old."

"How old is he?"

Masa hummed. "I'd say early forties."

"Is he married?" Theo's tone went flat.

"Nope. Babe, are you jealous?" Theo's shoulders tightened under Masa's hands, but he didn't say anything. "You don't have anything to be jealous about."

"Is he attractive?"

"Well, yeah, he is, but—"

"Then shouldn't I be jealous? He's smart, successful, good looking, and you get along well. He's someone you can be proud of."

"Theo, I'm going to stop you right there. First of all, I'm glad you told me this instead of just thinking it, but you're so far off the mark it would be funny if you weren't seriously feeling doubt. Dr. Kirstein is all those things you mentioned, but guess what, so are you. Maybe you missed the part the other night where I told you I was falling for you, so I'll say it again; I'm falling in love with you. *You*, Theo. Not Dr. Kirstein or anyone else, just you. The more time I spend with you, the more I know it to be true. I don't want you to say anything back, just tell me you hear me."

Theo released a breath he hadn't realized he'd been holding and relaxed his shoulders. "I hear you, Masa."

"Good. Now get up here and I'll give you a foot rub." Masa leaned back and patted the couch.

Theo left his shirt on the floor and climbed up onto the couch and sat at the other end, propped up on a few pillows on the armrest. He kept one leg bent at the knee and outstretched the other into Masa's lap. A devious thought crossed his mind, but teasing Masa without being able to eventually get him off didn't sound like a fun idea to Theo.

Masa's hands were warm against Theo's cold feet. He

worked his thumbs deep into Theo's arches, taking care not to press hard enough to cause pain. "Have you thought any more about what you're going to do about work?"

Theo sighed and rubbed his hands on the tops of his thighs. "Not really. Every time I try I just want to shut down and go for a smoke if you're not around."

"Wait, you smoke?" Masa said with raised eyebrows.

"Not cigarettes. I smoke weed sometimes when I can't sleep or if I need to calm my mind."

"Huh. I wouldn't have pegged you for it."

"Is it a bad thing?"

"No, not at all. I'd be lying if I said I didn't enjoy it from time to time. I was just surprised because I've never seen you do it, let alone smelled it."

"I only do it on the balcony. And it's only ever been when I'm alone. I don't really have a problem relaxing around you and don't need it when you're here."

"And it helps? With the bad dreams?"

"Usually, yes. That first night, I was actually smoking on the balcony when I noticed you outside."

"So you really did feel bad about kicking me out? So much so that you couldn't sleep? I *knew* it," Masa said with an all-knowing grin.

"I said I was sorry about that, okay? I shouldn't have done it."

"Want to tell me more about why you did?"

"It's a bit more than what I said that night. After Isaac died I was a wreck. I wasn't eating properly or sleeping. I barely bathed and didn't leave my condo. Jamie came over and hauled my sorry ass out of bed after two weeks of me moping around. After that I thought a lot about the last things Isaac said to me. He made me promise I'd take care of myself. He was healthy and got sick anyway so when I finally decided to enter the world of the living again, I guess I took it to the extreme. I still didn't want to be out and around people. I don't really think I knew how. But I had to try for Isaac and Jay.

"I did some research on healthy diet and exercise and stuck to that religiously. Pushing myself physically also distracted me from all the memories I was experiencing. It still does. After about a month of the new diet and workout regime I started getting more energy, but no drive to do anything with it. I spent every spare moment thinking a lot about how shitty of a person I was, especially at the end when I broke up with Dani and lied to Isaac so he could die in peace." Theo swallowed hard and rubbed his arms as if he were cold, despite the heat being on in the unit. "It hurt so much. I felt like I was trapped in my mind. I pushed myself harder physically, but the negative thoughts got worse. I wanted to die, but that seemed like the easy way out. I deserved to suffer for hurt I'd caused.

"I had to keep up appearances and couldn't do anything that would alert others. With Isaac gone, I could finally admit to myself that my attraction to men wasn't just limited to him, so I took that and twisted it. I downloaded Grindr and a guy messaged me right away. We met up at a bar and went back to his place after a couple drinks. I told him to do whatever he wanted and, my God, it hurt like you wouldn't believe. I didn't tell him it was my first time, I didn't see the point. I wanted pain and got exactly what I'd been looking for.

"So that's what I did from then on. I met guys for casual sex, sometimes several times a week. No names, no personal information, and never more than once. Anything more than that and things get complicated. I wasn't able to give more and I didn't want to."

"And that's what you wanted from me?"

"At first, yes. I was looking for someone at the club who

could hurt me. I saw you standing there eyeing me like you owned me. You looked tall and strong and that's exactly what I wanted. After I made an ass of myself I was completely thrown and I lost control of the situation. I got swept up in your pace and I couldn't say no. I knew I should, but I just couldn't. Then after we had sex I panicked."

Masa stopped rubbing Theo's feet and moved up to his calves. "Did I hurt you? Was that it?"

"No, quite the opposite, actually. I got scared because it felt too good. No one had ever touched me like that before. Dani loved me, and she was sweet to me, but it wasn't like it was with her. I didn't know what to do."

"I get it, baby. I'm sorry you had to go through feeling like that for so long, but I'm glad you took a chance on me. Not just for bringing me in from the storm, but for letting me in past your defenses. I know it wasn't easy, but I plan on making it worthwhile for you for as long as you'll have me." Masa smiled at Theo and rubbed his legs, not just soothing his muscles, reassuring him.

"You're the best thing in my life right now. I don't do a good job of showing my appreciation for you and I'm trying to work on that." Theo looked at Masa apologetically and bit his lip.

Masa released Theo's legs and motioned for him to come to him. "Get over here." Theo leaned forward and lay between Masa's legs, resting his head on his chest. "You're doing just fine, *nounours*. Thank you for telling me all of this. Is that why you made that comment earlier at the gym? About you kissing me not being a surprise to people?"

"Yes. I've hooked up with several guys from that gym. It was dumb, I know. But it was convenient. I'm sorry. This probably isn't what you want to hear about me."

"Don't be silly. I want to know everything about you.

You're still a bit of a mystery sometimes. But it keeps me guessing so it's all right."

Theo balled his fist into Masa's shirt and pulled at it. "You're too damn good for me, I hope you know that."

"Oh, shush. Do you mind if I offer you my opinion on your dad?"

"Of course not."

"I think you need to talk to him. Be completely forthright with him and take control before he has the chance to spring an attack and catch you off guard again. What he's doing isn't right morally, but he also doesn't have a leg to stand on professionally either. You told me your dad is the head of your department, are you on decent terms with anyone higher up?"

"My uncle is the CEO. He's always been good to me."

"Use that. Talk to him before you talk to your dad. Tell him everything that's going on with you. If you take the ammunition away from your father he'll have nothing left to attack you with and his hand will be forced to at least be civil with you at work. If he doesn't, it's only going to reflect poorly on him. I don't mean to tell you what to do, but it's what I would do. Or what I hope I'd do."

Theo rolled what Masa said over in his head a couple times before a hopeful smile spread across his face. "You're a genius. I knew there was a reason why I was keeping you around."

"*Just* one reason? Ah, you wound me."

"Shut up," Theo said with a smile.

CHAPTER EIGHTEEN

T HE NEXT MORNING Theo called Leah and had her schedule an appointment with his uncle for Friday afternoon. It took some negotiating with his assistant to make room in his schedule, but Leah pulled it off, just like Theo knew she would. He could have called his uncle directly, but he didn't want to be treated preferentially just because he was family. Leah was fully capable of securing him a meeting through official channels—or whatever mysterious means the support staff operated under.

When Theo got off the phone he and Masa headed out to look at a couple apartments Masa called about earlier in the week. Within three hours they looked at five apartments varying in price and distance from UIC. Everything in budget was, for lack of a better term, a shit hole, or in a less than savory neighborhood. Theo vetoed anything that might endanger Masa unnecessarily, but he made up other excuses for why he didn't like those places. Anything in budget and nice required living with roommates or was a long commute, which Masa wasn't keen on. The rail system in Chicago was great, but Masa voiced that he was hoping to be a little closer to school. Closer to Theo.

After the monumental failure of the apartment hunt, Masa decided to postpone the search for a couple weeks. With just a couple days left in November, it was unlikely that he'd find the right place before December first. He had more than enough savings to afford the hotel longer, but Theo knew he wanted his own space. If anything, he'd said he'd switch to a cheaper hotel instead of the luxury one he was currently staying in. It had been nice thus far, but he'd said it was a bit frivolous of him to spend more than completely necessary when a different hotel would suffice just fine.

He tried to hide how disappointed he was that he didn't find a place, but Theo noticed and suggested something that always made Masa feel better: food. Theo swallowed his pride and took Masa to Olive Garden. When he pulled into the parking lot Masa whipped his head around and faced Theo so fast that Theo was scared he was going to hurt himself. The neutral look on Masa's face was quickly replaced by a wide smile that crinkled the corners of his eyes. *This* was the Masa that Theo liked to see. Enduring one commercial meal that would make an Italian chef recoil was a small sacrifice to see Masa so genuinely happy.

"Are you serious right now?!"

"Calm down. What if you don't even like the food?"

"Unlimited. Breadsticks. How am I not going to like that? That's crazy talk. You're hot, but you're crazy."

"Okay, do you need a timeout to relax?" Theo teased.

"I'm sorry. I'll try to take it down a notch."

Theo laughed to himself and looked at Masa. He couldn't imagine not wanting to see Masa like this; he was so amused by the smallest things and that was one of the many things Theo loved about him. He gave him a hard time about it, but he wouldn't change it for the world. Theo put his palm to Masa's cheek and rubbed his thumb over the upturned edge of Masa's lips. The sun caught Masa's eyes just right—at this point, Theo was convinced any time was "just right"—and he was everything. Everything Theo had wanted and could want and more. Theo wanted to voice this to Masa, but his breath caught so he crashed his lips to Masa's to tell him another way.

Whether or not Masa got the message, Theo wasn't sure, but he kissed him back with all of the passion and intensity Theo was trying to convey. It wasn't fevered and lustful as much as it was sweet and tender. It was a kiss to show affection and appreciation, things Theo had trouble putting into words.

Theo pulled back and smiled shyly at Masa. Masa smirked at him in return and said, "You say so much without parting those gorgeous lips. Well, I guess that's not true. Your lips were definitely parted just now. I can still taste you on my tongue."

A shiver went down Theo's spine and sent a jolt straight to his cock. "Jesus, Masa. Come on; let's go before this turns into a scene."

"I'd love to make a scene with you. But unlimited breadsticks, ugh," Masa whined.

"Come on, I know you're dying to get inside."

"More than you know," Masa mumbled. Theo rolled his eyes, opened the door, and got out of the car.

If Theo thought Masa was excited at IHOP, he was ecstatic at Olive Garden as soon as the server brought the first basket of breadsticks. He inhaled one so fast that Theo wasn't sure he had even had a chance to taste it and quickly took a bite of another. "OhmyfuckingGod, these are *soooooooo* good. Are they truly unlimited?"

"Since we ordered food, yes. I suppose they'll bring them until you're done."

"This place is heaven." Masa scoffed down the rest of the breadstick and reached for another. He stopped before his hand touched the basket and looked up at Theo. "Do you want one?"

Theo waved his hand in front of him and shook his head. "I'm good. You have all you want."

"Won't you try one? For me?" A darkness Theo recognized well clouded over Masa's eyes.

Theo sighed and conceded, but when he reached for the basket Masa grabbed the last breadstick. With his elbow resting on the table, he broke a piece off and held it between two fingers across the table toward Theo.

"Come get it." Theo started to reach for the bread but Masa spoke again. "Nah-uh. No hands."

Theo groaned and looked around to see if anyone else could see them. The restaurant wasn't terribly busy and no one seemed to be paying them any mind. Theo leaned across the table and took the bread from Masa's fingers with his front teeth. His lips touched Masa's fingers and he felt a short, purposeful, graze across his top lip before he pulled back. His mind melted after the touch and he swallowed the bread after barely chewing it, causing him to choke a bit. Theo coughed and grabbed his glass of water while Masa doubled over in a laughing fit.

"I'm glad you find humor in me dying."

"I'm sorry, babe. Are you okay?" Masa tried to steady his voice, still uneven with glee.

"You're still laughing, asshole."

"I'm sorry. Are you all right?"

"I'm fine," Theo muttered.

"Ah, *nounours*, don't be mad."

"I'm not mad."

"You are, but I think I can make it up to you."

Theo raised an eyebrow at Masa. "Go on."

"What time are you going to be finished at work tomorrow?"

"The meeting with my uncle is at four. It shouldn't last more than an hour. I'll leave after that."

"Good. Call me when you're heading home, and I'll meet you there."

Theo eyed Masa suspiciously. "That's all you're going to give me?"

"Mhm. It'll be worth your while to accompany me into the unknown."

"You're weird."

"You like it."

"Is everything okay here?" the server asked in a cheerful voice.

Masa looked up at her and smiled in a way that would normally knock Theo on his ass if he wasn't trying his hardest to be cross with him. "Everything is great, thank you. Could we maybe get another basket of these awesome breadsticks?"

WHEN THEO STEPPED off the elevator and rounded the corner in the hallway, Masa was at his door dressed in a black suit with a pale grey button-up and a black skinny tie. He held his bag in one hand and he was pacing. He looked a bit nervous, though his face lit up and the tension in his stance faded when he laid eyes on Theo.

"You look gorgeous, babe."

"Thank you. Why are you wearing a suit? You look amazing, but why are you wearing a suit? Did you have a meeting at the university this afternoon?" Theo asked.

"Nope, I'm taking you out."

"In a suit?"

Masa laughed and kissed Theo's forehead. "Yes, in a suit."

Theo unlocked the door and they walked inside while they continued the conversation. "So, where are you taking me that requires you to be dressed up?"

"You'll find out soon enough."

Masa pulled out his cell and called a cab to Theo's address. Theo walked into the kitchen and filled a glass of water. "You do realize that I have a car and we don't have to take a cab." He drank half the glass.

"You driving isn't part of my plan." Masa walked around to the kitchen bar stools and set his bag down on the closest one to the door. "The cab will be here shortly."

Theo finished the water and set the glass in the sink. "Lead the way."

The cab stopped at the corner of Willow and Halsted at a place called Willow Room. Theo had driven by it many times but had never been inside. The tables appeared to all be full and Masa guided Theo downstairs to a cozy wine bar with burnt orange velveteen chairs lining the bar and a long matching booth lined against a brick wall. Glossy wooden tables sat in front of the booth with wood-backed chairs opposite the wall-lining booth. Masa pulled a chair out for Theo at the bar and took a seat next to him once Theo sat down.

Theo glanced around the bar then up at the mirrored ceiling to see Masa was looking at his face. He turned his gaze to Masa and stared into his eyes without realizing he hadn't said anything since they arrived.

"What are you thinking about?" Masa asked.

"You," Theo blurted out. Masa cocked an eyebrow and Theo blinked and looked away for a moment. "What I mean is you continue to surprise me. We're at a wine bar right now and I know it's not for your deep-seated love of a good vintage. You're wearing a suit, which *definitely* favors you, but it's not what you'd prefer to be wearing. And I can't begin to describe how beautiful your eyes look in this room. The honey and warm tones are just... And when you smile at me like that," Theo tilted his head, "it makes me feel like I matter to you. I can't try to pretend I don't see it anymore because right now it's all I can see."

"Jesus, babe. You might not say a lot but when you do it sure packs a punch."

"Sorry."

"Don't be. When you say things like that to me I can tell you mean them and aren't just saying them to fill the silence. It makes them that much more special and meaningful for me. And you really do like the suit? I bought it this morning. I wanted to take you out, but I didn't have anything suitable for the type of place I wanted to take you. I figured you might like this place."

"I do."

"Okay, good, because I don't know what I'd have done if you didn't," Masa said in a panicked rush.

Theo laughed and picked up the wine list. "Of course I like it. It's really nice down here. It's got a refined feel without being pretentious and stuffy. It's upscale yet comfortable."

"Oh, thank God. Are you hungry?"

"I am. I could also use a drink after today so good call on the wine bar."

"Do you want to talk about how it went?"

"Can we wait until after a bottle is uncorked?"

"Sure thing. Do you know what you want? Order a bottle of whatever you want, and I'll have that too. We both know I know shit-all about wine, but I trust you." Masa rubbed his hand around Theo's knee and smiled at him in that disarming way Theo tried to describe earlier. "Oh, and I do plan on feeding you tonight as well, so don't worry about that."

Theo set the menu down and said flatly, "Is that supposed to be a sex joke?"

Masa burst out laughing, seemingly caught off guard by Theo's bluntness and shook his head. "I really didn't intend it to be one, no. But it's nice to know you're thinking about it."

"I am not!" Theo whisper-shouted indignantly.

"Mmmhmmm," Masa drew out. "It's okay for you to admit that I'm irresistible. It's only natural you'd be thinking about me that way."

"Oh my God."

"Sorry about the wait. Can I get you gentlemen some-thing to drink?" The bartender was a neatly dressed man about thirty years old with fitted black clothing and rolled sleeves.

"Yes, please," Theo said quickly. He picked up the menu again and gave it a quick once-over. "Can we get a bottle of the Coyam Reserve, please?"

"Good choice, I'll be right back." The bartender spun around and disappeared through a doorway to the wine cellar. He returned a few moments later with a bottle with a white label and red print. He uncorked it in front of Theo and Masa and placed two stemmed wine glasses on the bar. He poured just a taste in each glass and set them in front of his patrons. "Would you like to try a sample?"

"That's fine, thank you," Theo replied.

The bartender nodded and filled the glasses to a socially acceptable level and set the bottle down between Theo and Masa. "I'll leave you to it, then."

"Thank you."

"Thanks," said Masa. Once the bartender left to tend to another customer, Masa picked up his glass and turned to Theo. "Why this one?"

"You'll know when you taste it. Malbecs are pretty smooth. This can be enjoyed with or without food, so I figured it would be a good start."

"Oh, right, food. I got distracted earlier when you were thinking about sex."

"I was not thi—"

"We are getting food after this. We have a reservation in," Masa pulled his phone out of his pocket then slid it back in, "just over an hour."

"Upstairs?" Theo asked before taking a sip of the wine.

"No, someplace else. It's a secret so don't bother asking," Masa said with a self-satisfied smile.

"You win. I'll stop asking questions."

"Good. I want you to just sit back and enjoy tonight. It's my gift to you."

"Wait, you don't hav—"

"It's my gift to you. Now tell me about your day." Masa took a sip of wine and his eyes went wide. "Holy shit, this is good."

Over the next hour Theo explained the positive outcome of the meeting with his uncle and he and Masa discussed a course of action for Theo to employ when he approached his father next. When Theo asked about Masa's day he wouldn't answer beyond saying what a chore finding a suit was. He was hiding something, but Theo assumed he'd find out what it was and wasn't concerned about it.

When Masa asked where the wine was from and Theo told him Argentina he told Theo several stories about when he travelled to South America after completing his first degree. He'd gone with a couple friends for a month and spoke of how he regretted not being into wine at the time because he truly loved the one they were drinking.

The hour drew near its end when the bottle finally ran

dry. Masa pulled his phone out again to check the time. "Are we going to have enough time to get to the reservation?" Theo asked.

Masa pocketed his phone and grinned knowingly. "Oh yes. It's not far." Masa looked away from Theo in the direction of the bartender. "Excuse me. Could I get the bill, please?"

"Masa—"

"Don't start," Masa interrupted. "I told you, I wanted to do something for you. Let me treat you just this once, okay?"

Theo was about to tell Masa that he already does more than enough for him just as the bartender came over with the bill, so he kept quiet. Masa got up and cleared the bill and they headed back upstairs and into the cool night.

"Shit, it's cold. Remind me to get my coat out of storage when we get back."

"Will do. Come on, it's not far, I promise."

To Theo's surprise, it truly wasn't far. They crossed the street and walked through a set of lights and arrived at another place Theo had seen dozens of times.

"Are we going to Boka?"

"Yes, we are. Have you been before?"

"I haven't. This place is supposed to be really nice."

"I hope so."

"No, like, Michelin star nice."

"I know! Isn't it exciting? I've never been in a restaurant of that caliber." Masa opened the door and ushered Theo inside. They were greeted and seen to in a matter of moments then taken to the table reserved for the Kuroki party of two. The restaurant was stunning. Filled with dark wood, textures, creams, and gold, it was an ideal date spot. The place was nearly at capacity and most of the patrons appeared to be on Friday night dates.

They were seated at a cream-colored booth with black

wood trim, curled around a dark stained wooden table. It was elegant, clean, and dimly lit. And romantic. So very romantic. Theo tried his best to mask his inner panic, but Masa noticed and leaned in to his ear.

"Is this too open? I can ask for a table instead if you'd prefer that," he whispered.

Now Theo felt like an ass. He wasn't embarrassed to be seen with Masa and he didn't want him to think that. He was uncomfortable with the public intimacy, *not* because they were two men, but because he didn't want anyone else to see what Masa did to him. He took a deep breath and shook his head lightly.

"This one is great."

Masa didn't look convinced, but he said, "Okay, babe." He lingered in close for a moment too long and Theo thought Masa was going to kiss him. In fact, he was hoping he would, almost as much as he feared what it would do to him. But Masa did not kiss him. He pulled back and smiled at the server before sliding into the deepest point of the semi-circle booth. Theo slid in next to him and they sat close enough that their knees touched under the table.

Sitting down was better for Theo. He no longer felt like he was a spectacle and he would have started to calm down if not for Masa. Masa was uncharacteristically quiet, and his body was stiff—probably not enough for a stranger to notice, but with one look Theo could see that Masa was troubled by something. He knew exactly what it was and felt terrible for the miscommunication. He couldn't bring himself to explain to Masa that he wasn't embarrassed to be there with him, but he had to do something to demonstrate that that wasn't an issue.

Having made up his mind, Theo sighed and grabbed Masa's tie, pulling him in for a kiss. Masa was shocked and took a second before he returned the kiss. The tension bled out of him immediately once he did. Theo released Masa's tie and pulled back from him to grab the menu. The eight-course tasting menu featuring grilled charcoal beets, shaved foie gras, and roasted venison immediately caught Theo's eye.

He casually said, "The tasting menu looks exceptional." He turned to Masa with a smile and asked, "What do you think?"

Masa's eyes were glassy and his mouth was still parted from the kiss. He was clearly still floored by the fact that Theo had not only kissed him, but by the manner in which he did it. There was zero room for doubt for anyone that saw that they were together. Masa licked his lips as one might do to savor the last drop of a good wine.

"You really do speak volumes without talking."

"I'm glad you got the point. Now look," Theo pointed to the menu, "this looks amazing."

Masa just smiled and sighed. "I don't know what half of that is, but I trust you. Do you want more wine? Or do you fancy a cocktail?" Masa said as he shrugged his brows and flipped to the drink menu. Theo rolled his eyes and knocked his knee into Masa's. "I think you should pick the wine. This is overwhelming and I don't know what I'm doing."

Theo giggled to himself and took the expansive wine list. It was many pages long and *very* impressive. "Hmm, would you prefer a red or a white?"

"What goes better with the food? You're the expert here."

"Well, we could go for either. Some things are going to pair better with a red and vice versa so it's a matter of prefer-ence," Theo said in a matter-of-fact manner.

"Why not just get one of each?"

"Brilliant."

When the server came by Theo ordered an Argentinean malbec-cabernet sauvignon blend and a Canadian chardonnay from Pearl Morissette and Masa ordered the food. The wines came out first and they went through the tasting ritual before the bottles were left on the table.

Theo and Masa made easy, light conversation that faded into silence when the plates of starters arrived. When the server was out of earshot, Masa has used the term "food porn" to describe what was in front of him and Theo had to agree. It tasted just as good as it looked, as did every course that followed. Both bottles of wine were gone by the time the dessert course wrapped up.

When the last plates were removed from the table, Masa slid closer to Theo and rested his head on his shoulder and his hand on his thigh. "I didn't think I would be, but I'm full. That was so good."

"Yeah, you picked a great place. But I think I drank too much."

"Nonsense. It's not too much if I say so."

Theo snorted a laugh. "I think you've had enough as well."

"Whatever," Masa whispered into Theo's neck. "I've got one more surprise for you back at your place." A shiver shot down Theo's spine and he shifted, suddenly ultra-aware of Masa's hand rubbing his thigh. The server returned to the table with the bill and Masa sprang back to life and snatched it up before Theo could get a look at it.

"Do you mind calling us a cab while I take care of this?"

Theo smiled and nodded.

Calm the fuck down.

Theo and Masa stumbled through the entryway, laughing, and shushing each other. Theo tossed his keys on the kitchen counter and sauntered over to the couch, collapsing into the cushions. He leaned all the way back and ground his head into the cushions, moaning in satisfaction. He heard Masa ruffling around in his bag, some rustling paper, then his heavy footsteps approaching the couch. Theo opened his eyes and smiled at Masa kneeling in front of him. He had one hand behind his back and the other brushed his bangs from his face.

"You're really hot," Theo said.

"Wow, and you must be really drunk. But thank you."

"That was my first impression of you when I saw you at the bar. When I saw you it just struck me, and I knew you were the guy I needed that night. And I wasn't wrong. You were hot, hotter now." Theo pulled on Masa's tie, but fumbled and couldn't loosen it.

Masa grabbed his hand and kissed it before setting it down on Theo's chest and loosening the tie himself. "Can you sit up for me?"

"Ugh, no."

"Come on, baby, please? Just for a minute."

"Fine. Only because you're hot. And nice. Hot and nice." Theo groaned as he hauled himself into a seated position, pulling off his blazer while Masa bowed his head and smiled. "I'm up now."

"I have something for you. It's not anything big, and I probably should have done this earlier, but here we are." Masa pulled his hand from behind his back and presented a bundle of brown paper to Theo.

"Packing paper?" Theo asked.

"You're drunk so I'm going to forgive your adorable stupidity. Open it."

Theo scoffed and took the bundle from Masa. There was a piece of tape holding a flap over the top down, so he tore it open and gasped when he saw the contents. Inside were some flowers, bright, vibrant flowers. Theo carefully and wordlessly tore off the rest of the paper and saw that the flowers where tied together with a black ribbon. He looked up at Masa and didn't know what to say. Normally he'd hoped he'd have said thank you, but all that came out through the haze of wine was a declaration of the obvious.

"You bought me flowers."

"I did." Masa nodded his head and nervously asked, "Do you like them?"

"Of course, they're gorgeous. No one has ever given me flowers before."

"I wasn't sure if you'd like them, so I waited until after dinner to give them to you. The orange roses represent passion and pride. Two things I feel deeply for you." Masa licked his lips and pointed to one of the other orange flowers. "These are snapdragons. They signify strength. The blue ones are irises and they mean hope. And the red ones are amaryllis—worth beyond beauty. They all remind me of you."

"Masa, did you pick these out for me?" Theo's voice caught on the last word.

"I did. It's what I did after I got this suit. I wanted to get you flowers but I don't know shit about them. So I did some research and went to a couple shops to see who had what and what looked good together."

"They're perfect. Tonight has been perfect. Thank you for everything." Theo leaned out and Masa met him halfway in a kiss. Theo set the flowers on the table behind Masa and wrapped his arms around his neck. He ran his fingers through Masa's hair, spread his legs wider, and deepened the kiss.

Likely to keep things from getting out of hand, Masa pulled back and brushed his thumb over Theo's kiss-swollen lips. "I'm glad you enjoyed tonight. Do you wanna watch a movie or something before bed?"

Or something. "Yeah. That's probably a good idea. You pick." Theo picked up his discarded blazer and Masa took it from him. He took it over to the bar stools and hung it up along with his own. He returned to the couch and put his hands on his hips while he looked down at Theo.

"You wanna be the big spoon or the little spoon?"

"I want to lie on you," Theo said sluggishly.

Masa climbed in behind Theo and draped a hand over his chest once Theo was against him. He put on one of his favorites, *The Matrix*. Theo had seen it before and really liked it, but he was having trouble getting into it. Since kissing Masa, all he could think about how was much he wanted Masa to pin him down and fuck him senseless. He knew he couldn't have that right now, but that didn't stop his mind from drifting there anyway. Within ten minutes of the movie being on, Theo had worked himself up to the point where he felt like he might explode. The sound of Masa breathing, and the warmth of his body was enough to make Theo rock hard. He closed his eyes and tried to relax. He tried to focus on anything other than Masa's steady heartbeat and how his hands felt on his body. While Theo was battling with his self-control, Masa must have noticed his eyes were closed.

"Are you awake?" Masa asked.

"Yeah. I should go to bed. You can finish the movie." Theo stood up and adjusted his erection out of Masa's sight.

Masa turned the TV off and stood up next to Theo. "Don't be silly, I can watch this any time."

Theo picked up the flowers and went into the kitchen to look for something deep enough to hold them. "Shit, I don't have any vases or anything."

"Don't worry about it. I bought one. I've rummaged through your kitchen enough to know you didn't have anything close. Just go to bed and I'll take care of the flowers."

"You thought of everything."

Masa shrugged. "I tried."

Theo went to his room and stripped down to his trunks.

A shower would have been great, but he just wanted to lie down and go to sleep and forget about the throbbing erection in his trunks. Or at least hide it from Masa. He sat down on the edge of the bed and pulled the blanket up over his lap just as Masa entered the room. He undressed and cocked his head at Theo.

"What are you not saying?" he asked Theo.

Theo eyed Masa up and down and swallowed the moan that almost escaped his lips. "I..."

Masa walked over to the edge of the bed and stood in front of Theo. He brushed the backs of his fingers down Theo's cheek and asked, "What are you afraid to say?"

"I want you to..."

Masa brushed his thumb over Theo's trembling bottom lip while Theo looked up at him. Theo shifted back further on the bed and the blanket slid down to his thighs. As Theo hoped they would, Masa's eyes immediately flicked down and he inhaled a sharp breath when he saw the bulge in Theo's trunks. Masa stared at it for a moment then lifted Theo's chin so they made eye contact and licked his lips.

"What do you want me to do?"

Theo dropped his eyes from Masa's and whimpered when he saw the growing erection in Masa's trunks. "Masa, I-I can't."

Masa rubbed his hands along the top of his chest then down over his abs. Theo watched, seemingly transfixed and now panting. Masa moved one hand over the front of his trunks and squeezed his semi. "Is this what you want?"

Theo nodded.

"Tell me. Say it."

Theo swallowed hard and bit his lip. "I want to watch you."

"Watch me what?" Masa said then slipped his hand

under the waistband. His breathing hitched, and his teeth clattered for a moment. "Say it, baby."

"I want to watch you come."

"Like this?" Masa asked as he slid his hand up and down his fully erect cock.

"Yeah, just like that. Can you take those off? I-I want to see you."

Masa pulled the underwear down and kicked them off. "Where do you want me?"

"On the bed."

Masa sat down in front of Theo and put his legs on either side of Theo's. He leaned back, propped up on one arm and cupped his balls, giving them a quick tug. Theo's cock twitched, and he reached for it without a thought. "Ah, sorry." Theo put both of his hands on the tops of his thighs.

"Don't be sorry. I'd like to watch you too."

"You could just fuck me."

Masa groaned and squeezed the base of his cock. "Theo, please."

Theo slid his trunks off and started stroking his aching cock while he watched Masa's foreskin slide over the tip of his length repeatedly. It was something Theo had only seen in porn and he couldn't bear to look away. His body burned with electrifying intensity, jolts shot through him with every stroke. Masa rubbed his thumb over his tip and Theo nearly fell apart. He wasn't going to last much longer.

"Come here," Masa said as he leaned forward and wrapped his free hand around the back of Theo's head, pulling him in for a kiss. "Come for me, baby," Masa said between kisses. Theo moaned into Masa's mouth and stroked himself faster until he gritted his teeth and grunted as his orgasm roared through him.

Masa pulled back and licked a streak of cum from Theo's chest before he pushed him flat against the mattress. He climbed in Theo's lap and straddled his hips. He rubbed his right hand through the cum on Theo's stomach then resumed working his cock. The wet sound alone was nearly enough to get Theo hard again. As much as he wanted to come again, it was too soon.

Masa's breathing picked up and he started fucking his hand in earnest. Theo turned his attention from Masa's cock to his face and watched the subtle twitches and movements he made. They locked eyes and all Theo saw was fire. Masa grabbed Theo's throat with his free hand and applied just enough pressure for Theo to be conscious of each breath. As he drew closer to coming, Masa jerked faster and squeezed harder. Theo was now struggling to take small breaths, but he didn't fight, he just stared into Masa's eyes as if to say, "I'm yours." Masa ground out a strangled cry and shot his load all over Theo's chest while Theo gasped around his tight grip. Masa released his hold on Theo's throat, tipped his head back, and kissed from his throat, up across his jaw, and finally on his lips. When he caught his breath, he rolled off Theo and flopped onto the bed.

"*Crisse*, we shouldn't have done that."

"It was fucking hot."

"Yes, but I said I wouldn't."

"But you didn't touch me."

"Since when did you become so literal?" Masa asked, catching his breath.

"Since you told me you wouldn't fuck me. I know, I get it, but it doesn't stop me from wanting you. I want you more now than I ever did before."

"I want you too, *nounours*. I think about you every time I jerk off. Do you think about me?"

"I think about you all the time. But I don't really jerk off much. I haven't had much of a healthy sex drive this past year."

"Jeez, coulda fooled me," Masa muttered. Theo whacked Masa's chest with the back of his hand and shook his head. "My bad."

"You're not sorry."

"No, not really, but I didn't say I was." Theo whacked him again, harder, and smiled deviously. "Jesus, you've got a sadist streak in you."

"Oh. That's rich coming from you."

"Yeah, but you liked it. I guess you've got a masochist streak too."

"Shut up."

CHAPTER NINETEEN

"WHAT DO YOU WANT?"

Theo closed the door behind him, walked up to his father's desk and took a seat. "We need to discuss the Madero file, as well as a few others."

The older man rolled his eyes, a crass gesture Theo hadn't seen him employ before. "We have already been over this and the matter is settled. Speaking of which, Jane has brought it to my attention that you have not yet sent over the requested files."

Theo tipped his head then held it up high after taking a deep, steadying breath. *Just like Masa and I rehearsed, just breathe.* "Look, Da—Mr. Rey, I'm not going to surrender any of my files without undue cause. You can hate me in our personal lives as much as you want, that's fine. But the fact that you've allowed your narrow-mindedness to affect our working relationship is, frankly, disappointing. I am the best employee in this department and I'm not going to roll over and concede to what you've proposed."

Jim Rey sat across from his son with a relaxed grin on his face, a testament to his haughty disdain. "Is that it? Did you think I'd be swayed by you, for once in your life, standing up to me? This isn't a game, Theodore. My position over you in this company is absolute. If I say I'm not satisfied with you, I don't require any further reason to reassign the cases that *my* department oversees. I'm not sure what you're trying to accomplish today, but I no longer have the patience for it. Leave now and send the files down at once." Jim turned his attention to an open file on his desk, his classic way of saying "get the fuck out, you've overstayed your usefulness."

But this time Theo didn't budge. He sat up straight with his legs crossed and his shoulders set back. Theo believed in what he was saying, but he wanted to flee—to cower like he was so used to doing. What kept him in place this time was Masa. He believed in Theo and that was something Theo did not want to lose.

"Theodore, if you don't leave of your own volition I'll have security escort you out." His voice was calm and unwavering.

"On what grounds? You're being grossly irrational right now and not displaying the qualities of a competent manager."

"Excuse me?" Jim's words were knives.

"I've been to see Uncle Charles." Theo waited for a reaction but didn't receive one. "I told him all about me and explained that you and I were having a bit of a... disagreement on a few things. He gave me his full support and offered to intervene if things continued to be unprofessional, but I asked for another chance to speak to you to see if we could resolve this."

They sat in a heavy silence for a few moments before his father spoke again. "Keep the files. Make one slipup and I will reassign them and ensure that you never move up in this company. Your revoked invitation to the house still stands. Now get out of my sight."

Theo smiled tightly and pushed himself to his feet. "I'm sorry it had to be this way. I'll tell Uncle Charles that we've resolved our disagreement and—"

"*Get out.*" Jim's upper lip twitched, the movement slight enough that anyone would probably pass it off as a muscle spasm, but Theo knew his father was livid. Jim Rey was not a man who easily showed his anger, especially not in public, yet Theo caught a rare glimpse of it. This was the first time he'd won against his father and he wanted to relish it, though he knew better than to linger any longer. He left his father's office to update Leah and called Masa.

THE NEXT WEEK at work was easy for Theo. He didn't hear a word from his father and he felt a newfound sense of joy and pride in the office. Being able to be fully open with Leah took off an enormous weight from Theo's shoulders that he didn't realize was there. His private life was going better than ever as well. He and Masa went on a couple dates but spent most evenings staying in and talking, watching movies, and cuddling. Theo would never admit that he liked cuddling, but he loved being close to Masa and spending any time with him he could. Cuddling accomplished this better than any activity he could think of.

Almost any activity.

Theo and Masa still weren't having sex and hadn't done anything nearly as ambiguously grey as what happened after their Boka date night—not for a lack of Theo trying. By Wednesday Theo realized just how serious Masa was so he stopped trying to seduce him and gave more thought to why Masa believed this had been a good idea. He tried to see the situation from Masa's perspective and understood why he felt this was necessary, but that didn't stop Theo from wanting him so much that he couldn't think straight sometimes. Instead of continuing to push, Theo gave in to Masa's plea for temporary celibacy and just focused on enjoying his company and getting to know him more. After a few days, they settled into a comfortable routine and Theo wondered how he was ever able to pass the time and keep his sanity without Masa around.

After staying in for a few days, Theo took Masa to the Morton Arboretum on Sunday. It snowed the night before, so the trees were all adorned in a fresh coat of white. Masa was cranky from being woken up before dawn, but Theo promised him it would be worthwhile. And also he promised him pancakes after, which instantly improved his mood on the half hour drive to Lisle.

Upon arrival at their destination, Theo pulled two scarves from the back seat and they got out of the car to go get tickets. It was just after seven and the admissions office just opened so there wasn't a line or any crowds. Theo paid for them both before Masa had a chance to protest and they strode off, heading toward the main trail. Masa looked around wide-eyed with a huge smile on his face that warmed Theo, despite the cold.

A sudden gust of wind and snow reminded Theo of just how chilly it was, and he wrapped one of the scarves around his neck. Masa was several paces ahead of him, buzzing around excitedly and taking pictures of the snow-covered trees. Theo called out for him and he walked back to him.

"This place is awesome! Running here in the spring and summer months would be amazing."

"I used to go for runs here in the summer with Isaac," Theo said with a sad smile. "The place is huge so it was perfect for stamina training. I haven't gone for a run like that in years."

Masa stepped in closer to Theo, slid an arm around his

waist, and cupped the side of his face. "Do you think you might want to go with me sometime?"

"Absolutely. But you'll have to go easy on me."

"Never. I'm gonna wear you out then take advantage of you," said Masa with a devious smile.

Theo leaned in close to Masa's ear and whispered, "You probably shouldn't disclose your evil plans if you want them to work."

"It's going to work."

"What makes you so sure?" Theo countered.

"The simple fact that you're still in my arms. And the smile you're trying so hard to suppress. Don't even try to deny it. You're trying to look cool and steely, but I can see through it. Your eyes are beaming." Masa dropped the timbre in his voice and continued. "I wouldn't be surprised if you were imagining just what I might do to you right now."

Theo's lip trembled. Busted. "That's inconsequential." Masa erupted into laughter and stepped away from Theo to double over. "It's really not that funny." When Masa stood up straight again Theo hooked the second scarf around Masa's neck and pulled him in close, planting a soft kiss once they were close enough. "Behave or no pancakes."

"Yes, Daddy," Masa teased. Theo's nostrils flared, and his eyes went wide. Masa grabbed his wrist and pulled the sleeve of Theo's coat back to kiss the inside of his wrist. "I'm just playing, baby."

"You're not funny."

"I'm a riot. Come on, let's go explore this place."

IT'S A BEAUTIFUL day for a run. Dawn is just breaking, and Isaac and I are stretching before taking off down the deserted trails of the arboretum. We've got a race coming up in a month so

we've been going hard on training to make sure we smash the competition. Just like we always do.

I don't mind running, but it's not my favorite activity. Especially not on weekends. Isaac even drags me on runs before school, and I'm a glutton for his punishment so of course I go. I'm not the most agile guy on dry land, but I do my part in the water. Isaac excels at both. I've got the edge on him in the pool because I'm stronger, but he's so much faster than me when we race on land.

I stand up after holding my toes for long enough that my hamstrings are on fucking fire and glance over at Isaac to see he's got his head back and his eyes closed. He's stretching his arms behind his back and giving me an eyeful of his body through the oversized sleeve holes of his baggy tank. Well, he's not trying to be sexy for me, but it's an inevitable side effect. It's going to be a hot day and I'm praying Isaac keeps his barely there shirt on. The last time he took it off my stupid ass got distracted and face-planted in the dirt. I was met with an eruption of unrestrained laughter from Isaac. Seeing his smile and abs convulsing... ugh, I'd just about died that day.

Today is going to be a scorcher, but it's super early so I shouldn't have to worry about it. We finish up stretching and Isaac comes over to wish me luck and fist bump me before he ties his hair up in a messy knot. Then we're off. We're off to a slow pace to get warmed up and the cool morning air is already burning my lungs. My strides are longer than Isaac's, but he's adjusted his so that we're running side by side. After a mile he looks over at me, cocks his head forward and we're off. Isaac sets a fast pace and I trail just behind him. At the quarter mile mark, he looks back at me and smiles then pushes harder. We go faster every quarter mile then dial it back once we hit mile two.

That's how it usually happens.

But today he doesn't stop. I don't think much of it since we have a race coming up, and I keep up behind him. We've been *running for two more miles and Isaac hasn't looked back. My legs are on fire, but I can't stop. I'd follow him to the end of the world if I could. If I thought it would save him.*

Save him?

I stop dead in my tracks and look around. I'm not in the arboretum any longer and Isaac isn't within sight. I call out but hear nothing in response except my own voice echoed back to me. I'm surrounded by white, nothing discernable but stark white. I close my eyes and take several deep breaths and try to think rationally. When I open my eyes I still see white, but once my eyes focus it's actually florescent lighting. My gaze travels down and I see I'm in a familiar hallway. It reeks of disinfectant and coffee and I know exactly where I am.

I run down the hall, feeling like my heart is going to explode at any moment. I stop in an all too familiar doorway at the end of the hall and walk in expecting—dreading—to see Isaac. But the bed is empty. I walk over to the pile of messy blankets and touch the cot. To my surprise, it's still warm. I spin around and run into the room's bathroom, but Isaac isn't there. He isn't out in the hall, he isn't anywhere.

I sit down on the vacant bed and wait. I wait for him to come back to me, so I can tell him who I really am and how I really feel. I'm still hot and sweaty from my run in the arboretum and the air in here is too stuffy and stale. A nurse walks by and spots me in the room. She shuffles in with a clipboard in hand and eyes me up and down.

"Can I help you with something, young man?"

"I'm looking for the patient in this room. Isaac Jones. I'm family."

She looks around nervously then right in my eyes. "I'm sorry to tell you that Mr. Jones passed away last night."

"What? No. I was here when… when it… I was—" I slam my eyes closed and bury the heels of my hands into them. I drop my hands in my lap and they ball into tight fists. "Please. Please

just tell me where Isaac is. I-I need to see him." My voice doesn't even sound like mine. Weak and pleading and cracked.

"Son, I'm sorry. But Mr. Jones is gone. Come on—let's go find your parents."

"My parents? That doesn't matter, why are you—" I'm cut off by the alarm on my watch for school. I haven't worn this watch since high school, though, so I'm just staring at it and trying to process what's happening while that nurse is looking at me like I'm a fucking lunatic. And maybe I am. I shouldn't be here. I was running with Isaac. We were seventeen. We were happy, and he wasn't sick. Now he's gone, and everything is wrong. My pulse is pounding so fast and hard that I feel like my veins might burst under the pressure. I suddenly feel dizzy and lie down with my knees pulled tight to my chest. The nurse is saying something, but I drown her out and whisper to myself to wake up.

Wake up.
Wake up.
WAKE UP.

Theo woke panting and sweaty. Once he was oriented enough to realize he was in his room, he glanced over his shoulder at Masa, who was soundly sleeping. Theo rolled over to face Masa, taking in his relaxed features. His hair hung messily in his face, so Theo gently brushed it back so Masa's face was no longer obscured. He wanted to touch him, just to ground him to something tangible, but he didn't want to wake him. Typically working out for a couple hours would be enough to tire Theo out, but that would be too loud to do at home, and leaving Masa alone for that long was not something Theo wanted to do. He slowly and carefully climbed out of the bed, retrieved the black box from the nightstand drawer, and made his way out to the balcony, wrapped in the couch throw.

It was a lot colder than when Theo first met Masa, he'd have to start wearing a shirt and pants when he went out to smoke. Theo quickly smoked three joints then went back inside. The cold was bearable, but he wanted to be back in bed with Masa as quickly as possible. He tossed the throw back on the couch and climbed back in bed next to Masa. Masa stirred and blinked the sleep out of his eyes.

"Where'd you go?"

"I couldn't sleep. I just went out for a quick smoke."

Masa moaned and nestled into Theo's neck. "You smell like weed."

"I'm sorry, I should have showered first."

"S'okay. I don't mind the smell. I just like your smell better." Masa squirmed closer to Theo and jumped when he connected with Theo's cold limbs. *"Crisse, t'es gelè.* Did you wear anything out there?"

"No. I'm sorry, I really should have showered."

"Shh, calm down and come 'ere." Masa rolled onto his back and lifted his arm for Theo to snuggle in. "Did you have another dream?"

"Yeah."

"You should have woken me up."

"You looked so peaceful, I didn't want to disturb that," Theo said quietly.

Masa rubbed Theo's arm and kissed his forehead. They lay in a comfortable silence for a while before Theo sighed and spoke again.

"I'd like you to meet Jamie. If you want to, I mean."

A wide smile spread across Masa's face in the darkness and he pulled Theo closer. "I'd love to meet him. I like hearing you talk about him."

Theo exhaled a deep breath and relaxed against Masa. "Good."

"Did you think I'd say no?"

"I'd hoped you'd say yes."

"That's not really an answer."

"I'm happy you said yes."

"You don't play fair, *nounours*."

"Holyfuckingshit," Jamie blurted out.

Theo sighed in exasperation before even entering Jamie's apartment. "Hello to you too. Are you going to let us in?"

Jamie zapped out of his awed state and opened the door, beckoning Theo and Masa inside. "Shit, my bad. I was just… shocked."

Theo took his coat off and draped it over a bar stool. He turned to Masa, smiled nervously at him, and said, "Masa, this is my brother, Jamie." He turned to face Jamie. "Jay, this is Masamune."

Jamie stood stock-still and stared at Masa with his mouth agape and his eyebrows furrowed. Masa smiled back at him awkwardly then stepped forward to greet him. "It's a pleasure to meet you. Theo's told me a lot about you." Masa extended his hand to Jamie, which was left hanging in the air.

"Jesus, Jay." Theo turned around and whacked Jamie on the side of his head.

"Ow, fuck, dude." Jamie rubbed his head then hurriedly reached out and shook Masa's hand. "God, I'm sorry I'm being such a space cadet. It's just…"

"Are you not as okay with this—with me—as you initially thought?" Theo asked, his voice not quite hiding his hurt.

"Oh, fuck, no, no, no! I swear to God it's not that." Jamie looked between Theo and Masa apologetically then settled on his brother. "I meant everything I said, Theo. It's just that you," he stepped forward and pointed at Masa, "shocked the hell out of me."

Masa cocked his head and looked down at Jamie's outstretched finger then to his eyes. "Excuse me?"

"Ah, shit, no." Jamie waved his hands in front of him. "I'm fucking this up. Redo. I'm Jamie, and it's a pleasure to meet you, Masamune."

Theo raked his hand through his hair then grasped Jamie's shoulder. "What the hell is up with you right now? Are you high?"

"No! I was just surprised."

"About what?"

"Well," Jamie eyed Masa up and down, "about him. When I asked you about him you said he was *cute* and *adorable*. Naturally I pictured someone a bit more... cute and adorable, whereas the guy standing in my kitchen right now is a total knockout, holy shit." Jamie leaned into Theo's space, put his hand up to the side of his mouth, and whispered, "And he's huge!" A snort made its way out from Masa accompanied with a cocky smile Theo was accustomed to seeing. Jamie dropped his hand and raised his voice back to a normal speaking volume. "And apparently he's not deaf. Dude, look, I'm sorry I wigged out on you. Take off your jacket and stay awhile."

"No worries, man." Masa took his jacket off and draped it on the stool over Theo's. He placed a hand on Theo's lower back, startling him. "You okay, babe?"

Before he could reply or even nod, Jamie sucked in a sharp breath, garnering both Theo's and Masa's attention. "Oh, don't mind me, I'm just freaking out over this whole dynamic. Please, do go on."

Theo cleared his throat and unbuttoned the sleeves on his white dress shirt. "Can we please go sit down before I pass the fuck out?"

Jamie sat in the chair adjacent to the couch where Masa

and Theo sat side by side. Theo was rigid and chewing on his bottom lip. Masa placed a hand on his thigh and rubbed it in an attempt to ease Theo's nerves but it didn't seem to be effective.

"Masamune, once again, I apologize about how I reacted earlier. Don't worry about Theo; he'll be fine in a bit. But I suppose you already know that." Masa smirked and nodded his head. "Can I get you a drink?"

"What have you got?" Masa asked.

"Everything. I keep a fully stocked bar."

"Some whisky would be good."

"My man." Jamie smiled and made his way over to the kitchen to fetch three tumblers and a bottle of platinum label Johnnie Walker. Jamie poured for his guests first, filling the glasses above the halfway point.

"*Crisse,* are you trying to get me drunk?"

"I'd be lying if I said no. Drink up. You too, Theo, I know you love Johnnie Walker."

Theo picked up his glass and drank half of it in one large gulp while Masa and Jamie stared on. "Okay, I think I'm good."

Jamie leaned over and clasped Theo around the back of his neck and bumped their foreheads together. "Welcome back to the land of the living, big bro."

"Shut up. Jesus, I think you win the award for being the most tactless human."

"Come on, I said I was sorry. But are we really going to gloss over your utter shit skills at describing people?" Jamie shifted his attention to Masa and added, "No offense, man."

"None taken."

"It's really not that big a deal. I was drunk before," Theo replied defensively.

"Wait, you don't think I'm adorable and cute?" Masa asked seriously.

"Nah, he totally does. I can tell just by looking at you two. He leans into you whenever you touch him. And just the very fact that you're here. Oh, and he's nervous as hell and holy shit, if looks could kill."

Despite Theo's sheer embarrassment over being discussed so brusquely, Masa seemed to be utterly tickled by the entire exchange and giggled like a schoolgirl. "You know, I wasn't sure about you at first, but I *definitely* like you now," Masa said.

"Meeting the boyfriend and winning him over? Naaaaaailed it. By the way, that sweater is fucking dope and you have to tell me where you got it."

Dope? Oh, sweet Jesus, they are *the same.*

Masa looked down at the tiger sweater Theo despised then grinned at Jamie. "Right?! Isn't it? That's exactly what I said when I saw it."

"It's perfect for you. The gold really makes your eyes pop. It's kinda striking to be honest."

"Jeez, thanks." Masa smiled shyly. "Theo bought it for me a couple weeks ago from, um… babe, where was it?"

"Nordstrom," Theo mumbled.

"Yeah! There were so many nice clothes, but I thought I was going to die when I saw the prices. Theo was very generous and bought me a bunch of really nice things, including this sweater he hates."

"Why does that not surprise me? My dear brother has always had a more reserved, classic style. It suits him, or at least I thought it used to. I have to wonder what other surprises could be in store." Jamie cocked his eyebrows at Theo and slung back his whisky.

"Oh, piss off, there are no other surprises," Theo said as he reached for the bottle to top up everyone's glasses.

"You sure? You kept some pretty colossal shit from me. One day you were gay and—"

"I always was, Jay."

"Yes, yes, but in my world it was a sudden thing. So one day you're gay and you have a cute and adorable boyfriend you lied about as well."

Theo leaned forward and rested his elbows on his thighs. "I didn't lie about that."

"You told me you weren't dating. Masamune, when did you and Theo start going out? You know, doing the whole boyfriends thing. " Jamie took another drink and held the glass to his chest.

Masa cleared his throat and looked to Theo questioningly. Theo shrugged apologetically in response. "What Theo told you technically isn't wrong. We were seeing each other casually at that point."

"So when did things become official?"

"Um, I guess, maybe a few weeks ago after we got in a fight."

When Masa finished speaking he grabbed his whisky and drank several large gulps. He shot Theo a pleading look, so he spoke up and came to Masa's rescue. "Well, we haven't actually talked about exactly, uh, what we are." Jamie wrinkled his forehead and sucked in a breath, as if he were about to say something when Theo continued. "That sounds bad. What I mean is we haven't expressly said what this," Theo motioned between Masa and himself, "exactly is. We've talked about… us a bit and I think we're on the same page."

"Theo. I know this is all new for you and everything, but come on. I'm not going to lecture you, bro. Although I hope you amend this whole situation when you get home. I won't make you do it here, but you better make this official instead of just leaving Masamune in limbo."

"Shut up. I know." Theo flashed Masa a tight smile and Masa squeezed his thigh.

Jamie sniggered and addressed Masa. "This one here," he

motioned to Theo, "tells me to shut up all the time when he knows I'm right or if he's at a loss. It's his backwards way of telling me he loves me. He can come off as being a bit prickly, but once you learn Theo-speak you'll be fine." Masa looked at Theo with wide eyes and Theo instantly felt heat creep up from under his collar. Theo quickly looked away and caught Jamie brushing his wavy bangs out of his face. A perfect opportunity to change the subject had just presented itself.

"You need a haircut."

"You need to shave. It's cold out there; Masamune doesn't want your prickly whiskers ripping his skin off."

Masa choked on a mouthful of whisky, nearly spraying it all over the table. He fell onto his side in a fit of laughter and coughing while Theo shot daggers at him. Theo kicked him and turned back to Jamie. "My beard is *not* prickly. And whiskers? Really?"

"Masamune, be honest here."

Theo and Jamie both turned to Masa and stared expectantly. "I like the beard. I think it's really sexy."

"Buuuuuuuuut…" Jamie probed.

Masa nudged Theo's leg with his own. "It does tickle a bit. I think you'd be hot whether you had a beard or not. I'd like to see pictures of you clean-shaven sometime."

Theo stroked his beard and sighed. "I can shave it if it bothers you at all."

"Were you even listening to me? I think it's sexy. And yes, it tickles sometimes but it's a nice sensation on my skin, especially when—"

"Hey! Easy there, tiger," Theo rushed out.

After polishing off the bottle of Johnnie Walker, Jamie retrieved another and ordered a couple pizzas. All of the tension and awkwardness from earlier dissolved and the three of them conversed with ease and familiarity. Theo sat back and outwardly scowled and groaned over how like-minded Jamie and Masa were. They talked about everything from music to movies to shoes. Apparently Yeezys, or something equally ridiculous sounding to Theo, were a hot commodity and Jamie had a few pairs, which Masa fawned over. Truthfully, he loved how well they were getting along. He had been dreading the possibilities of what would happen if they hated each other, but his worries were rendered nil by the time the pizza was gone. All of the pizza save for the slice on Theo's plate. Another thing Masa and Jamie had in common; they were both bottomless pits. Theo took a bit of the meat-lovers slice—Jamie thought it was *hilarious* given the company—and lapped up the stringy cheese.

Unbeknownst to Theo, a tendril of cheese caught in his beard. Jamie mentioned it, but Masa was on Theo before he could do anything about it himself. Masa simultaneously kissed Theo all over his mouth and jaw and ate the offending string of cheese. He smiled and nipped Theo's nose before leaning back over and tending to his drink.

"I'm happy for you. You're glowing. And before you throw a hissy fit, yes, you are glowing. You just seem so much... happier, dude, something. And you're to thank for that, Masamune." Jamie smiled at Masa.

"Please, call me Masa. I like to think I'm part of why Theo is happy, but I can't take all the credit."

"It's mostly because of you," Theo said sheepishly.

"No, babe, it was mostly you."

"No, I—"

"Ooooooooookay," Jamie interrupted. "Can we not get in a figurative dick measuring contest over who affected more change over Theo? Thanks in advance, guys."

"I second Jamie's sentiments," said Theo while he swirled the amber liquid in his glass and took another drink.

"Whatever. Figurative or literal, I'd win anyway," Masa muttered.

"Excuse me?"

Jamie raised an eyebrow and smiled in the same devious way Theo sometimes did. "Oh, now we're getting somewhere."

"I was just joking, babe."

"Good. You'd have been wrong otherwise."

Masa brushed his hair back and rested his hand behind his head. "How do you figure?"

"My dick is clearly bigger than yours." Masa's eyes went wide and Jamie roared with laughter.

"Um, I know it's been a minute since you've, uh, seen *it*, but I think you're misremembering what my dick looks like."

"*No*, I've got a good inch on you at least."

Masa scoffed and waved his hand to dismiss the notion. "Please, girth is far more important than length and I *dare* you to say I don't win that contest. Or perhaps you need a reminder?"

Theo flushed, but the whisky kept him in fighting spirit. "We're talking about length. Any other measurements are inconsequential."

"*Mon cul!* It should go by what's most important."

Theo rolled his eyes and turned around to face Jamie. "You be the judge. Do we go by length or girth?"

Jamie grinned so hard Theo thought his face might crack. "This is so fucking great."

IMMEDIATELY UPON GETTING HOME, Theo drunkenly shaved off his beard and endured endless cheek-to-cheek nuzzling from Masa. The next morning Theo was filled with regret over shaving and letting Jamie's ribbing get to him, though Masa seemed to genuinely like him clean-shaven so he tried to carry on and forget about it, despite feeling fifteen again. Masa assured him he was *très beau*—as well as some other, likely obscene, French terms—which helped.

Theo was also nervous about what Jamie had said about love. It wasn't something he was aware he did, but the more thought he gave to it, the more plausible it became. Masa didn't mention it so Theo decided to leave it alone for the time being.

A few days after the alcohol-poisoning-inducing night with Jamie, Theo planned a dinner date for Mass after reading up on Quebec during his downtime at work. Finding a place that served authentic Quebec food proved to be a challenge in Chicago, so Theo picked a burger bar uptown that offered Montreal-style poutine. He kept where they were going a secret and had only told Masa to dress casually. He opted for one of the new shirts, a Ted Baker paisley and floral print t-shirt with varying shades of red, grey, and blue. It was a bold choice, but one that Theo thought Masa pulled off effortlessly. With it he wore black jeans, black high tops, and his leather jacket. Theo opted for a vertically ribbed black cashmere sweater and medium wash jeans with his Armani suede boots.

The bar had a very relaxed setting with deep ochre walls surrounding round and square dark wood tables. The second Masa opened the menu and saw the starters his eyes flew to Theo's and his expression was one of pure happiness. The server came by to take their orders not long after and they both got poutine to start and bacon cheeseburgers with fried egg. Theo had never tried egg on a burger, but Masa said it was "dope," so Theo gave it a try. Theo ordered a couple craft beers for them to try as alcohol was more his area of expertise. Masa liked beer in general which made it easy enough to choose.

The beer came first and the food about ten minutes later. Two rectangular plates of burgers and fries and two squared bowls of poutine were placed on the table. At Masa's insistence Theo tried the poutine first. He was a bit skeptical how fries, gravy, and cheese curds would be the life-changing event Masa was promising, but he was pleasantly surprised.

"This poutine is *really* good. I'm going to have to work twice as hard tomorrow to atone for all this." Theo motioned to the food in front of him.

"You don't need to punish yourself after an infrequent cheat meal. Although, I admire your discipline and dedication, and your body is," Masa swirled his tongue around the tip of his thumb, licking off a spot of gravy, "sexy as hell."

Theo swallowed hard and shifted his legs slightly to try to accommodate his swelling cock. "It wouldn't be if I ate like this often."

"First, you don't eat like this often so stop fretting and enjoy it. Second, don't think I don't notice when you dodge my compliments." Theo met Masa's gaze and the panic on his face made Masa laugh. "It's okay, I'm not mad or anything. I just want you to know that I'm serious when I say things like that. No ulterior motives. The thought crosses my mind and I just blurt it out. If that makes you uncomfortable, I can try to hold back." Masa's voice carried a vulnerability Theo didn't hear in it often.

"No, don't stop." The words came out faster than Theo intended. "I said it before and it still holds true, I like how you speak your mind and I'd hate for you to change that on account of me or anyone."

Masa smiled and nodded his head. "All right, enough talk. Dig in and take a bite of that burger."

"I'm still not sure how I feel about egg on a burger, but okay."

"You're going to like it."

Theo picked up the burger and took a large bite. His taste buds were bombarded by the succulent taste of the meat mixed with the yolk spreading across his tongue. The taste was everything Masa said it would be, but Theo hadn't anticipated that the yolk would be so runny. He scrambled for his napkin as the viscous yellow substance ran down nearly all of his fingers and over his palms and knuckles. Theo frantically chewed the meat and swallowed as he rubbed his hands clean.

"Holy shit. That was really good but way messier than I expected." Theo looked up at Masa and noticed him staring back at his face. "What is it?"

Masa bit his bottom lip and had a look in his eyes Theo knew well—lust. He was intently watching Theo. Theo sat completely oblivious as to why while Masa reached across the table and gently cupped his chin. In a slow, smooth glide, he swiped his thumb across Theo's chin and collected a stray trail of yolk. He drew his hand back and slid his thumb between his lips, softly moaning while tasting his thumb and maintaining eye contact with Theo. The erotic sight sent a flush across Theo's bare cheeks and pulsations through his dick.

"Delicious."

Fuck me sideways.

After dinner Masa came back to Theo's condo. Being a work night for Theo, it was too late for a movie so they decided to just go to bed instead of finding something short to watch. Theo sent Masa off first to get ready for bed while he waited patiently on the edge of the bed, scrolling through work emails on his phone.

"Bathroom's all yours," Masa's voice called out.

Theo looked up to see him walking around to the other side of the bed wearing a pair of black lounge pants. He plopped down in a heap of graceless limbs and nuzzled Theo's side. "Okay. I think I'm going to take a shower. It's been a long day."

Masa detached himself from Theo's abdomen and rolled onto his back. "All right. I'll wait up for you."

Once Theo was alone in the bathroom he locked the door and stared hard at his reflection, as if it would unveil some truths. It had been about three and a half weeks since the night Theo and Masa fought and three days since they saw Jamie. They hadn't had that defining conversation about their relationship when they got back to Theo's place that nigh. Theo tried and failed to find a way to express what was on his mind. Masa said he understood and told Theo not to worry about it and that he could take his time to truly figure out what he wanted to say. Jamie had good intentions, but Masa told Theo he wanted him to go at his own pace and that they would talk when he was ready.

The truth that Theo saw staring back at him was that he was still a coward. He knew exactly what he wanted; he was just too afraid to let himself have it. Even now that he and Masa were together, a part of him still feared what would happen if he gave himself over to Masa completely. But the prospect of what joys it could bring also pulled at Theo.

He'd committed himself to do better and be honest with Masa. It was time to deliver on that.

With his hair still damp, Theo walked into his bedroom, clad in a towel draped low across his hips, and sat down on the edge of the bed. Masa was lying on his side facing Theo, typing away on his laptop. It wasn't anything flashy to say the least; there was a two-inch-long crack on the left side of the lid. Masa paid it no mind, though, and assured Theo it didn't affect the functionality of the unit. He finished typing out then slammed the computer closed and set it down on the floor. He eyed Theo sitting there in a damp towel and sat up next to him. Theo was staring off into nothing and was anything but relaxed.

"What's up, baby? You feel okay?" Masa placed a hand on Theo's lower back.

Theo nodded his head and looked Masa in the eye. "I want us to have sex."

CHAPTER TWENTY

"Ah, Theo—" Masa started.

"I know, I know. Just hear me out, okay?" Masa sat up next to Theo and kissed his shoulder quickly before leaning away to see him clearly. "I've been thinking a lot."

"About what?"

"Everything. You and me, Isaac, what I want for myself... I just... I spent half of my life following Isaac. And I did love him, I really did. But what I felt for him is a lot different than what I feel for you right now. With Isaac I knew that we would never be together. Continuing to love him after accepting that truth was cowardly on my part."

"We can't help who we fall for, Theo."

"No, we can't. But I certainly didn't help the situation. I didn't once try to get over him. I threw myself into wanting him completely, knowing full well nothing would ever happen. And I think I did that so I wouldn't have to deal with the fact that I was gay." Theo's voice faded to a whisper on the last word. "If it wasn't Isaac then it would have been some other guy. A guy that could potentially love me back. What the fuck would I do then? I've just now come to terms with me being attracted to men. I couldn't pretend anymore even if I wanted to after I met you." Theo rubbed the new stubble on his jaw and glanced over at Masa. He wore a serious expression and was intently listening to Theo's every word. "When I'm with you I don't feel like I'm being complacent. You challenge me in all the best ways to be honest with you and myself. I've known for quite some time now how I felt about you, but, like always, I was too fucking scared to say anything. And too afraid to act.

"When you suggested we stop having sex I was terrified. It was something else I couldn't hide behind. I was forced to accept that what we have wasn't just physical. I already knew that, but now... after spending all this wonderful time with you, I have nothing left to hide behind and no reasons to second-guess myself and what I want. I-I love you, Masa. I really do. I don't want to follow you; I want to be there next to you. For as long as you'll put up with me. I don't want to have sex because I'm horny, I want to because I want to be with you. I can't stand the thought of being away from you any longer. Just saying it feels kind of cheap. I want to show you as well. I-I know I didn't go about this in the most romantic way, but it really wasn't planned."

Masa drew his brows closer together and bit his bottom lip. "Do you really love me?"

"More than I've ever loved anyone."

Masa inhaled sharply and nodded his head while he rubbed his palms on his thighs. "Holy shit. Thank you for telling me, baby." Masa leaned over and kissed Theo softly on the lips. It was short and sweet and they both smiled against each other. Masa pulled back from the kiss, put his hand around the back of Theo's neck, and touched his forehead to Theo's. "I hope you know that I love you too. I love you so much that I can't think logically sometimes. I just want to hole up with you, forget there's anything other than you."

Masa brushed his thumb along Theo's jaw, causing him to shudder. "Theo, I love you so much."

Theo slammed his lips to Masa's, kissing and licking every inch of his mouth he could. Masa started to move closer to Theo, but Theo pushed him back and climbed into his lap. Masa stared up at him and panted through parted lips. Theo returned his gaze and slowly ground his hips into Masa's, making his own eyelids flitter and a desperate sigh fall from his lips. Theo kissed Masa and rubbed against him, making Masa suck in a quick breath. Masa bit Theo's lip and squeezed his ass in response to his movements. Theo rocked his hips again, coming down harder on Masa's hardening cock. A needy groan resonated between their connected mouths.

"Baby, it's been the better part of a month, if you keep doing that I'm going to come before we're even naked."

Theo leaned back and dragged his hand down Masa's bare chest until it reached the waistband of his pants. "We should get these off then." Theo swung his leg and settled on the bed next to Masa. He slowly pulled his pants down and suppressed a whimper when he saw Masa's fully erect cock spring free. He cast the pants off onto the floor and got back in Masa's lap. Theo kissed along Masa's jaw and dragged his tongue down the side of his throat. He scooted down Masa's legs a bit and pushed him flat against the bed. Masa flinched when Theo took his nipple into his mouth and circled it with his tongue. Theo was nervous as he hadn't ever done it before, but Masa's encouraging moans reassured him. He wanted to make Masa feel as good—as appreciated and loved —as he did whenever Masa touched him.

He pinched Masa's nipple between his teeth and Masa's back shot up off the bed. He cried out unrestrained and fisted one hand in the sheets and the other in Theo's hair. "Oh, fuck, that's good."

So he likes nipple play—noted. Theo kissed over to Masa's other nipple and circled his tongue around it for a while before he sank his teeth in. He tugged on it gently and the whimper from Masa made pre-cum leak from his tip. Theo gave his dick a squeeze then kissed and licked his way down Masa's stomach. Masa moaned in a longing way Theo hadn't heard from him before. He sounded vulnerable and he was; for the first time since they met Theo was in full control, which was exhilarating and terrifying. Masa was pliant and responsive to Theo's every touch. He watched Theo with heavy-lidded eyes as he kissed further down his stomach.

Theo hesitated when he reached Masa's pubic hair. He licked his lips and looked up at Masa's face. He could tell what Masa wanted, what he needed. He wrapped a hand around the thick base of Masa's cock and slowly brought it up to the tip then back down again. A low moan rumbled in Masa's throat and his hips jerked off the bed. Theo tightened his grip and continued to stroke while Masa fucked his fist. Seeing Masa come undone from just his hand was driving Theo crazy. He needed more. He needed to give Masa more and he needed more from him. Theo licked his lips again and leaned down to take Masa into his mouth, but he was stopped by a hand holding his hair.

"Theo, you don't have to," Masa said through ragged breaths.

"Shut up. I know." Theo swatted Masa's hand away and took Masa's cock into his mouth. He knew Masa was big, but stretching his lips around him really made it apparent. Masa was hot in his mouth and Theo had a moment of panic where he wasn't sure how to best proceed.

He tried to mimic what Masa did for him and took him all the way in to the back of his throat. Masa made it look easy, but Theo choked and pulled off to cough. His eyes stung but he was undeterred. Before he started choking Masa had made the most wanton moan Theo had ever heard. Masa started to ask Theo if he was okay and Theo answered by taking Masa back into his mouth. To ensure he didn't go too far again, he gripped the base to limit how far down he could go. He stroked Masa while he slid his cock past his lips, adding the occasional swirl of his tongue when he reached the tip. Theo's movements were unsynchronized and unrefined, but it was enough to make Masa writhe and whimper uncontrollably.

After gaining some confidence, Theo took Masa a bit deeper into his mouth. He felt the need to gag but overcame it and continued to slowly slide up and down Masa's length with his hand and mouth. The gliding sensation from Masa's foreskin was unlike anything Theo had ever felt and he loved it.

"Baby, stop, I'm gonna come soon," Masa warned.

Theo flicked his eyes up to Masa's and saw fire within them. He worked Masa's cock faster and squeezed harder, ripping the orgasm out of him. With a strangled cry and bucking hips, Masa fisted his hand in Theo's hair and shot into his mouth. Theo was surprised by the volume and suddenness of it all, but swallowed everything Masa gave him. He continued to suck until Masa started to soften. Theo gave him one last quick lick from root to tip before sitting up.

Masa trembled and winced from the sensation. "Ah, wait, I'm way too sensitive."

Theo rubbed his jaw. "Sorry."

"S'okay. Come 'ere," Masa said as he beckoned Theo over with a finger. Theo climbed up so he sat on Masa's hips and leaned down to meet him in a kiss. Masa grabbed the back of Theo's head and held him close. He had to taste himself on Theo's lips and the thought made Theo moan into Masa's mouth. Masa kissed him fiercely while he ran his free hand down Theo's back. When he reached the top of the towel he broke the kiss and smiled seductively at Theo.

"Why are you still wearing this thing?" Masa asked as he tugged on the damp towel. Theo leaned back, pulled the towel off with one hand and dropped it on the floor. Masa growled and licked his lips, eyeing the pre-cum dribbling from Theo's fully erect cock. "Oh, fuck. I wanna suck you off, baby." Masa slid his hands up Theo's thighs and gave his balls a light squeeze and tug. Theo gasped and stood up when Masa let go.

"If you want it, come get it, tiger."

Masa's lips twitched and he leaned up and wrapped his hands around the backs of Theo's thighs. In an instant, he took Theo all the way to the back of his throat and moaned when his nose connected with Theo's pubic hair. Theo threw his head back and cried out when Masa swallowed around him. Masa squeezed Theo's ass hard and hummed around his cock. Theo shuddered and rolled his head down to watch his cock disappearing between Masa's lips. When Theo noticed Masa was erect again, he pulled him off his dick by his hair, leaned down and kissed him hard. The kiss lasted for only a few moments before Theo raised his foot to Masa's chest and pushed him down, flat on his back.

"Where are the condoms?" Theo asked with his foot still pressed to Masa's heaving chest. Wordlessly, Masa stared up at Theo in awe and blindly reached for his bag next to the bed. He managed to find the box of condoms and tossed them on the other side of his body. "Stay," Theo ordered as he stepped over Masa and jumped off the bed. He opened the top drawer of the nightstand and pulled out the bottle of water-based lube. He kneeled onto the bed and made his way over to Masa, his eyes instantly settling on Masa's erection. He fumbled the box of condoms in his distracted state and dropped them on the bed. Theo snapped out of his lust-induced haze long enough to retrieve a gold wrapper from the box, open it, and roll it down Masa's length. He popped the cap on the lube and drizzled a liberal amount in his palm before stroking up and down Masa's cock.

Theo climbed back into Masa's lap and squeezed out more lube onto his fingers. He tossed the bottle aside and placed one hand on Masa's chest. He reached around with the other and slowly inserted two fingers into himself. The sudden intrusion made Theo inhale quickly, but he relaxed after the initial push. Masa gazed up at Theo with his lips parted and his hair flowing wildly in his face. His breathing was rough and ragged, like he was just barely clinging to his sanity. Theo raised himself up with a hand holding Masa's cock in place and started to lower himself on it when Masa grabbed his legs then leaned up.

"Wait, let me stretch you some more, it's been a while."

"It's okay, I uh, took care of it in the shower."

"Fuuuuck."

"I just want to feel you, Masa." Heat spread across Theo's cheeks as Masa's eyes went wide and he bit his lip. Masa lay back and a low groan rumbled through his chest and throat. Theo took a deep breath to steady himself and slowly sank down onto Masa's slicked cock. He could have done with a bit more preparation as it stung like hell, but he knew his body would adjust and he couldn't stand to wait any longer. Theo lowered himself all the way down and placed both hands on Masa's chest while he took a few moments to let his body adjust. He could feel Masa pulsing inside of him and see how much effort it was taking to restrain himself. Theo started to move, but it was still too soon and he winced.

"Baby, it's too tight."

"I'm fine. Just give me a minute." Theo took a few more deep breaths and slowly started to move. He leaned up several inches on his knees then relaxed back down to rest on his shins again and again. Once the pain subsided, Theo went a bit faster and shifted a bit to get more comfortable. The new angle drove Masa's cock right into his prostate causing Theo to shiver. Masa squeezed Theo's thighs which only spurred him on more. He tried a few tentative rolls of his hips and shivered again at the sensation. Theo's breaths started coming faster and he felt his skin flush from his cheeks, spreading down to the top of his chest. He felt like he was being split in two in the best possible way. Each time he slammed down waves of pleasure rolled through his body. He could feel the familiar pressure building at the base of his spine and in his balls. Theo lasted a couple more blows to his prostate before he cried out and shot all over Masa's chest. He stopped moving and let his climax take over until he was nothing more than a twitching mess of a man on top of Masa. He tried to apologize for coming before Masa was able to get off, but he couldn't find the words. His head spun and so did the room.

Wait, what? I'm moving…

Masa wrapped an arm around Theo's lower back and flipped them over so he ended up on top. He pulled out of Theo, gathered up the cum from his chest, and smeared it all over the condom before sliding it back inside Theo's hole. Theo slammed his eyes shut—still reeling from his release— as Masa slung Theo's legs up onto his shoulders and thrust into him as deep as he could. Theo was overly sensitive so he was feeling a mixture of tortuous pain and pleasure, but it wasn't anything he couldn't handle for Masa. It wasn't long before Masa's breathing caught, and he stilled on top of Theo as he filled the condom with this release.

Masa released Theo's legs and collapsed on top of him, boneless and sweaty. He nuzzled into the side of Theo's neck, planting quick pecks and taking a few tastes before he took a deep inhale. A satisfied groan rumbled in Masa's throat and he turned his head so his lips were facing Theo's ear. "I love you so fucking much."

"I love you too, but you really are heavy."

"I love you even though you're a grumpy ass sometimes."

"Shut up." Theo pushed Masa's forehead away and he sat up on his knees. Theo rolled over onto his side of the bed and Masa grabbed his phone from his bag then plopped down beside Theo. He held up his phone with the front-facing camera on and nestled closer to Theo. "What are you doing?"

"I don't have any pictures of you. Or us." Theo started to protest, but Masa silenced him with a finger to his lips. "And I want to remember this moment for the rest of my life." Theo's cheeks burned, and he couldn't quite contain the smile that pulled at his lips. Masa angled the phone just right and snapped a few shots of them smiling and looking thoroughly fucked.

"All done," Masa announced. "That wasn't so bad, now, was it?"

"I'm all sweaty and gross right now."

"You're anything but gross, *nounours.*"

"You have a biased opinion," Theo grumbled.

"I'm a researcher. I aim to be unbiased."

"That is a load of—hey!" Masa leaned in and kissed Theo's cheek, shocking him out of his train of thought and speech. "Oh my God, are you still taking pictures?!" Theo reached for Masa's phone, but he yanked it away over the edge of the bed and giggled as Theo struggled. "Give me the phone, Masa."

"Hmm, let me think about it… No." Masa dropped his phone in his bag, stole a quick kiss from Theo's pursed lips and rolled out of bed.

"Where are you going?" Theo sat up on his elbows.

"Just getting cleaned up a little bit," Masa answered as he

glanced down to his flagging erection. "I'll be right back." Masa disappeared and Theo reached out and touched his side of the bed, feeling the fading heat. *His side. As opposed to my side...* When Masa came back in he was carrying a glass of water and a damp cloth.

"I thought you might be thirsty," he said as he handed Theo the glass.

"Thank you."

Masa slid in next to Theo and held up the cloth. "It's still warm if you want to get cleaned up a bit."

Theo reached for the cloth, but Masa pulled it back. "Do you mind if I do it?"

"You're asking now all of a sudden?" Theo asked with a raised eyebrow.

"I fucked you into oblivion the other times, there was no way you were moving. And I, ah, I like doing it. I like touching you. So, do you mind if I do it?"

Theo's ears burned red. He didn't want to answer but Masa was looking at him so earnestly he had to. "I don't mind."

Masa smiled and sat up with the cloth in hand. He started on Theo's arm, gently wiping Theo's skin and planting soft kisses in the cloth's wake. He did Theo's neck and chest next, following up with kisses on his clean skin. Theo tried to lie still but his skin was hypersensitive everywhere Masa touched him. He even flinched in anticipation of his touch, seeking it. Needing it.

Masa followed the cloth and kissed Theo's foot, his calf, the inside of his thigh. Theo gasped when Masa kissed the crease where his thigh connected to his groin and tried to close his legs, but Masa held him open.

"Oh God, Masa, please."

"Please what?" Theo tried to close his legs again, but Masa just pushed them further apart. Theo shuddered and broke out in goose bumps across his arms and chest. "We're not finished yet. I've still got another leg and some... sensitive regions." Theo tried to calm his breathing as Masa touched his skin, but everything felt so hot. Masa held Theo's leg up on his shoulder while he pulled the cloth along Theo's inner thigh. He leaned down to lie on his stomach and wrapped his arms up under Theo's spread legs. He kissed Theo's inner thigh and slowly licked the crease.

"Masa," Theo pleaded. He could feel Masa's hot breath on his balls, tickling him in the wickedest way. It was a tease, but it was enough to stir Theo's cock back to life.

Masa pulled back a bit to look up at Theo. "You know, the cloth is a bit cold now and this skin," Masa flicked his tongue across the top of Theo's semi, "is very, very sensitive." Theo whimpered and tried to buck his hips up to seek more contact. "Calm down, baby, I'll make sure I clean every inch of you." Masa smirked before sinking down on Theo's cock. He gave it a few good sucks and teases with his tongue until Theo was hard then he did what Theo had tried and took him all the way down and swallowed around him.

"Ah! Fuck!" Theo hissed and moaned while Masa continued to work him over with his tongue and throat. Masa slowly pulled off Theo and buried his nose in his pubic hair. He ground his nose against Theo's pelvis and licked a trail up his stomach.

"Baby, I wanna fuck you again. Can I?" Theo made a desperate sound somewhere between "yes" and a cry and Masa took him back into his mouth. He grabbed the bottle of lube and another condom while he teased Theo's cock. Once he had the condom in place and wet with lube he pushed two slicked fingers inside Theo and brushed his fingers over his prostate.

"Ah! Masa, please."

"Please what?" Masa said as he withdrew his fingers.

"Please fuck me." Masa smiled and rammed his cock into Theo. Theo shouted and his eyes went wide but Masa didn't stop. He gripped Theo's thigh and hip tight enough to bruise and continued to pound Theo as hard as he could. He jerked Theo off while he nailed his prostate on every hard thrust. Masa was getting exceptionally good at ripping orgasms out of Theo and this was no exception. Theo came with a cry that almost sounded pained. He contracted around Masa in a series of spasms and threw his arms around his neck, gripping his hair. Masa kept slamming his hips into Theo—one, two, three times more—before he froze and Theo felt him pulse inside, filling the condom with a breathless moan.

Masa collapsed on his back next to Theo and sloppily brushed his hair from his sticky forehead. Theo dragged himself closer to Masa and leaned his head against Masa's shoulder.

"Fuck me," Theo sighed through gasping breaths.

"Again? Really?"

"No, no. Just speaking figuratively. I don't think I could come again right now if you paid me."

"That sounds like a challenge. I bet I could get hard for you again."

"Shut up. You're twenty-four—your refractory period, or rather lack of one, astounds me."

"I just want to make you happy."

"This is the happiest I've ever been," Theo whispered.

"Do you mean that?"

Theo nodded against Masa's shoulder. "Yes, I do."

"Shit, you're going to get me worked up again."

"Can we just take a shower?" Theo offered.

"Together?" Masa asked optimistically. Theo nodded and climbed out of bed, a bit unsteady on his legs. He took a shaky step and tumbled back down onto the bed.

"Perhaps we can go in a few minutes once I can feel my legs again."

"Are you just weak in the knees thinking about getting all wet and soapy with me?" Masa asked with a smug smile.

Theo scoffed and rubbed his hands up and down his face. "You're lucky you're so damn cute."

Masa crawled over the bed on his hands and knees and stopped with his face above Theo's and his arms on either side of Theo's head. His hair hung down a few inches from Theo and framed Masa's face in a sea of flowing obsidian. "You really think I'm cute?"

Theo reached up and brushed the tendrils out of Masa's face, gently tucking them behind his ear on one side. "I think you're beautiful."

THE NEXT MORNING Theo received a call from Dr. Kinley's office while he and Masa were lounging in bed. The receptionist said his test results were available to be picked up. Theo had inquired about hearing them over the phone and was told that it was office policy not to disclose results over the phone. Theo disconnected and texted Leah for Dr. Kinley's cell number. He apologized for making her work on a weekend, though she insisted it was no big deal. Theo made a mental note to have flowers delivered for her on Monday morning as a thank you. While Theo dialed Dr. Kinley's number, Masa propped up on one elbow and shook his hair from his face.

"What kind of tests did you have done?"

The phone rang in Theo's ear. He switched it over to speaker and set it down on the bed between them. "You can hear for yourself."

"You don't have to tell me—it's a private thing."

The phone rang again. "I don't have anything I want to keep from you."

The phone picked up on the third ring. "Dr. Kinley speaking."

"Good morning, Dr. Kinley. It's Theo Rey calling."

"Oh, good morning, Theo. What can I do for you, son?"

Masa looked up at Theo and mouthed the word "son" with a warm smile. "The receptionist called this morning to tell me my test results came back in. I'd asked to hear them over the phone, but she said it was against office policy. I was wondering if there was any way I could get them now."

"Ah, of course. Give me one second here to grab your file." The sound of a drawer opening and shuffling paper filled the space between Theo and Masa until Dr. Kinley's friendly voice returned. "All right, long story short, you're one hundred percent healthy. All of your blood work came back in order."

"And the STD tests?" Theo flicked his eyes up to Masa's.

"You're all clear, son."

"Thank you, Dr. Kinley. I'll be by this week to collect the results."

"No problem. Take care of yourself, Theo."

Theo disconnected the call and tossed his phone onto the nightstand. He turned back toward Masa and shrugged, not sure of what to say.

"I guess now is as good a time as any to talk about this. So, your tests all came back negative. That's fantastic, babe. Before I left for the US I was tested for everything and the results were all negative. I haven't been with anyone but you since I was tested. I get that it's a lot to take my word on, so I have no problem getting tested again for you."

So fucking direct, my Masamune.

"I-it's okay. I believe you, Masa."

"I don't want you to say what you think I want to hear,"

Masa said softly while he played with the waves in Theo's hair.

"It's not like that. I trust you. I know we haven't really known each other for long, but it's just a feeling I have. I *know* that I can trust you."

"You don't understand how happy that makes me."

"No, I think I do." Theo chewed the inside of his cheek for a few moments before looking up at Masa's contented smile. "So what do I call you? I've been thinking about what Jamie said, and I'm sorry I've been such a clueless ass. I don't want to be with anyone except for you. I want to be yours. And I'd like you to be mine."

"Jesus, that was hot. I couldn't have said it better myself. I want us to be exclusive. Boyfriends if you will."

"I can do that." Theo smiled, and Masa leaned in for a quick kiss then pulled back. "So," Theo started, "since we're both clean and going to be exclusive, does that mean we stop using condoms?"

"Ah, that's a big step. It's definitely one I'd like to take with you, but there's no rush, *nounours*. If it's something you want too, we'll get there."

"Okay." Silence fell between them and Theo began to wonder if he'd said the wrong thing. Masa looked like he was deep in thought, maybe even a bit serious. Theo wanted to bury his face in Masa's chest and pretend he wasn't having a minor mental meltdown, but he'd said he'd be open and try, so he swallowed the lump in his throat and pressed on. "Did I say something wrong?" The words scraped out low.

Masa's features relaxed and he turned his attention to Theo. "What? No. Why are you asking?"

"Things went quiet after I proposed the whole no-condom thing and you looked really serious just now."

Masa started to laugh but coughed and stifled it. "Ah, hell. I thought I was being inconspicuous. After you said that, all I could think about was fucking you raw and I was focusing really fucking hard to not get a boner and ruin the serious talk we were having." Theo's eyes widened at Masa's unfiltered honesty. "I'm going to apologize in advance for not being able to last. But I promise I'll make it up to you on round two."

"Oh, God. You're too much."

"In all seriousness, I've never had unprotected sex before. So it really is a big deal for me. But it is something I want with you."

"I have. Had unprotected sex, I mean. It was with Dani. She was on birth control and I couldn't find a good reason to say no when she proposed it. What am I saying… this isn't what you want to hear." Theo shook his head and pressed his palms into his eyes.

"I really don't mind. I told you that I wanted to know everything about you and I meant it. I don't want you to be embarrassed or ashamed of anything you've done."

Theo sat up and turned to face Masa with his legs crossed and the sheet draped over his lap. "I want to give you everything, Masa. I wanted to convey that last night but because I suck at talking about shit sometimes—"

"Most of the time," Masa mumbled with a smile.

Theo huffed out a laugh and nodded his head. "Yes, most of the time. But I feel like this needs to be explicitly said."

"This is one time where your actions and words are in sync. I truly feel like you've given all of yourself to me and it's awesome."

"Awesome? Really? That's what we're going with?"

"Yeah, totally awesome. Was that your first time giving head?"

Theo flushed. *Way to change the subject.* "Was it bad?"

"I came in your mouth if you don't remember. You did

really well for your first time. Oh, don't make that face, I mean it."

"You make it look easy," Theo muttered.

"Well, it's a skill I've been working on since I was seventeen. You'll get there with practice. And I'm here any time, day or night, you feel like practicing."

"Jeez, how selfless of you," Theo said dryly.

Masa shrugged his shoulders exaggeratedly. "What can I say? I'm a giver."

"Does that make me a taker?"

"It makes you mine."

Theo leaned down and kissed Masa. Against his lips he whispered, "I like the sound of that."

ANOTHER WEEK comfortably went by before Theo saw his father again. Theo scheduled a meeting with his father to discuss the family's Christmas plans. He didn't like discussing private matters at work, but it was neutral territory.

The meeting went about as well as Theo had expected. Jim was standoffish and refused to look him in the eye, though he listened to everything Theo said regarding work. When Theo switched gears and mentioned Christmas his father held up a hand and stopped him. He informed him that he wouldn't be invited over for Christmas and wasn't to set foot inside the house again. At that point, further talk was pointless so Theo bowed his head and went back to his office.

He sat at his desk and texted Masa about how things with his father went.

M: I'm sorry things turned out that way, baby.
T: It's okay.
T: Well, it's not. But I'm okay.

M: I can come over after work if you need some cheering up...

T: I'll come see you. I'll bring dinner.

M: I'll be waiting.

Theo backed out of the conversation with Masa and opened up a new message from Jamie.

T: Hey, Jay.

J: Whaddup, bro?

T: When can I see you next? There's something I need to talk to you about.

J: Ouu, it sounds juicy.

T: So when are you free?

J: Thursday morning. Brunch at the usual place.

T: Okay. I'll meet you there at 10.

J: 11.

T: Fine.

Theo tucked his phone into his pocket and stared at his closed laptop. He had plenty of work to do, but there was someone he needed to talk to. He pulled his phone back out and dialed the number to his childhood home. The phone rang four times before Theo's mother answered.

"Hello?" Her warm voice filled Theo's ear.

Theo's leg shook with nerves and his voice was quiet. "Hi, Mom."

"Theo, love? Is that you?"

"Yeah. I-I'm sorry I haven't called or visited sooner. I'm sorry for everything, Mom."

"It's okay, honey." Her voice trembled, Theo was sure she had started to cry.

"It's not okay. I've been horrible to you and I am so sorry. I promise I'll make it up to you soon."

"I'm just happy to hear your voice. Don't worry about the rest."

Theo slammed his eyes shut and swallowed hard. "I'm going to fix this, I will." More sniffling over the line. "I talked to Dad today. I'm sorry, but I'm not going to make it home for Christmas this year. I'm really sorry."

"Your father told me, honey. I don't share his opinion. You're always welcome at home. But I do understand if you choose not to come this year. Your father has been worse lately than usual. He might just need some time to cool down."

Theo shook his head even though his mom couldn't see. "Thanks, Mom. But I don't think Dad is going to change any time soon. I don't want to cause more trouble."

"You were never trouble, Theo."

"I met someone, Mom. His name is Masamune and he really means a lot to me. I'm sorry I never told you about… how I am before. I was afraid of so many things."

"You don't have to apologize for who you are, honey. You would have told me when you felt ready."

Theo took a deep breath and rolled his shoulders. "Thanks, Mom."

"I'd like to meet him someday. When you're ready, of course."

"I'd like that too." A knock at the door made Theo sit up straight. Leah walked in a moment later holding several old files Theo had asked her to retrieve from storage. "Mom, I have to get back to work now."

"Okay, honey. Please, call me again soon. I love you."

"I love you too, Mom. I'll call you in a couple days." Theo hung up his cell and set it on the desk in front of him. Leah walked up to the desk and smiled.

"Sorry I interrupted." She placed the folders on the desk.

Theo cleared his throat and sat up straighter. "It's all right. Did you find everything okay?"

"Yeah, no problem at all. It's almost noon, what would you like for lunch today, boss-man?"

Theo snorted then grinned. "Surprise me."

"Where's Masa?" Jamie asked. He sat at a small square table wearing jeans and a white and navy blue sweatshirt Theo had purchased for him a couple years prior. It was a bit worn and had a couple small holes on the cuffs, but Jamie still wore it often and claimed it to be his favorite article of clothing.

"It's nice to see you too, Jay. Masa had a meeting this morning." Theo sat down across from Jamie.

"I thought he hadn't been accepted yet?"

"It wasn't about admissions. There's this professor there he loves. They've been going for coffee once a week for the past few weeks."

"Good for him. But I *am* a bit bummed he's not here. I guess I'll make do with just you."

"Gee, thanks," Theo murmured. Theo scanned the room with his eyes and took in the familiar setting. They were in a small, quaint café on the main level of an old house. The place only seated about twenty people and it was their favorite spot for brunch.

Jamie flipped open a menu and aimlessly browsed the selections, as if he didn't already know what he wanted to order. "Come on, you know I love you, but Masa is a lot more fun."

"I won't argue that point."

Jamie folded the menu closed and set it to the side of the table. He scanned his eyes up and down Theo and grinned.

"You look happy, dude. Like, really happy. I take it Masa is treating you nice. Or maybe you're treating him nice. Hmm, one has to wonder."

"I'd tell you it's none of your business, but we both know you won't pay any heed to that." Theo sighed. "Things have been going exceptionally well with Masa. I took your advice and we talked. About everything. I, ah, I told him that I loved him."

"Bro, this is huge! You're legitimately in love? Hoooly shiiiiiit. Why are we having brunch? Where is the scotch?"

"Calm down, Jay. It's a little early for scotch," Theo replied with a smirk.

"Yeah, you're totally right. It's not, however, too early for mimosas."

As if on cue, the eighteen-year-old daughter of the owner came over with a notepad and two cups of ice water. "The Rey boys are back. We haven't seen you around in over a month, thought maybe you guys found a new place."

"And miss out on seeing your beautiful face, Izzy? Neeeever."

Theo rolled his eyes at his brother and smiled at Isabel. "Good morning, Isabel. I'm sorry we haven't been around as much. Things have been pretty busy at work."

"That's okay, Theo. I always knew you'd be back. So what'll it be today? The usual?"

Jamie swept his bangs out of his eyes and sat up straight. "Yeah, we'll get the usual stuff, only give Theo extra bacon and we'll take four mimosas." Isabel winked and strode off to the kitchen to give her dad the order.

When she was out of earshot, Theo leaned forward toward Jamie and cocked an eyebrow. "Four mimosas?"

"Yes. We're downing two as soon as they hit the table. Soooooooooo," Jamie drew out the word, almost enough to grate on Theo, "what did you want to talk to me about?"

Theo sat back in his chair and forced a smile. "Maybe we should wait for the mimosas."

The drinks were brought to the table by Isabel's mother and the first two were gone before she left the table. Theo relayed the details of the meeting with their father, to which Jamie had some choice words. When the food arrived, Jamie took a bite of his chocolate chip waffles and jumped forward, startling Theo.

"I've got it! We're going to have Christmas at my place! You and Masa can come over and I'll cook, it'll be great."

"Since when do you cook?" Theo asked disbelievingly.

"Okay, maybe I'll hire a caterer. Just say you'll come over. It would be so much fun. I can go see Mom on Christmas Eve and give Dad a piece of my mind."

"You don't have to confront Dad. He's made his stance very clear. As for Christmas, let me talk to Masa about it first, okay?"

"Riiight, it's your first Christmas together. He might have something romantic planned." Jamie winked at Theo and stuffed a large forkful of waffle and syrup in his mouth.

Theo bit back a laugh and reached for the hot sauce on the table. "Something like that." He drenched his three-egg omelet and took a bite of the warm, fluffy egg. They finished eating with light conversation, mostly surrounding Masa at Jamie's insistence. Theo finished his second mimosa just as Jamie's third and fourth arrived at the table.

"What else did you want to talk about? I can tell there's something else, Theo," Jamie said before sipping on a fresh drink. "You were always a shit liar. Well, except for the whole," Jamie dropped his voice and whisper-shouted with his hand shielding his mouth from the restaurant, "gay thing."

"Yes, well, it's related to the whole gay thing." Jamie took another drink and sat up straight, ready to listen. "I did a lot of lying for a long time and it didn't really hurt anyone other than me, until I made the decision to drag Dani into my mess. I owe her an apology, Jay. I was hoping you could give me her new number or an updated email."

Jamie set his drink down and nodded. "I can do that. I can give her a heads-up too, if you'd like."

"No, that's okay. I need to do this on my own."

"You don't, you know. You're not alone and I'm never going to let you forget that. I get it this time. I'll text you her number and leave you to it. But, Theo, you can talk to me any time and about anything."

"Thank you, Jay. Really, thank you." Theo's phone suddenly rang in his pocket over his last words. "Ah, sorry." He reached in his pocket and pulled the phone out with the intent of ignoring the call, but the call display made him freeze. "It's Masa."

"And? Aren't you going to answer it?"

"He's never called me before." Theo's temperature spiked and his palms started to get sweaty.

"Well, gee, I don't know, maybe it's important," Jamie deadpanned.

"Fuck, right," Theo answered the call and held the phone up to his ear. "Hello?"

"Hey, baby. Are you still out with Jamie?" Masa's voice warmed Theo, even over the phone. He couldn't help but grin.

"Yes, he's sitting across from me." Theo flicked his eyes up at his brother to see him leaned over the table, intently eavesdropping. "Did you want something from him?"

"No, I just didn't want to interrupt you."

"It's fine!" Jamie yelled.

Theo sighed. "Did you catch that?"

"Loud and clear. Hey, Jamie," Masa said with his voice raised. He sounded like he was smiling.

"Dude, Theo has been a complete bore. He won't tell me any of the good stuff and it's driving me—"

"Enough, Jay. Was there something you needed, Masa?"

"Well," Masa paused briefly, "I kind of did a thing just now." Another pause. "I just signed a lease for January!"

"Oh, shit. That's great. But wait, I thought you were having coffee with Dr. Kirstein right now?" Jamie silently mouthed "who?" but Theo waved him off.

"I am, well, was. I'd mentioned the lack of success we had in finding me a place and he told me about a basement apartment one of the English professors was renting out. I think you're going to love it."

Theo licked his lips and stroked his stubble. "I can't wait to see it. Is it," Theo lowered his voice, "private?" His efforts were in vain, Jamie heard him and sniggered.

"That's the best part. It has its own entrance. And it's an old house so there's an antique claw foot tub."

"Masa," Theo warned.

"I know, I know. I'll be good for now. Can I see you later today?"

"Of course. Text me when you're finished."

"Okay. I love you, *nounours.*"

Theo flushed and looked up at Jamie, who definitely noticed. He lowered his eyes from Jamie's and disregarded the jubilant look on his face. "I love you, too."

Theo called Dani when he got home and asked if he could see her. She was taken aback by the request, though she agreed to meet him when her rotation allowed it in a few days. To make it easier on her, they arranged to meet at her family's restaurant. Theo stood in front of the entrance to *Ciao Bella*, nerves wracked. After standing in the cold for a few minutes, the biting wind won out over his nervousness and he opened the door. The restaurant was the same as it was the last time he'd been there over a year ago. It was warm and simple with the emphasis being on the authentic home-cooked-style Italian food from recipes passed down from Dani's great-grandparents. It was just after ten so the place was empty as they didn't actually open for another hour and a half.

Theo walked toward the kitchen to look for Dani when she came walking down a hallway to his left. Her hair was pulled back in a high ponytail and she wore jeans with a green hoodie. Unsure of how to act, Theo flashed a nervous smile, which she returned.

"Hi, Daniella," Theo greeted nervously.

She folded her arms and sighed. "You can still call me Dani, Theo."

"Right. Sorry."

Dani tilted her head to the side, seemingly amused. "Come, come, we can talk in the office. You never know who's listening around here." Dani started down the hall, presumably toward the office. Theo glanced around the restaurant again before he followed her into a small room at the end of the hall. She sat down on the edge of the desk in front of a chair and crossed her arms across her chest. "Close the door behind you." Theo did as he was told and took a deep breath.

"Look—"

"Theo," Dani started, "relax and take a seat." Theo nodded and sat down in the empty chair, his leg bounced absently. "You wanted to talk to me for a reason, so let's get to it. I don't want you to be nervous."

Is everyone in my life direct? "Okay. I'll be straight to the point. I wanted to apologize to you."

Dani uncrossed her arms and gripped the edge of the desk. "Ah, Theo, come on. You don't have to do that. I'm sure Jamie told you I'm fine."

"It's not about us breaking up, not entirely. I... I'm gay, Dani. I'm gay."

She lifted her head and huffed to herself. "I had a feeling you might be."

"Really?" Theo stilled his leg.

"Yeah. There were small signs, like you not being all that interested in sex, despite seeming to like me." Dani crossed her arms again and looked up like she was remembering something. "But the real giveaway was how you were around Isaac. Were you in love with him?"

"Jesus Christ." Theo sank into the chair and squeezed the back of his neck. "I was, yes. I thought I did a pretty decent job of hiding it, though."

"A woman always knows. That night that we told him about us moving in was when I really knew. But I was in love and I wanted to be wrong, so I ignored it. If that's what you came to apologize about, you're not solely at fault."

"You haven't changed a bit, Dani. No bullshit, uncompromisingly blunt. It's refreshing."

"I can't say the same about you. You're like a completely different person. Are you seeing anyone?"

"I am actually. It's new, but he's... he's everything."

"I'm happy for you. Consider yourself forgiven in my eyes. I don't want you carrying around any guilt when it comes to us." Theo nodded and released a breath he didn't realize he was holding. Dani tapped her nails on the desk then stopped suddenly. "Did Jamie know about you?"

"No. No one did," Theo replied.

"How did he take it when you told him?"

Theo rolled his eyes and groaned. "How do you think?"

"There would have to be cursing, over excitement, and alcohol."

"All of those things. He took it really well, actually.

Although he was a bit hurt that I didn't tell him sooner. But he's been great."

"Good. I work hard to keep him in line; I'd be livid if he acted up when I'm not around."

"Your efforts haven't been in vain. He told me you were seeing someone."

"Do you really want to hear about that? If the answer is yes, I wouldn't mind making you my nonna's gnocchi. I know you used to love it."

"Will you let me help?"

Dani pushed off the desk and shoved Theo's shoulder as she walked past him. "Not a chance. I'm not letting you steal the secret recipe."

Theo stood up, grinning. "Am I so transparent?"

Dani turned back to him in the doorway. "You were always a terrible liar, aside from the whole gay thing and even that was questionable."

"Jesus, Jamie said nearly the exact same thing." Theo and Dani spent the next hour talking and laughing while Dani made the gnocchi from scratch. Theo tried to take note of what she was doing, but was too caught up in listening to her stories about Jamie and her woes with her new boyfriend. He told her about Masa and caught her up on the past year, which is when Dani poured them a glass of Valpolicella. It wasn't the morning Theo prepared himself for, but he was thankful to have Dani back in his life.

CHAPTER TWENTY-ONE

"ARE YOU SURE you want to do this? We can just go back and spend the day in bed." Theo and Masa stood in front of Jamie's door holding wine, bags of gifts, and a homemade *tarte au sucre*. Rock music could be heard through the door.

"Shush, *nounours*. We're here and we're going to have a great time with your brother. Although, I am a bit nervous." Masa said as he ran his hand down his black tie.

"Why the hell are you nervous? Jamie loves you already."

"Today just feels different. I don't know... important. It's Christmas and we're spending it with your family."

"We're spending it with my no-filter-having, binge-drinking little brother," Theo deadpanned.

"You're including me in your family holiday," Masa said quietly.

Theo nudged Masa's arm to get him to look at him. When Masa did, Theo looked him in the eye and said with absolute certainty, "You are part of my family, Masa. I want you here more than I could ever manage to say."

Masa pressed his forehead to Theo's and kissed the tip of his nose. "Thank you. Do I look okay?"

"Oh my God, Masa. We went over this before we left about a dozen times. You look great, but you're definitely overdressed." Masa had on a grey and dark grey checkered button-up shirt with a black tie. Theo convinced him to wear jeans and boots and not wool slacks and loafers, but it hadn't been easy. Masa had refused to part with the tie, claiming he wanted to make a good impression. Theo dressed in a striped, knit, cream pullover with light wash jeans and suede boots.

"Nah, I should have gone with the wool pants. I totally should have."

Theo shook his head and knocked on the door. They were greeted a few moments later by Jamie, bright-eyed, with his hair a bit wilder than usual. Most shocking of all was his attire; he was wearing a brown teddy bear onesie.

"Hey! What took you guys so long? I've been dying to open the Christmas scotch." Jamie stepped aside and walked over to the fridge. He took out a bottle of Dom Pérignon and set it on the kitchen island next to an empty one, all before Theo and Masa entered.

As if frozen in place, Theo and Masa stood in front of the open door and gave each other side-eyed glances. "Are you sure you don't want to spend the day in bed?" Theo asked playfully.

"I am so overdressed."

"I tried to tell you," Theo said as he edged past Masa and stepped inside, setting the bags down on the counter. Masa trailed in after Theo, closing the door behind him, and setting his bags and the pie down next to Theo's bags. Theo eyed Jamie up and down as he carelessly filled three champagne flutes while swaying to music heavy enough that one should not sway. "Sorry we're a bit late. Masa couldn't decide what to wear." Masa narrowed his eyes at Theo then flicked his gaze over to Jamie and shrugged.

"I think you look awesome, Masa. You've got this whole sexy professor thing happening with the tie and your hair in a knot. I dig it." Masa laughed and pulled the band off of his hair, letting it fall on his shoulders. "Althoooough," Jamie motioned to Masa's head and shoulders, "*this* is a great look too."

Masa smiled and looked down then back at Jamie. "Thanks, man." Jamie winked at him and slid two flutes across the island.

"What the fuck is going on here? Am I in the Twilight Zone or something?" Theo toed out of his boots. Masa did the same.

"Oh, calm down, bro. I'm just trying to ruffle your feathers a bit. Seeing you jealous is equal parts weird and amusing." Jamie waggled his eyebrows as he drained the flute in his hand.

Theo crossed his arms and looked away while muttering, "I'm not jealous."

"Come on, *nounours.*" Masa wrapped his arms around Theo's waist and pulled him against his body. He leaned in close to Theo's neck on the right side—shielded from Jamie's sight—and kissed him just behind his ear then gently nibbled on the lobe. "I think it's hot that you're jealous. But you don't need to be. I only want you," Masa whispered. Theo looked up at Masa and smiled, unconsciously leaning into his touch.

"Don't move," said Jamie. He held up his phone and snapped a picture of the embrace. "Poifect."

Theo stepped back from Masa and reached across the counter to grab Jamie's phone. He missed. "Jamie," Theo warned.

"I'm not going to delete it so don't even ask."

Theo slumped down on the counter, defeated. "You're going to drive me to an early grave."

"You just need to lighten up."

"What if Masa isn't okay with it?"

Jamie shifted his stance toward Masa. "Masa. You cool?"

Masa looked between Theo and Jamie before settling on Jamie. "I really don't mind. Actually, if you could send it to me I'd appreciate it." Theo groaned, eliciting laughter from his boyfriend and brother.

"Lighten up, bro. Finish your bub and I'll hook you up with a refill."

Masa smiled at Theo's dejected state and lifted his glass to his mouth. His eyes lit up when the champagne passed his lips. "Holy shit, this is great."

"First time having Dom?" Jamie asked. Masa nodded his head excitedly. "Drink up, there's plenty more in the crisper. The roast should be done in," Jamie checked the timer on his phone, "forty-seven minutes, so we've got plenty of time to get lit."

"Awesome." Masa drank the rest of the gold fluid in one go and set it down on the island next to Theo, who'd managed to sit upright during their exchange. "Where can I put these presents?" Masa said as he pulled several giftwrapped boxes of various sizes out of the cloth bags.

"Around the corner, under the tree."

Theo perked his head up. "Tree?"

Jamie clapped his hands together on outstretched arms and grinned like a madman. "I wanted to make this a special Christmas since it's a first for all of us in a lot of ways so I bought a tree. Because, like, Christmas needs a tree and shit. Before you panic, I'll have you know that Dani forbade me from going wild so it's modest and decorated with just lights."

As if on cue, Theo and Masa each grabbed a pile of boxes

and rounded the corner to the left of Jamie's open living area. Tucked in the corner by the windows was a small fir tree, about five feet tall, adorned with red, blue, yellow, and green lights. Atop the tree sat a red and white Santa hat that looked like it had seen better days. Theo eyed the hat closely and lightly closed his fingers around the white trim. He turned around to see Jamie standing behind them with his hands clasped behind his back.

"This hat," Theo swallowed hard, "is it...?"

"Yes," Jamie answered with a small grin.

Masa set the presents he held under the tree and relieved Theo of the ones he held. He stroked Theo's cheek with the backs of his fingers with his free hand. "What is it, baby?"

"This is the hat I used to wear every Christmas. I stopped after I met Isaac. We'd only been friends for a couple months but..."

"But they were pretty inseparable," Jamie finished.

"Yes, inseparable. His uncle had to work on Christmas and that was all the family he had. I didn't want him to be alone, so I invited him over. And this very quickly became his hat. He came over every year for Christmas and wore it. Last Christmas he was in the hospital, so Jay brought it over when he came to visit the day before. I'd forgotten all about the damn holiday." Theo's voice trailed off at the end. He rolled his shoulders, sniffled, and shook off what he was reminded of: pain.

"Hey, hey, don't do that. Don't close yourself off, please? It's just me and Jamie here." Masa wrapped his arms around Theo and he returned the embrace.

"Sorry. I didn't even realize I was doing it," Theo said quietly.

"It's all good, baby." Masa leaned in and pressed his mouth to Theo's for a slow, reassuring kiss. The tension in

Theo's body dissolved and he kissed Masa back to communicate that he was okay.

"Fuck me; you guys are the cutest thing. I think more drinks are in order." Jamie clapped his hands once and rubbed them together. "What'll it be, boys?"

Theo sighed and shrugged. "Anything is good."

"Oh, you're not watching your carbs today?" Jamie mumbled. Just as Theo was about to react, Jamie continued with, "Kidding! What would you like, Masa?"

"More of that champagne for sure," he replied, failing to disguise his eagerness.

"Coming right up. Make yourselves comfortable." Jamie rounded the corner back to the kitchen while Theo and Masa finished dropping off the gifts and walked over to the couch. The source of the music was Jamie's record player, sitting on a long table flush against the back of the couch. It was connected to Bluetooth speakers scattered about the apartment for comprehensive sound.

Theo sat down on the end of the couch closest to the kitchen so that Masa could be closer to Jamie, who always sat in the chair at the other end of the couch. They got along better than he'd have hoped and figured they'd enjoy being able to chat easier while he sat back and relaxed. Masa took his tie off, unbuttoned the top two buttons on his shirt, and rolled his sleeves up mid-forearm before he sat down. He rested his head in Theo's lap and looked up at him with a contented smile. Theo ran his fingers through Masa's hair while he watched every subtle movement of Masa's face.

"Why are you smiling at me?" Theo asked.

"I'm just happy. And you were totally right about dressing casual."

Theo snorted and cocked his eyebrows. "I swear, he's never worn a fucking onesie to any family holidays before. I'd have given you a heads-up for *that*."

"I like it. It's really cute and it gives me an idea of what you might look like in one."

Theo wrinkled his forehead and cocked his head. "How so?"

"Well, you guys don't look exactly alike or anything. His nose is different, and his eyes are a bit lighter, but you still resemble each other. Especially when you were all smooooth," Masa said as he swiped his hand over the short stubble on Theo's jaw and chin. "I think you'd be irresistibly cute in a onesie."

Theo laughed at that and traced his thumb over Masa's top lip as the sound of champagne popping off overpowered the music for an instant. "That's never going to happen."

"Never say never."

"I'm saying it."

Jamie didn't have a dining table so they opted to eat at the kitchen island on high stools. Jamie seated Theo and Masa and filled plates of mashed potatoes, stuffing, green beans, carrots, and slow-cooked roast beef. To Theo's surprise there was even delicious-smelling gravy. Skeptical of his brother's newfound cooking prowess, Theo eyed the normal-looking food and asked Jamie if he actually made it. Jamie proudly boasted that he made absolutely everything, and that Dani had helped him via Skype, texts, and calls. He followed her instructions diligently and ended up with a meal that everyone thoroughly enjoyed.

"Look, I don't want to say I'm an amazing cook, buuuut..."

"Dinner was amazing, Jay. Those were better than the potatoes from the caterer we usually use."

"Yes, thanks for hosting us," Masa added with a smile.

Jamie pulled his tumbler away from his lips. "Don't give me that super polite BS. You guys are welcome any time. I'll have onesies for everyone next time." Masa snorted and choked on his mouthful of scotch—the Christmas scotch Jamie had been saving—while Theo just rolled his eyes. Jamie nodded to the foiled-over pie at the end of the counter. "So, what did you bring me for dessert?"

Theo inclined his head toward Masa and took a drink. Masa leaned across the island and pulled the pie back with him. He uncovered it and watched Jamie's face contort. He snorted a laugh and said, "It's a *tarte au sucre* from Quebec. Or sugar pie in English. I know it doesn't look like much, but it packs a serious punch."

"Okay, I'll bite. What does it taste like?"

"Death by sugar, basically. It goes really well with vanilla ice cream."

"Death by sugar? Sign me up. And I gotchu—there's ice cream in the freezer. Slice it up and I'll get some plates."

Masa cut the pie into pieces about two inches wide at the crust and plated them while Jamie retrieved the ice cream. Theo sat back and watched Masa. He wasn't looking at anything in particular, just taking in everything: the way his hair hung in his face, the shape of his slightly parted lips, the tease of his chest tattoo, the flexing muscles in his forearm as he scooped out ice cream onto two of the three plates. When he got to the third he looked over at Theo.

"Do you want ice cream, babe?" Theo nodded, and Masa scooped him out some before sliding the plate over to him and one to Jamie. "I hope you guys like it."

Jamie rubbed his hands together then took a big bite of pie with a small bit of ice cream. His eyes went wide, and a smile immediately spread across his face. "Holy fuck, that's sweet as hell. It's so rich." Jamie went back for another bite and moaned in that not-acceptable-for-public way that he and Masa so often did. Theo shook his head and cut off a piece of pie without ice cream and popped it into his mouth. He'd assumed that Jamie had been overreacting—as Jamie often did—but after tasting the pie, he realized he was not.

"This is really good, Masa."

"I'm glad you guys like it. I've had this for Christmas every year since I can remember."

Jamie swallowed the last bite of his pie and licked the back of the spoon. "Bruh, you can make that for us for every Christmas from now on. Or any occasion for that matter."

Masa turned his head toward Theo, who'd been already staring at him after Jamie's comment. Theo turned up the corner of his mouth and tried not to look as anxious as he felt. Masa smiled at him easily. "I'd love to do that, Jamie."

Theo cleared his throat and shifted his attention to Jamie. "I think it's time for presents."

"Yes!" Jamie cried. He grabbed the half-empty bottle of scotch off the counter and abandoned the empty plate. He plunked down on the floor in one ungraceful swoop next to the tree as Theo and Masa rounded the corner and joined him a few moments later. They sat down on the floor with Theo in the middle. "So who wants to go first?"

"I will," said Masa. He picked up a large, flat, square box wrapped in red and silver striped paper with cartoon penguins and handed it to Jamie. "First gift for the host."

"Aw, thanks. You didn't have to get me anything, man."

"Theo said the same thing. But it's okay. I wanted to get you something. It isn't a lot, but I hope you'll like it." Jamie grinned from ear to ear and tore into the neatly wrapped paper, uncovering a white cardboard box with a lid. He set the box down and placed a hand on either side of the lid.

"Drumroll please!" Jamie proclaimed.

"Shut up. Just open it."

"Whatever, bro. You're no fun." Jamie lifted the lid on the box and smoothed aside the red tissue paper, revealing a vinyl LP. "Oh, shit, you got me a record?!" Jamie picked it up and uncovered a second one in the box. "Oh, shit, two!"

Masa and Theo laughed at Jamie's reaction and Masa pointed to the box. "There are two more albums in the box."

"Duuuude, I love vinyl. How did you know?"

"Well, I figured you were a fan when I saw the framed album art. I asked Theo to be sure and gauge your taste in music. Three of those are alternative rock and one prog metal. They're all great Canadian artists I think you'll enjoy."

"Alt and prog? I'm down for that. Thanks, man. Do you guys mind if I play one of these after Sleddin' Hill?"

"Sleddin' Hill?" Theo asked.

"The music, bro. August Burns Red?"

"Whatever. Here," Theo reached out and slid a flat rectangular box wrapped in gold and red paper toward Jamie, "this one is from me."

Jamie lifted the box and shook it lightly. "Hm, no real sound. Interesting." He set the box down on his lap and tore into the paper. He opened the white box beneath and pulled out a white and blue sweater, identical to the one he already had. "You replaced my sweater."

"The other one is pretty beat up. I figured you could use a new one. You wear it all the time so I figured you liked the style."

Jamie snorted and folded up the sweater in his lap. "You dummy. I wear it all the time because you gave it to me. I like the sweater just fine on its own—I love it because it's from you."

"Oh." Theo's cheeks flushed, and he scratched the back of his head.

"I love you, bro. I mean it." Jamie leaned over to Theo and held out his fist. Theo bumped his fist to Jamie's and Masa looked on with a smile.

"I love you too, Jay. There's, ah, more in that box for

you." Jamie dug through the box and found an envelope at the bottom. He opened it and pulled out four tickets.

"Dude, are these VIP tickets for Muse?" Theo nodded, still a bit flushed from earlier. "Thank you. You guys killed it with this stuff. Okay, my turn. Masa, can you grab that big box there with the candy cane paper? That bad boy is for you."

"You didn't have to get me anythi—"

"Shush, grab the box."

Masa huffed out a laugh. "All right, thank you." Once the paper was removed his hands froze and he stared at the box then at Jamie.

"Go on and open the box, dude."

Masa hooked his finger in the cutout in the box and pulled out the inner tray containing a pair of solid black sneakers. "Oh my God, you didn't." Masa picked up one of the shoes and visibly shuddered. "Oh my God, you did."

"Am I missing something here?" Theo asked, looking between the shoe, Masa, and Jamie.

"Um, these are Yeezys and they're very expensive. Goddamn, Jamie, you seriously did not have to get these for me."

"I'm glad you like them. I was gonna get you the black and white striped ones, but I felt like Theo would hate me less if I went with solid black."

"Good call," Theo added.

"Here, Theo. Open this while Masa has a moment with those sneakers." Jamie handed Theo two gift bags and something heavy and flat. Masa set the box of shoes down and shifted his attention over to the bags Theo was holding. "Open the big bag first, then the small bag." Theo did as he was told and pulled out a frosted bottle of absinthe from the larger bag. "That's real absinthe. I picked it up while I was in Amsterdam last year. I was saving it for a special occasion because when I had it there I tripped fucking balls, so I know it's the good stuff. But due to some new developments," Jamie winked at Masa, "I think you should have it."

"I had this stuff once in university. It was… messy." Theo winced at the memory causing Jamie and Masa to laugh.

"Next bag. It'll make things easier for you." Theo reached into the bag and pulled out a large jug of lube with a pump top. His eyes went wide, and he audibly gasped before whipping around toward Jamie. Once he made eye contact with his brother he realized he didn't even know what to say. He turned to Masa and saw he was red-faced and holding his hand over his mouth, trying—rather poorly—to contain his laughter.

It'll make things easier. *Oh my fucking God.* Theo cleared his throat and slid the jug back into the bag then set it down to the side. He forced a smile, but was pretty sure his lips quivered and thanked Jamie. As if on cue, Jamie and Masa burst into roaring laughter and Theo wanted to cease to exist.

Once Jamie had reigned himself in, he clapped his hand on Theo's shoulder and gave him a good shake. "I'm sorry, I'm just fucking with you, bro. You really need to learn how to lighten up again. I'm putting you in charge of that," Jamie said pointing at Masa. "Here," Jamie placed the third gift in Theo's lap, "this one is for real. I promise." Theo huffed and shook his head as he tore into the paper. He was taken aback by the sight of himself underneath it. He held in his hands a framed photograph from many years ago of him and Jamie laughing and covered in mud.

A smile worked its way across Theo's face and he looked up at Jamie fondly. "Do you remember this day?" Jamie nodded and leaned back to rest on his palms. Theo turned to Masa and held out the picture. Masa scooted closer to him and took hold of it.

"Oh, wow. You guys were just kids. And pretty adorable, albeit filthy."

"This was taken when we were visiting our grandparents one summer. I was eleven, and Jay was five. Our grandparents had a really large country property and Jay wandered off when I was supposed to be watching him. When I found him he was rolling around in a mud pit with the biggest shit-eating grin on his face. That one right there," Theo said tilting his head over toward his brother.

"This is just my face, man," Jamie said in mock offense.

"Anyway, he wanted me to play with him when he saw me. We needed to get back, but he was calling out to me in his little voice, 'Teo! Teo!' so I got in there with him. When we got back to the house we were laughing and saw Grandpa first. He took this picture and sent us to get washed up before Dad could see us. Unfortunately, Dad found us inside and was furious. I said it was my idea and got grounded for a month."

Masa took Theo's hand in his and kissed it. He brushed his thumb over the back of Theo's hand and gave it a soft squeeze. "You'll have to tell me more about your childhood sometime. That was a beautiful memory. Well, up until you got grounded."

"It was," Theo replied with a smile.

"That's my favorite memory with you, you know. I honestly didn't remember the part about Dad getting mad at you. Sorry. For me that day was the best. I lost my shoes in the mud and you gave me a piggyback ride home and I remember wanting to be just like you when I grew up. As we got older you stopped giving me piggyback rides and we didn't play in the mud anymore, but you were still my favorite person. I've always admired you and that rings true today more than it ever has. When I thought of what to get you as a gift I came up with a serious blank—after I'd already bought the lube, of course. What could I get for the guy who has everything he needs? The answer I came up with is reinforcement. I love you lots, Theo. I just wanted to remind you that you'll always have family. You can't get rid of me no matter what." Jamie's eyes glassed over but he grinned and held up his fist to Theo. Theo bumped it with his own and shook his head.

"You're crazy and I want to smother you sometimes, but I'm glad I have you, Jay. I love you, too." Theo smiled at Masa and gave his hand a squeeze.

"Tender times. Now you guys exchange!"

Theo looked at Masa and felt his temperature rise. He was suddenly a mess of nerves. Masa must have seen it on his face and offered to go first, much to Theo's relief. He handed Theo a gift remarkably similar to the one he'd just opened. He tore back the paper and once again came face to face with himself. Held within a solid black frame was the picture Masa had taken of them in bed.

"You were right to want to capture this moment, Masa."

"I didn't know what Jamie was getting you, I swear. This picture represents a first for us, in many ways. Your second gift is, well… they kind of go together. I'll let you open it." Masa gave Theo a square box that just fit in his hand. He opened it and pulled out a smaller box. A ring box. Jamie gasped, and Theo's eyes darted to Masa's while his pulse spiked. "Open it, baby." With trembling fingers, Theo flipped the box open to reveal two silver rings with a satin finish in the middle and polished angled edges.

Theo set the rings in his palm and traced the edges with his fingers. "These are beautiful."

"I'm glad you like them. I don't want to freak you out, any more than I already have. These aren't engagement rings. But they are very important to me. Where the photo represents our beginning, these are the future I'd like with you."

Masa pushed his hair back and picked up one of the rings from Theo's palm. "These are tungsten. I chose it for its strength and weight. I want us to have an unbreakable bond. The weightiness of the ring is to serve as a reminder. If you're ever feeling lost or sad I want you to be able to feel it on your finger," Masa brushed his thumb over Theo's right ring finger, "and be reminded of how much I love you."

I love you so fucking much.

"You're not saying anything. Is it too much?" Masa asked. Theo's hand was still in his.

"Shit, no. I'm sorry; I thought I was talking out loud. The rings are beautiful, what you said about them was, and fuck, so are you. I love you, Masa."

Jamie gasped again but he clapped his hands over his mouth and kept quiet.

"I hope I can be everything you deserve," Theo continued.

"*Idiot nounours.* You already are." Masa pulled Theo's hand up to his lips and kissed his right ring finger. "Can I put it on you?" Theo nodded with a smile and Masa slid the ring onto his finger.

"It's a perfect fit," Theo said, surprised.

"Ah, yeah. I kind of measured your finger while you were asleep. Tungsten can't be sized so I needed to be sure."

Theo held his hand up and admired the ring and how it felt on his finger. It definitely possessed a presence he couldn't ignore. The foreign feeling was one he welcomed, and it made him smile even wider. "The other one is for you, isn't it?"

"Yes," answered Masa.

"Same finger?" Theo asked. Masa nodded, and Theo picked up the ring then slid it on Masa's finger. They joined palms and entwined their fingers and looked at each other lovingly until the sound of whining caught their attention.

"Look, I'm sorry, but I can't keep quiet any longer! Let me see those rings now!" Jamie leaned forward and crawled on his hands and knees to get a closer look. "Fuuuuuuck me, those are sexy. You did great, Masa. But, guys, just remember to take those off before you use my gift. We don't need any embarrassing trips to the emergency room to retrieve them."

"Jamie, I swear—"

"Time for Theo's gift for Masa! The suspense is killing me." Theo groaned, but leaned forward and pulled a large rectangular box into his lap. He handed it to Masa feeling every bit as nervous as he'd been before he opened the picture of them.

Masa glanced at Theo once more and bit his lip before he tore into the paper and uncovered a MacBook Pro. "*Crisse*, babe."

"Do you like it?" Theo asked.

"I do, I definitely do. It's just a lot. These are damn expensive. You didn't have to do that."

"It looked like you could use a new computer for school. I wasn't sure what you'd need, but the guy at the store assured me you'd be set with this one."

Masa laughed, still clutching the box. "That's definitely true. Holy shit. I didn't think I'd ever get one of these, I couldn't really justify the price."

"If there's ever anything you need I'd be more than happy to help you out," Theo said quietly.

"Time-out," Jamie called. "Theo, does he not know how much money you make?"

Theo shook his head. "It hasn't really come up."

"Oh. Masa, dude, I love you even more now, man. You have my blessing to wed my bro, welcome to the family."

"Jamie, rein it in. I'm not finished yet." Jamie's lips formed in a silent O and he sat back down and mouthed "sorry." "Masa, I don't want you to worry about the cost of the computer. I can afford it just fine, okay? Same goes for our dates. Keep your savings for school, don't spend them on me. I want to help you any way I can. I know you didn't ask me to, nor do I think you expect it. This isn't that. This is me genuinely wanting to help you succeed. I know you can do it without me, but I'd like to help you if you'll let me."

Masa snorted a laugh. "I can't really say no when you put it like that. Thank you, baby."

"There's something else I want to give you." Theo reached into his back pocket and pulled out a shiny, new key. "I don't have a profound speech planned. I-I just want to fall asleep and wake up with you every day. You've breathed life into me again and the time I spend without you feels empty. So, if you want to, I'd love it if you moved in with me. Ah, or if you don't want to, you're welcome any time to come visit. Whatever you want."

The smile left Masa's face and his eyes went wide while his lips silently parted. With his brows raised and his lips trembling ever so faintly, he looked every bit as raw and vulnerable as Theo felt. Still holding the key in his hand, Theo brushed his free hand through his hair and bit his bottom lip. "Masa, I need you to say something—you're freaking me out."

Masa's lips stilled, though his staggered breathing continued as he penetrated Theo to the core with nothing but his gaze. Without warning he leapt up from his seated position and tackled Theo onto his back, kissing him so fiercely Theo couldn't breathe. The key went flying and bounced on the floor, but that was far from the most pressing thing on Theo's mind. Masa buried his hands in Theo's hair and devoured him. Theo in turn wrapped a hand around the back of Masa's head, pulling him down and deepening the kiss even more.

When Masa pulled back they were both panting and kiss

drunk, regarding each other through heavy-lidded eyes. Masa brushed his thumb against the corner of Theo's kiss-swollen lips and smiled at him. *"T'es vraiment sérieux?"* He planted a lingering kiss on Theo's forehead and a quick one again on his lips.

"Can I take that as a yes?"

"Fuck yes, baby."

"Can I be excited now?!" Jamie blurted out, looking like he was about to explode with joy. Masa sat up between Theo's knees and shrugged his eyebrows, looking like the happiest guy in the world. Jamie lunged forward, effectively tackle-hugging Theo and Masa in a tangle of limbs.

"All right, all right, you guys are heavy as hell and I can't breathe." Theo leaned his head back against the cool floor.

"Bro, we're like, having a moment. Don't be a buzzkill."

"Call me Captain Buzzkill then. Get off." Jamie groaned and rolled off of Theo while Masa snickered and did the same. Theo sat up and took a deep breath to steady his racing pulse. He looked down at his finger, now adorned with the beautiful ring Masa had given him. In that moment he truly understood the weight it carried and looked forward to the future instead of feeling like he didn't deserve one.

When he looked up Masa was watching him with a knowing grin on his face and happiness in his eyes. Jamie bombarded Masa and Theo with congratulations and asked a million questions about when they were moving in and if they planned on getting a bigger place. Without giving a chance for Theo or Masa to wedge in, he spouted off the several great areas close to UIC so Masa's commute would be short then abruptly stopped.

"Um, so when do you find out about school anyway?" Jamie asked.

"I actually found out a couple weeks ago. I told Theo not to tell you so I could do it in person." Masa smiled wide.

Jamie howled and jumped up. "Aiight, boys, it's time for more Dom. We're celebrating!"

I'M ON MY WAY back to Isaac's room when I pass Dr. Thiessen in the hall. She smiles meekly and nods her head at me as I pass by her. Just a couple weeks ago she told us Isaac had about a month left and that there was nothing more that could be done. Isaac took the news with a weak smile and thanked her, probably as a show for my benefit more than anything. I, on the other hand, was a complete and utter wreck. I cried and shut down like a child and Isaac, weak as he was, consoled me. I am supposed to be his support and he consoled me. I really am a terrible person.

The door to Isaac's room is closed when I approach. I gently knock on the door to announce my arrival then enter. He's asleep in the small bed so I quietly tiptoe over and take a seat in the stiff chair next to the head of the bed. The chair creaks when I settle into it and Isaac stirs. He blinks the sleep out of his eyes and furrows his brow trying to focus on me. The rounds of chemo have really done a number on him. His once vibrant hazel eyes are now dull and clouded over with cataracts. The right is a lot worse than the left, so I'm always careful to approach him on his left if I don't announce my arrival first. When his hair started to fall out he had me shave his head. It's a good thing I'm not a barber because I fucking botched it, though he insisted it was perfect and wouldn't let me call someone else to fix it.

I lean over the side of the bed to get a good look at him. His golden skin has also turned pale and grey and he's terribly thin, but he's still my Isaac. I've thought so many times about telling him about me. About how I feel. At this point, it just seems pointless. I don't want him to hate me or even worry about me right now, so I can't tell him. I can't handle the possibility of him shutting me out. I'm just too selfish and weak.

I lean in closer so I can hear his shallow breathing over the beeping of machines and I realize that he's feigning sleep. "I know you're awake, Isaac."

"You're always watching me sleep. I'm convinced you're going to smother me one of these days and put me out of my misery."

"That's not funny."

"Oh, come on. Let me indulge in a little bit of gallows humor. It's all I've got left at this point." Isaac laughs but it turns into a violent cough. I get him a glass of water from the bedside table and lift his head to get a drink.

"You still have me."

"Yeah, I guess I do. Dani must be pretty angry with me for once again monopolizing your time."

"She understands, don't worry about it." I haven't even told him I broke up with Dani when he got worse. I don't want him to ask why. "Jamie said he's going to come by tomorrow to see you in the morning."

"So what you really mean is he'll be by around three."

I laugh. Isaac can always make me laugh. "Yeah, that sounds about right."

"You guys don't have to visit as often as you do. I won't hold it against you, you know."

"Shut up. There's nowhere else I'd rather be."

Isaac smirks at me and places his hand over mine. "I appreciate it, man. Even if I do feel a bit selfish."

I wave my hand in front of me and shake my head. "Enough of that. I brought some food if you're up for eating. It's in the fridge on this floor so it won't take me long to go grab it."

"Thanks. I'm good for right now, though. I haven't been able to keep much down today and I'm just really tired."

"Shit, I'm sorry I woke you. I tried to be quiet."

Isaac laughs again. It sounds pained, but his laughter is still a beautiful sound to me. "Dude, you're not graceful or stealthy. Unless you're in the pool."

"I'm not sure how good I'd be anymore."

"You should pick it up again."

I shake my head immediately. "I don't want to race. It's been too long."

"No, not competitively. Just for leisure. It took some convincing to get you in the pool, but I could tell you really loved it." Isaac coughs again and I give him another drink.

"Yeah, I did. I might try it again."

Isaac whacks me on the chest, but there's no strength behind it so it feels more like a tap. "Don't give me that non-committal bullshit. Promise me you will. You don't do shit for yourself anymore and I want you to start again."

When I'm gone. That's what he's not saying. I know better than to argue with him so I nod my head and smile. "Okay, I promise."

"You're a shit liar, but what else is new." We both genuinely laugh, and Isaac has another coughing fit. "Shit, this fucking sucks." I look up and open my mouth to say that I'm sorry for the millionth time, but Isaac holds up his hand and I shut up. "Don't even think about apologizing to me."

I shrug and lean my head down against his arm. "Busted." He yawns, and I notice his blinks becoming longer so I sit up and pull the blanket up to his neck. "You should get some more rest. We can talk more when you wake up."

"You don't have to stay. It's Christmas, man."

"Yeah, it is. That's why I'm here. There's nowhere else I'd rather be."

Isaac closes his eyes and his voice is barely a whisper as he says, "You already said that."

"I meant it. Merry Christmas, Isaac." I lean back in the chair and close my eyes. The last thing I hear before sleep takes me is the steady beeping of machines.

I'm woken up by one of the nurses on this rotation I've come to know well, Steph. I smile when I see her and blink the sleep out of my eyes. It's then I notice that she looks distressed and I immediately look over at Isaac. His eyes are open, but his body is still. Too still. Then it hits me: the steady beeping which has lulled me to sleep countless times is now a constant note, drawn out in the worst way. I know what it means, but I don't want to believe it. I can't believe it. Yet there he is, so close to me yet gone from my life. A shrill sound cuts through the room. I feel hot tears run from my eyes and my lungs burn; I realize the sound is my own screaming. My happiness, my love personified, my best friend, is gone. And I don't know what to do other than hold his cold hand and cry.

THEO WOKE up sweaty and in Masa's arms. He could feel tears welling in his eyes and slid out of bed, careful not to disturb Masa. He slipped on some briefs and made his way out to the couch, plunking down and wrapping himself in the black blanket. He wasn't sure of the time as he'd left his phone on the dresser, but the sun had not yet begun to rise, leaving the room shrouded in darkness. He replayed his last conversation with Isaac over and over while cursing himself for not being there more.

The sound of Masa's footfalls at the end of the hallway, slowly getting louder, brought Theo back to the present. "What are you doing out here?" Masa asked. His hair was a mess and he was completely naked.

"I couldn't sleep. I didn't want to wake you up," Theo said distantly.

Masa walked over to the couch and yawned. "Ah, *nounours*, I'm sorry to tell you that you're not very stealthy. I thought you might just be going to the bathroom and waited for you to come back, but you never did. Do you mind if I sit? I'm freezing my balls off right now."

A smile pulled at Theo's lips and he flung the blanket back for Masa to climb in. Masa was freezing cold and snuggled in against Theo's chest while Theo draped the blanket over his body. Theo rubbed Masa's arm to generate some heat. "Jesus, you're freezing cold."

"I was sitting up in bed waiting for you for at least half an hour. When I reasoned that you weren't coming back I came out to see what was wrong."

"It's December, Masa. You can't just walk around naked."

"Pfft, says you. So," Masa paused before continuing, "do you want to tell me what's wrong?"

"It's Isaac. He died a year ago today."

Masa leaned up and kissed Theo's forehead while he cupped his cheek. "I'm sorry, baby."

"I don't know what I was expecting to happen. I thought maybe I was getting better. Being with you makes me so happy, yet when I close my eyes all I see is pain and the past."

"You've been harboring this pain for a long time, even before Isaac got sick. It's not going to go away overnight. You being happy now is going to help, but it's still going to take time. Healing always does, babe."

"Right now it feels like I can't. It feels like no matter how much I want you, this will always be over my head. I dreamt about him last night. It was the night he died. We just talked like it was any other night then it got kind of serious. He got stern with me and told me I didn't do anything for myself. I promised him I'd start swimming again but then he died and I felt like I did too. Swimming was the last thing on my mind; I just wanted my best friend back." Theo's voice cut out at the end and tears welled in his eyes. He tried to maintain his composure while he was speaking, but now that he was finished his cheeks were wet with fresh tears.

Masa kissed Theo's tears then reversed their positions and pulled Theo against his chest. "You're going to move past this. You've already made a lot of progress in a short time. I won't let you fail, neither will Jamie." Masa hugged Theo tighter and told him that he loved him while Theo clung to him and cried in his arms. When Theo calmed down Masa licked his lips and traced his finger along Theo's jaw. "Have you ever thought about talking to someone about Isaac?" Theo went rigid against Masa, but Masa just rubbed his back when he continued. "Calm down, babe. There's a lot of stigma surrounding therapy, but I think it would really help you. That doesn't mean I don't want you to talk to me, because I do. I just want you to be happy."

Theo relaxed again under Masa's touch and nodded his head slowly. "If you think it will help I'll do it." Theo lowered his voice and rested his hand on Masa's chest. "I'll try anything for you."

"If you don't like it we'll try something else." Masa kissed Theo's forehead and traced small circles on his shoulder. "Can I ask you something about Isaac?"

"Anything."

"Where was he laid to rest?"

Theo shook his head. "Ah, he wasn't. He wanted to be cremated. He'd had it in his head that if he were cremated he could be a badass phoenix in his next life. It's silly and I'm pretty sure he said it for my benefit more than anything, but I like the idea. It suits him. I wanted to scatter his ashes in California in the ocean, but I've been too much of a wreck to manage that."

"Where are his ashes?" Masa asked, still stroking Theo's back.

"Jamie has them. He said he'd hold onto them for me until I was ready."

"When you're ready, I'd like to go with you when you

scatter them, only if you want me there. I'll be there for you in whatever capacity you need." Theo nodded and smiled against Masa's chest. "I have an idea in the meantime."

"Oh?"

Dripping from just having been in the shower, Theo stood at the edge of the UIC pool watching Masa tread water. The familiar scent of chlorine brought him back to his racing days the moment he'd entered the facility. He was anxious on the drive over—as he'd been every time he thought about getting back into something he shared with Isaac—but now, standing at the edge, Theo felt no trepidation. In its place was anticipation and, as he looked on at Masa's smiling face, he realized he also felt hopeful.

"Come on, baby," Masa ushered with an ear-to-ear grin.

Theo smiled at him, raised his hands, and dove in headfirst.

EPILOGUE

D R. KATRINA HOOPER sat across from Theo with her legs crossed and a notepad in her lap. She was always impeccably dressed during their sessions, with today being no exception. Despite the January cold, she wore a pale grey skirt with a matching blazer atop an olive green satin blouse. What stood out to Theo most were her shoes: black suede ankle-strap stilettos in the middle of winter. She watched him with piercing blue eyes as he silently contemplated the practicality of his therapist's footwear in an attempt to not think about what had been plaguing him since Christmas.

"Do my shoes intrigue you, Theo?"

Realizing he'd been caught, Theo flashed a nervous smile. He'd been seeing her for just over a year and could hide nothing from her. "I'm sorry."

She tapped her pen on her notepad a few times before casting it aside and brushing her auburn bangs from her field of vision. "You seem distracted today. Not just right now, but earlier as well, when you arrived. Has something changed at home or work?"

At the beginning of the weekly session Theo relayed the

events since his last session, including updates on Masa's classes at UIC and how he'd had lunch with his mother. His relationship with his mother was in a much better place thanks largely to Dr. Hooper's assistance and Masa's support. Theo saw his mother several times a month and they discussed everything except for Theo's father. The man did not speak to Theo outside of work and tried his damnedest to avoid it in the office where possible.

"No, nothing has changed. Work is still going great; my father hasn't caused any new problems." Theo licked his lips and ran his palms over his thighs. "I'm actually nervous about Valentine's Day. I want to do something special for Masa, but we kind of agreed to keep it low-key, like last year. He's been so busy researching for his dissertation on top of taking a few classes. I'd like to do something nice for him." Masa was taking three extra classes taught by Dr. Kirstein simply because he was so enamored with the man. Theo admired Masa's passion for his studies, but he also couldn't deny that he was a touch jealous. Theo and Dr. Hooper had touched on this many times over the past year. She assured him a bit of jealousy was an understandable response, though Theo still hated that he felt that way.

Dr. Hooper pondered this for a moment before replying. "Have you discussed this at all with him?"

Theo shook his head. "I already know what he'd say. He would say he doesn't need anything fancy or expensive and that... he only wants me." Theo's ears burned red with embarrassment over speaking those words and his chest swelled with a comfortable warmness he'd become accustomed to feeling whenever he spoke of Masa.

"Do you believe him?" Dr. Hooper asked neutrally.

"I know what you're doing, Katrina. I *do* believe him. And I know that I don't need to buy him things, but I really want to. And I want it to be a surprise. Surprising him on

Valentine's Day is cliché, but the timing is perfect. And he kinda likes cliché. Ah, I'm having lunch with Jamie next week, so I'll probably bounce some ideas off of him." Theo smiled to himself. Talking about Masa in his therapy sessions was always easy. He could go on at length about the man he loved and he knew that Dr. Hooper knew this as well. She often probed about Masa to lower Theo's guards before broaching more sensitive topics.

"I'm glad to see you so comfortable and happy, Theo. I think Masa appreciates everything you do for him, just as you appreciate what he does for you."

Theo nodded his head. "He does a lot more for me than money could ever buy."

"Do you still tell him about your dreams?"

It's coming. "Yes."

"How many have you had this past week?"

And there it is. "Ah, two. Tuesday and Saturday," Theo said quickly.

Dr. Hooper tilted her head and squinted her eyes at Theo. She waited a few moments before she spoke again. "Was there something unusual about them this time?"

"One was just a normal memory, Isaac and me getting drunk after a race. The other was," Theo swallowed and tried to find some moisture in his suddenly dry mouth, "the sort I used to have before I met Masa. It's a dream I've had dozens of times; I was standing on the edge of my balcony looking down at the ground below. I know it's a dream and that I have to jump. I always jump and wake up feeling like that's the answer to my problems. This time, Masa was there on the balcony with me."

"Did he say anything to you?" Dr. Hooper asked.

"No. He didn't speak. He just looked at me and he was sad about something. I-I wanted to go to him, but I felt a pull toward the edge, some sort of magnetism drawing me away."

"Then what happened?"

"Nothing." Theo threw his hands up in front of him in a gesture. "Masa woke me up. I guess I was talking and thrashing in my sleep. I woke up with his voice in my ear and his arms around me."

"Okay." Dr. Hooper's neutral expression softened and Theo thought for a moment she might smile at him. Instead, she turned her attention to her notepad and scribbled down what appeared to be several sentences.

Theo glanced at his watch, a Christmas present from Masa, and noted that there were still twenty minutes left of the session. "Look, Katrina, I know it's early, but I was hoping we could call it a day? Masa will be home early and we're having dinner. I wanted to get to the gym prior to that and be home before him."

She smiled knowingly at him and gently nodded her head. "That's not a problem, Theo. I'd like to discuss this particular dream a bit more next week, okay?" Dr. Hooper rose to her feet and Theo did the same, smoothing down his tie before extending his hand to her. She took hold of it and Theo thanked her before he left for the gym.

STILL WEARING HIS GYM CLOTHES, Theo entered his condo and was greeted by the smell of something savory coming from the kitchen and loud electronic rock coming from the Bluetooth speaker Masa got for his birthday. He toed out of his sneakers and dropped his gym bag at the door then walked into the kitchen to see Masa clad in just a pair of black Armani trunks—*his* black Armani trunks—and a black apron. His hair was tied up and he was chopping something on the cutting board while several pots simmered on the stovetop. Theo had protested when Masa brought home the apron, but he'd grown to develop an appreciation for it, as well as some of Masa's other spirited fashion choices.

Theo snuck up on Masa and waited for him to put the knife down. A few moments later he finished chopping what was on the board, set the knife aside while he reached across the counter for a container of strawberries. Theo stepped in close and pressed his body firmly against Masa's. He slid his arms around Masa's waist and nuzzled into his exposed neck. A jolt of surprise shot through Masa's body at first contact then he relaxed and melted against Theo, sighing at the soft scrape of Theo's beard against his nape.

"You're here early," Theo said, mouth just below Masa's ear.

"Yeah, I finished my paper and thought I'd get dinner started." Masa turned his head toward Theo and sucked in a sharp breath. "Did you just come from the gym?" His voice was thick.

"Yes. I wanted to get here first and surprise you."

Masa lowered his hips and ground his ass into Theo's crotch, surely feeling Theo's stiffening cock through his thin sweatpants. Theo tightened his grip on Masa's smooth skin and lolled his head back as a rough groan passed his lips. "I'm sorry I ruined your surprise." Masa turned in Theo's grasp and kissed him, just a soft, slow press of lips. He dragged his nose along Theo's jaw, down to his neck, and inhaled deeply. "I can think of a few ways I can make it up to you."

"You've done enough thinking today, I'll make it easy for you; take me to bed and remind me why I keep you around." Theo bit his bottom lip and grinned.

Masa scoffed out a laugh and shook his head. "I made you dinner and you've got jokes? So cold, *nounours*."

"I love you," Theo whispered against Masa's cheek. He

pulled back to look him in the eye and added, "Even when you steal my underwear."

"Ah, yes. That's one of my boyfriend perks." Masa slid his hands down Theo's sides and cupped his ass. He gave it a good squeeze and pulled Theo's hips flush against his so their hard cocks were aligned. "Mm, this is another boyfriend perk." Masa waggled his eyebrows to signal Theo then slid his hands just under Theo's ass and pulled him up against his stomach in one heave. Theo wrapped his legs around Masa's back and hooked his arms around his neck. Masa stared into Theo's eyes and licked his lips. "*Crisse*, you got heavier."

Theo's eyes flew open in shock and Masa started to laugh. "School's made you soft," he countered teasingly.

"On the contrary; I'm rock hard right now. I'll thoroughly demonstrate just how much for you for the next," Masa craned his neck to look at the timer on the stove, "forty-eight minutes."

"Come on, tiger. Show me what you've got."

Despite the bravado and playfulness of their earlier exchange, Theo and Masa made love without haste, savoring each other as much as they could. Masa lay behind Theo and held Theo's leg up while he slowly rocked his hips, sliding his cock into him. He kissed Theo's shoulder, behind his ear, and his neck—any of the flushed skin he could reach. When Theo's breaths started to come out ragged, Masa sucked on his earlobe, treating Theo to the occasion nip between flicks of his tongue.

Theo came with Masa's arms around him and his lips on his neck, licking the salty, sensitive skin. Masa's own orgasm followed shortly after, ripped out of him from Theo pulsing around his cock. He stilled as he shot his seed deep inside then thrust in a few more times, making them both moan. Once he came down from his post-orgasm daze, he slowly pulled out of Theo and rolled them both over, pulling Theo into his arms.

"I need to take a shower," Theo said, but he made no efforts to get out of Masa's embrace.

Masa sighed and Theo could tell by the sound that he was smiling. "Not yet. Just stay with me for a bit."

"Okay. But you have to change the sheets before bed."

"Please, any trace of a wet spot will have dried by the time we go to bed," Masa replied sleepily.

"I'm not sleeping on crusty sheets because you got lazy."

"Agh, *nounours,* I'll change the sheets later, okay?"

"Okay," Theo said, trying—rather unsuccessfully—to suppress a snicker.

Masa groaned at his obvious defeat and dragged the tops of his fingernails gently up and down Theo's back. "There's something I wanted to talk to you about."

Theo froze. "Oh?"

"Calm down, it's nothing bad, babe. It's about Valentine's Day. Was there anything in particular you wanted to do?"

Does he know? No, he can't know. I haven't even mentioned it to Jay yet. "Ah, I haven't really thought too much about it. I figured you'd want to do something small like last year." Theo tried to sound casual.

"That works for me. Can I just ask that you keep the night open?"

Theo drew his brows together and looked up at Masa's face. "Where else would I want to be?"

"No, I mean, don't plan anything or book, like dinner or anything like that. Leave planning the evening to me."

Satisfied that Masa was oblivious to his half-baked plans, Theo relaxed and enjoyed about fifteen seconds of snuggling with his boyfriend before the timer on the stove went off signaling that snuggle time was over.

A FEW DAYS later Theo met Jamie for lunch back at the Mexican restaurant in Downers Grove. Jamie didn't have a prior engagement there this time, but it was a spot they both enjoyed and had returned to several times throughout the past year. Salma smiled and brought over water to their table, not bothering with menus. Every time Jamie and Theo came they ordered beef and chicken fajitas respectively. Salma greeted them and they made comfortable small talk for a few minutes before she confirmed that they'd be having their usual orders.

The food came, as well as beer, and Theo and Jamie ate and made easy conversation over Jamie's interviews with med school and his plans for the rest of his lax fourth year. When the plates were taken away, Jamie took a long pull from his beer and set it down overly forcefully on the table, garnering Theo's full attention.

"All right, bro. Why are we really here?"

Theo sighed, feigning annoyance. "Can't I just want to spend time with you?"

"Nah-uh." Jamie over-exaggeratedly shook his head. "Not this close to Valentine's Day, dude."

Theo groaned and slumped back in his chair. "I don't know what to do. We said we'd keep it pretty low-key."

"But…"

"But Masa has been working really hard on his dissertation and the extra classes. I'd like to do something nice for him."

Jamie scoffed through his perma-grin. "You lavish him any chance you get, so good job setting the bar ridiculously high."

Theo winced. "I know. I'm terrible and he keeps telling me to stop, but I just can't help it."

"Look, I get it. He's kinda loveable and humble—"

"Did you just say he was *humble*?"

"Let me finish, you dick. He's humble when it comes to material things. He appreciates everything you get for him, but he would love you all the same without it." Jamie took another drink. "And that's fuckin' great, man."

"So what can I get him that would be special?"

"Oh, easy! I take back what I said about this being difficult. Book a trip somewhere tropical." Jamie held up his hand and extended his index finger. "One, it's cold and miserable here this time of the year." He flicked up his thumb. "Two, we already know that Masa likes to travel. Hell. He was going to travel across the country before he fell for your stupid ass." Theo flipped Jamie off but Jamie ignored it and continued his count. "And three, you guys haven't been away together. Picture this: a week in the sun with your guy and enough rum and tequila to forget about everything else."

"Shit, that does sound good."

"I'm a genius, trust me, I know." Jamie finished his beer and waggled his eyebrows at his brother. "And now you can thank me by taking me to Neiman Marcus. I could go for some new clothes."

Theo shook his head. "Some things never change."

Jamie caught Theo's gaze and earnestly smiled at him. "Yeah, but some things do, and I'm glad for it."

"Come on, Masa is waiting for me."

"Oh, I'd hate to keep true love waiting."

"Shut up."

"You're right, some things never change."

VALENTINE'S DAY was on a snowy Thursday. Masa didn't

have class on Thursdays, but Theo had to go to work for a last-minute department meeting his father had called. The meeting wasn't anything that couldn't have been relayed via email, but Theo figured that his father was trying to soil the day for him by calling the meeting and dragging it out as long as humanly possible. A direct confrontation would be far too uncouth for Jim Rey.

As Theo looked his father in the eye from across the boardroom table he saw a flash of arrogance on his father's face which confirmed what he'd suspected: his father derived some sort of twisted satisfaction from this. As frustrating as it was, Theo didn't let his irritation show and played the role of dutiful employee and disregarded his role as scorned son. He felt bad that the rest of the team had to suffer because of his relationship with his father, but there wasn't much he could do about it except be compliant to speed things along.

When the meeting finally drew to a close, Theo grabbed Masa's gift from his office closet, texted Masa to let him know he was on his way, and headed straight home without a wayward thought.

The condo smelled of the crème brûlée-scented candles Masa picked up a few weeks ago, although there was some-thing else under it. Theo couldn't quite place it and figured the candles were to mask the scent and not spoil the surprise. The kitchen lights were turned off and a soft acoustic ballad could be heard coming from the living room. Theo followed the sound, holding an eight-by-eight inch square box wrapped in white and gold paisley paper Leah had picked out. As he walked into the living room, Masa was nowhere to be seen, but a flower bouquet on the living room table caught Theo's eye. Theo set the box down on the table next to the source of the music and one of the candles and gently touched one of the silky petals of what he'd come to know as lilies. The red, orange, and white flowers were beautiful in the dimly lit room. As lovely as they were, Theo longed to see the man who gave his life renewed purpose. He started down the hall and called out for him.

"Ah, you're home," Masa yelled back. "Just give me, like, thirty seconds and I'll be right out."

"Okay." Theo expectantly went back and sat down on the couch. Masa came down the hall wearing his black cotton overalls he liked to lounge in. As usual, he didn't have a shirt on under them and his tattoo was on full display—as were his nipples, not that Theo was looking. Leering would be a more appropriate term. Theo wondered if there ever would come a time when Masa wouldn't leave him breathless. As Masa got closer to him and smiled Theo knew for certain that the answer to his prior thought was a definitive no.

"Hey, baby. I didn't hear you come in. I'd meant to change into something... well, *more*, I guess." Masa looked shy in that moment, the set of his shoulders suggesting that he was nervous.

Theo stood up to meet him and pulled him into a hug. Up this close he noticed that Masa's hair was damp and smelled of exotic oils, the source of which being a shampoo and conditioner set Jamie, of all people, gifted Masa. Theo thought it was an odd gift, but it made Masa's hair so damn soft that he couldn't stop playing with it.

"You look amazing, Masa. You don't have to dress up for me," Theo whispered in his ear, sending a tickle down his neck. Theo pulled back and looked around the candlelit room then at Masa. His eyes looked like honey in the lighting. "It looks and smells great in here."

"I'm glad you like it. Are you hungry?"

"I'm starved. I skipped lunch today."

Masa frowned. "Leah let you do that?"

"I gave her today and tomorrow off so she could do the whole romantic-getaway-weekend thing."

"Take off your tie and jacket and have a seat by the kitchen." Masa pecked Theo's lips and nose then made his way into the kitchen. Theo admired the muscles in his back and longed to trace the moons on Masa's spine with his tongue. *Later.* He ripped off his tie and tossed it and his jacket on the arm of the couch and took a seat on a stool at the bar. Masa still seemed nervous and prefaced dinner by saying it was something he hadn't made before. He made Theo close his eyes while he arranged the food. When Theo was allowed to open his eyes he first saw an empty plate with chopsticks lying in the middle. Beyond the plate were white Chinese takeout cartons and two glasses of white wine.

"Chinese food?" Theo asked.

Masa bit his lip and nodded. "It's not just any Chinese food, though. I made everything here. So again, I'm really sorry if it sucks."

"Shit, are you serious? What's in these?" Theo looked from Masa to the cartons.

"Your favorites. I didn't want to try anything too daring and risk you not liking it."

"You mean too authentic?"

Masa laughed and seemed to relax a bit. "Well, yes. So, I made beef and broccoli, chow mein, Szechuan chicken and peppers, steamed rice, and," Masa slid a container directly in front of Theo, "these."

Theo smiled and opened the container, revealing his favorite cheat food. He gasped and his nostrils flared. "You made me chicken balls." It was an obvious observation, but Theo was too happy to say anything remotely intelligent. "God, I love you. Get your ass over here and eat with me before I devour them all."

"You haven't learned the virtues of patience and temperance yet in your old age?" Masa teased as he grabbed a fork for himself and walked around the counter to sit beside Theo.

"You're one to lecture me about temperance, Mr. Zero-Self-Restraint."

"Touché."

After dinner and a bottle and a half of wine, Theo and Masa relaxed on the couch to exchange gifts. With dinner out of the way, and Theo having loved it, Masa was back to his usual self. He explained to Theo that the red, orange, and white lilies represented passion, pride, and devotion, respectively. Theo loved them all the more for the thoughtfulness, but he could always expect that from Masa. Masa kissed the back of Theo's hands then reached over the side of the couch and handed him a small flat box adorned in powder pink paper with red hearts.

"Cute paper," Theo said as he tore into it. He opened the box and pulled out an insanely soft, black jock strap. He held it up and read the print on the waistband. "Charlie, huh?"

Masa wore an expression that can only be described as being up to no good. His smile was wide, crinkling the corners of his eyes, which had now darkened. "Charlie by Matthew Zink. I'm not saying I want you to wear that for me, but I totally want you to wear that for me."

Theo dropped his hand with the underwear in his lap and his shoulders trembled with laughter. He was powerless against Masa; of course he'd wear them. "I think I can make a concession for you."

"Damn, I knew I should have ordered more. I'll be honest, that's not really your gift, that's totally more for me. Your real gift," Masa reached into his pocket and pulled out a small box, "is right here."

Theo cocked his head and took the box. It was too flat to

be a ring box and Masa looked way too relaxed for another ring so Theo eagerly ripped into the paper. The box was branded Givenchy and Theo made an "ouu" sound and grinned at Masa before he flipped the lid open. The box held a pair of silver shark tooth cuff links and Theo nearly squealed. He bit it back, though a small squeak still slipped out. He beamed at Masa and leaned over to meet him in a kiss.

"These are perfect. Thank you."

"They screamed 'you' to me, so I hoped you'd like them."

"I love them." Theo set the open box on the table and rubbed his palms on his thighs. "Ready for yours?"

Masa nodded and Theo set the box in his lap. Once the paper and lid were removed Masa smiled at the box full of pink and white origami sakura flowers. He pulled out several and smiled at Theo. "Baby, did you fold all these?"

Theo nodded. "Keep going."

Masa found an envelope at the bottom of the box. "Hm, what are you planning?" He eyed Theo suspiciously while he opened it then directed his attention to the two tickets to Japan he now held in his hand. "*Decrisse! Mon dieu*, babe."

"I don't want to take away from your surprise, but I love it when I shock you into speaking that sexy, filthy French."

"Is that why you booked us a trip to Japan," Masa looked at the tickets closer, "in April?"

"No, I chose April because it's reading week for you and it also happens to be sakura season. I figured it would be something you'd like to see."

"Fuck, I love you." Masa dropped the tickets and climbed into Theo's lap, pushing him down into a lying position while he assaulted him with fevered kisses. He ground his hips into Theo's several times, getting them both semi-erect. Masa pulled back with a faint growl and licked his lips. "Don't think you're off the hook for another expensive gift.

I'm just too fucking happy and horny to care about lecturing you right now." He kissed Theo again and unbuttoned his dress pants with one skilled hand. He cupped Theo's ass and gave it a hard squeeze causing Theo to quiver. Theo jerked when Masa slid his hand under the waistband of his trunks and ran his fingertips over his hole.

"Masa, wait a second."

"What's up? Are my fingers cold?" Masa asked, his voice heavy with lust.

"There's something I want to ask you."

Masa propped himself up on his elbows. "Yeah, what is it?"

"Do you…" Theo looked down for a second and swallowed. "Do you mind if I top you tonight?"

Masa's lips parted wordlessly then he kissed Theo again. "Seriously?"

"Is that okay? I know it's not something we've ever talked about." Theo's voice was all nerves.

"Of course, baby. I told you on the first night we met that I was vers and okay with whatever you wanted to do. That's even more accurate now than before."

A scarlet flush crossed Theo's cheeks. "I must have missed that when I was ass-up on the bed waiting for you."

Masa smirked and hummed in delight. "And what a magnificent sight that was." A blush spread down to Theo's neck and Masa kissed him once more, slow and sensual. "I'm yours, Theo."

Theo pulled off of Masa's cock and withdrew his fingers from inside of him. He'd taken the time to prepare Masa the way he was used to Masa preparing him. He was nervous and wanted it to be good for Masa so he spent probably more time than he needed stretching him. Judging by the sweet sounds he was making, Masa hadn't minded the thorough treatment and relished Theo taking such loving care of him.

Theo pumped out more lube and rubbed it against Masa and along his own length. He edged closer to Masa so that the tops of his thighs touched the back of Masa's. Theo gave himself a few quick strokes to ensure that he was sufficiently lubed up as well as to steal a moment to calm down. The sight of Masa spread and bare and writhing was almost too much. He stared up at Theo through heavy-lidded eyes, hair a mess, and pre-cum dripping from his tip. He was debauched and shamelessly pleading for Theo's cock in a mixture of English and French that guaranteed Theo would not be able to last long.

Theo lined up his cock and suddenly remembered something that hadn't occurred to him. "Do you want me to wear a condom?"

Masa lifted his head and raised one eyebrow. "Of course not. We don't even have any anymore."

"I didn't want to assume."

"It's okay, baby. But if you don't fuck me soon, we might have a problem." Masa squeezed the base of his thick cock and moaned. "I'm gonna blow any minute and I want your dick in me when I do."

Fuck me. Theo swallowed hard and his cock twitched at Masa's words. This was *definitely* going to be over quickly. He took one more steadying breath and slowly pushed inside. Once he breached the initial resistance he slid right in all the way to his balls. Theo whimpered while Masa sucked in a sharp breath and fisted both hands in the sheets.

"Oh, sweet fuck," Theo muttered mindlessly.

Masa gripped his cock again and started stroking himself off. "Theo," he pleaded.

Theo pushed Masa's legs toward his chest and leaned down to kiss him. He started rocking his hips slowly into

Masa, completely overwhelmed by the heat and tightness. Masa moaned into Theo's mouth with a vulnerability Theo hadn't heard from Masa before. Masa's soft cries and his hand moving faster between them gave Theo enough encouragement to thrust faster and deeper.

The feeling was unlike anything he'd felt before, emotionally and physically. It was too overwhelming for Theo and he felt the telltale signs that a fast orgasm was imminent. He tried to slow down to draw it out, but Masa growled in his ear.

"Faster, baby."

"I'm not gonna last," Theo choked out between breaths. He shifted to get more leverage then fucked Masa as fast as the position would allow. Theo teetered on the edge, ready to self-destruct at any moment.

Masa breathed in Theo's scent then bit his earlobe and ground out, "I'm so close, fuck me harder." And that did it. Theo stilled as his orgasm roared through him, igniting all of his nerves at once. He cursed and moaned as his cock pulsed again and again. He dug his fingers into Masa's hips and thighs hard enough that there would surely be bruises in the morning. Masa stroked himself to climax with a smile, shooting streams of hot cum all over both of them. Breathless, he flung his head back to rest lifelessly against the pillow.

"I'm sorry. I promise next time I—"

"Baby, shut up. Don't ruin the moment." Masa pressed his finger to Theo's lips. Theo let his head collapse on Masa's chest and they enjoyed their post-orgasm bliss, feeling each other's heartbeats slowly return to normal. "Are you really taking me to Japan?" Masa asked quietly.

"Only if you want to go. I'd take you anywhere you wanted to go, Masamune."

Masa flung his arms around Theo and giggled excitedly.

"I can't believe it." His laughter died in his throat abruptly. "Oh, shit."

Theo lifted his head and looked at Masa's face. "What?"

"I need to learn how to use chopsticks. I can't go to Japan and ask for a fork everywhere we go."

Theo snickered and leaned up to kiss Masa's worried jaw and lips. "Don't worry, I'll teach you."

"What if I'm a lost cause?"

Without missing a beat, Theo smiled at Masa and said, "Then I'll use a fork with you."

"You really do love me, don't you? You're my ride or die."

"I love you more than anything, but please never say *that* again."

"Fine. But only because I love you and you're the baddest bitch." Masa tried and failed to contain his snickering.

"Oh my God, shut up. You've been spending too much time with Jay."

"Maybe, but you love me anyway."

Theo shook his head, a wide smile plastered across his face. "Always."

ACKNOWLEDGMENTS

To Cass and Jenny for alpha reading from day one.

To Steven for helping me with all things Chicago—among other details.

To Jess for translating Masa's filthy French.

To Jay Aheer and Judy Zweifel for a gorgeous cover and awesome proofreading (and tips!).

To everyone who supported me and put up with me (mostly my mom) while this book consumed my life for over nine months.

ABOUT THE AUTHOR

Serene Franklin lives in Halifax (Nova Scotia, not California), but has fallen in love with Chicago through research and writing. She has a political science degree, and—more importantly—two adorable and mildly irritating dogs: Tai the Goldendoodle and Fynnian the Irish Wolfhound.

When not writing, she enjoys reading, cooking spicy food, thrashing to music, losing at crib, and watching movies. Serene is a proud otaku and collector of anime figures in addition to novels and yaoi manga.

Serene currently writes contemporary MM romance, but has plans to branch out into other subgenres.

Email: sfwrites801@gmail.com

instagram.com/serenity_darko